John Dickson Carr and The Murder Room

>>> This title is part of The Murder Room, our series dedicated to making available out-of-print or hard-to-find titles by classic crime writers.

Crime fiction has always held up a mirror to society. The Victorians were fascinated by sensational murder and the emerging science of detection; now we are obsessed with the forensic detail of violent death. And no other genre has so captivated and enthralled readers.

Vast troves of classic crime writing have for a long time been unavailable to all but the most dedicated frequenters of second-hand bookshops. The advent of digital publishing means that we are now able to bring you the backlists of a huge range of titles by classic and contemporary crime writers, some of which have been out of print for decades.

From the genteel amateur private eyes of the Golden Age and the femmes fatales of pulp fiction, to the morally ambiguous hard-boiled detectives of mid twentieth-century America and their descendants who walk our twenty-first century streets, The Murder Room has it all. >>>

The Murder Room
Where Criminal Minds Meet

themurderroom.com

John Dickson Carr (1906–1977)

John Dickson Carr, the master of the locked-room mystery, was born in Uniontown, Pennsylvania, the son of a US Congressman. He studied law in Paris before settling in England where he married an Englishwoman, Clarice Cleeves, and he spent most of his writing career living in Great Britain. Widely regarded as one of the greatest Golden Age mystery writers, his work featured apparently impossible crimes often with seemingly supernatural elements. He modelled his affable and eccentric series detective Gideon Fell on G. K. Chesterton, and wrote a number of novels and short stories, including his series featuring Henry Merrivale, under the pseudonym Carter Dickson. He was one of only two Americans admitted to the British Detection club, and was highly praised by other mystery writers. Dorothy L. Sayers said of him that 'he can create atmosphere with an adjective, alarm with allusion, or delight with a rollicking absurdity'. In 1950 he was awarded the first of two prestigious Edgar Awards by the Mystery Writers of America, and was presented with their Grand Master Award in 1963. He died in Greenville, South Carolina in 1977.

By John Dickson Carr

(Titles in bold are published in The Murder Room)

Poison in Jest (1932)
The Burning Court (1937)
The Emperor's Snuff-Box (1942)
The Nine Wrong Answers (1952)
Patrick Butler for the Defense (1956)
Most Secret (1964)

Henri Bencolin

It Walks by Night (1930)
Castle Skull (1931)
The Lost Gallows (1931)
The Waxworks Murder (1932)
 aka The Corpse in the Waxworks
The Four False Weapons, Being the Return of Bencolin (1938)

Dr Gideon Fell

Hag's Nook (1933)
The Mad Hatter Mystery (1933)
The Blind Barber (1934)
The Eight of Swords (1934)
Death-Watch (1934)
The Hollow Man (1935) *aka* The Three Coffins
The Arabian Nights Murder (1936)

To Wake the Dead (1938)
The Crooked Hinge (1938)
The Problem of the Green Capsule (1939)
 aka The Black Spectacles
The Problem of the Wire Cage (1939)
The Man Who Could Not Shudder (1940)
The Case of the Constant Suicides (1941)
Death Turns the Tables (1941)
 aka The Seat of the Scornful (1942)
Till Death Do Us Part (1944)
He Who Whispers (1946)
The Sleeping Sphinx (1947)
Below Suspicion (1949)
The Dead Man's Knock (1958)
In Spite of Thunder (1960)
The House at Satan's Elbow (1965)
Panic in Box C (1966)
Dark of the Moon (1968)

Historical mysteries

The Bride of Newgate (1950)
The Devil in Velvet (1951)

Captain Cut-Throat (1955)
Fire, Burn! (1957)
**Scandal at High Chimneys: A
  Victorian Melodrama (1959)**
**The Witch of the Low Tide: An
  Edwardian Melodrama (1961)**
The Demoniacs (1962)
Papa La-Bas (1968)
The Ghosts' High Noon (1970)
Deadly Hall (1971)
The Hungry Goblin: A Victo-
  rian Detective Novel (1972)

Short story collections

Dr Fell, Detective, and Other
  Stories (1947)
The Third Bullet and Other
  Stories of Detection (1954)
The Exploits of Sherlock
  Holmes (with Adrian Conan
  Doyle) (1954)
The Men Who Explained
  Miracles (1963)
The Door to Doom and Other
  Detections (1980) (includes
  radio plays)
The Dead Sleep Lightly (1983)
  (radio plays)
Fell and Foul Play (1991)
Merrivale, March and Murder
  (1991)

Writing as Carter Dickson

The Bowstring Murders (1934)
Drop to His Death (with John
  Rhode) (1939)
  aka Fatal Descent

Sir Henry Merrivale

The Plague Court Murders
  (1934)
The White Priory Murders
  (1934)
The Red Widow Murders (1935)
The Unicorn Murders (1935)
The Punch and Judy Murders
  (1936)
  aka The Magic Lantern
  Murders
The Ten Teacups (1937)
  aka The Peacock Feather
  Murders
The Judas Window (1938)
  aka The Crossbow Murder
Death in Five Boxes (1938)
The Reader is Warned (1939)
And So To Murder (1940)
Murder in the Submarine Zone
  (1940)
  aka Nine – and Death Makes
  Ten, also published as Murder
  in the Atlantic

Seeing is Believing (1941)
  aka Cross of Murder
The Gilded Man (1942)
  aka Death and the Gilded Man
She Died a Lady (1943)
He Wouldn't Kill Patience (1944)
The Curse of the Bronze
  Lamp (1945)
  aka Lord of the Sorcerers
  (1946)
My Late Wives (1946)
The Skeleton in the Clock (1948)
A Graveyard to Let (1949)

Night at the Mocking Window
  (1950)
Behind the Crimson Blind (1952)
The Cavalier's Cup (1953)

Historical mystery

Fear is the Same (1956)

Short story collections

The Department of Queer
  Complaints (1940)

Deadly Hall

John Dickson Carr

This edition published by
The Orion Publishing Group Ltd
Orion House
5 Upper St Martin's Lane
London WC2H 9EA

An Hachette UK company
A CIP catalogue record for this book is available from the British Library

ISBN 978 1 4719 0543 8

www.orionbooks.co.uk

To Macon Fry, who showed how it could be done

1

Towards one in the morning he faced the fact that he couldn't sleep. Not yet, at least.

He rolled on his left elbow, right hand finding the chain of the little bedside lamp. Light revealed the subdued luxury of Stateroom 340, on the sun deck at the stern of the steamboat's starboard—no, not starboard: its two-whistle side. Its open window (never call windows portholes) overlooked the huge red-painted paddle-wheel, whose drowsy churning ought to have lulled him. And he was alone here, having paid for both beds.

They *were* beds, not berths, for the most sybaritic accommodation on the river. Time, twelve-fifty by his watch on the bedside table. The tiny leather-edged travelling calendar showed the date as Monday, April 18th, of this year 1927. By this hour it was now Tuesday, April 19th. The Grand Bayou Line's *Bayou Queen*, bound down the Ohio and the Mississippi for New Orleans, had left Cincinnati at noon on Monday. Their first stop would be Louisville, some time today.

Jeff Caldwell, who would be thirty-three years old in the middle of July, had many questions on his mind. Of sedentary habits, though neither ill-looking nor unathletic, he might have been considered too studious, too much a loner, if it had not been for his sardonic sense of humor. But the damned situation kept tormenting him. And he wanted a breath of air.

Light painted the shiny white walls a pale gold. The door of the little bathroom stood ajar. The other door led to the open deck on the two-whistle side. Jeff swung his legs out of bed, thrust his feet

1

into slippers, and pulled a dressing-gown over his pajamas. Then, automatically lighting a cigarette, he made for the open.

Main deck, cabin deck, texas deck, sun deck: this atop all, under a fresh breeze and the edge of a moon. Except for the paddle wheel's churning, the soft slap of water past the side, hardly any noise. A scattered light or two, remote and ghostly; no other sign of life.

"Not even half full, this trip," they had told him at the company's office in Cincinnati. "You know how it is. People with plenty of money don't discover America, as a general thing; they travel abroad. We'll be full up June to September, 'cept maybe the luxury staterooms. Or maybe you don't know. First visit to New Orleans?"

"I was born and brought up in New Orleans."

"You don't talk like a Southerner."

"I was educated, if it can be called that, almost entirely in the North."

"Live at New Orleans now?"

"I don't even live in this country."

"Well, it's none o' my business . . ."

'No,' Jeff had thought, 'it's not.' And he had said no more.

Now, leaning one elbow on the railing, shielding the fire of the cigarette in his other hand, he still pondered. Jeff Caldwell could not have denied that he did have plenty of money. With the Dixieland Tobacco Company continuing to prosper, as it had been prospering since his great-grandfather founded it in North Carolina well over a century ago, neither he nor Uncle Gil, his late mother's brother, need fear the future. He and Gilbert Bethune, now New Orleans's District Attorney, were the only surviving members of the family. But then Dave and Serena were the only surviving Hobarts.

As for what old Ira Rutledge had meant, no less than what Uncle Gil meant . . .

The questions in his mind, far from being answered, were not even fully formulated. After crossing the ocean, he had gone by train from New York to Cincinnati for the slow journey by boat to his native city. Why was he doing this? Why did he think it

2

necessary? Had the destiny of Dave and Serena Hobart, that strangely contrasted brother and sister, in some fashion become entwined with his own? Considering that his grandfather had once been so close a friend of old Commodore Hobart, *their* grandfather . . .

Or it may have been so unexpected, half-frantic a letter from Dave.

On the *Bayou Queen*'s sun deck, under smoke blown wide from her single chimney, Jeff Caldwell found his thoughts moving back not only over the past day or month, but over the past ten years. After all, how little he really knew either of New Orleans or of the relatives and friends of his extreme youth! How little time he had spent there!

Northern preparatory school from an early age, with only Christmas vacations at home. His father had died in '13, his mother a year later; he and Uncle Gil had sold the Caldwell house in the Garden District. Then, despite all his trouble with mathematics, he was admitted to Yale. He had not finished his junior year at New Haven when in April, just over a decade ago, the United States entered what must forever be called the Great War.

"You'll do, I suppose," Uncle Gil commented, "what you think you ought to do; or, rather, what you think you want to do. If I were a younger man, I should probably be damned fool enough to do it too."

And so, combining Creole Bethune with Anglo-Saxon Caldwell, Jeff had enlisted. First the long grind of basic training, then the long grind of officer's training; always, for one reason or another, some delay. Easy-going, imaginative, Second Lieutenant Jeffrey Caldwell was shipped to France. He had not yet gone to the front, never having heard guns fired in anger, when news of the false armistice immediately preceded news of the true armistice in the second week of November, 1918.

Shipped home to be demobilized the following May, Jeff afterwards went to New Orleans for a conference about his future. Gilbert Bethune had always resolutely refused to touch the family financial affairs.

"When any lawyer tries to handle his own family's finances," said

3

Uncle Gil, "it means friction at best and bad blood at worst. Let Ira Rutledge deal with it, as he always has."

But Uncle Gil had sat in on the conference about his nephew's future. Jeff never forgot that day in 1919: himself not quite twenty-five, Uncle Gil lean and hatchet-faced at just on forty, Ira Rutledge lean and grizzled at what then seemed an advanced age, the perfect picture of a family lawyer who advised so many of the well-to-do, in Mr. Rutledge's dusty office above Canal Street.

"Now that we can take up our normal lives again, Jeff," the family lawyer said, "you'll be returning to New Haven?"

"No, I think not. They shouldn't have admitted me to begin with, and I can never graduate."

"But your academic record—!"

"Yes, that's what I mean."

"Well?"

"My dislike of mathematics or any form of science, sir, isn't mere dislike. It's full-blown hatred and lack of aptitude that today they'd call pathological. What difference how high a grade I make in English or history if I can't understand the simplest algebraic problem or proposition in geometry, let alone the more advanced math (plus one science) I need even to take an arts degree? Rightly or wrongly, taking a degree seems of no importance at all."

"Well, what do you intend to do?"

"What about finances, Mr. Rutledge? How's Dixieland Tobacco?"

Mr. Rutledge assured him that Dixieland Tobacco had never been in better shape, and that (always within reason, of course) whatever sum he required could be paid in monthly at the bank of his choice.

"I'm afraid I must still ask, my boy, what you intend to do."

"Live abroad for a while, I think. With a base in Paris, but visiting London as often as possible."

"Of course," Ira Rutledge said drily, "there's no real reason why you *should* work."

"Oh, I intend to work, sir, though some mightn't call it that."

"Just as you please. What do you want to do?"

"I want to write historical romances, as I always have. Swashbuckling stuff, not altogether free of gadzookses or the like, but at least historically accurate. France and England are ideal backgrounds for that. There's one other kind of novel I'd rather like to try, though I don't think I ever can."

"Indeed? And what is that?"

"Detective stories, about who killed whom and why. There's always a market for blood and thunder, and I love it!"

"Now there," Uncle Gil had interjected with some heartiness, "you're really speaking my language. Our friend Ira wouldn't touch a criminal case if they accused his own son of murder, and yet it's what *I* love. By all means write historical romances, provided you don't turn out the oversugared confectionery we get so much of. Why not detective stories too?"

"Because I don't think I've got enough sheer ingenuity. You need a first-class, brand-new idea, with all the tricks of presenting it. Whereas the historicals can be managed. I'm probably going to make a hash of it. But I think I can write readable English, and I'm game for all necessary research."

"Let it be Paris, then," sighed Mr. Rutledge, "since you seem to have made up your mind. Whether you succeed or fail, from a practical standpoint, is of little consequence. When would you wish to go?"

"As soon as possible. There'll be quite a hullabaloo before they've finished the Versailles peace conference, but it needn't interfere with my daily life. Besides, being here won't be pleasant if they pass their so-called prohibition law, and close up New Orleans worse than Josephus Daniels and his ilk closed it up during the war."

Gilbert Bethune looked thoughtful.

"They'll never close it up completely," he said, "whatever they try. Speaking of detective stories and ingenuity, however, remember that here on our own doorstep . . ."

Uncle Gil had paused there, and had not resumed. Long afterwards Jeff wondered if he had been referring to the Hobarts, an Anglo-Saxon family as old and respected as the Caldwells, and to the doubtless imaginary but still picturesque legend of Delys Hall.

Jeff could not remember old Commodore Fitzhugh Hobart, C.S.N., dead these many years. There had been only a nodding acquaintance with the late Harald Hobart, the commodore's son, father of David and Serena. Even flighty Dave and completely self-possessed Serena—the former his own age, the latter five or six years younger—could hardly be called close friends. What of others from the past? What had happened to Penny Lynn (nobody ever thought of her as Penelope), to whom he lost his heart during the Christmas vacation when he was seventeen, and had seen on only two occasions afterwards?

But such reflections had been far from him almost eight years ago. He took ship for France, chose a small residential hotel behind the Champs-Elysées, and, after much poring over documents at the Bibliothèque Nationale, he wrote his first novel.

He did not try to employ a literary agent, knowing none. Instead he sent *The Cardinal's Jester* to an acquaintance at the old New York firm of Keane & Sons. To his gratified astonishment they accepted it at once, as did Justus of London.

Whatever he did, work or laze, he must go his daily round. Jeff was no bohemian, except insofar as bohemianism may be practised by the clean and well tailored; he shunned the companionship of the left bank. Though too much a loner to make many friends, he made friends who liked him. There had been other contacts of a different sort: the French *midinette*, the English girl dabbling at sculpture, the bored American heiress who found something to interest her. During those early years, despite the awkward Channel crossing, he spent almost as much time in London as in Paris. Today, with both Air Union (French) and Imperial Airways (British) maintaining regular flights Croydon-Le Bourget, travel had become as easy as it was pleasurable.

At first, for all his long days at the typewriter, he had no success. The books, favorably reviewed, failed to sell. As novel followed novel into the nineteen twenties, each with its background of France or England in a different century, he told himself he must not chafe so much.

"Be grateful," he said aloud, "you've got an independent income."

Still, though with few aspirations towards best-sellerdom, he wanted to write one story somebody wanted to read. Then, for whatever mysterious cause, his fifth try, *My Friend Fouché*, actually showed some profit. *Witch's Eye*, its successor, did better. In January of this year, before he had finished *Till the Great Armadas Come*, the publishers offered a new two-book contract at improved terms. He had hinted, they wrote, that he might be in New York that spring to deliver the manuscript. If he had been serious . . .

Well, why not?

This notion of delivering the book in person had been with him for some time. He corresponded fairly regularly with Uncle Gil, hearing little from or of anyone else. Since '24 Uncle Gil had been Mr. District Attorney Bethune. Detective fiction, which Jeff had never tried, took the thesis that the prosecution is always wrong, the defense is always right. It delighted him that a lawyer so fond of mystery stories as Gilbert Bethune should find himself in that fictionally unrewarding office. Early in March, this year, Uncle Gil did write with news.

> You may or may not have heard that Harald Hobart died of a heart attack last week. Yes, 'Harald' is correct; the old commodore's wife was a Danish beauty; hence the Scandinavian name. His father left him very well off, though they found no hidden hoard. If Harald never seemed particularly astute in business, there should still be quite a substantial inheritance for Serena and Dave.

Ten days later came a business letter from Ira Rutledge, in that dignitary's most discreet manner.

Subsequent to the demise of Mr. Harald Hobart, said the letter, there had arisen a somewhat delicate situation involving Jeff and one other person outside the family. As the Hobarts' legal adviser, of course, Mr. Rutledge could always explain by letter, which he proposed doing with the other interested party. However, since he had been led to believe Jeff would visit New York before the end of April, and would doubtless choose to visit New Orleans as well, he preferred to communicate in *propria persona*. Trusting he had been in receipt of no mistaken information, and would cause little inconvenience by the suggestion, he remained, very sincerely . . .

It left Jeff fuming. What situation, delicate or otherwise, could possibly involve himself and one other person unspecified? Old Ira, rot his law-books, made discretion the better part of coherence.

As though that were not enough, the letter from David Hobart exploded soon afterwards. It had been handwritten on notepaper stamped with the crest of the Delys family, the Delys family being Hobart relatives not Creole but Norman English. Dave himself, fair-haired and wiry and intense, seemed to be there in the room.

If you're surprised to hear from me after all these years, Jeff, it's not because I've never wondered how you were getting on, or forgot the days when we were opposing debaters at Lawrenceville. You said you could write, and you've proved your point; more power to your elbow.

My reason for appearing out of the blue is this. I hear you'll be in America come spring . . .

So they'd all heard it, had they?

For God's sake, Sabatini, you've *got* to be in New Orleans before May 1st at the latest! There's something wrong with the Ice Maiden, our Serena herself. I might even have said there's something wrong with *me*, only I'm such a sober, steady-going customer that nobody would believe I've got any nerves. Don't ask me what I'm talking about; it's all too indefinite. Just get here!

You may miss your Uncle Gil; there's a big political do at Baton Rouge about that time. Though he hates politics, or says he hates politics, I swear they're grooming him to be Senator Bethune or Governor Bethune. You can stay with us, can't you? Jeff, this is so *infernally* important—

He had already decided to go. But he told nobody except Mr. Sewall of Keane & Sons. To Ira Rutledge he wrote in terms as veiled as that pundit's own, saying he hoped to be present but must refrain from promises. To Dave Hobart he was equally noncommittal. To Uncle Gil, whom he hoped to surprise, he wrote nothing at all. If Uncle Gil happened to be absent, he would neither stay at Delys Hall nor disturb old Melchior by invading his uncle's apartment; he would put up at a hotel.

He finished *Till the Great Armadas Come*, getting three copies made. At Cherbourg he boarded his favorite liner, the *Aquitania*, which landed him at New York just before the middle of April.

In New York, where Henry Sewall entertained him at dinner and the sales manager entertained him at a speakeasy, prohibition was not so much flouted as ignored. At speakeasies the patrons drank almost anything. In private they drank bathtub gin, home-compounded of alcohol, water, and juniper drops, which they drowned with Hoffman's Pale Dry or Hoffman's Lime Dry to kill the taste. Jeff, who liked beer and wine, learned at one session to beware of this gin.

Easter Sunday would fall on April 17th. Although a native New Orleanian, Jeff Caldwell had never seen much of the river. The Grand Bayou Line would get him from Cincinnati to New Orleans in five days. On the 16th he took a night train to Cincinnati, spent Easter Sunday in the Queen City and that night at the Netherland Plaza Hotel.

The following morning was cool without being chilly enough for a topcoat. After making his one-way reservation at the company's office, Jeff boarded the big stern-wheeler: four decks glistening white against slate-gray water, under white pilot-house and black chimney.

He made himself comfortable in his room, starting to unpack. Shortly before departure time, amid a straggle of other passengers getting their bearings, he descended to the ornate forward lounge on the cabin deck. And into the lounge marched Serena Hobart.

Serena's manner said, 'Accept me as I am, please, or don't bother me.' Determinedly no-nonsense as well as determinedly athletic, nevertheless she had charm hard to resist. Sleek honey-blonde hair framed a pretty face which seemed almost overdelicate, despite the firmness of the jaw. Serena wore fashionable batik, its skirt knee-length, and carried an alligator-skin handbag.

"Hel-*la*, Jeff!" she greeted him, polite without being cordial. But she did not seem at ease. "It's been a long time, hasn't it? Now don't say you're surprised to find me making the journey by boat!"

"I wasn't going to say that. Good to see you, Serena."

"Really, now, why shouldn't I go home this way? If it comes to that, why shouldn't either of us?"

"No reason whatever, of course. Sorry about your father."

"We were all sorry. But it's a fact of nature; it can't be changed;

9

let's not get pious and platitudinous. After all, why should I be in such a hurry to get home? There's no cause for hurry, until—" She stopped.

"Until when?"

"Oh, just 'until'! Until any time you choose, I mean."

"Serena, what's been happening at New Orleans?"

"Nothing much, as you'll soon learn."

"Well, how's Dave?"

"Pretty much as usual. Poor Dave! He's my brother and I'm fond of him, but he does think too little and talk too much. As for what I'm doing here," she continued, with a sudden rush, "I was visiting a friend. Jeff, do you remember Helen Farnsworth in the old days? No; I think she was after your time. Anyway, she's Helen Westerby now; married somebody else you don't know. Which reminds me . . ."

At her side now loomed a large, shambling, sandy-haired young man in a tan suit of plus-fours with diamond-pattern stockings. Serena touched the newcomer's sleeve with her left hand and raised candid blue eyes.

"Speaking of people you don't know, Jeff, I'd better do the necessary." She wagged her handbag. "Charles Saylor, Jeff Caldwell."

"It's a pleasure, Mr. Caldwell!" said the large young man, shaking hands heartily. "You see, Mr. Caldwell . . ."

"All things considered," Serena appraised both of them, "hadn't you two better get on a first-name basis? Under the circumstances . . ."

"I'd heard about you, Jeff, though I never expected to meet you quite so soon. You see, I'm—" And *he* stopped.

"Yes, Mr. Saylor or Charles? Must everybody make cryptic remarks?"

"Nothing cryptic about it; tell you later. Can't say I'm very familiar with this part of the world, or with New Orleans either; my bailiwick is Philadelphia. Never mind! We'll be under way in a minute or two. And then lunch. And then . . . !"

Mr. Saylor's gesture seemed to conjure up unimaginable joys. They did get under way soon afterwards, with something of a flourish from the pilot-house, and presently went down to their excellent lunch in a white-and-gilt salon called the Plantation Room. Each table had been set for four. Serena commandeered one such table, graciously acting as hostess.

"If anybody else tries to sit with us," she instructed them, "just wave him away and tell him it's reserved. I knew Jeff was here; I saw him come aboard. There'll be somebody else joining us, though not today. And it's all right; I've already seen the steward.

"Now, Jeff," Serena warned, indicating the white-jacketed Negroes in attendance, "mind you don't refer to the *waiters* as stewards. There's only one steward: an officer; he has charge of waiters, porters, busboys, maids, and so on. We don't use ocean-going terms on the river, you know."

"I do know, Serena. I'm from New Orleans too."

But he learned nothing, either then or at dinner that evening. Whenever he so much as hinted at questions on his mind, Serena changed the subject or turned it off with some remark designed to show he must be an ill-mannered Paul Pry. Charles Saylor, whom he was further instructed to call Chuck, seemed to have adopted very similar tactics.

Following dinner, they played desultory three-handed bridge in the after cabin lounge. Once a burly, red-faced, genial-looking man, with four gold stripes round the sleeve of his uniform, strode through the lounge and greeted Serena in passing, but did not stop. At length Chuck Saylor, as though now taking charge, porten-tously said: "Follow me!"

He led them to a double stateroom on the same deck (all the rooms were double), which he shared with some passenger not at present in evidence. Here he produced a quart of colorless liquid calling itself Gordon's Dry Gin, together with a bottle of ginger ale more conventional than any sold under the Hoffman label in New York. He rang for glasses and ice, which were promptly brought.

The room grew thick with cigarette smoke. Serena and their host each had two drinks. Jeff, after valiantly finishing his first glass of what could only have been the Philadelphia variety of a familiar beverage, declined a second. Serena had already declined a third.

And still Jeff learned nothing. Once Serena, abstracted, had muttered a name that sounded like 'old Merriman.' Since Dave in the letter had called him Sabatini, presumably Rafael Sabatini, he wondered if Serena with equally heavy facetiousness meant the pen name of the author who had written historical romances as Henry Seton Merriman.

But he did not pursue this. Whatever they said or refrained from saying, a feeling of tension persisted and increased. At half-past eleven he took his leave.

He ascended to his own room, donned night-gear, and sat down to read. A friend in England had sent him bound page-proofs of a book, eagerly awaited by Jeff but not yet published, which had arrived at his New York hotel on Saturday. He had also the most recent number of the *American Mercury*. But tonight even his favorite detective fiction failed to hold him. The *Mercury* he could not face.

At just before midnight he turned in. An hour later, still scratchily awake, he gave it up and went out on deck.

So here he stood, in breezy night over the broad Ohio, on what Serena would have protested to hear him call the starboard side of the sun deck. There was no sound from the engines, hardly even a vibration: only churning, splashing water under the great stern wheel. If for some reason Serena must be secretive or cryptic, what did he already know?

Comparatively little. Everything seemed to turn on the death of Harald Hobart towards the end of February. The late Harald was always reputed to have been somewhat erratic, though not so romantically erratic as old Commodore Fitzhugh, who, paying heavily to get brick replaced on brick, had imported his mansion from across the sea. Commodore Hobart . . . that legend of a secret hoard . . .

Jeff flung his cigarette over the side and whipped round, staring into shadows towards the stern. There was nobody there, of course; there could *be* nobody there. Yet the sensation of someone standing there and watching, eyes fixed on the back of Jeff Caldwell's neck . . .

You could imagine anything at this drugged, drowsy hour of the morning. He returned to his cabin and closed the door. Sleep still seemed impossible. As again he took up the bound page-proofs, it was not imagination that footsteps approached along the deck outside, and someone knocked lightly but insistently at the door.

"Yes?" Jeff almost shouted. "Come in!"

The door was opened by David Hobart.

Dave, the 'artistic' member of the family, wore pajamas, slippers, and a lightweight black dressing-gown patterned with silver dragons. Of middle height, thin but muscular and virile, he had the brooding look we customarily associate with dark-complexioned persons rather than fair. A lock of fair hair had tumbled across his forehead, and he fiddled at his chin.

"Well—" he began.

"A while ago," Jeff said, "I thought I heard somebody prowling around outside. Were *you* prowling around outside?"

"What do you mean, prowling around outside? I've just come up from the texas, that's all. Got a few things to tell you."

" 'For this relief much thanks.' I'm going to get some solid facts," Jeff vowed, "if I have to use the torture of the rack. What's the matter, Dave? What's wrong?"

Dave hesitated.

"There's all hell to pay, I'm afraid," he answered. "Delys Hall may not really be Deadly Hall. But a whole volcano is going to blow up in a few days. That's what I'm here to tell you."

2

"Just a minute, Dave!"

"Yes?"

"At our table in the dining-room, there's a seat reserved for somebody who's supposed to be joining the boat later. Does that mean you?"

"Good God, no! Besides, I'm already aboard."

"So I see. But Serena said—"

"Serena?" Dave stared. "Don't tell me she's here too?"

"I do tell you."

"What's *she* doing up north?"

"Visiting a New Orleans friend whose name used to be Helen Farnsworth. Her married name is . . ."

"Westerby? Helen Westerby?"

"That's it. Serena said—"

"Then it's funny, it's damn funny. Mind, I don't say the gal lies in her teeth; I don't say that at all; but it's funny. Still, Serena likes to be mysterious just for the sake of being mysterious. Travelling alone, as I am?"

"Not exactly alone. She's travelling with, or at least in the company of, a character called Charles or Chuck Saylor, S-a-y-l-o-r. From Philadelphia."

"Never heard of him. Who is he? What does he do?"

"That's what I can't find out, though Serena says there's some reason why Saylor and I ought to be *en rapport*. Between 'em they've got a trick of turning every straight question crooked; it's like lunging at a fencer. Are you going to do the same thing?"

"No, not on your life! I'm here to impart information."

"Then you might begin imparting it. If you didn't know Serena's a passenger, does she know you're a passenger?"

"I don't think so; I've taken pretty good care she can't. Listen, Jeff. I trust you; I've always trusted you. When I saw you walk on board this morning . . ."

"There seems to be some lack of mutual confidence between the Hobarts. You say you trust me. Does that mean you don't trust your own sister?"

Dave raised his hand as though to take an oath.

"Old son, of course I trust her! Serena's in this too, however it eventually turns out. You see, I've been on a little mission for the good of the family. At the moment you might call me a kind of stowaway, a paying stowaway."

"Paying stowaway?"

"Like this," Dave said with great intensity. "I'm in 240 below on the texas, directly under this one; booked the whole room, as you seem to have done too. I sneaked on board early this morning, before passengers are usually allowed; I've been sort of hiding there. But I've squared everything with Captain Josh."

"With whom?"

"Captain Joshua Galway, always called Captain Josh. The Grand Bayou Line is owned by the Galways, who've been on the river for generations."

"Is Captain Josh a thick-set, red-faced man with a broad grin?"

"Yes. I made him swear he'd keep my presence a complete secret."

"And he agreed?"

"Well, he read me quite a lecture; said I'd have to do my own bribing of the help if I wanted food delivered in private. But he's a hell of a good fellow, and an old family friend, so . . ."

Jeff looked at his companion.

"Did you use an alias too? Dave, for God's sake! Sneaked aboard? Hiding there? Complete secret? Food in private? Why are *you* being so damn secretive?"

"Now I think of it," Dave drew a deep breath, "no real reason at all. We'll reveal the light of my countenance tomorrow morning.

Meanwhile, let me repeat that I've got things to tell you. And this deserves a drink in honor of your return. It's a little late, but that doesn't matter. Come down to my quarters with me, and I'll break out a bottle."

"If this is more bathtub gin—"

"It's not gin at all. It's Scotch, imported stuff. It may have been cut, but at least it's drinkable. And I've already got the makings. Don't argue, now; just come *on!*"

They went out on deck, dressing-gowns flapping in the breeze, and down the outside stairs on the two-whistle side.

Stateroom 240, somewhat smaller than the one above, was equally comfortable. All the lamps had been left burning here; in full light Dave Hobart looked haggard, even a trifle ill. Two tumblers stood on the bedside table, together with a bowl of melting ice cubes.

Dave set out a pint bottle, poured generous potations over ice, and added tap-water. If it did not quite live up to the label, it proved a fair approximation. They both lighted cigarettes, each taking one of the armchairs.

"Jeff," Dave began with the same intensity as before, "how familiar are you with my family history?"

"Not very familiar. I've heard the general outline, but very few details."

"That's what I thought. Some people might imagine that you, the history fiend, would have investigated a wild story so close to home."

"I haven't investigated, I suppose, *because* it's so close to home."

"Fair enough. But it's very important you should hear the details, or such details as are now known. I've got to take you back a long way, almost three quarters of a century, to the year 1860. That's the year my father was born, and my grandmother died in childbirth. My grandfather, generally called Commodore Hobart, Confederate States Navy, as he afterwards was . . ."

"He had not become C.S.N., you mean, because that particular navy didn't yet exist?"

"Right!" Dave sipped, set down his glass, and pointed with the cigarette. "Fitzhugh Hobart was born October 31st, 1827, and died

16

late in 1903, at just past seventy-six; I can only faintly remember him.

"Most people think of him as the dashing captain of the Confederate raider *Louisiana* or as the bearded patriarch his portrait shows. In the summer of 1860 he was thirty-two years old, ten months married to Ingrid De Meza of Denmark, and, though mad-keen on all things nautical, had become commodore only of the Delta Yacht Club. But that summer, not learning either of his son's birth or his wife's death, one of the world's great romantics had set forth on a romantic dream. With his own schooner he went after sunken treasure in the Bahamas."

"That's just the point, Dave. Did he find any treasure?"

"He did; there's no doubt of it."

Here Dave sprang to his feet.

"You know me, Jeff: I'm a fairly useless sort of fellow. In my extreme youth I thought *I* wanted to write, as you did. You meant what you said; for me I knew it would never be. But in this family matter I really *have* assembled the facts, as carefully and conscientiously as though I could make sense of 'em, which I can't.

"As far back as the seventeenth century," he continued, "fifteen Spanish treasure-galleons, homeward bound for Cadiz from South America, foundered and sank in a gale off the Ambrogian Reefs at the tip of the Bahamas: British territory. Their cargo consisted mainly of gold bullion in the form of ingots, with additions of specie and jewels. A British adventurer had recovered some of the loot, though very little in proportion to its over-all worth; my grandfather hauled up some more. But the great bulk of that treasure, estimated at a value of some nineteen million dollars, has never been found and is there to this day. Are you following me?"

"Closely."

"Old Fitzhugh was an ingenious devil; his whole career proved it. Maybe we think of nineteenth-century diving expeditions as being crude, half-baked attempts. That's a mistake. Jules Verne could write *Twenty Thousand Leagues Under the Sea* in 1870. If you study the subject, you'll find that sixty-odd years ago their

17

diving equipment—canvas-and-rubber suit, metal helmet, with air pumped down through a tube from above—was only a less sophisticated version of what we've got today.

"And adventurers had quite a piratical style at that time. If my esteemed grandparent had reported his discovery to the British authorities, he'd have been lucky to keep any considerable part of what he recovered. But he never told 'em; he never meant to. He slipped in and out so nimbly, so secretly, that they never even knew he'd been searching for treasure, let alone had found it. So he and his crew sailed home in triumph with the loot.

"We know what he did. The specie . . . minted coins, that's to say . . ."

"I understand what specie is. Well?"

Dave assumed an air of profundity.

"Specie and jewels he sold on the q.t. for what they'd fetch. The gold he hid, and hid with such craft that nobody's ever been able to lay hands on the stuff. Where he hid so much gold, how he *could* have hidden it beyond detection, has baffled shrewder wits than mine. This much, ancient friend, we actually know."

"All right, but how do we know it?"

"From notes left by the commodore," said Dave, beginning to pace the room, "and from what he told my father. There are clues to the problem, which I needn't explain now, for those who want to have a try at it. And the story has two parts, as you'll see. At this point they momentarily divide before uniting again.

"In those days the family had a considerable number of business interests. Not that these much interested Fitzhugh, who hated business and said he couldn't be bothered with it. Still, he did pretty well. Among the business interests was a big sugar plantation fifteen or sixteen miles upriver. Now you've heard, haven't you, we're distantly related to the Norman English family of Delys?"

"Yes, I seem to have heard it somewhere."

"Cut the sarcasm, old son! Fitzhugh himself bought that plantation, also on the q.t., before leaving to look for treasure. But he couldn't be bothered with growing sugar either. At the end of the eighteen-fifties an indigent younger son of the Delys clan had emigrated from England with his wife. Fitzhugh set 'em up as master and mistress of Faracres, the plantation, in a big pillared house that's now dust. Though my grandsire owned and continued to own the place, he let everybody think the real owner was Arthur Delys.

"Then came the Great Unpleasantness of '61–'65.

"It's important to mention that at this time Fitzhugh Hobart, who soon became Captain Hobart and then Commodore Hobart, had two great friends. One remained his friend, the other didn't. The first of these, who remained his friend, was the grandfather for whom you were named: Colonel Jeffrey Caldwell of the 4th Louisiana." Dave stopped pacing. "Let me think, now, Jeff! Didn't you yourself see service with the infantry during the late Great War?"

" 'See service' is much too strong a term; I never got near the front. I wound up as a shavetail in the 18th Connecticut."

Dave straightened up.

"Got a very slight heart condition," he declared, "that kept *me* out of the navy! Never mind; back to old shades. Fitzhugh's other crony, who didn't stay a crony very long, was a financial genius named Bernard Dinsmore, seven or eight years his senior.

"Trouble between 'em flared up even before the outbreak of hostilities. Fitzhugh called him a damn Yankee-lovin' traitor, and told him to go north with his goddamn friends.

"Fitzhugh never forgave him. My father, only a baby then, later took steps to investigate the quarrel. My father always said the accused had been badly misjudged, and that right should have been done. Bernard Dinsmore, though a sharp businessman, just wanted the South to forget war. But he got into such hot water that he had to go north. If he didn't join the Yankees in any active sense, he did make a fortune there. Bernard's only surviving relative is his grandson, who must be a good deal older than either of us: Horace Dinsmore, a very pious and sour-faced Boston clergyman."

Dave had begun pacing again.

"You'll soon see, Jeff, how all this affects us today. The war storms rolled, wrecking so many Confederates but leaving the Hobarts untouched. Any bitterness is forgotten now, although one or two still gripe about what they did to Georgia in '64. In New Orleans *we* had 'em on our necks from '62 until the last carpetbagger was chased out in '77.

"Once Hobart fate hung in the balance when 'Spoons' Butler, the Federal commander, wanted to take over that plantation house upriver. Why they wanted a house so far from town I can't tell you, but then Spoons wanted anything he could get, including the silverware. If they had known the place belonged to Fitzhugh, who had been playing hell with Union shipping . . . ! But Arthur Delys swore Faracres was his own, and maybe by that time Arthur believed it.

" 'I am a British subject,' he said truthfully. 'Unless you care to provoke an international incident, sir, you will keep your hands off my property.' Spoons thought better of it.

"Then, presently, Commodore Hobart returned. He didn't return to Faracres, where he'd lived with my grandmother; probably he expected some carpetbagger would grab it. Jeff, why do we think men who had beards couldn't have had any emotions? He never remarried, cherishing his wife's memory. His son, whom he'd called Harald in her honor, was brought up by a nurse until the boy grew old enough for boarding school. Fitzhugh took furnished rooms in the Garden District, which he made his home for many years.

"Arthur Delys and Mrs. Delys died in a fever epidemic at the end of the eighteen-seventies. With the last carpetbagger gone, my grandsire sold Faracres, safely reinvesting his considerable profit. In the spring of 1882, at the mature age of fifty-four, he went abroad; he went to England, where he'd spent his honeymoon. It was partly a sentimental pilgrimage, and partly to call on the head of the Delys family at Delys Hall, Delys, Lincolnshire.

"There it stood in the fen country: a sixteenth-century Tudor manor house, dark-red brick, many windows, with the date 1560 cut in stone over the front door. But the old boy's Delys kin, once so wealthy, had fallen on hard times; they wanted to sell. And Fitzhugh conceived another romantic dream.

"He had already bought that big tract of land outside New Orleans, upriver but quite close to town, meaning to build a home there for his old age. Now he'd do better. He would buy Delys Hall and have it taken apart for transportation, to be set up again beside the Mississippi.

"And that's what he did. Apart from gaslight for modern illumination (people were already talking electric light, but hadn't got to it), and a few other improvements like up-to-date bathrooms, there were no alterations in its history of more than three centuries. There it stands now, windows and tall chimneys and all, as you've seen it a thousand times in the past."

Jeff, who had been smoking one cigarette after another, crushed out the latest.

"I don't like to interrupt you, Dave . . ."

"Then why interrupt?"

"Because I don't understand!"

"What don't you understand, for Pete's sake?"

Jeff stood up and faced him.

"This family history is fascinating; to one with my turn of mind, anyway. But how *does* it affect the situation today?"

"Eh?"

"Dave, you're as jumpy as a cat; you've been acting like a wanted criminal. You say there's all hell to pay, and that something bad or dangerous will explode very soon. What has the commodore's story, or your father's story, got to do with some trouble that threatens you now?"

"Everything! You don't see it?"

"No. And that's not all."

"If you'd just shut up and let me get to the point," Dave told him pettishly, "maybe you *would* see. You've still got reservations; all right! If I promise to prove I'm not talking through my hat, may I have the liberty of saying what I want to say?"

"Of course. I didn't mean—"

Dave made a magnanimous gesture.

"Though it's true my father had little to do with it, I'd better include him. He was in his early twenties when they transplanted the Hall, and looked on as the workmen made those few alterations under the commodore's direction. My father studied engineering, but never finished at M.I.T. All he did, mostly, was help handle

21

financial affairs before the commodore died, and handled 'em entirely later.

"Four years after the old boy kicked the bucket, both my father and my mother were afraid they'd have to get repairs done to the fabric of the Hall. That damp climate, remember, can be rough on old brick and wood. But the architect they consulted said it wouldn't be necessary; any house that could stand the English fen country could stand Louisiana. They made no changes except to install electric light, and the architect watched it done."

"Is this relevant too?"

"Strictly relevant. Don't forget old Fitzhugh's hidden treasure."

Dave crossed to the door giving on the texas deck. He opened the door, peered out, then closed it softly and returned.

"That place," he went on, "never seemed incongruous in its new demesne, as it might have seemed. It looks old; it *is* old; it was bound to gather legends. Ever since the commodore did his transplanting job, finished in 1883, there's been a persistent rumor you must have heard because so many have heard. Delys Hall, they'll whisper, contains a secret room, a hidden room, and that's where my grandsire put his Spanish gold. Isn't there a story like that about some place in Scotland?"

"Yes, about Glamis Castle. But Glamis Castle is a huge place where almost anything might be hidden. The Hall is large, admittedly, and yet . . ."

"You needn't argue, Jeff; I agree. Another story says there's no 'room' in a technical sense, but that the gold has been stashed away between two of the walls."

"Just a minute, now! The commodore found his gold, you tell me, more than two decades before he ever set eyes on Delys Hall. If he insisted on stashing it away in some place or other, where did he stash it during those twenty-two years?"

"I don't know, and it doesn't matter. Our subject is the Hall; let's stick to it. Well, there's no gold stashed away between any of the walls; I can testify to that."

"How so?"

Dave's excitement had grown along with his nervousness.

"The workmen," he replied, "went into the walls when they put in the electricity and the telephone. And that architect had got interested enough in legends to watch everything. I was only twelve years old then; Serena was younger. Neither my father nor the architect would tell me what they kept muttering about. But little pitchers *have* big ears and eyes; I've since verified what I thought. And you needn't take my word for it. The architect in question is still very much alive; why not ask him? Nothing between the walls. At the same time," Dave sighted along his pointing forefinger, "the damn gold has got to be *somewhere* in the house!"

"Sure of that?"

"Dead sure. The commodore left notes in a big ledger he called his log, as I started to remind you. It's now available for inspection. He also talked to my father, who long afterwards talked to me."

"Gold bullion in the form of ingots, was it? How much gold?"

"The weight is roughly in those notes. I asked a friend of mine at the Planters & Southern Bank, putting it as a hypothetical question about America's gold supply, what would be the value of that weight in bullion. It works out at just under three hundred thousand dollars."

"As much gold as that?"

"As much gold as that; no kidding! 'It's here,' the old boy once said to my father, meaning in our house. 'It's not buried; in one way it's not even concealed. It's in plain sight, when you know how to look for it.' "

"He didn't say, 'When you know *where* to look for it'? He said, 'When you know *how* to look for it'? "

"His very words. Pretty wild, isn't it?"

"It's more than wild; it's against nature!" Jeff stared at him. "Dave, do you understand your own grandfather? We might reconcile the hard-boiled with the sentimental; that seems to have characterized his generation. But he left your parents one fortune, didn't he? If he salted away another fortune in some hiding place that's not a hiding place, why had he kept it so secret? Why didn't he just tell 'em?"

Dave swaggered a little, thumbs hooked at the lapels of his dressing-gown.

"To my way of thinking, the ingenious old devil enjoyed making it a challenge."

"Suppose he's been stringing everybody for all this time?"

"No, Jeff; grandpop wouldn't have lied. By all accounts he never lied, though he did get a kick from making misleading statements inside the truth, like one of those mystery stories that play fair. You used to read a lot of mysteries, didn't you?"

"I still do."

"Yes, my father liked 'em too. The old commodore would have been a fiend for the stuff, if in his day there'd been anybody to read about besides Sherlock Holmes. He never thought our family would need that gold, you know. We don't really need it now, of course, but what a triumph if somebody could read the riddle!"

"That's not the only riddle in this affair, Dave, or your grandsire's conduct either. Your own conduct is just as odd as his."

"*My* conduct?"

"Yes, yours. You say you'll explain the jitters that so patently affect you, and make everything clear. But not one word of explanation have you uttered so far!"

"Oh, I don't know. There must be some reason, mustn't there, why Delys Hall has been called Deadly Hall?"

Jeff, who had sat down, jumped up.

"Now hold it right there! Gabble away as much as you like and welcome, but I won't have that!"

"Oh, Lord, what's on your mind *now?*"

"What's been on my mind for some time. A certain book on the stately homes of England, Dave, devotes one whole chapter to Delys Hall before it was transplanted. As an amateur historian of sorts, *I* can tell you something about the place and the Delys family too."

"Well?" demanded Dave.

"Your Delys kin, who built their house two years after the accession of Queen Elizabeth, were good old stock. They were also sober, unspectacular stock: sound Protestants of Henry the Eighth's Anglican Church. They avoided squabbles, religious or political, before then and afterwards. By some miracle they even contrived to stay neutral during the English Civil War. And their private lives were just as unspectacular. No murders, duels, or tragic love affairs leading to suicide."

"Suppose *you* explain now?"

"Delys Hall had been called Deadly Hall in England. It got that name through a natural habit of our common language; 'Delys' would instantly suggest 'deadly' to the primitive sense of humor. It didn't acquire the names from anything that ever happened there, because no such thing ever happened. Has it ever been called haunted, sinister, or of ill repute in any way?"

"Not in England, maybe. But—"

"Well," Jeff pursued, "doesn't the same apply to its history on this side? The place exudes antiquity, as you've pointed out—"

"It exudes jitters, as I do myself. Damn the business, Jeff . . . !"

"Still, can you name one sinister aspect? Did anything violent ever occur there?"

"Yes, once!" Dave burst out. "Aren't you forgetting what happened that night in the fall of 1910, when you and I were both away from home for our first term at preparatory school?"

"If you mean the family friend who tumbled down the stairs in the main hall and broke his neck, it's not even violence of the sort we've been discussing. And it attracted almost no attention. That staircase is solid oak, but the treads are worn and apt to be slippery. A guest who was drunk or even careless . . ."

"Wrong in everything, old son!"

"Wrong in everything?"

Dave checked off the points on his fingers.

"You can't call Thad Peters a family friend; he had some very slight business dealings with my father. He was never careless and he couldn't have been drunk: he didn't drink. Thad Peters, in fact, was a noted athlete with a perfect sense of balance. You see, Jeff . . ."

Again Dave's eye had strayed towards the door; suddenly he went rigid. Dave darted at the door and flung it open. Then, taking one long step outside, he paused, turned towards his left, and stood staring forward along the deck.

"Good God!" he muttered.

25

3

Night murmurings, water noises: no more. Jeff, who followed Dave a moment later, also crossed the threshold to stand beside him.

Any lights in the roof over the deck had been extinguished. And Dave had already closed the little curtains at the deck window. Only a glow from the open door fell across scrubbed boards outside. Glancing forward, Jeff could see, some sixty feet from them, the indistinct shape of a woman who seemed to be leaning her elbows on the rail as she gazed out towards the vague Indiana shore.

If Dave thought he had heard somebody just outside, he must have been mistaken. The figure was too far away to have covered that distance in a second or two.

"Kate!" Dave called.

As the woman turned, still indistinct, he lifted his forefinger and crooked it, beckoning. Evidently unsurprised, but giving a little gasp none the less, she approached at a graceful walk that was not quite self-conscious.

The newcomer emerged from gloom as a tallish, handsome brunette, her figure well developed despite current fashion, in a white dress with the shortest of skirts under her long, fleecy coat, and hair confined by a cloche hat. If her manner could not have been called furtive, it had a touch of the stealthy. Beautiful brown eyes seemed to lurk in ambush. The woman called Kate might have been thirty-odd.

"Dave Hobart, as I live and breathe!" she said in her throaty voice. She extended her hand, which Dave took briefly. He did not appear over-cordial.

Kate ignored this. Her gaze, combining the soulful with the sensual, searched Dave's face. She dropped her hand on his left shoulder, then let it wander down to his chest.

"When I passed once today, do you know, I *thought* I saw you hiding in there—positively hiding, poor boy—as though you didn't want to be seen! Silly of me, wasn't it, being only poor little me? But . . ."

"Hiding? Who's hiding, for God's sake? I'm very much in the open, as always. And I do want to present a very old friend of mine, also bound for our destination on the levee. Mr. Caldwell, Mrs. Keith. Jeff, meet Kate."

"*Such* a pleasure, Mr. Caldwell!" carolled Mrs. Keith. "I've heard of you, of course. You're—" Her attention returned to Dave. "Is Mr. Caldwell your roommate for the trip?"

"No; we're each travelling alone. Have *you* got a roommate, Kate?"

"Davey-boy, I'm alone too! Anyway, what girl *would* travel with an old widow woman like me? Returning to the city of your fathers, Jeff?"

"Only for a very short time, I'm afraid," Dave answered for him. "However, I think I can persuade him to stay with us at the Hall."

"How terribly nice! Or at least I expect it is. *He* won't fall downstairs and break his neck, I hope? Oh, dearie me," Kate exploded, "there I go again! *Such* a blabbermouth, they tell me, with no more tact than an Arkansas farmer. I hadn't intended to mention that, Dave, and I swear I'll never mention it again!"

"Somebody's going to mention it, Kate, maybe talk about it a lot."

"Well, *I* won't!" she assured him. "I never met the poor man who got killed. And of course it happened a long time ago, when I was only a little girl. But I've never forgotten that part about the plate and the big silver jug!"

Here Jeff glanced at Dave, who refused to meet his eye. Instead Dave glanced into the room behind them. Whatever he may have been feeling, he did not forget his manners.

"I apologize for the informality and the dressing-gowns, Kate. Still, no use standing out here, is there? Care to join us in a drink?"

For a moment Kate Keith seemed badly upset.

27

"I'd *love* to, honey, as you know very well! But I was only walking to make me sleepy; it'll be all right now. So I'd better not; *truly* I'd better not!" After one last twist at a button on Dave's pajama-coat, she stood back, her eyes never leaving his face. "I need more sleep than some people, unless I find better pursuits to keep me occupied. Good night, good night, good night!"

Away she went, heels rapping, forward along the texas deck. Dave continued to watch the retreating back of the lissome, *soignée* widow who left so little doubt of what motivated her. Jeff, drawing back into the doorway, also watched until Mrs. Keith, so far towards the bow as to have become invisible, opened some very distant door, beyond which a small lamp glimmered, and slid herself inside.

"What stateroom would that be, Dave?"

"It's not a stateroom at all; it's one entrance to the texas lounge. Somebody's left a light on. Well . . ."

They both re-entered Dave's room. Dave closed the door and then shook his fist in the air.

" 'Po' li'l me!' " he mocked savagely. "Po' li'l this, po' li'l that! What about the po' bastard who hears her?"

"Kate Keith," Jeff was musing. "K.K. There ought to be a third initial, oughtn't there?"

"There is. Her maiden name was Kettering, if you can imagine her as maiden in anything."

"She's got designs on you, obviously."

"Kate's got designs on any male currently available. She may be alone now, but she won't be alone for long. She makes this trip as regularly as the river gamblers did in my grandfather's time. Damn her, Jeff! Damn her to hell and back!"

"Easy, Dave. She's a very attractive woman."

"Oh, Kate's attractive. And she's got all the right skills, if only she'd keep from talking. But the variety of things she wants, and how often she wants 'em . . . !"

"Since when did *you* start preaching sermons?"

Dave seemed to struggle within himself.

"I don't want to sound like a Christer, which I'm not. I couldn't preach sermons if I wanted to. There's a gal in my own life, as there usually is. It doesn't seem to affect many of us; it does affect me. When I think of something I oughtn't to do . . ."

"That doesn't prevent you from doing what you oughtn't to do; it just prevents you from enjoying it?"

"My damn guilty conscience is all over me! Yes, there's a gal on my mind right now. But, though I mustn't sound like Kate either, I don't want to talk about *that*."

"Never mind." Jeff soothed him. "This slight family acquaintance, Thad Somebody . . ."

"Thad Peters, of Danforth & Co., Baton Rouge."

"Thad Peters, of Baton Rouge, the one who fell downstairs and broke his neck. Do you mind talking about him?"

"No; is there any reason I should mind?"

"That's the point, Dave. Since it happened seventeen years ago, or almost seventeen years ago, why does it affect you now?"

"It doesn't, as a rule. I haven't even thought about it in years. Recently, though, I remembered some peculiar circumstances that didn't become generally known at the time . . ."

"Peculiar circumstances? You never passed 'em along to me."

"No, you bet I didn't! I was told to keep my mouth shut or lose my allowance."

"They made us shut up about everything in those days. Anyway, what's all this about a plate and a big silver jug?"

Dave, who seemed about to preach or at least to lecture, made illustrative gestures.

"That very large, ornamental silver water pitcher, with its silver tray. It used to be on the sideboard in our dining-room, which everybody calls the refectory. Remember the pitcher and tray?"

"I probably saw both, but didn't notice. There was a lot of stuff on the sideboard. Here's the problem, Dave. Is there anything so very peculiar about a guest falling on those stairs? The athletic Mr. Peters starts downstairs—in the middle of the night, if memory serves—he misses his footing . . ."

"No, Jeff; wrong again. He wasn't on his way downstairs, you see. He'd *been* downstairs, and was on his way up again, when . . . Want to hear about it?"

"I've been waiting to hear."

"It happened," Dave began oracularly, "in November of 1910; the exact day doesn't matter. I was away at school; Serena had been visiting Aunt Betsy upstate. Apart from servants, there was nobody in the house but Thad Peters and my parents. Oh, and old Ira Rutledge, who'd been spending the night, though he doesn't count.

"At two o'clock in the morning they heard one hell of a metallic crash, which woke everybody up. The whole house was dark. They found Thad Peters, in sweater and sports flannels and tennis shoes, lying at the foot of the main staircase with his neck broken. He had a flashlight in his pocket, but doesn't seem to have used it. The silver pitcher and the tray, both fairly weighty, lay some distance away where he'd dropped 'em.

"Well, *why?*" demanded Dave, squaring himself. "You see what he did and must have done. In the small hours he left his bedroom; he went downstairs. Didn't I tell you the pitcher and the tray were kept in the refectory: nowhere else? For some unknown reason, carrying a massive empty pitcher on its tray, he had started upstairs when he came to grief. And echo still answers, why? Those are the real facts, though they didn't get into the press or come out at the inquest."

Jeff found his wits whirling.

"There was a police investigation," he said, "but the evidence didn't get into the press or come out at the inquest?"

"For one thing, both the District Attorney and the coroner were family friends."

"Still, even if they were both playing favorites . . . ?"

Backed against the dressing-table, Dave again sighted along his pointing forefinger.

"Incredible as this may sound, they weren't playing favorites or hushing it up. The whole business was handled by a capable police detective, Lieutenant Trowbridge, who afterwards made his name with some affair out at Bayou St. John. He's retired now. In the case of Thad Peters, clearly an accident, the D.A. didn't think any good purpose would be served by too much publicity. They had reached the worst possible *impasse.*"

"Oh?"

"They had found the truth, but the truth made no sense. It's as

30

though something on those stairs grabbed the victim and threw him down."

"That won't do," Jeff retorted, "and you know it won't."

"But—!"

"You can't be suggesting some malevolent force or presence on the stairs? I don't believe that; you don't believe it either. In fact, Dave," he held his companion's gaze, "it's something else, isn't it? There's something else behind all this, isn't there, that's really been worrying you for so long?"

"Maybe there is. I thought I could tell you and get it off my chest, but some matters aren't easy even to approach. If I do tell you, it'll have to be by easy degrees. God knows I've got my reasons! Then, too, there's Serena."

"Serena? What about her?"

"I said in my letter, I think, that the Ice Maiden's had *her* moments of brooding. Listen, Jeff. If I tell you something in strictest confidence, you won't tell Serena you know?"

"No; I'll respect your confidence."

"Visiting Helen Westerby, was she?" demanded Dave. "Helen *used* to live just outside Cincinnati; her husband's a big noise in some big manufacturing firm. Just less than a year ago he was transferred to Jacksonville, Florida. Whoever Serena's been seeing up north, it can't have been Helen. Who was it?"

"Any ideas?"

"None at all; that's part of the confidential information." Dave hesitated. "I can't help knowing, Jeff, she's always had the reputation of being a teaser, or something very much like a teaser. You're supposed to biff any man in the eye, aren't you, if he suggests that about your sister? But I've got a pretty shrewd idea it's true, or has been true in the past. I don't think it's true now. I think she's got a boy friend, and has fallen hard at last. Who the hell he could be is another question. This fellow Saylor you mentioned . . . ?"

"Possibly, Dave, though that didn't seem to be the atmosphere. If Serena does have a boy friend, anything or anybody is possible. He may be Saylor; he may be the Prince of Wales or Douglas Fairbanks or Joe the Dog-Catcher. Is there any earthly reason she *shouldn't* have a boy friend?"

31

"No, of course not! But what's worrying her so much?"

"Well, what's worrying you?"

Whereupon Dave the mercurial seemed suddenly to alter his mood.

"Do you know, Jeff," he burst out, "this unrelieved gloom of ours is the worst possible medicine we could take. If all the news from my camp is depressing, can't we see any hope from yours? Are you going to find New Orleans dull after Paris? Or are you looking forward, just a little, to revisiting glimpses of the moon? Don't you ever think about any of the gang you used to know?"

Jeff tried to catch at the same mood.

"As a matter of fact, Dave, only tonight I thought about little Penny Lynn. Penny was always such a charmer, though, that she must have married years ago."

"Wrong for the umpteenth time, me bucko! She's still there, and still unattached; won't listen to any of her suitors. Serena thinks Penny's carrying a torch for you. Do you understand what I mean by carrying a torch?"

"Yes, I understand. But I can't think of anything less likely."

"Why so unlikely?"

"I have seen Penny only three times in my life. Two of those occasions were disastrous."

"Disastrous, eh?"

"By a couple of sheer accidents, one of them not even remotely my fault, she became convinced I only wanted to embarrass her in the worst possible way. It wasn't true, naturally; I was as embarrassed as she was, or more so. But I couldn't persuade her of that; I couldn't even get past her parents to see her."

Dave left the dressing-table and sat down in the chair he had previously occupied.

"Got any objection to telling me?"

Jeff had met Penny, as he tried to explain, during the Christmas vacation when he was seventeen, and the Lynns had just moved to New Orleans from Kentucky. There had been a very formal, heavily chaperoned dance at the home of old Madame de Saure. An image of Penny returned to him from the past: the fleecy yellow-brown hair, the gray-blue eyes vivid in so pretty a face, the whole concentration of femininity.

"She's younger than I, and seemed very young, but so mature of face and figure she couldn't have escaped notice. She wore a foamy, frilly evening-gown, lilac-colored, that there's some cause to remember. We were getting along at a great rate; I thought I'd lost my heart and had begun to lose my head.

"As we finished about our tenth dance, I failed to notice my left foot—part of it, anyway—was on the hem of her gown. The music stopped. Penny jumped back to applaud the orchestra. Her gown split wide open from neckline to waist, and was yanked off her bodily. She had on underwear, of course; they all did in those days. But it left her in her underwear before the whole ballroom. Penny didn't say anything. For a second she just stood there, paralyzed, then burst into tears and ran off the floor.

"Well, that was bad enough. The other occasion . . ."

"Yes, I do seem to have heard something about your second meeting. Tried to undress her again, didn't you?"

"No, of course not! And it isn't so very funny, Dave."

"I know; sorry if I started to laugh. That sort of thing is funny only when it happens to somebody else. What's the truth of the matter?"

Their next encounter had been harmless, and had occurred during the Christmas vacation two years later. Staying at Uncle Gil's because the family home had been sold, Jeff was crossing Lee Circle one afternoon when Penny and her father had driven past in the latter's Pierce Arrow. Penny had raised her hand in recognition, giving an uncertain half smile; even her old man condescended to nod. Judging himself forgiven, the culprit had telephoned and requested her company at some function the next week.

"It was a big do at the St. Charles Hotel. This episode also concerns a staircase, though not tragically except to dignity. I mean those broad, high stairs in the lobby of the St. Charles, from the lobby to the mezzanine floor. They used to be covered with thick, smooth red carpet . . ."

"They still are. Well?"

"Penny and I had been in one of the rooms on the mezzanine floor, and had started downstairs. I didn't jostle her; I didn't so much as touch her, in spite of what they said afterwards. She was walking rather fast, and she slipped. All of a sudden, before I could catch her, she pitched straight forward and rolled. It may have been something on the stairs; it may have been something in her corsage. This time her gown, a silvery-tissue sort of thing, ripped apart from corsage to hem. She scrambled up too quickly afterwards, before she realized it wasn't only her dress she'd begun to lose. The underwear was torn too, and fell off down to the waist. Penny caught the underwear before it had slipped below her waist, but it did fall that far. And there weren't many people in the lobby, but they did include her mother.

"Penny cried out: 'What'll you do to me next time, not that there'll ever *be* a next time? Strip me completely?' That was all, except for the uproar. Again she burst into tears and ran. Yes, the woes of adolescence are always supposed to be funny. But if you laugh I'll break your neck!"

"I wasn't laughing, Jeff," Dave assured him. "You say you couldn't smooth her down?"

"Not then; not afterwards. She wouldn't see me again. When I did reach her by phone, her old man intervened and cut us off. I tried again later, but her mother broke it up with the same tactics. I tried several times, once when I could feel reasonably sure both parents were absent, and Penny sent word by the maid that there was nothing she cared to discuss. The psychiatrists, our modern witch doctors, might say she'd been through a traumatic experience. Probably she still holds it against me."

"After all the time that's elapsed?" scoffed Dave. "Don't you believe it, son. Don't you believe one word of it!"

"What do *you* know about the business?"

"Nothing, but I know women. Penny's much too good-natured to have remembered for long. And if she *is* carrying the torch, as I suspect, she won't really care what you did then or what you may do in the future. Anything else I can explain for you?"

"Yes. You can explain what's worrying both you and Serena."

A deep, hoarse blast of the steamboat's whistle went vibrating up. And at that moment Serena Hobart herself, in the dark semi-formal dress she had worn at dinner, opened the door and entered from the deck.

"Really, Dave—" she began with strong disapproval.

The whole emotional atmosphere had altered. Dave sprang up, instantly defensive.

"It's all right, Serena! I haven't said one word of what mustn't be said!"

"That's a relief, if I can trust you. There's at least one matter," and a glance passed between them, "that must never be touched on or so much as hinted at, no matter how curious your friends may be. When I learned you were favoring us with your presence . . ."

"All right, all right! Sit down and make yourself comfortable, then. How'd you know where to find me?"

Blonde Serena, as poised as a Michael Arlen heroine, allowed herself to be installed in Dave's armchair, and regarded him with pitying indulgence while he prowled and fussed.

"Not long ago," she said, "I was sitting by myself in the texas lounge, thinking of this and that, when who should walk in but Kate Keith. I hadn't seen her at lunch or dinner; apparently Kate hadn't seen me, though she'd hardly have missed you. She said you were here, among other things." Serena lifted one shoulder. "Of course I had to pretend I knew it all along, and knew what you were doing in this part of the world. Incidentally, Dave, just where *have* you been?"

"I went to consult the expert, that's all! Then, since neither of us need be home much before May 1st, this seemed easily the most pleasant way to travel."

"Pleasant, Dave? I'd have said so too, until this morning. Now I'm not at all sure." Serena's cool smile swept round. "Jeff here is something of a privileged character, let's admit, but he mustn't carry it too far. Still feeling so insatiably curious, Jeff?"

"I am curious," Jeff retorted, "because I have been given considerable reason to feel curious."

"Oh, really? What particular reason, for instance?"

Jeff looked at her.

"First Ira Rutledge writes me a letter, saying he wants to see me in New Orleans about some delicate situation (unstated) involving me and one other person (unnamed) outside the Hobart family. Then Dave writes in the same vein, but with more urgency, insisting I've got to be there because it's so very important. The nature

35

of this situation, or how it can concern one other non-relative besides myself, is never so much as indicated. Finally, what mystic significance attaches to the date of May 1st?"

"May 1st, Jeff?"

"Ira mentioned some date before the end of April. Dave specifically said May 1st, which he's just quoted again. In short, what's it all about and why May 1st?"

Dave whirled towards him, fuming.

"Now listen, Sabatini—!"

"The Hobart sense of humor," Jeff pointed out, "is never long in abeyance. You called me Sabatini in the letter, if you remember. Earlier tonight, Dave, Serena herself muttered a name that sounded like 'Merriman.' She didn't seem to be looking at me, but I've got a feeling she meant the late Henry Seton Merriman. If you both find endless amusement in christening me with the name of some comparatively recent historical novelist, alive or dead, you might vary the list. There's Stanley Weyman, there's Charles Major . . ."

Serena laughed with very evident sincerity.

"No, Jeff. That's not funny, agreed; you can't seem to see what *is* funny. It's your whole verbose tirade, which would be a bore and a nuisance if it weren't so completely ludicrous." Then her mockery rang. "Delicate situation, is it? Delicate situation, indeed! We'd better tell him, Dave."

"But—!"

"We'd better tell him, I say, or he'll only hear from Ira and draw the wrong conclusions. It's not delicate; it's not important; it's nothing at all."

"That part of it, you mean?" asked Dave.

"That part of it, of course. As technically head of the house now, you'd better tell him yourself. Then two of his hideous perplexities, my supposed clumsiness of speech and the awful date May 1st, will both be resolved at once. Speak up, King David of Israel! Indulge your habitual loquacity, for once with my blessing."

Dave seemed to brace himself.

"All right; *I* was being funny about Sabatini! But, if Serena did refer to anybody called Merriman," he looked at Jeff, "she didn't mean the Seton Merriman who wrote *Barlasch of the Guard*. She

36

meant Earl G. Merriman of St. Louis, Missouri. He may be a barbarian of sorts, but he's made us a very fair offer and we've promised him our decision by May 1st. You see, Jeff, we're probably selling Delys Hall."

4

When Jeff went down to breakfast at shortly past nine on Tuesday morning, few questions had been answered and few attitudes
made clear.

It had been two A.M. before he left Serena and Dave sitting
moodily in the latter's room, a thick restraint on them both. Nor
were tempers improved by thrashing round and round in the same
old circle.

"No, really, now!" Serena had said, with a shivering kind of
airiness. "I can see what you must be thinking, Jeff, but you're
wrong. There's *no* financial difficulty, truly there's not! Father may
have made one or two small investments that weren't wise, but the
bulk of the estate remains untouched. We can still be supported in
the style to which we're accustomed; Dave needn't find a job and
I won't have to take in washing."

"All the same," protested Jeff, "to sell Delys Hall . . ."

"Of course we're selling, my poor romantic idiot! I'm bored and
fed up with the place; I've been bored and fed up for a long time.
It's so phony, so essentially bogus—!"

Here Dave had intervened.

"The Hall has its disadvantages; I agree we ought to sell. But
what's phony or bogus?"

"Dressing the place up with a lot of period furniture? Pretending
we're feudal lords of the manor with centuries of history behind
us?"

Dave brooded.

"There's been a great joke," he reminded her, "about the *nou-*

veau riche countryman of ours, real or imaginary, who imported a fourteenth-century castle for his Idaho estate. But I've always felt a sneaking kind of sympathy for the fellow, who must have been very much like Earl George Merriman. Anyway, it's not the same thing."

"No, Dave?"

"No, Serena. As Jeff and I have both remarked, the Hall looks old and is old; it's never seemed out of place where it is, as a feudal castle would seem in Idaho or anywhere else. Those three and a half centuries of history (more than three and a half!) aren't a joke or a myth; they're real. Don't look so damn superior, little sister! *You're* the one who—"

Dave stopped suddenly, as though he had almost made a slip, and turned towards Jeff.

"But this is just arguing in a vacuum, old son! Does it make any difference whether or not we sell the place?"

"It does to the question under consideration. You may be selling the Hall; you may be selling anything. Regardless of that, where's the delicate situation or the matter of great importance?"

"There isn't any," Serena told him. "It's only Ira Rutledge's lawyer talk, you know."

"It's Dave's talk too, don't forget. Whatever you sell or don't sell, how can it possibly affect me and one other person outside the family?"

"More lawyer talk, I daresay." Serena drew herself up. "If there *should* turn out to be a *little* something behind it, no doubt you'll have your curiosity satisfied at the proper time. *I* wouldn't tell you even if I knew; you're too horribly impatient for your own good."

And so, presently, Jeff had left them.

He slept well, if he slept for little more than six hours. In a morning of bright sun on the water outside, he shaved, showered, and dressed at leisure. He was headed for breakfast when he remembered leaving his wrist-watch on a shelf beside the shower-stall in the little bathroom. But he need not go back for the watch now; he could always get it after breakfast. And Jeff noted something else at the same time.

He had gone indoors again on the cabin deck, entering the

forward cabin lounge on his way to the Plantation Room below, when he became conscious of a stocky, middle-aged, bald-headed man seated alone near the purser's office on the one-whistle side.

Jeff's eye passed on incuriously. He had reached the grand staircase, a sweep of brass-bound mahogany treads between curving mahogany banister-rails, and had taken one step down when something made him glance across the lounge. The middle-aged man, who wore a heavy moustache more suited to some past generation than to the clean-shaven present, had stood up and was looking in Jeff's direction with a concentration of interest as obvious as inexplicable. Finding himself observed, he instantly sat down again and became busy at lighting a cigar. Jeff hastened on down to the Plantation Room.

Though most passengers had finished breakfast and gone, some few still lingered amid a light murmur of talk. At his own table Jeff found Serena Hobart and Charles Saylor sitting over the last of their coffee. At another table for four across the room, also alone, Kate Keith and Dave Hobart seemed to be conferring.

Serena did not look as though she had slept well; last night's shadow still haunted her. But she greeted the newcomer with much of her customary *aplomb*.

"Dave's found a place for himself, as you see. Dave usually does, even if it's the wrong place. Sit down, Jeff. I must run along in a moment, but Chuck here wants a word with you. You'll use discretion about what you tell him, I hope?"

"With your example in mind, Serena, I could hardly do anything else."

As he finished ordering bacon, eggs, toast, and coffee, Jeff saw Serena's gaze move past his shoulder towards the stairs. Briefly he craned round.

The heavily moustached man of the lounge, cigar still unlighted between the fingers of his left hand, stood on the steps and surveyed the other side of the dining-room. After a moment's further inspection, he turned and tramped upstairs.

"That character with the moustache, Serena . . ."

"Yes?"

"As I passed him on my way down, for some reason or other he had his eye on me."

"You're not the only one, you know. When he was having breakfast not long ago, he very much had his eye on *me*. I may have imagined it, but I don't think so."

"Any idea who he is?"

"No, none at all. But I can easily find out. And now I *must* run. *A'voir*, good people! See you later!"

Away she went, trim in a gray tailored suit, the alligator-skin handbag under her arm.

Large, friendly Mr. Saylor did not speak until Jeff had finished eating, though he seemed to hover as though awaiting opportunity. At length he offered his companion a cigarette, took one himself, and lit both.

"There, that's better! Serena's right, you know. I do want a word with you; I wanted one yesterday. But it seemed kind of crude to remind you at once. And, anyway, I promised Serena I wouldn't. The fact is, you see . . . *do* you mind if I call you Jeff?"

"No, not at all."

"The fact is, you see, I'm a writer too. Magazine articles, mostly: that kind of thing. Not a bad deal, either, since I've been lucky enough to make the big slicks."

"Magazine articles, you say? Are you on an assignment now?"

The other's strong sense of drama kindled at once.

"Stately homes of our own country!" he proclaimed. "Why go abroad for history and legend, when we've got 'em right here at home? 'On the left bank of the Mississippi, not far from picturesque New Orleans . . .' "

"Delys Hall, naturally?"

"Delys Hall, naturally, among others. You can do most of the research at any good public library, without needing to bother people very much. But I'm going to feature Delys Hall. So much has been written about the place, not only in New Orleans, that I was pretty well informed before I decided to go down the river and soak up atmosphere. On Sunday evening, when I met Serena at the Netherland Plaza Hotel in Cincinnati, and learned who she is . . ."

"We were all at the Netherland Plaza, it seems. How has Serena taken your questioning so far?"

Saylor looked uncomfortable.

"She hasn't been very cooperative, I admit. But then she hasn't warned me off either."

"If you can't get answers from a member of the family, what sort of answers do you expect to get from me?"

"None at all! Nothing, that is, you yourself wouldn't be allowed to publish if you got permission. So help me God," swore the large young man, with an air of virtue beyond corruption, "I won't even ask to go *inside* the infernal place, if she doesn't want me to! Listen, Jeff," he continued, crushing out a cigarette he had only just lighted, and immediately lighting another, "I've never got anybody sore by one word I've ever written, and I'm proud of the record."

"Well, that's something."

"You bet it is! What really interests me, and would interest any number of readers, is this tale of a secret room, or a secret hiding place of some kind. There's only one man in America who's a real authority on architectural tricks like that; if the worst comes to the worst, which I hope it won't, I can always write to him.

"Then, again, there's the story of a mysterious death seventeen years ago. Some visitor named Peters or Peterson was carrying a load of silverware up the stairs when he fell and broke his neck. Quite a business, eh?"

Sudden alarm rang at the back of Jeff's mind.

"Where did you pick up *that* story?"

"Oh, not in the newspaper files; there's no confirmation about the load of silver. However, a friend of mine—he's an old man now, but he used to live in New Orleans—gave me the real dope. He said it was just one of those things always known to anybody really in the know, but not published or talked about. Jeff, what imaginative treatment could do with a killer force on a haunted staircase . . . !"

Jeff rapped the table with his knuckles.

"Now just a moment, Mr. Thoroughgoing Researcher! Though I'm not very familiar with magazines or their requirements, are you sure you know what you're doing? Suppose you prepared your account of the mysterious death, adding every grisly detail you could dig out or dream up, would any responsible editor publish such a tale when you couldn't substantiate the most important part?"

Sandy-haired Chuck Saylor regarded him in horror.

"You don't think I intend to write about it, do you?"

"Isn't that the idea?"

"No, it is not the idea. Sweet, suffering Moses, never in this world! Serena's father died only a few months ago. She didn't take it much to heart, as you may have noticed. But that's got nothing to do with the price of eggs. Am I such a heel that I'd risk upsetting the girl by talking about *anybody's* mysterious death, though it wasn't a death in the family and occurred as far back as 1910?"

"Thanks. That's better."

"Whereas," argued Mr. Saylor, concentrating his energies, "the business about a secret room is very different. Serena's grandfather was an old crook, a pirate on the Spanish Main or something; I must be sure of my facts. If he did have such a thing built at Delys Hall, or found one there when he took the place apart, I want to know what's what. The report of a secret room has never been any secret at all, has it?"

"No very deep secret, at least. You won't make yourself widely popular if you describe Commodore Hobart as an old crook, but . . ."

"Don't let it worry you, Jeff. I won't describe the old bastard as anything that could be offensive. And I can show legitimate interest in the secret room, hideyhole, or whatever it is. Much the same story, only more elaborate and with trimmings, has been told for centuries about Glamis Castle in Scotland."

Jeff rose to a point of order.

"Not Glam-is, if you don't mind. The name is pronounced Glams, in one syllable to rhyme with psalms."

The other uttered a wail of agony.

"These damn British pronunciations!" he cried, groping as though dazed. "They just won't say any name the way it's spelled!"

"Don't we do exactly the same thing? Judged by spelling alone, how would any erudite foreigner pronounce Connecticut or Arkansas?"

"We do it occasionally, I admit. They do it *all* the damn time, and get sore if you claim it's nuts. Cholmondoley is Chumley, Cavendish is Candish . . ."

"Not Candish, again if you don't mind. They said Candish in Thackeray's time; we have Thackeray's testimony they did. In London today, if you asked the way to Cavendish Square and called it Candish, they'd either correct you or ask which square you meant."

"Look!" urged an excited investigator, keeping his voice down but speaking with powerful persuasiveness. "Let's not argue about it, shall we? But Glamis, which I'll call Glams to please the Old South, opens up a new line of thought. Glams was one of Macbeth's castles, I seem to remember, though it mayn't have been the place where they bumped off King Duncan. Still, old Macbeth was a great one for rubbing 'em out and leaving no witnesses. Now if there should be a murder at Delys Hall, or if the killer staircase worked again . . . !"

"*Murder?* Who said anything about murder?"

"Not your obedient servant; I haven't opened my mouth, and I'm not going to. Anyway, that would be news; I don't deal in news. Again don't worry; it's not going to happen, and wouldn't be very funny if it did. But I was just thinking that—" Suddenly he broke off, listening. "Here! What's that?"

Jeff also listened.

"If you mean the music or alleged music we hear from outside —*Beautiful Obio*—it comes from a famous steamboat institution: the calliope."

"Steam calliope, eh? Like the one in circuses?"

"Something like that. If you care to go up on deck, you can watch the steam as well as listen. It plays as we approach or leave river towns."

Saylor pondered for a long moment.

"One Christmas Eve, back in West Philadelphia years ago, some pious souls or would-be humorists hired a circus-wagon calliope to roll through the streets as late as possible, waking everybody up with its deafening version of *Silent Night.* Where they found a circus-wagon towards the end of December would make a story in itself.

"Yes," he added, stubbing out his cigarette and getting up, "I figured it must be the calliope. Also, from what Serena was telling me, our first stop will be Louisville. Going ashore?"

"Not this time, I think. You?"

"Yes; I'd like to stretch my legs a little. Well . . ."

Jeff glanced across the room; both Kate and Dave had gone.

"Well, old sobersides," prompted Saylor, still hesitating, "will that be all? Any further hints or instructions for my benefit?"

"Only one. When you meet Serena, or her brother either, you might curb that feverish fancy of yours. Don't tell 'em what you wouldn't for a moment think of saying, especially about murders and a killer staircase."

The other ruffled up his sandy hair.

"How many times," he insisted, "must I tell you to quit worrying? It's all right. I'm not one to make irresponsible suggestions or misinterpret facts, as must be very plain. And I don't want trouble for anybody, least of all for myself. Just trust Uncle Chuck to handle things, which will then be as merry as a marriage-bell. And so," he concluded, as though making himself radiantly clear, "until Townsend finds that secret room and we all meet together on a peak in Darien, fare ye well with full consciousness of good works!"

Away went Saylor, making faces over his shoulder.

Jeff ordered more coffee. He sipped it slowly, and continued to sip as the *Bayou Queen* slid to her landing-stage at the left bank, where tall warehouses cut off any immediate view from the Plantation Room windows. An offstage bustle began; thuds, creaks, chain-rattlings attested the activity of the deck crew.

Presently Jeff finished the coffee and nodded to their waiter. Mounting the stairs in his turn, he sought first the open air of the cabin deck on the side away from shore, then the open air of the texas above. Here Kate and Dave Hobart accosted him at once. The latter, wearing a blue blazer, tennis flannels, and the look of one spiritually rumpled, laid a detaining hand on Jeff's arm.

"Easy, Dave! What's the matter?"

"We're being followed, that's what. Not right now, maybe, but you should have been here a while back."

"Followed?"

"This tub," Dave explained, "is two hundred and fifty feet long, two hundred and eighty-five if you count the paddle-wheel. Kate

45

and I thought we'd do ten circuits of the deck as a slight constitutional. And there he was behind us, twenty feet back but keeping up a steady pace . . ."

"*Who* was, Dave? What are you talking about?"

"Nobody seems to know who he is. Might be a naval petty officer or an army sergeant in mufti. Might be an old-fashioned bartender, with that moustache. Looks a little like all of 'em."

"Ah, our own man of mystery! Yes, I've seen him. Well? What happened?"

"Nothing actually *happened*, in the way of definite action."

"If you ask me—" began Kate, who again wore white.

"If you ask *me*, woman," Dave interrupted, "he had his eye on me and not you, though that's an odd one for anybody's book. When we slowed down," Dave continued, turning again to Jeff, "old mystery man slowed down and didn't overtake. All of a sudden we did an about-face and marched in the other direction. Then, after a little while to make it less obvious, so did he."

They stood well forward near the texas lounge, whose windows formed a three-sided wall with deck-chairs ranged underneath. Dave turned his back to the lounge.

"Maybe I'm a bit jumpy this morning. But, when mystery man had been on our trail for what seemed like half an hour, it was getting me down. I stopped; I went straight up to him and said, very politely, 'Anything I can do for you?' He just said *he'd* been taking a constitutional, and drifted into the lounge there."

Glancing through the nearest window, Jeff could see three sides of an oblong mahogany counter dispensing soft drinks and soda water either as drinks in themselves or to mix with alcohol provided by passengers. One heavy moustache could also be discerned.

"Dave, you poor boy!" Kate cried in sympathy. "If only you'd do what I want you to do . . . !"

"Whenever I do what you want me to do, pet, it leaves me in worse shape than I am now. Seriously, though," Dave addressed them both, "it's not an easy situation to deal with, you'll admit. There's nothing I can complain about or bawl him out for; the pursuing phantom's got as much right here as we have. It's this spooky feeling of being watched or spied on, that's all! And it can't go on all day, or I'll see Captain Josh and have some steps taken. Meanwhile . . ."

"We haven't *done* ten rounds of the deck, you know," Kate reminded him. "Shall we go on walking, all three of us?"

"No, thanks; I've had enough. Meanwhile, as I was saying, the boat won't stop here for long. In what ought to be a very short time—" Dave broke off, galvanized. "Yes, of course! Jeff, what time *is* it?"

Automatically Jeff thrust out his left wrist before remembering.

"Watch!" he said. "I left my watch on that ledge beside the shower; I'd better run up and get it before it disappears. No, don't trouble yourselves to follow; back in just one moment."

At least, he hoped as he hastened towards the open stairs aft, he had silenced Chuck Saylor for as long as the latter's assurances should last. It might prove no great respite. Mr. Saylor, irrepressible, would return inevitably to the image of the killer staircase he had conjured up. Killer staircase? What poisonous nonsense!

'There's been one staircase in my life,' Jeff told himself. 'I don't want something lethal, in addition to that idiotic business thirteen years ago.'

Idiotic, yes. As he thought of Penny Lynn, so shapely and yet so angry at the St. Charles Hotel, he knew he should have dismissed that incident from his mind long before he had done so. Youth's inexperience and youth's self-consciousness, encountering unforeseeable if ridiculous accident, had made them both behave as youth will.

But it was all past and done with; it could become almost a tender memory touched with nostalgia. When he reached New Orleans, he need not even try to avoid Penny. The combination of circumstances which so embarrassed her must be unique among all mishaps; it *was* unique; it could never recur.

In this frame of mind, intent only on recovering his wrist-watch, Jeff ran up to his room, opened the door, and closed it behind him. The little cubicle which housed toilet and shower had been built in the far corner of the left-hand wall, between that wall and the partition separating Room 340 from Room 339 on the other side of the sun deck. He need not even switch on the light in the cubicle;

enough sun entered through both windows.

He dashed into that confined space, reaching out for the ledge with his watch and glancing into the shower-stall on his right, just as someone turned on the shower. He saw a bathing cap of yellow rubber, he saw vivid gray-blue eyes, and he saw female flesh. He saw this one split second before her sudden gasp became a cry, before the shower curtain was yanked shut and the water turned off.

Jeff retreated in haste, shutting the bathroom door. It had been a shock, but he must not let it throw him. He leaned towards the closed door.

"This time, Penny," he called, "not even your parents could say I'm guilty. It makes quite a change, doesn't it?"

5

Penny hesitated long before replying. When she raised her soft voice, it was with less of stunned outrage than he had been expecting, but with a tendency to stammer.

"You—you *didn't* know I was here? Can't you see that chair near one of the beds?"

Over the back of the straight chair she meant hung a light-brown cloth jacket, a skirt of the same material, an orange-colored cashmere sweater, and a white silk slip. The chair's seat carried folded tan stockings and a pair of garters, with tan shoes underneath. On the nearby bed a very small soft-leather travelling bag had been opened to show further feminine apparel. Jeff addressed the door.

"There wasn't time to notice anything, Penny. May I offer one suggestion, though? If you must take a shower in someone else's quarters, you might latch the bathroom door or at least close the shower curtain."

"Someone else's—" Stupefaction momentarily choked her. "But it's *my* room! I'm to share it with Serena!"

"Did Serena tell you so?"

"I haven't s-seen her! I thought she'd m-meet me, but I haven't even s-seen her! She phoned long-distance when I was in Louisville . . ."

"In Louisville?"

"It's my home town; I was born here! Don't you know that?"

"I knew your family came to New Orleans from Kentucky, not where in Kentucky. What did Serena tell you, then?"

"She hadn't made the reservation when she phoned. But she said

49

it'd be the large stateroom at the stern of the sun deck, something about a 'back porch.' It's ex-expensive, she said, and never t-taken at this t-time of year!"

"There are two staterooms at the stern of the sun deck, opening on opposite sides. There's this one, 340, which is mine . . ."

"You—*you* . . ."

"Do you doubt it's my room? On the ledge outside the shower you'll see my watch, which I charged in to get. If Serena's been occupying 339, on the other side of the partition, she hasn't mentioned it to me."

"And they told me this was her room! An officer in uniform told me. I—I wondered why they hadn't brought up my big suitcase; I was carrying the little bag myself. It may even *b-be* your room, but . . . !"

"Once more I apologize, Penny, for what couldn't have been helped. Do you want to finish taking your shower?"

"No; I—I couldn't! I've been in enough hot water already, for one cause or another. Honestly, Jeff . . . !"

"Then I'll clear out and let you dress in peace."

Retreating to the open deck, carefully closing the outer door, he came face to face with Serena Hobart as she rounded the back of the deck from the one-whistle side. The fair-haired girl showed concern, but also a certain self-satisfaction.

"Serena—"

"I know, Jeff. I was on my way here in any case; the windows are open; I know what happened this time. And I must say . . ."

"Whatever you say, Serena, kindly don't tell me I stripped her clothes off and threw her under the shower. Isn't it time we ended this fable about my passion for undressing Penny on every possible occasion?"

Up went Serena's eyebrows.

"I had no intention of making any such remark. When I say I know what happened, I mean I can tell you exactly what happened and how it happened."

"Then you might tell me."

"Very well. I meant to meet Penny when she came on board. But I was in the purser's office with Mr. Learoyd, the purser, asking questions about that man with the moustache; and it took longer than anybody would have expected."

Serena shook her head, musing.

"Really! For a person born in Louisville, brought up both here and in New Orleans, Penny knows less about the river than you do. She knows nothing, absolutely nothing!"

"Well?"

"When she did come aboard, instead of making reasonable inquiries at the purser's office on the cabin deck, the poor dear girl wandered down to the main deck again. Ernie Aspern, Mr. Learoyd's assistant, was sent down on some errand. Penny met him in the hall between the Plantation Room and the Old South Lounge, and said, 'Miss Serena Hobart?' Ernie, who'd seen her on the cabin deck only a few moments before—Penny does take a man's eye, as *you're* aware—just made a gesture and answered, 'Up there, miss.' He meant the purser's office, where I actually was. Since they were standing in the hall on this side forward, and she knew my room would be on the back porch at the top, Penny thought that's what he meant.

"But would she ask anybody to show her or conduct her? Oh, no! She must find it for herself.

"Ernie came back up to the office, and told us a young lady had been looking for me. That's where I began to see what must be happening. I asked about her luggage. Ernie said she hadn't been carrying anything except a tiny little bag that might have been a visitor's. But I've known Penny well for some time. I knew she'd have taken her big suitcase, which is marked P.L., when she went to visit her grandparents. So I told them to have a porter find that suitcase, wherever it was, and hoick it up to 339 in a hurry. I also started to wonder."

"About a possible mistake?"

"Naturally; what else? I'd gotten Room 339, the one I wanted. Still, I thought I'd better come up. But I'm no prophetess or crystalgazer. Until I heard you two talking in there, I couldn't have guessed in what state she'd be when you walked in on her.—In heaven's name, Jeff, what's the matter? Have you taken leave of your senses?"

It may have been loss of dignity; it may have been near-loss of her balance. Unceremoniously he had seized Serena's wrist and yanked her some distance away along the deck.

"If you could hear Penny and me in there," he said, "she can just as well hear us now. There's no need to let on you've learned everything!"

"You were both shouting, you know; you were positively *shouting.* I have been speaking in a low, self-restrained tone hardly above a whisper; she can't have heard, and I won't tell her later. My dear, good idiot, exercise your own self-restraint! Nobody really thinks you're a wandering rapist on the prowl. Besides,"—and sudden, unexpected sympathy warmed Serena's manner—"she can't have been so very *dreadfully* upset, now can she?"

"Since I lose whichever way I answer that question, I'll take a tip from you and avoid answering. Have they found the missing suitcase?"

"Yes; it's in my room now. As for the sinister character with the moustache . . . ."

"Learned anything?"

"If it's about old mystery man," interposed Dave Hobart, bounding up the steps from the deck below and joining them, "I want to be in on this too. Well, Serena?"

"I can tell you his name, which is Minnoch, and his destination: New Orleans. He's travelling with another man called Bull, also for New Orleans. That's all anybody can say about either of them. Mr. Learoyd never saw or heard of Minnoch before this trip. Even Captain Josh, who usually knows everybody, can supply no information whatever."

"But—!" protested Dave.

"On the river, after all, you don't have to show a passport or establish your identity; it's enough to pay the fare. Mr. Learoyd thinks Minnoch is just a businessman and a busybody. Whatever his game may be, it needn't trouble any of us. He may be a bore and a nuisance; he's scarcely very menacing."

"Why not, little sister?"

"My poor Dave, the lout's so *obvious!* He couldn't have shown less subtlety if he'd used a battering-ram or thrown a custard pie."

"Who were you expecting, Dr. Fu Manchu? He won't have to pour poisonous spiders through the window before he gets on my own nerves. It'll be a fine state of affairs, won't it, if I can't even make a pass at Kate without finding old mystery man in the wardrobe?"

"Is that what happened, Dave? Were you and Kate—?"

"No, and I'm not going to! I was only saying, for the sake of argument . . ."

At this point Penny Lynn, entirely self-possessed in the brown-and-orange outfit Jeff had already seen, opened the door of Room 340 and smiled at them.

"Hello, Serena! Hello, Dave! Beautiful day, isn't it?"

Dave pantomimed astonishment.

"Hel-lo to *you*, Penny; and at least the sun's shining." He looked at Serena. "Is this the one with the place reserved at your table? Yes, I see it is. You didn't tell me Penny would be honoring us, Serena."

"No, Dave, and I didn't tell Jeff either. I thought it would be a pleasant surprise for you both."

"It *has* produced some surprises, hasn't it?" smiled Penny. "But, before we all go downstairs or whatever we do, may I please have a word aside with Jeff?"

If for the moment he felt a certain reluctance about approaching her, Penny herself showed no reluctance. She had never seemed so alluring as when he met her again that morning after almost thirteen years. She retreated before him into the room, sweater and skirt defining her figure, gray-blue eyes raised, and he followed.

"You'll close the door, won't you, Jeff?"

He closed it.

"I hope you don't think, Penny, I'm going to refer to . . ."

"Well, I'm going to refer to it. You don't imagine *I'm* angry, do you? When I got over the surprise of seeing you, which may have taken all of two minutes, I knew I wasn't angry in the least. I was glad."

"Glad?"

Penny shook back her soft golden-brown hair, worn in a long bob that caught the light from the windows.

"Because I know now what I should have known all along. Those other times, when I lost my dress or when I lost my dress and part of my underwear too, *weren't* your idea of a huge joke, as some said. That was what I couldn't bear: to have *you* think it was funny. And you never did think so, did you? Are *you* angry with *me?*"

"No, of course not; why should I be?"

"For acting like the silly, bad-tempered little beast I must have seemed! When I think of the outrageous things I said and did or was made to do . . . !"

"Incidentally, Penny, how are your mother and father?"

"Subdued these days; very subdued. They don't rule my life as though they were keeping a very strict boarding-school; I'm glad to say they don't even try. Those past events I distorted so much were simply accidents that pursued us then and are still pursuing. If I could just make you understand how much I've thought about it, how often I've thought about it . . . !"

Penny clasped her hands together. Suddenly tears glimmered on dark lashes that accentuated the gray-blue eyes and luminous whites. He had to restrain an almost overpowering impulse to take her in his arms.

"Sorry!" said Penny, moving back. "It's only my equally silly way of showing I'm happy. But I mustn't start blubbering on your shoulder, must I? Or those people out there might hear me and misunderstand."

"You're certainly unpredictable, young lady. Never mind! Choose your mood or change it; weep, laugh, or whatever pleases you. It's sufficient for me just to be with you again."

"Do you really mean that?"

"You know I mean it, don't you?"

"Well, I—I hoped you might. *Your* life, at least, has been a success through your own efforts. You chose the course you wanted; you wouldn't be put off or diverted by too much 'sensible' advice; and you've become the distinguished author you always wanted to be."

"I'm not very distinguished, Penny. But I may make a living from it if I stay on the job."

"Hasn't the work itself been a great satisfaction? All those books have been good, Jeff; two or three of them are awfully good."

"Romantic foolery, for the most part!"

"What's wrong with romantic foolery, if it's well done or realistic of its own kind?" Penny raised her eyes. "In *The Inn of the Seven Swords*, for instance, I've never forgotten that fight on the battlements of Falworth Moat House. And the love scene with Lady Phillida in the garden might have been in the garden behind Delys Hall. Speaking of Delys Hall . . ."

He did not tell her that the character of Lady Phillida Falworth had been suggested by Penny Lynn. Penny wandered over to the deck window and peered out.

"They've gone!" she reported, turning back. "Both Serena and Dave have gone. Speaking of Delys Hall, I was saying, would it seem too out of place if my up-in-the-sky mood contained a touch of depression or gloom?"

"Gloom?"

"I'm worried," confessed Penny. "I'm worried about Serena because Serena herself is so worried and distraught that sometimes she hardly knows where she is or what she's doing."

"Does anything ever worry Serena?"

"Don't be misled by that manner of hers! She puts on a great show; she always has. Underneath the la-di-da it's different."

"Well, what would worry her?"

"I don't know, though I might make a guess. She hasn't confided in me, please understand! Serena wouldn't confide in anybody about something that really mattered to her, and I couldn't even mention it if she had. But—"

"But what?"

"She does talk to me a *little* more than she does to other people. In things that concern her own affairs, of course, Serena's so reticent that . . ."

"Serena—and Dave too, under his own show—are not only reticent about things that concern their own affairs. They're equally and mysteriously close-mouthed about what doesn't concern 'em at all, but affects somebody else."

"Somebody else?"

"Me."

For some time he had been conscious of the stir that heralded departure. To distant, indistinct orders, with a great churning and foaming of paddle-wheel, the *Bayou Queen* vibrated, moved, and backed from the dock.

As once more they headed downstream on the Ohio with *My Old Kentucky Home* played on the calliope, he told Penny about the letter from Ira Rutledge and the letter from Dave.

"What this soberest of family lawyers has to communicate to me, and with whom else he must communicate as well, remain profound, inexplicable secrets."

"It does seem odd, doesn't it?" Penny wrinkled her forehead. "Have you heard, Jeff, that they're probably going to sell the Hall?"

"Yes; it's no secret; they told me. The prospective buyer is one Earl George Merriman of St. Louis; the decision will be handed down May 1st."

"Serena won't like that; she won't like it at all. Well, we're under way now, at least. How's the time going?"

Jeff went into the bathroom, retrieved his watch, and strapped it to his wrist.

"Just past eleven," he said. "Does it matter?"

"No, not really. But we mustn't stand here gossiping, must we? We'd better join the others, or they'll think I want to monopolize you."

"I do want to monopolize *you*, Penny; at some not too distant date I must tell you just how and how much I want to monopolize you. In the broad, mundane light of near-noon, however, we'd better present ourselves for inspection. Have you travelled by this boat before?"

"No, not by any steamboat."

"Before we join the others, do you care for a conducted tour? At least I can show you what little I've learned myself of our temporary floating home. Would that be agreeable?"

"Jeff, I'd love to! I've repacked the little bag; just let me drop it in Serena's room, and I'd love to! Will *that* be agreeable?"

"It will be excellent, my pocket Circe. Sending you to the wrong room was only a misunderstanding by the purser's assistant; your suitcase has been restored. This way, then, and in a few moments more . . ."

Presently, with Penny attentive at his side, they circled the sun deck ("Those are the officers' quarters forward; we mustn't wander there"), they descended to the texas deck and looked into the texas lounge without even encountering overcurious Mr. Minnoch. On the cabin deck, where passengers still lingered at the rails, Jeff led her inside and down the grand staircase.

"I've been *here* before," Penny told him. "This is the Plantation Room, where we eat. Through there, beyond that hall, is the Old South Lounge."

The Old South Lounge—panelled in Confederate gray, with a great shield of the stars and bars above its dummy mantelpiece, as well as overstuffed furniture and a good many round tables down its length—looked dusky despite sunlight outside. At a table near the middle they found Serena, Dave, and Charles Saylor, the two latter in a state of some emotion. Serena and Dave were seated; Mr. Saylor stood up to face them, as though in mid-flight of narrative.

"Shall I go on?" he asked.

"My dear fellow," said Serena, who seemed to be stifling a yawn, "I can't think of anything that interests me less. Still, if it gives you any pleasure . . ."

"I don't say it gives me any pleasure! But you're not sore, are you? I mean, you don't think it's funny?"

"Not having a warped sense of humor . . ."

"I didn't mean funny ha-ha, dammit! I meant—"

"Yes, Chuck, you needn't interpret." She broke off to present him to Penny, and then settled back again. "We're quite well aware of your good intentions; you've already explained often enough. He's been telling us about G-l-a-m-i-s, which he's been careful to call Glams in the most precise way."

"Of course he calls it Glams," cried Dave, "if he's done anything like the right research! Go ahead, Chuck. Nobody's stopping you."

"I don't know whether it's a fact or only part of the legend," Saylor pursued, "but it's mentioned in every account of Glams Castle that's ever been written. They were looking for the secret room, see?" he continued, including the two newcomers. "Out of every window in the castle they hung something white and conspicuous, like a towel or a pillow-case. It's a big building, of course . . ."

"Big?" echoed Serena. "It must be positively enormous, if they could find as much linen as that."

"For the sake of argument," Dave demanded, "couldn't we stop quibbling long enough to hear this?"

Saylor indicated phantom windows.

"When they'd done that, according to the story, there was one solitary window without a marker. They searched and searched; they've gone on searching to this day. But they still can't find the lost window of the lost room. Quite a story, eh?"

"Yes, it's quite a story," agreed Dave, "except that such tactics wouldn't work at Delys Hall either."

"Why not?"

"In the first place, we've got no reason to assume it's a room in any conventional sense, or that there's any window at all. What we want is a secret hiding place of some kind, which is not really hidden if you know how to look."

"In that case, Dave," up went Saylor's forefinger, "there must be a way to it from inside the house."

"Well, where do you start looking for a way?"

"If you let me call the shots, I'd start looking somewhere in the neighborhood of that killer staircase."

"Killer staircase?" repeated Penny, her voice faltering. "I expect I've been at the Hall as much as anybody has, but what on earth do you mean by killer staircase?"

"He doesn't mean anything," Jeff snapped, "except that he never means anything he says."

Saylor had retreated, left arm lifted as though to ward off a blow.

"All right, all right! I said I wouldn't talk about it and I wouldn't have, only Dave went on and on until he got it out of me. That's the truth; ask Serena! And it's only a wild fancy of mine, nothing to alarm or upset any such pretty ladies as these two."

"It doesn't upset *me*, thanks very much," Serena assured him. "I'm shock-proof and free of fancy, at least of superstitious fancy. Have you any sensible suggestion?"

"Yes, I have. I was telling Jeff at breakfast I might write to somebody; maybe that's your own best course."

"Oh?"

58

"There's one man in America who's *the* authority on secret hiding places, secret passages, that sort of stuff. He's studied 'em all over the British Isles and on the continent of Europe; in this country too. There are more of 'em abroad than here, though we've got some good 'uns on our own soil. So this fellow's the man for you."

"Do you by any chance mean Malcolm Townsend?" asked Dave.

"Yes, I mean Malcolm Townsend; he wrote a book that's the standard work. You've already heard of him?"

"Oh, I've heard of him. A couple of years ago he wrote to father and asked permission to have a try at the Hall. Father, you remember," Dave glanced at Serena, "didn't want anybody messing around at that time. He wrote back courteously and said he feared it would be impossible. But Mr. Townsend's letter is still there, with his address in Washington. Why do you think I've made a special trip to Washington now, if not to see him about the same matter?"

"And did you see him, Dave?" inquired Serena.

"Would I go all that distance and let myself be put off? Well, I wasn't put off. He's got a lecture to deliver, and the meeting of some antiquarians' society too. But it's all right! He's coming by train; he'll be in New Orleans Saturday morning, only a day after we get there ourselves. Then we ought to see some action. I still think the secret's in that logbook grandpa left, if somebody can just spot the clue."

At the entrance of the lounge appeared the burly blue-uniformed figure and red face of Captain Joshua Galway, with Kate Keith clinging solicitously to his arm. Kate whispered something in her companion's ear. They had taken only a step or two inside the door; both instantly wheeled round and went out again.

There was a little space of silence.

"The Galways," observed Dave, "have been Yankees for about a hundred years. So naturally, of course, they'd decorate this lounge in a way that would have gladdened the hearts of Jefferson Davis and Robert E. Lee. What do you think, Serena? Is our Kate making up to Captain Josh too?"

"She'd better not be," Serena said, "or Mrs. Captain Josh will take an axe to somebody. Aren't you jealous, Dave? Aren't you—"

Whereupon Serena's languid manner underwent a complete change.

"Really, Penny," she cried, getting up in haste, "there's something I *must* tell you. I must tell you at once, and apart from the hearing of these good but obtuse people. You wanted a word in private with Jeff; you must please allow me a word in private with you. It won't wait; it can't wait! Don't argue, dear; just come along!"

Penny, her face protesting but as good-natured as ever, allowed herself to be swept out of the room.

Dave spoke as though inconsequentially.

"Well, how do you like that?" he said. "There goes the gal with no notions or fancies. But they're all alike, when you get right down to it: Serena, Penny, every daughter of Eve since the beginning of time!"

"Yes, very sudden," Saylor conceded, "and might bear thinking about. Hardly to the point at this moment, though."

"No, not to the point at all; let's see where we were. This coming Saturday will be April 23rd. That gives us a full week to search. If the expert can come up with something really good, we mightn't even . . ."

But Chuck Saylor would not permit Dave to finish. Saylor, clearly, already saw himself as one of the searchers.

"If we find the secret room, Dave . . ."

"What's the matter with you? Hoy!"

The other's eyes, set rather close together above a long nose, had wandered towards infinity. Now his gaze returned, hesitant but determined.

"I was just thinking . . ."

"Let's hear it!"

"If we find the secret room, and it's somewhere near that staircase . . ."

"Well?"

"It would be the height of something or other, wouldn't it, if we found another dead man inside?"

6

When Jeff Caldwell afterwards reviewed subsequent events of that journey downriver, between lunch on Tuesday until their arrival at New Orleans late Friday afternoon, he realized that he had seen or sensed little except the obvious. Apart from one or two trifling incidents, nothing in particular seemed to happen before the last night afloat, when too much threatened to explode at once.

The boat could slow down or increase speed at will, her whistle bidding hoarse hello to passing craft. Below Louisville they negotiated the Ox Bow Bends of the Ohio. Then, presently, the broad Ohio became the still broader Mississippi.

He did not go ashore at Memphis, high on the Fourth Chickasaw Bluff of the left bank. He did not even see Vicksburg, which they passed during the small hours of Thursday morning. Natchez, he decided, should be another matter.

Time also passed in much talk with little said. At the insistence of Jeff, backed up by Serena, Penny, and even Dave, they managed to dissuade Chuck Saylor from too much speculation about the alleged secret room at Delys Hall. But sandy-haired Mr. Saylor must always speculate about something, usually the sensational. He related every grisly detail of what the newspapers had called a love-nest strangling in New York, and dealt slanderously with all concerned.

Jeff's only real difficulty, as unexpected as unexplained, occurred with Penny.

Ever since Serena's communication before lunch on Tuesday, Penny had altered. It was not that she tried to avoid him or showed any lack of friendliness. But she seemed no longer responsive, eager, or particularly interested. Some sort of wall had been built up between them, keeping her beyond reach. The more he knew himself to be falling for Penny, the less encouragement he received. He tried tentative questions as early as Tuesday night.

The boat's amenities included a white orchestra, five active young men in maroon jackets, black trousers, white shirts, and black ties. Following dinner, most evenings, they played for dancing in the after cabin lounge.

On Tuesday evening, to the thump of a lively fox trot from *Hit the Deck*, Jeff and Penny were circling the far from crowded floor when she said she didn't care to go on deck for a breath of air.

"Is anything wrong, Penny?"

"Wrong? Good heavens, no! What could be wrong?"

"That's what I've been wondering. Have I offended you again? Or did Serena tell you something to cause a change?"

"I haven't changed one bit! It's got nothing to do with *you*, not really. Serena's your friend, Jeff. She's fond of you; in private she shows it. And I'm just the same as I always was. You're not often absurd, but you're being absurd now."

Then, too, there had been that conversation with Dave before dinner, when he and Dave finished cigarettes on the texas deck as twilight gathered.

"Dancing tonight," Dave had announced, humming a bar or two. "It's not formal any night, unless you want to dress for the captain's ball later. Penny, at least, won't go formally. She won't wear an evening gown, I mean, or you'd probably tear the whole thing off her before the end of the first dance."

"For God's sake, Dave, won't anybody drop that tedious joke?"

"What's tedious about it, or a joke either? If *you* never wondered how Penny looked in the nude before you actually saw her that way, you're not the man I take you for! *I've* wondered often enough, I can tell you!"

"Just a minute, now! This guff about seeing Penny . . . seeing Penny . . ."

"In the nude, you mean? Only this morning, I understand . . ."

"But—!"

62

"Yes, I know! It was a mistake; Serena told me it was a mistake. They'd directed Penny to the wrong room when you walked in."

"But, Dave—!"

"It happened, didn't it? So it had to happen somehow. You're not likely to have smashed the door down, and I don't see her inviting you in to watch her take a shower. Kate Keith would, and others might too; not Penny!"

Dave, of course, would never have referred to it if Penny had been present or within hearing. Nor, so far as Jeff knew, had he commented to anyone else.

But could any aspect of that unfortunate shower business explain her present attitude? Though Penny had denied this almost as soon as it happened, she sometimes made remarks contradicted in both directions by her behavior afterwards. He had debated the issue before his tentative approach that night resulted only in a denial of everything.

During Wednesday night's dancing he almost questioned her again, but decided to refrain. With Penny technically in his arms if spiritually miles away, he must not allow himself to grow light-headed and babble. Easy, Caldwell! Don't rush your fences or jump the gun!

Wednesday's dancing was both preceded and concluded by one incident that might have provoked argument. After dinner a little procession trooped up from the Plantation Room and through the broad hall, where stateroom doors opened inwards rather than on deck, towards the after cabin lounge at the far end. Kate Keith and Dave went first; Penny followed, with Jeff at her side; Serena and Chuck Saylor lingered a little way back.

"Mrs. Keith!" called Saylor, who had been treating Kate with powerful gallantry ever since they were introduced. "Mrs. Keith!"

Kate, in semi-formal yellow, disengaged her arm from Dave's and turned.

"Today, Mrs. Keith," Saylor intoned, "you went ashore at Memphis. You went on your own, disdaining company. When you returned, it's whispered in Gath, you were carrying a paper bag with the distinct outline of a bottle inside. I mustn't be Mr. Buttinsky; if I'm getting out of line, madam, just tell me to go fly

63

a kite. However, if you *should* invite us to your room for re-freshment . . . ?"

"Are we such a gang of topers as that?" asked Dave, eyeing him without favor. "Do we need liquor to sustain us before we can face the evening? If I were you, Kate, I'd ask at the gift shop whether they've got any good kites."

"Sorry, Dave!" Saylor threw off apology in haste. "But you all know how it is."

" 'Deed and I do know how it is!" breathed Kate. "Later, of course, would be *much* better!"

The dancing swayed and wheeled, mostly fox trots varied by the occasional waltz, with a sufficiency of partners for every girl in their party. Penny, chatting lightly, to Jeff seemed more remote than ever. Well before midnight, when the orchestra would call it a day, they adjourned up to the texas lounge and claimed one of its oblong mahogany tables.

Disappearing for no great time, Kate returned with a paper-wrapped parcel which she passed to Saylor under the table and whose contents, surreptitiously inspected, proved to be a square-faced bottle labelled London Dry Gin.

"Tells us a good deal about the lady's character," muttered Say-lor, as Kate drew Dave to another table. "Among other things, she doesn't lack generosity. Let's see: it'll be Natchez tomorrow, eh?"

It was. They reached Natchez towards noon on Thursday.

Throughout these days, except at meals, they had seen almost nothing of enigmatic, heavily moustached Mr. Minnoch. With his travelling companion, another middle-aged man as lean as Minnoch was stocky, having smooth gray hair in contrast to Minnoch's bald-ness, he champed his way through many courses at the table of some amiable elderly couple who beamed on everybody. Other-wise Messrs. Minnoch and Bull kept to themselves, evincing no curiosity at all.

Jeff finished the book of detective short stories which had de-feated him that first night, finding them well up to their author's high standard. And it fascinated him merely to watch the river. Just when you thought it only muddy brown, you caught tinges of green, of blue, of both, or of all three together. But his preoccupation with Penny had not lessened. If he could persuade Penny to accompany him ashore at Natchez, he must see how she behaved away from this atmosphere.

Penny readily agreed to go. Though Serena and Dave elected to stay aboard, Saylor would escort Kate Keith. They held a conference before the sightseers left.

"Dave was saying something about the captain's ball," Jeff remarked. "Since we're due in New Orleans tomorrow, do they hold that tonight?"

"Either Dave misunderstood you," said Serena, "or, as usual, he wasn't thinking at all. This is a kind of cruise, you know; most passengers will return upriver. They won't hold the captain's ball until they're almost back at Cincinnati. Have fun, you people!"

If New Orleans might be called a mingling of elements, polyglot style, ancient Natchez seemed the Old South itself in every road, every house, every tree, from the slope that made it Natchez-under-the-Hill to the stately Greek Revival mansions beyond.

Under a drowsing sun, warm but not too warm, their party of some dozen visitors was driven by motor coach to inspect several stately homes amid shaven lawns and gardens aflower. At the Garden Club, in itself a stately home, Jeff saw on the wall an oil painting of a woman, some bedizened beauty from the court of the second Charles, which he could have sworn was the work of Kneller.

And more than once, from Penny, he caught a flash of that eager responsiveness she had shown before the change. If he did not understand, it contented him to accept. They were soon on their way back; and Penny, beside him in the bus, herself made a suggestion.

"We've had so little opportunity to talk, have we? To talk by ourselves, I mean. Since this *is* our last night, couldn't we talk this evening?"

"On deck, by any chance?"

"Yes, of course! On deck by all means, if you don't mind. You won't forget?"

"The risk of my forgetting, Penny, would get you all kinds of odds at Lloyd's."

He returned to the boat so buoyed up, so stimulated, that he hardly heard Saylor's question; Saylor wanted to know who had engaged in the bloodiest duel ever fought below the Mason-Dixon Line.

Again the paddle-wheel churned in foam and spray; once more they were off. Some time afterwards, when twilight had begun to smudge the sky, Jeff went up to wash before dinner. Still in his exalted mood, still hurrying, he ascended the outside stairs, threw open the door of his room, took one step over its raised doorsill, and stopped short as though he had almost trodden on a snake.

What he had almost stepped on was only a small sheet of the boat's notepaper, headed with a color picture of the craft itself, such as might be found at any writing-desk in the forward cabin lounge. Pushed under the door in his absence, it bore nothing more than a line and a half of small, neat typing done by some practised hand.

At your convenience, try 701b Royal Street. Fear nothing, but remember the address.

That was all. No greeting or signature; merely an address which had no meaning for him, with the equally mysterious injunction not to be afraid. Why *should* anybody be afraid of some given number in Royal Street: house, shop, whatever it might be?

But there was something so unpleasantly furtive about that little note, so full of secret suggestion like a whisper, that Jeff didn't like it at all. He picked it up, carried it to the nearer window, and tilted it against the light. He was still holding it when a tap at the door heralded the entrance of Dave Hobart, followed by Chuck Saylor, both in dark suits with ties of restrained color.

Jeff showed them the note and told them where he had found it.

"Royal Street?" demanded Saylor, alert at once. "Where's Royal Street?"

"If it means New Orleans, which presumably it does," Dave answered, "Royal Street is a famous thoroughfare of the Vieux Carré.

"Well, *what's* Royal Street?"

"As a shopping center," replied Dave, "it's been called our own Fifth Avenue. There's a difference. You can buy the most expensive jewelry or antiques, and you can also buy the inexpensive confection known as pralines. Does the address ring any bell, Jeff?"

"No. I seem vaguely to remember that, if you stand in Royal Street with your back to Canal Street, facing the direction of Esplanade Avenue, the even numbers are on the right-hand side of the street and the odd numbers on the left. Number 701, therefore . . ."

"It says 701b!" Saylor pointed out.

"Ordinarily," explained Dave, "the 'b' for *bis* would mean two separate establishments, families or businesses, on different floors of the same premises. In our French quarter, at least, it doesn't mean that: 701b will mean a separate building, next to 701 but occupied by somebody other than the tenant of 701.

"Hold on, now!" he cried, suddenly clutching at his head. "*I'm* beginning to remember. I can't tell you what's at 701b. But I can tell you what's very definitely at 700, and what used to be at 701 across the way."

"Well?" prompted Jeff.

"It's true about the even numbers being on the right-hand side. Number 700, at the northeast corner of Royal Street and St. Peter Street, is one of the celebrated sights of the town: the Labranche Building, sometimes called the lacework building, from the elaborate iron lacework, entwined oak leaves and acorns, on every gallery above the street. It bristles with 'em; it's got more iron lacework than any other house in the district; you seldom pass the place when somebody's not photographing it. Beginning to remember now, Jeff?"

"Yes. And across the way . . . ?"

"Across the way, the red-brick building at 701 used to be a well-known bakery, Cadet Molon's bakery, early in the nineteenth century. I can't say who's got it now, still less who or what may be at 701b next door. I'm just nailing it down for you, in case you feel any overwhelming urge to go there and see."

"Yes," Jeff held up the paper, "but what sort of joker would send a note like this? And, if it must be sent to somebody, why send it to *me?* It looks as though it's been written on a portable typewriter."

"It does look like that," Saylor agreed briskly. "The joker did it on your own machine, did he?"

"I'm not carrying a typewriter; I don't like portables."

"Well, I am and do. But it wasn't written on my Corona; you're welcome to look at mine and compare the type." He appealed to Dave. "Jeff's right, though. Whether it's a joke or not, who sent it and why? Any ideas, Dave?"

"No, nary an idea. Surely *you* have a suggestion, haven't you?"

"You couldn't call it a suggestion, exactly. But I was just thinking . . ."

"Yes, Hawkshaw?"

"Isn't there, or wasn't there, a whole district of New Orleans where prostitution could be practiced within the law?"

Dave struck an attitude.

"Yes, my fount of no suggestion, there used to be. For thirty-eight blocks of the Vieux Carré, no less, the fancy women rode high, wide, and handsome, free from all interference provided they didn't raise hell or rob anybody. It was the wisest move local government ever made; it operated with great success for twenty years, from 1897 to 1917. Then some damn bluenoses and Christers from Washington thought it might corrupt our holy servicemen in the war to end war, and got Storyville closed forever."

"All right, all right! But if at that address, for instance . . . ?"

"In Royal Street?" demanded Dave. "*Royal Street*, for God's sake? Even in the free and easy days, take it from me, you'd no more have found any broad with a Royal Street crib than you'd have found the whole choir of angels twanging their harps at Tom Anderson's saloon.

"Now look here, George Horace Lorimer," Dave pursued in a more reasonable tone. "I've told you I don't know what Jeff will find at 701b. But I can tell you what he won't find there, which is any joint of the kind you've got in mind. As for the note, I don't think we'd better even mention it to the women. It's hard to say what we could tell 'em if we did mention it. So, however great the temptation, just keep your lip buttoned and we'll all stay quiet about the note. Agreed?"

"Yes, agreed. We don't want to worry 'em."

"We certainly don't, although that note's got me worried enough as things stand. It's got me worried and buffaloed, in fact, because it makes no sense. But then nothing in this whole blasted business makes any sense at all!"

And so, after another long debate which established nothing, eventually they went down to dinner.

At the dinner table Jeff devoted so much attention to Penny that it excluded other considerations from his mind. Though they said little to each other, Serena and Saylor doing most of the talking, they more than once exchanged a glance; he had not lost the sense of communication from that afternoon.

Later their whole party drifted upstairs, and were waiting when the orchestra began. Saylor took the floor with Serena, Jeff with Penny, Dave with Kate. In addition to current dance numbers, the musicians sometimes whaled into tunes from several years gone, *Down on the Farm, Barney Google, Nobody Lied,* and even reached as far back as *Dardanella.* All the party had changed partners quite a few times, each returning to the partner with whom each began, when Jeff and Penny re-established communication at last.

Penny, a vision in oyster-colored silk, more than once had begun to speak. Jeff began to speak, also in a kind of rush, at exactly the same moment, and then they both stopped.

"What are they?" he asked now. "Shall I offer you a penny, Penny?"

"No, don't! They're not worth it. I—I don't really *mean* they're not worth it! I mean—"

"Care for a breath of air now?"

"Yes, please; I'd love to!"

As he guided Penny off the floor, Kate leaned past Dave's shoulder.

"Don't be gone too long, you two! It doesn't matter how long you're gone, does it? Just remember," Kate never avoided platitudes, no matter how often repeated, "don't do anything *I* wouldn't do!"

"That's unlikely, me dear," Dave reminded her. "I will not be ungallant enough to enlarge on the theme, being the strong, silent man I am. Let me merely say . . ."

The departing couple failed to hear what he would merely say. They went out into the open on the two-whistle side, Penny disdaining any scarf or handkerchief to keep her hair from blowing. But hardly a breath of wind stirred. As they ascended first to the texas deck and then to the sun deck, moving forward, the river stretched shadowy, mysterious, very faintly light-spangled under a strengthening moon.

The same sense of expectancy seemed to touch them both. They were almost at the bow when Penny gestured towards her left.

"There's the calliope," she said. "That's the keyboard of the calliope, I mean; the valves that make it work are on the roof just above. The same side as your room, only forward instead of astern. I hope I've got those names right; Serena keeps correcting me."

"Serena keeps correcting everybody."

"On the river, she says, they don't even call it a calliope; they call it the steam pie-anna. When we left Natchez this afternoon, remember, it played *Meet Me Tonight in Dreamland?*"

"An invitation hereby heartily endorsed. It's a good deal like dreamland, Penny; it could be still more so."

"You must tell me how." Penny raised her eyes. "First, though, may I make a request?"

"Of course. Anything at all."

"Dave's been at you already. When we get to New Orleans, Jeff, he doesn't want you to stay with your uncle or at a hotel. He wants you to stay at the Hall. And you will stay at the Hall? You won't be put off by any mad talk about haunted staircases or a killer force. You *will* stay at the Hall?"

"Nothing would give me greater pleasure, Penny, if that's your request. Have you any particular reason for requesting it?"

"Well, yes. We—we've moved to our own summer place on the river, only a short distance above Delys Hall. You could meet me, and I could meet you, much more easily than if you were anywhere in town. Whether or not that's an important consideration, of course . . ."

"It's a very important consideration to me. I didn't think it could have any importance to you. Ever since Serena imparted certain information on Tuesday . . ."

"Yes, Serena did say something. But I've told you it had nothing to do with you, not really. And, anyway, I should have told Serena at the time that I didn't care, which I don't. As for meeting you not being important to me," the soft voice faltered, "oh, Jeff, if you *knew* how very important it is . . . !"

They were standing near the forward railing of what at sea would have been the starboard side. Penny's nearness, already intoxicating, tilted the balance as she wavered towards him. His left arm went around her shoulders, his right hand to her waist. Penny, unresisting and cooperative, had allowed herself to be drawn close when a small crash behind Jeff's back made them spring apart as though they had been burnt.

Somebody, little more than a stocky shape discernible by moonlight, stood there peering.

"Well, well, well!" said a musing voice.

The flame of a pocket lighter, its wheel spun by somebody's thumb, rose up to illumine the blunt features and heavy moustache of the man called Minnoch, a cloth cap pulled down on his head.

"Well, well, well!" he repeated. "Didn't mean to butt in or startle you: accident. But—"

Penny fled. As though blindly, uttering no word, she ran across the front of the deck and round the corner towards Room 339 on the other side. A door slammed; Jeff gritted his teeth and waited.

"Didn't mean to butt in or startle you, I say," the newcomer resumed in his heavy voice. "And I'm sorry; I'm right sorry! Maybe I'd better introduce myself."

"Yes, undoubtedly you had. Some explanation of your actions also seems called for."

"It does, don't it? Reckon some kind of an explanation's just about due. My name is Minnoch, Harry Minnoch, Lieutenant Minnoch.—New Orleans Police," he added. "I'm a cop."

"*A cop?*"

"That's right; you've got it. You're Mr. Gilbert Bethune's nephew, they tell me. Yes, I'm a cop; and I'm not such a bad guy when you get to know me."

"Most of us could forgo that pleasure. This explanation you mentioned . . . ?"

Lieutenant Minnoch lowered the lighter-flame to inspect something at his feet, then blew it out and straightened up.

"Wouldn't think, now," he said agreeably, "a good cherrywood pipe would smash to pieces just falling on the floor? It'd gone out, though; no danger o' fire. What I was saying . . ."

"If you expect commiseration for a broken pipe, it's addressed to the wrong man. You might explain why you're shadowing us again."

"Well, now, I wouldn't call it shadowing, exactly!"

"Then what would you call it?"

"Now, now, young fellow, don't get your dander up! No offense was intended; would I insult the D.A.'s favorite nephew? Me and Fred Bull—he's Sergeant Bull, see—were at Cincinnati on a professional job. I had some leave due; so had Fred; that's why we're here. We had to use some cop tactics to make everybody aboard this boat shut up about us *being* cops. Maybe we exceeded our authority; yes, I guess we did. If you think I've been pestering you, you could get me in all kinds o' trouble just by complaining to your uncle."

"Any complaint, Lieutenant Minnoch, will be addressed to you alone. And it doesn't matter about pestering me. But when you pester Miss Hobart and her brother, to say nothing of Miss Lynn tonight . . ."

"For the love of the sweet Jesus, Mr. Caldwell," Lieutenant Minnoch sounded a hoarse note of appeal, "will you just keep control of that temper and try to relax? Can't we talk about this sensibly?"

"We can't seem to talk about it at all. Still, if you insist on a truce . . ."

"That's better. That's much better!"

"Do you suspect one of us, or all of us, of being concerned in some crime?"

"Did I say I suspect anybody of anything? Leastways, of anything that's ever likely to get into court? The answer is: I don't, and that's a fact."

Lieutenant Minnoch approached the railing along the side, leaned his elbows on it, and looked out over the water. Jeff did the same.

"Howsoever," Minnoch went on, "I've been wondering if I oughtn't to speak to you. I've heard a good deal about you from your uncle; you're the one who writes the books, and he thinks a lot of you. Mr. Bethune says I lack subtlety. Subtlety, is it? If I understand what he means, subtlety's just about the last thing any cop ever needs or can use.

"My idea of a good police officer has always been old Zack Trowbridge; they promoted me to his job when he retired. Now Zack's smooth; he's as smooth as all get-out. And he's a great reader, too, though I finished high school and he didn't. It was a writin' fellow helped Zack with the most important job he ever tackled; he admits it. Not that I think you can help me; your uncle's the man for funny business. All the same, I've been wondering . . ."

"You've been wondering," Jeff prompted, "if you oughtn't to speak to me about what?"

"Well, now, that's the point. I can't tell you much about it 'less Mr. Bethune does. But I can tell you this much. We've had information that could cause the biggest hullabaloo and uproar since that Axeman business at the end of the war. Somebody wants us to reopen what our informant swears is a still unsolved case of murder."

73

7

The big car, bound for Delys Hall, sped along the River Road outside New Orleans at just past six on that afternoon of Friday, April 22nd, with a Negro chauffeur at the wheel and three passengers in the back.

Seated between Serena and Dave, Jeff found himself thinking back again as he talked.

"For most of our journey," he reminisced, "we sailed so much nearer the left bank than the right bank, or even mid-channel, that I felt sure I could get a look at the Hall as we passed."

"Nobody could have seen the Hall," Serena reminded him, "even if anyone had cared to see it. Do I need to elaborate? That rain . . ."

Yes, rain. Beginning at breakfast time on Friday it had rained almost without interruption, sometimes lightly and sometimes in great whirling sheets that obscured all view. Less than half an hour before arrival at New Orleans, after the capricious fashion of this climate, the rain vanished. Under a placid blue sky breathing of evening, with the calliope playing first *Waiting for the Robert E. Lee* and then *There'll Be a Hot Time in the Old Town Tonight*, they had made majestic approach to their mooring at the Grand Bayou Line's wharf on the levee.

Dave Hobart, now at Jeff's left hand in the Packard limousine on the River Road, referred to this among other matters.

"You'll see the Hall soon enough," he said. "But I'm glad you decided to accept our hospitality instead of going elsewhere. Up to this morning I couldn't get a straight answer out of you."

"If it won't be too much trouble . . ."

"It won't be any trouble at all. When we landed, Jeff, I wonder whether you saw something I saw?"

"Well?"

"The first person off that boat, as soon as they lowered the what-dyecallit on its chains, was your little friend Penny. Did you notice?"

"Yes, I noticed."

"There was the venerable Cadillac I swear they've had for years, almost as long as the venerable Pierce Arrow of yore. There was old Bertie Lynn," thus did Dave describe Penny's father, "waiting all agog. There was her Uncle Gordon, a host in himself. They whisked that gal away as though they thought somebody wanted to kidnap her."

"Maybe somebody did."

"In the general bustle of landing," Dave pressed his hands over his eyes, "everything got sort of confused and mixed up. Where was Kate? I didn't even see Kate. What happened to Kate?"

"Kate," Serena answered, "was with Chuck Saylor. Chuck's been giving her quite a play for several days. He was to give her a lift in his taxi, or she was to give him a lift in hers: something of that sort, anyway." She gestured towards the Negro chauffeur beyond the glass panel. "When I saw Isaac waiting on the levee, and knew he must have brought the car as I'd wired him from Cincinnati to do, I realized I *couldn't* offer a lift to everybody! We might just have squeezed in the whole party, but we couldn't possibly have accommodated the luggage. There's enough of our own as it is. As for Chuck Saylor . . ."

"Oh, Saylor! Forget Saylor, can't you? *Has* it been established whether Kate was, or was not, making up to Captain Josh Galway?"

"No, Dave, she certainly was not," Serena assured him. "Captain Josh did have something on his mind and still has, but it wasn't anything to do with Kate."

"How do you make that out?"

"He wasn't in the pilot-house when we landed, as we all observed. He didn't oversee bringing the boat in; one of the pilots attended to that. You don't often meet Captain Josh without a smile on his face. But this afternoon he stamped past me as though he had the weight of the world on his shoulders. And he said something. He didn't say it to me; he didn't say it to anybody; he was a strong man in agony. He just muttered, 'How many of 'em? Dear God in heaven, how many of 'em?' and stamped on. I can't think what on earth he meant."

"I can tell you that," volunteered Jeff. "When I talked to Minnoch last night . . ."

"Ah, Minnoch!" Dave said ecstatically. "Good Lieutenant Minnoch! Old Nemesis Minnoch, the Grand Bastard of the police force! All roads lead straight back in a circle to Minnoch. Suppose, Jeff, you just repeat every word he said to you?"

Serena drew herself up in protest.

"Really, Dave! Since breakfast this morning we've been over all that at least twenty times. Surely," and she gave him a smile almost coquettish, "you don't want Jeff to repeat it *again?*"

"Yes, little sister, that's just what I do want; and with very good reason for wanting it. If you don't see how important that is and is likely to be, you're not the bright gal I've always thought you. Well, Jeff?"

Jeff looked at Serena.

"Captain Josh's attitude," he said, "is hardly mysterious either. Remember what's been happening. Early Monday morning, long before the boat leaves Cincinnati, Dave sneaks aboard with the idea of keeping his presence in Room 240 strictly secret all the way. He tackles Captain Josh, who doesn't like it but finally agrees as a family friend.

"Then Lieutenant Minnoch and his accompanying sergeant, one Fred Bull, waylay Captain Josh with much the same sort of request. Though they don't want their presence kept a secret, they make sure nobody on board will breathe a word about the fact that they're cops. They seem to have used threats of some kind. Dave changed his mind; they didn't. Captain Josh has had enough, hasn't he? He's had almost as much of it as . . . as . . ."

"Almost as much of it," interposed Dave, "as you've had encounters with Penny when she's been partially or completely undressed? But that's not the point. Listen, old son! I don't care two hoots whether they threatened Captain Josh with the law or bribed him with police funds or said they'd sink the boat in mid-channel if he refused to play ball. Minnoch didn't hide his presence; he did hide his job. Why?"

"Well . . ."

"What was the last thing he said to you, before you two parted yesterday evening? The very last thing?"

"He said, 'I can't stop you from telling your friends who I am, or anything else I've talked about. But we're so close to home it can't hurt much now.'"

"'It can't hurt much now.' And just before then, Jeff? What had Old Nemesis been going on about just before then?"

Jeff reflected.

"A few minutes ago, Dave, you said you couldn't get a straight answer out of me until this morning. I could no more get a straight answer out of Minnoch than I can get one out of you or Serena. But I've already given you the gist of it. Some unnamed informant has been stirring up both the police and my uncle about an old case, years ago, their informant claims was a case of murder."

"What was this alleged murder, and when did it happen?"

"Minnoch said he couldn't tell me that unless Uncle Gil told me first. All he'd say was that it would be seventeen years ago in November."

Dave uttered an exclamation of triumph.

"Seventeen years come November! Hear that, Serena? It's the United States Mint to a plugged nickel Old Nemesis meant our own home-grown business of Thad Peters breaking his neck on the stairs."

"Dave, that's silly!" Serena sounded outraged. "I'll indulge these fancies if you insist, but it's *silly!* A sheer accident that might have happened to anybody . . ."

"Can you name any other case that'll be seventeen years old in November? Yes, Iris March; we all know it was an accident. But if somebody wants to stir up trouble at the present time—" Dave broke off. "Didn't it occur to you, Jeff?"

"Oh, yes, it occurred to me. I said, 'Whatever happened, Lieutenant, why should you be interested in shadowing any of us at so late a date? In 1910 Dave Hobart and I were only fifteen years old. Mrs. Keith couldn't have been older; Serena Hobart was nine or ten at the outside, and Penny Lynn not as old. Why so much belated interest?' "

"And Old Hawkshaw's reply?"

"You've heard that too. 'Well,' he said, 'what could any of you be up to now? You yourself, or the Hobart children, or even the dark-haired lady with the figure? I won't include the other little lady with the figure. She's all right; she's like the daughter I never had. And I don't say there's anything to be interested in, mind. All the same, what *could* any of the rest of you be up to?' "

"Leaving it at that?"

"Leaving it at that."

"Really, Dave," Serena lifted one shoulder, "unless you're just trying to give us the creeps, in which you won't succeed, I do wish you'd drop this subject for good and all! And you needn't worry, Jeff."

"I needn't worry?"

"About Penny. When Dave suggests Penny may have been deserting you by getting off the boat so soon . . . ."

"So help me, Serena," Dave vowed, "I wasn't suggesting any such damn thing! Nobody else has got a chance with her when this gangling lout's around."

"You do appreciate it, then? Jeff, just before Penny's father and her uncle 'whisked her away,' to quote Dave, you and I know she called out to you and asked you to phone soon."

Jeff bent forward, pondering.

"There's one other call I ought to make. In a letter last month Dave predicted that Uncle Gil would be in Baton Rouge for some political do. He really is there, according to Minnoch, and won't be back until Monday. I meant to surprise him, but it doesn't seem such a good idea now. All things considered, I'd better ring his apartment and report."

Dave waved towards the right-hand side of the River Road.

"Our phone, old son, is at your disposal. And you'll be able to use it at any minute. We're almost there."

In England, perhaps, some sixteenth-century Delys had over-seen the building of a wall to enclose the grounds of the Hall. No wall existed here, nor would anybody have thought of one.

Set well back beyond live oaks carefully cleared of Spanish moss, Delys Hall faced south towards the river. Red brick and gray stone had darkened like the colors of an old painting. Though of only two main floors, with some few gable-end windows indicating smaller accommodation on an embryonic top floor, each main floor reared to good height, the lower one particularly high, above a flagged terrace with a stone balustrade. The gravel drive, which also enclosed a grass plot with stone pedestal and statue of Diana, divided into two branches before shallow steps leading up to the terrace.

Despite gathering dusk, the sun's afterglow caught a flash from ranked windows: diamond-paned, each window a panel of four lights separated by stone mullions. The lower parts could open out like little doors. Many on the ground floor were stained glass. Projecting from the brickwork between the panels of windows, upper floor as well as lower, stretched a row of ornamental iron brackets in *fleur-de-lys* shape.*

Was there something else too? Antiquity, yes. What about decay?

But Jeff had no time to speculate. Isaac, the young chauffeur, stopped the car beside the steps to the terrace. After holding open the door for his passengers to alight, he unstrapped suitcases from the grid and hauled down other luggage from the roof.

Dave, whom Serena tried unavailingly to shush, pointed towards a Model T Ford parked in the drive where it turned past the right-hand or eastern side of the Hall.

"Question for old residents!" Dave carolled. "In all New Orleans, what prosperous character alone still drives a Model T, and that particular Model T?

"Speaking of cars, Jeff," he added, "there are three of 'em in the garage out back: this royal coffin, for state occasions only; the

---

Lys, French for 'lily,' today we usually find spelled *lis*. But either version is correct.

touring car; and a Stutz Bearcat Serena and I use. You're welcome to share the Stutz, if that's agreeable?"

"Very agreeable, thanks."

Dave danced up the steps to the flagged terrace. He had barely touched the doorbell when the massive, arched, iron-studded oak door was opened by old Cato, who had been major-domo for as long as Jeff could remember.

The lofty lower hall, with its linenfold oak panelling, its famous staircase, and its smell of scrubbed stone, was now illumined only by the last light through stained-glass windows above the front door. Cato, unsurprised, greeted Jeff as though the latter had been calling there every day for years.

Dave, amid heaped luggage, cleared his throat like a master of ceremonies.

"There's a question before the house," he declared. "The room just over the door," and he pointed upwards, "is Serena's. It used to be the principal guest bedroom; but she bagged it in early adolescence and she's been there ever since. Here's the question, Serena: just where do we put this Caldwell fellow?"

"The Tapestry Room, I think." Serena became coolly practical. "Yes, the Tapestry Room; he'll like that. You might see to it, please, Cato."

And yet a certain air of constraint held both Serena and Dave. This only increased, for some reason, when still another person joined them.

To your right, as you stood in the lower hall, another massive door stood open on the drawing-room. Beyond lay the dining-room they called a refectory. Out of the drawing-room, tall, stooped, grizzled, cadaverous of both voice and appearance, wandered that esteemed family lawyer, Ira Rutledge.

"Ah, Serena!" he said, adjusting his spectacles and blinking in the twilight. "You've returned, then?"

"That should be fairly obvious, Mr. Rutledge. We took the steamboat at Cincinnati."

"So Cato informed me, when I telephoned about another matter. He informed me, to be exact, that *you* had taken the steamboat. I had not even been aware of Dave's absence."

80

Then, faintly anxious, he addressed them both.

"It has been necessary, for your own sake, to consult certain papers in the study. You don't mind, I hope? Since you both were absent . . ."

"For the love of Mike," Dave said heartily, "of course we don't mind! Consult anything; do anything! But your eyesight must be even worse than usual. Isn't there anybody else here you're acquainted with or have seen somewhere before?"

"That gentleman there . . . ."

"You mean you don't recognize Jeff Caldwell?"

"Indeed!" exclaimed the lawyer, bustling forward and shaking hands formally. "It's good to see you and welcome you, Jeff. Your uncle will be still more pleased, I know, when he returns from Baton Rouge. Is he expecting you?"

"Not to my knowledge, at least. Your letter, Mr. Rutledge . . ."

"Ah, yes. I wonder, Jeff, whether I can persuade you to call at my office tomorrow afternoon? Two o'clock, if that would be convenient? Saturday is a bad day, of course. But then lawyers, like doctors, may not study their own convenience. If it's also a bad day for you . . ."

"You may expect me, sir. At two on the dot."

"Good! Consequently, with the permission of you all, I had better get on home for dinner. The Ford is not what it used to be, one fears; and I mustn't worry Mrs. Rutledge, now, must I? Before I take my leave, however . . ."

Again he addressed Serena and Dave.

"Without wishing to touch on any delicate subject," he added, with a dry rasp in his throat, "may I ask whether you have come to some definite decision about May 1st?"

"There's no reason to call it a delicate subject," Dave shot back. "Serena and I haven't quite made up our minds; but the answer will probably be yes. Is that good enough?"

"May 1st," mused Mr. Rutledge, "will be a Sunday. If Saturday is a bad day, Sunday is a day so bad as to be downright awkward. But, having chosen the date yourselves, I daresay you should abide by it. At the same time, I was wondering . . . ?"

"Yes?"

"Forgive me, my boy. I seem to detect in you both more than a shade of embarrassment or uncertainty. If the subject is not delicate ..." Then, suddenly, he drew a breath of relief. "Come, this question should never have been raised! Perhaps I do see and do understand; no more of it. Whereupon, with best wishes for the future, permit me to bid you good evening."

Taking up his hat from a Jacobean table near the front door, he bowed to them and went his way, closing the door after him. There was a little space of silence in thickening dusk.

"For heaven's sake, Dave," Serena began too loudly, "don't call him an old mossback! He's far more shrewd than most people ever think."

"You needn't worry, little sister. He may be a mossback, but I've never taken him for a fool. And I like the old boy. As a matter of fact, I wasn't thinking about Ira at all."

Dave surveyed the flagstones of the floor. During that interval Cato, assisted by a youth who may well have been his grandson, had been so industriously carrying luggage that no luggage now remained.

Turning sideways for a dramatic pose, Dave levelled his forefinger at the back of the hall.

"There's the damn thing!" he said. "There's the staircase that seems to have caused all the trouble!"

Serena and Jeff also turned to look. Very broad, a single solid affair with carved banisters and treads somewhat worn, it stretched up into near darkness on the floor above.

"Haunt of ghouls and goblins, is it?" demanded Dave, still pointing. "On you, my sister, I would also urge a consideration. If I mustn't underestimate Ira Rutledge, don't you overestimate those stairs or their power to do harm. Don't let 'em affect you, gal. Don't be frightened or hypnotized."

"Dave, how many times must I tell you I'm not? The only ones who seem to be hypnotized are you and perhaps Chuck Saylor. Really, now ... !"

"There's a precedent, Serena. Something was said, I seem to remember, by Marmion on the home ground of Douglas. Yes, got it!"

Striking a pose still more dramatic, he soared into quotation:

" 'Here in thy hold, thy vassals near,
  I tell thee thou'rt defied!
  And if thou said'st I am not peer
  To any lord in Scotland here,
  Lowland or Highland, far or near,
  Lord Angus, thou hast lied!'

"But Marmion's tirade hardly seems to the point, does it? Let's try a tirade of my own."

Whereupon, as though completely carried away, Dave addressed the stairs.

"Ghoulies and ghosties and long-leggity beasties, every evil spirit that may hear, I tell thee *thou'rt* defied! Grab *me*, why don't you?"

And he darted towards the stairs, bounding up them.

"Grab me, trip me, sling me down on my ear to die! Come on; that's a dare!"

"Dave," Serena burst out, "what on earth are you up to? Do look out! It's almost dark; you can't see a thing; it would be easy to miss your step and—"

At the very moment she spoke, Dave did seem to lose his footing. He flung up his arms, reeled round, and pitched down headforemost. Rolling over and over, though with comparatively little noise, he came to the foot of the stairs and lay there.

Uttering a cry, Serena ran to the front door, found a little row of electric switches beside the door, and clicked one down. A crown of large electric candles, their massive iron frame swung on chains from the central beam of the ceiling, sprang into soft yellow glow.

Even as the lights went on, that recumbent figure stirred. Dave Hobart, completely unhurt and not even shaken up, bounced to his feet like an india-rubber cat.

"How was that?" he demanded. "Did it deliberately, of course. Trick fall I learned at the gym; every slapstick comedian knows and uses it, they tell me. You used to be a pretty classy gymnast yourself, Serena, before the doctor made you give it up. I've been wondering how Thad Peters, with his famous sense of balance, could have let any such spill become a fatality. Thad Peters—" He broke off. "Here, what is it? What's the matter?"

"What's the matter?" echoed Serena, staring at him. "You idiot! You beast! You absolutely hopeless something or other! You have the nerve to play a trick of that kind, and still ask what's the matter?"

"Nothing like a demonstration, is there? Had to see if *anything* would shake your composure. If I made it too realistic, I'm sorry; no harm was intended. Besides . . ."

For all Dave's attempted swagger, he did not make it convincing or even try hard to make it convincing.

"Don't take too seriously what I'm going to say now. I know I imagined it or dreamed it." He appealed to Jeff. "While I was on those stairs, old son, did *you* hear anybody?"

"Hear anybody?"

"Hear anybody present besides ourselves?"

"No; who would there be to hear? I heard you utter your put-on challenge to the spooks. I heard Serena tell you to look out or you might slip. That's all."

"Yes, that was all; and yet it's very peculiar." Dave made a mesmeric pass. "As Serena called her warning, and I turned for my trick fall, I could have sworn a little voice beside my ear also whispered, 'Take care.' I imagined it; I dreamed it; that's established! But I could have sworn I heard that voice, and for a second or two it scared me a little as I fell."

8

Little further was said about what might or might not be on the stairs. Serena and Jeff asked no questions; Dave volunteered neither information nor theory.

The Tapestry Room, a front bedroom at the southwest angle of the Hall, Jeff did remember having seen before. It seemed reasonably comfortable if also austere, the tapestries gray-green scenes of beruffed gentlemen at bowls or of beruffed ladies and gentlemen against formal backgrounds. Its bathroom, in which Jeff washed for dinner, would have been modern in the early years of the century.

When he went downstairs afterwards, Cato directed him to the one telephone in the house, at the back of the main hall. Information gave him the number of the Lynns' country place at no great distance from here. But the line was busy. So he phoned his uncle's apartment and reported his whereabouts to Melchior, that most efficient, fussy of servitors. He had just hung up the receiver when Cato announced dinner.

At dinner, by candlelight in the great, heavily raftered refectory, Serena was constrained and silent, while Dave talked twenty to the dozen without saying much.

"If you're looking towards the sideboard, Jeff," he remarked, "the silver tray and pitcher—that particular pitcher, anyway—are no longer in evidence. Even if they were there to be inspected, we couldn't tell much now."

The three of them shared a bottle of authentic Sauterne. Though French wines seldom travel well, this one proved excellent, fully as good as the meal.

"Yes," commented Dave, "Washington Jones is still our cook. His repertoire may lack variety; it has never lacked skill. The man's Southern fried chicken, as you can now testify, couldn't be bettered at Antoine's or *La Louisiane.*"

Afterwards they smoked a cigarette over coffee and Armagnac brandy, then wandered into the drawing-room. Thence, irresolute, they were drifting out into the hall when the telephone rang. Before it could be answered by a servant or anyone else, Serena flew at the instrument and snatched it up.

"It's for me!" she called out, cradling the phone against her breast. Though her voice remained noncommittal, her constraint seemed to increase and faint color tinged her cheeks.

To obscure the fact that they were both listening or half listening, Dave and Jeff began to examine the display of sixteenth- and seventeenth-century weapons against oak-panelled walls. Serena said little more before putting down the phone and hurrying to join them.

"Will either of you two," she inquired, "be going out tonight?"

"No, I don't think so," replied Dave. "I'm not, at least. What about you, Jeff?"

"That goes for me too. Unless Penny . . ."

"I ask," said Serena, "because I *am* going out. You won't mind if I take the Stutz, Dave?"

"No, of course not." Dave gestured towards the telephone. "Who was it, old gal?"

"Oh, nobody in particular; it doesn't matter. And don't ask where I'm going, either; only to town, that's all! But don't be surprised if I'm a *little* late."

Waiting only long enough to find her handbag, Serena left them in haste. A few minutes later they heard the hum of a car rounding the east side of the house and fading away down the drive. Dave turned to his companion.

"Are you thinking what I'm thinking?"

"I don't know what you're thinking, Dave."

"Then you ought to know, old son. Most definitely you ought to know. That gal—!"

"Excuse *me* just one moment."

Jeff himself marched to the phone, again asking for the Lynns' number. The deferential female voice which spoke to him, evidently a maid's, reported that Miss Penny wasn't there because she had gone out. Dave wandered to the telephone table.

"No luck, eh? Well, never mind. Since I know I'm not the brightest possible company tonight, Jeff, I wonder if you'd like to look at the commodore's logbook, the old ledger I've talked about at least once and probably more often? Care to see it?"

"Yes, by all means. Where's it kept?"

"Where my grandfather kept it, and my father after him. In the safe of the room they both used as a study."

"You know the combination of the safe?"

"Naturally, though nobody's needed to know the combination for years. It's never locked. If you will just follow me, Jeff, we can . . ."

His voice trailed away. The hum of a car, approaching up the drive at no great speed, grew louder as it neared the house.

"Well, how do you like that?" Dave exclaimed. "If my unpredictable sister has changed her mind and is returning . . ."

He strode to the front door and threw it open.

"It's not Serena," he declared, peering out, "because the car's not even a roadster. It's a sedan; it looks like a Hudson, and that probably means . . . Yes, Jeff, you'd better come here. It *is* Penny!"

The night, despite its promise of being fine, had turned cloudy. A great gust of wind swept up the lawn as the car swung and stopped broadside to the terrace. Leaving the front door wide open, Dave and Jeff crossed the terrace and descended to meet Penny, who was leaning out of the left-hand front window with a face of something like alarm.

"Where's Serena, please?" she began. "I must speak to Serena!"

"You can't, I'm afraid. Up to your own arrival, Penny, everybody except Serena has been missing everybody else." Dave seemed to catch a little of Penny's mood. "She got a phone message from some caller unnamed and ran out of here not ten minutes ago. Is it important?"

"I don't know, but I think it may be very important. Did she say where she was going?"

"Just somewhere in town. You know Serena; she wouldn't be

likely to say. Have *you* any idea where she went?"

"I don't know that either, but I may be able to guess. Nobody except myself uses this car much, so I was able to get it. It's even possible I can find her, if," and Penny looked out appealingly, "if Jeff will come with me?"

"I am at your service, as always," said the miscreant in question. "Shall I climb in the front?"

"No, Dave," Penny suggested, as Jeff went round the car and Dave made a move to follow. "This is only a wild guess, probably all wrong. And, under the circumstances, I don't think you'd better go with us. But, also under the circumstances, I also think you understand."

"Oh, I understand! Serena's affairs must remain her affairs, at least to another member of the family."

"I didn't mean—!"

"I know you didn't, Penny. If any of her friends are disturbed about what the hell she may be up to, they've got a right to be disturbed and I applaud 'em. In you get, Jeff. Do you want your— no, you don't wear a hat; nobody of our generation has worn a hat since we were in college. Good luck in your quest, both of you! I'll go and commune with the log."

Another gust of wind swirled up the lawn as Jeff got into the front seat and slammed the door.

"Like me to drive, Penny?"

"No, thanks; I'm more capable than I look."

They were rolling smoothly towards the main road when Penny spoke again. If flustered, she remained intent and somewhat remote.

"You know," she said, "this notion of mine may be even more ridiculous than I think it is! Can you bear it if we only get laughed at for what we're doing?"

"Easily, though I might prefer to learn what we're doing. Or is it your turn to be mysterious?"

"I'm not being mysterious, truly I'm not! Dave thinks there's a man in Serena's life; I'm almost sure there is, from certain remarks she's let fall. What did he mean, by the way, about communing with a log? Did he mean sitting on a log, or what?"

"He meant a log*book*, the log kept by the old commodore. Dave says it contains some clue to the hidden treasure."

"I wonder," began Penny, starting to turn towards him and then turning back to the wheel, "whether poor Harald Hobart really lost as much money as my father says he did? That wouldn't worry Dave, though it might worry Serena. And it's not the point I'm trying to make. Dave's afraid Serena, who's always been so careful about keeping suitable company, may have picked up with somebody most *un*suitable."

"We're looking for Serena, then. Well, where do we look for her?"

"Bourbon Street. It's a speakeasy."

"You in a speakeasy? *Serena* in a speakeasy?"

"Yes; why not?" Penny spoke rapidly. "There are speakeasies and speakeasies, you know. Some of them are dreadful, of course. The better ones, mostly restaurants where they serve good food as well as drinks, have become quite respectable. The place we're going is a kind of night club, also reasonably respectable. It's . . . it's . . ."

"Yes?"

"It's called Cinderella's Slipper, and is known as a coffeehouse. As for drinks, you get only absinthe served in coffee cups. If the management doesn't know you, you actually get coffee at an exorbitant price. Is it true, Jeff, that absinthe has been forbidden even in France?"

"Technically it's against the law, but they've got a legal substitute: some vicious green stuff called Pernod, with as deadly a wallop as real absinthe. I don't care much for it."

"I don't like absinthe myself, though I can drink some and make a show of finishing the rest. But Marcel knows me; it was Serena and Dave who took me there, so my escort oughtn't to be questioned." Penny shivered. "You do see, don't you? However enlightened I think I am, I couldn't have gone to the place *alone.*"

"The real question, Penny, is what we do when we get there. Suppose we find Serena, sitting over absinthe with a highly unsuitable character: some plugugly or even gangster? Do I stalk up to him and say, 'You are an unsuitable character, sir; get the hell out of here'?"

"Of all things, no! Good gracious, no! There's nothing we can *do*, even if we wanted to. Besides, the man in question won't be anything like that. I'm sure, from references made by Serena herself, he's somebody we all know. When I say 'all,' of course, I don't include you; you've been away too long. —What's the matter, Jeff? Have you got some reservation in mind?"

"Only that this seems a little like spying. Isn't the girl entitled to her own love life?"

"Yes, of course! But the man's being socially presentable, after all, is no guarantee she's not mixed up in a situation that could be unpleasant or even dangerous. Oh, I hope there's no such situation; I do hope so! Serena's so—so reserved, so terribly *fastidious* . . . !"

"Whereas you," Jeff asked with heavy sarcasm, "are neither reserved nor fastidious, I suppose?"

"I'm not a bit reserved! And, though it's a terrible thing to admit, in my heart I'm not even fastidious! That's what I should have told Serena straight out, when she told me—"

"When she told you what? Last night, before we were interrupted by the cop Dave calls Old Nemesis . . ."

"It was too bad, wasn't it?" Penny said with soft intentness. "And I behaved like an idiot again, as usual." Briefly she raised her eyes. "We must go back to last night, Jeff, and take up where we left off. But not now, please? Not *now*?"

"Whatever you say, Penny."

"No more reservations?"

"None at all. If it's your wish, my dear, I will cheerfully walk up to the devil and pull his whiskers."

They fell silent, each occupied with individual thoughts. After a fairly long drive, to Jeff all too short with Penny beside him, they were swallowed up by twinkling lights. Taking what she said would be a short cut, Penny drove in from northwest. It was past ten o'clock when he saw a familiar view.

Under high, pale lamps and flashing sky signs, Canal Street swept its great breadth south towards the river amid lessened traffic. You could not be five minutes in central New Orleans without catching the easy-going atmosphere or responding to the tolerant mood.

Since Penny would not take a car into the narrow lanes of the Vieux Carré, she left the Hudson in University Place on what some still called the American side. Afoot they crossed Canal Street to the French side. Passing Burgundy Street, passing Dauphine Street, they turned left into the thoroughfare they sought.

Bourbon Street and its denizens, after dark, wore that faintly shuffling, slightly furtive air which perhaps both may have worn since the street existed. On the left-hand *banquette*, with Penny's right shoulder touching his left forearm, he felt immensely protective as they strode along.

"What are you thinking now, Jeff?"

"My principal thought, as requested, I will file away for future reference. One secondary thought . . ."

"What's the secondary thought?"

"Prohibition!" exploded Jeff. Unspoken curses wrote a fine legible hand across his brain. "Prohibition, *here*, seems as unreal, as unnatural, as it would seem in Paris or Vienna."

"I don't doubt it's unnatural; it's certainly unreal. So much good liquor still comes in by boat that there's never been any shortage. Fishermen from the bayous meet inbound vessels and cover great loads of bottles with shrimp or oysters until they can dispose of the load in town. That's what my friends tell me; I'm not *au fait* with everything. Cinderella's Slipper . . ."

"Is the place far from here?"

"A fair little distance. But nothing at all, really. It's between Dumaine Street and St. Philip Street, not quite as far as Laffite's Blacksmith Shop. Jeff, why *will* they dream up such absurd tales? Either about the Old Absinthe House over there, or about the house that's supposed to have been a blacksmith's? There are enough peculiar places without having to invent legends about them."

Jeff made no further comment. A flighty wind whistled and piped across rooftops. As they passed the intersection of St. Peter Street, it occurred to him that he must be close to 701b Royal Street, whose typewritten address lay safely tucked away in his inside breast pocket, and which he meant to investigate next day.

At a point just beyond three short blocks farther on, still on the same side of the road, Penny drew him towards the wall. Between two rather ramshackle houses, faced respectively with gray and with yellow stucco, a brick-floored open passage led to the front door of a third house, lightless, looming indistinguishably through uncertain gloom.

As they groped along the passage, Jeff thought he could hear faint music. Penny pressed a bell to the right of the front door. When the door opened, you might have thought the interior also dark if you had not seen chinks of light through heavy curtains which hung like a barrier within three steps of the door.

The man who admitted them first closed the front door. After holding back the side of one curtain, a rich crimson, so that the glow fell on Penny and then on Jeff, he beckoned them inwards. He was a swarthy, thick-set young man in full evening kit of white tie and tails. Though Penny addressed him as Marcel, he looked more Italian than Creole.

"Good evening, Marcel. This gentleman is a friend of mine, Mr. Caldwell."

"Evening, Miss Lynn. Evening, sir. Good table for two near the band?"

"If you don't mind, Marcel, we'd like to glance through both rooms first. Is Miss Hobart here, by the way?"

"Miss Serena Hobart, ma'am? No, Miss Lynn. Haven't seen nothing of her; not tonight. *You're* a member, Miss Lynn; any friend of yours is welcome."

They had emerged into a hall or lobby, very broad but not at all deep, heavily carpeted and ornately decorated in crimson, white, and gold. At the *vestiaire*, behind the counter across a recess in the left-hand wall, presided a young lady who, far from sporting the traditionally scanty attire of hat-check girls in night clubs, wore a full skirted if low cut imitation-mediaeval gown to represent one of the beauties at the ball from which Cinderella fled.

"They hire various name bands here," observed Penny, pointing.

A placard on a gilt easel informed Jeff, supremely uninterested in bands, that Cinderella's Slipper now featured Tommy Some- body and his Boys. This immediately became evident. From the direction of an open archway at the rear of the hall, sound smote with a kind of religious fury, soon afterwards picked up by the Boys' tenor vocalist in revival-meeting exaltation.

> "When cares pur-sue ya, sing hal-le-lu-jah,
> And it will shoo tha blues a-way!
> When cares pur-sue ya, hal-le-lu-jah
> Gets ya through tha dar-kest day!

Again Penny indicated.

"Back there," she explained, "there are two rooms opening into each other, set in a line from right to left. The band's in the far room at the extreme left; that's why this entry is so wide. They haven't got a bar; I mean they haven't got a bar counter. You sit at tables to be served. That's it, Jeff; straight through."

With the solicitous Marcel hovering attendance, they made their inspection.

Both rooms, little more than one room separated by another open archway, were dark except for a meandering blue spotlight and a little glow from the throne dais which held the band. Each room contained a small dance floor surrounded by tables for two or for four. On the white cloth of each table stood a siphon of soda, cups, saucers and spoons as well as a small silvered bucket of ice cubes. In air thick with tobacco smoke and the damp aniseed breath of absinthe, both rooms seemed pretty well patronized without being crowded or even full. Nobody except the waiters or attendants wore formal dress. Most couples were dancing; some merely sat and listened with rapture.

After she had glanced at each table in the first room, Penny led her escort into the second. At a ringside table Jeff noticed one couple: the woman a well-shaped redhead with her back turned, the man heavy-shouldered and balding in his early forties. He should have looked of the utmost good nature, and didn't. But he raised his hand in salutation to Penny, who returned the salutation absently.

Still no Serena. Penny even opened a distant door adorned with a pastel sketch of Cinderella herself, disappeared for a few moments, and returned shaking her head.

"*Et alors, madame, monsieur?*" prompted Marcel.

"It's *rather* loud," said Penny, with which Jeff could heartily agree. "If you don't mind, Marcel, perhaps a table in the first room . . . ?"

When they had been installed at another ringside table, Marcel's place was taken by a waiter. Asked in French whether madame or monsieur wished to order something, Penny replied in the same language that both would have the specialty of the house. Removing two cups and saucers, the waiter soon returned with both cups half full of the greenish liquid Jeff had been expecting. He filled the cups with soda-water already so chilled that the beverage needed no further ice.

"Hadn't we better drink a toast to absent Serena," Penny suggested, "since we can't drink it to her in person? She's not here, Jeff; she's not *anywhere;* I ought to have known she wouldn't be."

"To Serena, then! But afterwards," said Jeff, when both had sipped and set down the cup without making a face, "why not a toast to ourselves? Or would you prefer to dance?"

"No; let's just sit here for a minute or two, shall we? Serena's not here and hasn't been here; Marcel wouldn't lie about a thing like that. Then, too, you don't meet your secret lover at a speakeasy; or, if you do, you don't stay there afterwards. Yes, to ourselves!" breathed Penny, giving him a glance of some intimacy. "But I could drink with more enthusiasm if this stuff were distilled from honest alcohol instead of wormwood! And . . . and . . ."

"What is it, Penny? What's the matter?"

"Ever since we've been here, Jeff, have you had a feeling somebody's been keeping an eye on us and watching us?"

"Yes, I know what you mean." Jeff had experienced the sensation without being able to define it, still less account for it. "At first I thought it must be good old Marcel himself, but I'm not sure. He'd have no particular reason for keeping an eye on either of us, surely? If not, who would?"

"I can't think; that's just what makes me nervous!"

"Whoever may be doing it, Penny, it's not that fellow in the other room."

"What fellow in the other room?"

"Big fellow, built like a football player a little run to fat. He's with the redhead in green, who always keeps her back turned as though to concentrate on him; you can see 'em both from here. He waved to you, and you waved back."

"Oh, him?" Penny said with relief. "It's all right, Jeff; that's only Billy Vauban. He's the managing director of Danforth & Co., a manufacturing firm of some kind. The woman is Pauline, his wife."

"Danforth & Co., did you say? I've heard that name recently, in some way related to the Hobarts. What's the connection, Penny?"

"I never heard there was one. Billy's very popular, and deserves to be; everybody likes him. Normally he's the best-tempered man on earth, but . . . is he drinking?"

"He's gulped down at least two since we've been here. One eye looked glazed when we passed; he didn't seem very pleased about something. And you can't polish off the green scourge as though you were swilling grape juice or soda pop."

"When Billy's been drinking, it's more than rumored, he can be quite impossible. Pauline Vauban is no patient Griselda herself. She keeps her attention on him so she can tell him off when they have one of their frequent spats. If Pauline cuts loose, apparently, she's got no inhibitions at all." Penny faltered. "That's in private, of course. They'd keep it to themselves; the Vaubans *are* an old Creole family. I—I don't think they'd have a row in public."

But they would.

The band finished its number on a soaring note, individual musicians settling back with the deflated air that betokened an interval. When loud applause drew no further music, the dancers returned to their tables. Soft lights glowed through both rooms.

Hitherto, under the buzz of talk in that damp, smoky atmosphere, both Pauline Vauban and her husband had been speaking in voices so lowered that they could scarcely have been overheard at the adjoining table.

Now it changed. Mrs. Vauban was leaning forward intently. Though she remained inaudible, she must have administered one more stab or goad. Even here Jeff could feel the shock as her

95

husband's temper blew to pieces. He lurched to his feet and stood swaying, a red-faced tower of menace. His hoarse voice tore through smoke and fumes.

"Now don't you start on my mother's people, either! Thad Peters was my uncle, the best offensive halfback Tulane ever had!"

The woman, still with her back turned, also sprang up.

"Offensive?" she shrilled. "You just bet you're offensive, every last one of you! Beginning with your drunken grandfather and ending with your drunken self, the double-dyed offensive worst!"

Guests at nearby tables, trying hard to pretend they saw and heard nothing, sat as though paralyzed. Billy Vauban paid no attention.

"I've had about enough of this!" he roared. "Shut your damn mouth, you hear me? How'd you like to be turned over papa's knee and get your tail smacked as you deserve?"

"You'd *like* that, wouldn't you?" shrieked his wife. "Every time you're crazy with booze, which is practically all the time, you'd like to hit me or get your filthy paws on me. But would you do it? Oh, no! Not with anybody else present! You wouldn't dare, not you, or they might lock you up in the asylum where you belong!"

Her husband did not reply; he seemed incapable of reply. Left hand a little extended, right hand back, he began to edge round the table towards her. Several waiters, black vests and white shirt-fronts, were converging on them without haste.

"I wouldn't, sir," the leading waiter advised quietly. "If it was me, honest, I wouldn't try to touch the lady. Because if you did, you know, we'd just have to stop you."

Drunk or not, overweight or not, Billy Vauban moved as fast as a striking leopard. Snatching up the chair behind him, holding the chair by its back, he whirled it aloft and brandished it in the air, defying everybody.

Shocking as the outburst had been, its aftermath was no less so. For, at the very peak and paroxysm of rage, another change occurred. A wheel seemed to go round behind his eyes. Wrath drained out of him. Lowering the chair, he sat down in it. With a waiter on either side of him, each with a hand near his elbow, he put both elbows on the table and his head in his hands.

Then, after a pause during which you might have counted six, Billy Vauban sat up as though partly waking from his daze.

"There, now!" he said in a different voice. "Did it again, didn't I? Made a damn fool o' m'self, or almost." Remorse, contrition shook him as he rose to his feet. "Poll m'dear, I ap—I 'pologize for everything! I 'pologize, too, to all these good pol—all these good ladies and gentlemen I 'ffended by my lout's goin' on! Poll m'dear, time we went home."

The woman, it was clear, had instantly become mollified. Producing a thick roll of banknotes, Vauban dropped several on the table. He extended his arm to his wife, who took it. Unsteadily, if not without a certain curious dignity, he led her through the other room and out.

The waiters, who had followed the offender as far as the lobby but had not tried to escort him, went their several ways. A brief buzz of comment swelled and died.

"Jeff," Penny said soon afterwards, "it's not late; it's not much past eleven o'clock. But do you really want to stay here with the specialty of the house?"

"Am I still forbidden to approach what I want to approach?"

"You're not *forbidden* anything. And possibly I'm thinking about it as much as you say you are. But this isn't the time or the place. Having dragged you here on such an utter fool's errand!"

"We haven't learned much about Serena's alleged boy friend, it's true. If *you'd* like to go—?"

"Please!"

Jeff called for the bill, and was surprised to find it reasonable. The band had begun to prepare for another number when they left the table. Marcel ushered them to the front door, volubly regretting their early departure and insisting, after the habit of the South, that they must soon return.

The door shut them into that brick-floored passage. Wind still piped across rooftops, though it did not penetrate down here. Penny lingered at the front door. Despite near darkness, she had opened her handbag to make sure of the car keys.

"Jeff, don't you still feel somebody's watching us?"

"No, that's gone now." Having moved a few steps to one side, he was inspired towards the oracular. "Let me repeat, Penny, that we haven't done well as detectives. We have learned only that one William Vauban of Danforth & Co., a nephew of the late Thad Peters, can go berserk and then recover before much damage has been done. What might have been an ugly incident blew over very quickly. The essence of the whole evening is that *nothing* has happened. It's peaceful, after all; it's so utterly peaceful that—"

He never finished the pronouncement. Some heavy, fairly large object, whushing down out of the air between them, landed with a smash on the brick paving. Both had instinctly recoiled; he heard Penny gasp.

Finding a box of matches in his pocket, he struck one and lowered its flame.

The large flower-pot of spring daffodils, which now lay in a ruin of reddish shards, brown earth, and ragged yellow flower fragments, would have crushed the skull of any person underneath. Jeff straightened up. He saw Penny's frightened face a moment before the match went out.

"Was it meant for you or was it meant for me?" she cried. "And why, oh, *why* should it have been meant for either of us?"

9

When Jeff finished breakfast on the following morning, an over-cast Saturday, he was not expecting more trouble within the next hour.

He had decided, or virtually decided, that the incident of the flower-pot at Cinderella's Slipper must have been the accident everybody said it was. Almost as soon as that weight fell, he had jabbed at the doorbell in a way that brought Marcel in some haste. But Marcel, though sympathetic, seemed to have deeper woes. Somebody, said the *maître d'hôtel*, was always leaving flower-pots too precariously balanced on the ledge around the little low roof. And they'd noticed the high wind, hadn't they?

A waiter, sent upstairs to investigate without being told what sort of horticultural item had almost done the damage, reported the absence of a flower-pot containing daffodils, adding that he himself had removed other flower-pots to a safer place.

With some intimation that it had better not happen again, since even one brained patron would be no very good advertisement, Jeff led Penny away.

He calmed her down, he thought. But she drove slowly and somewhat erratically on the return journey; she would not be drawn from her preoccupation. At past midnight, when she let him out at Delys Hall, the whole house seemed dark except for a gleam behind stained-glass windows above the front door.

Waiting until Penny had gone, Jeff found his way around the east side of the place to a modern brick garage at the back. Pushing back its folding doors, he discovered the light switch and kindled a

99

hanging bulb in the middle. The garage, which would hold four cars, at the moment held two: the dark-blue Packard limousine and a gray Marmon touring-car. The Stutz was still missing. He had no real curiosity; it was only by accident he touched the hood of the Marmon and found it faintly warm.

Jeff returned to the house, where a sleepy-looking Cato admitted him.

"Hadn't you better turn in, Cato?"

"Think I go now, suh. Mist' Dave, he gone a'ready; Miss Reen got her own key. Good night, Mist' Jeff; glad you back home!"

The returned wanderer slept heavily that night. Whatever shadows may have been in the house, they did not trouble his rest. It was past ten in the morning when he awoke, and almost ten-thirty before he finished dressing and went downstairs, to find Dave sitting over the remnants of breakfast in the great black-beamed refectory, with several of its window-lights set open on the warm, dampish day.

"How'd it go, old son? Didn't sleep very well myself," said Dave, who looked as though he hadn't. "Heard Cato let you in round about half-past twelve. Serena didn't get back until half-past one."

"She's not up yet this morning, I gather?"

"Oh, she's up. Up, and full of beans! Finishing her toast and coffee when I got down a little while ago. She's out in the garden now, but said she'd join me for more coffee when *I* finished. Well, old son, how'd it go? She volunteered no information; I asked no questions. Did you find her last night?"

"No, not a sign of her. Penny thought she might be at a night club called Cinderella's Slipper. But she wasn't there and evidently hadn't been there."

"For the sort of meeting I think it was, she wouldn't have been. Well . . ."

Jeff helped himself at the sideboard, which had been set out with some variety of dishes. While Dave kept glancing towards the open windows that faced south, his companion returned to the table and pitched into breakfast. He did not mention the incident of the flower-pot, seeing no point in bringing it up.

"Did you yourself go out last night, Dave?"

"Yes, for a short time. Remember the drugstore at Rupert's Corners up the road? I was running low on cigarettes, so I took the touring-car and went to get 'em before the place closed."

"Anything so very interesting out on the lawn?"

"I'm not interested in the lawn, old son; only in the driveway. It's Malcolm Townsend: the authority on old houses and architectural tricks, if you remember?"

"He's in New Orleans?"

"Very much so. Got in by the early train this morning. He's at the St. Charles now, and phoned me as I was coming downstairs. Of course I invited him to stay with us. But I think he prefers the freedom of a hotel, as you did yourself until somebody persuaded you. I should have said he was at the St. Charles when he phoned. I offered to drive in and get him, but he had a taxi waiting. He ought to be here very soon."

Jeff, eating steadily, had pushed aside his plate and gone to the sideboard for coffee when Serena, all in white for the tennis she may or may not have intended to play, strolled in from the drawing-room.

Dave had described her as full of beans, by which presumably he meant happy or even radiant. Jeff would have used no such description. But she did look determined, with a certain fixity in her blue eyes and perhaps a more stubborn line to the fragile jaw.

"May *I* have some of that coffee, Jeff? You might pour for me, please? Cream, but only one lump of sugar. —Thanks!"

Together they carried their cups to the table, where Dave had risen as though with some sort of protest on his lips.

"Look, Serena, you're not—?" He stopped.

"Not what? If it's in your own mind to ask a lot of questions about last night, Dave, I'd much rather you didn't!"

"Oh, we know that. And I don't intend to ask a lot of questions, which would only give you the chance to ask me twice as many. One query, though, that ought to be harmless. Was he very entertaining?"

"Was who very entertaining?"

"The man you went to meet."

"How do you know it was a man I went to meet?"

101

"Because I can be pretty damn certain it was nobody else! Whatever your tastes may be, little sister, we all know they're not Sapphic."

"*Really, Dave—!*"

"Any pretense of shock and outrage, Serena, becomes you still less. Since you object even to that question: as Ira Rutledge might say, I'll rephrase it. Did you spend an entertaining evening?"

Serena lifted one shoulder.

"Whether or not I found it entertaining," she replied, "I must say I found it both enlightening and profitable."

"Profitable?"

"That was the word. Can you and Jeff say the same?"

"Since I stayed at home and minded the store, I found it anything but profitable. I can't speak for Jeff; he went to a night club with Penny Lynn."

"Jeff went gallivanting to a night club? And with Penny? Tell me, Jeff . . ."

Serena did not finish. Through the open windows they could all see a Yellow taxi approaching up the drive, where it turned and stopped at the terrace steps. Muttering excuses, Dave left in haste. They heard him cross the drawing-room and cross the hall, then the opening of the front door.

Serena and Jeff drifted to the line of southern windows. Out of the taxi had climbed a figure in cream-colored suit and Panama hat, carrying a brief-case. Dave appeared on the terrace, descended its steps, and shook hands with the newcomer amid a murmur of unintelligible words. Serena's brow was wrinkled.

"Jeff, who *is* that? I don't think I . . ."

"His name is Townsend, Malcolm Townsend. Dave's been expecting him."

"Oh, the man who wrote *Secret Ways?* Yes, Dave's mentioned it more than once. But I never thought he'd *really* turn up. You never do expect something to happen, do you, when it's been planned beforehand?"

Motioning his taxi-driver to wait, the newcomer accompanied Dave up the steps, and they both entered the refectory. Seen close at hand, Malcolm Townsend proved to be a spare, middle-sized man of indeterminate age not ill-looking, with a narrow line of brown moustache. His manner combined the suave and the easy-going; you could not help liking him on sight. After Dave had introduced the others, Mr. Townsend declined breakfast or even coffee because he had eaten two hours ago. Then he turned to Serena.

"This is all the more a pleasure, Miss Hobart, since it's my first opportunity to visit Delys Hall. Your late father did not see his way clear to granting permission when I requested it. That's under-standable, of course; I must often seem the most unpardonable kind of interloper."

Serena decided to be gracious.

"You're no interloper now, at all events. Are you an architect, Mr. Townsend?"

"Not by profession, no. But I take some considerable interest in old houses, and I've picked up a little architecture on the way."

"It's most interesting, I'm sure," said Serena, who did not sound very interested. "Dave's told you what *he's* anxious to find, I imag-ine. How does one of your profession or hobby go about finding it?"

"Before any practical steps can be taken, it's as well to familiarize oneself with the history of the house, especially an old English house like this, and determine why some previous owner wanted or needed a secret hiding place. Invariably it was to hide some *person*, either during the days of religious persecution between Protestant and Catholic or during the days of political persecution between Roundhead and Cavalier. They didn't build such things for fun, you know."

"But that's just the trouble, isn't it?" Jeff interposed. "If the old Delys family were such strict conformists as they seem to have been, they'd have had no reason to hide anybody or anything."

"Exactly!" agreed Malcolm Townsend, as though rather pleased than otherwise. "But I gather from young Mr. Hobart that his famous grandfather may well have meant it as a kind of joke, humorous or otherwise. The first practical step, then, is to find some space that can't be accounted for. I have here," he held up the brief-case, "some measuring tapes and other easily portable gear."

"You know, this is real business!" exclaimed Dave. "Shall we get on with the search right away?"

"By all means, if it won't seem too abrupt."

"Oh, it won't seem too abrupt! We might begin with a look at those stairs out there. Coming, Serena?"

"If you'll excuse me, gentlemen, I think I'd better go about my own affairs. Just call me in case you find anything; I won't be far."

All three went on through towards the main hall. About to join them, Jeff glanced out of the window. Up the drive came bowling a Buick sedan, which parked at one side a little way behind the taxi. Out of the car unfolded the long, lean shape of Gilbert Bethune. Uncle Gil, well and formally dressed, took two steps towards the house, then turned and stood staring down the drive in the opposite direction.

Jeff hesitated. There was one small matter which, as a matter of mere courtesy, he must not neglect. He hurried out into the hall. Serena had disappeared; Dave was addressing some remark about the staircase to a fascinated Malcolm Townsend. Jeff ran up those stairs, hearing the peal of the doorbell as he reached the Tapestry Room, where he found the book of detective short stories he had brought with him.

When he returned to the lower floor Dave had admitted the second visitor of that morning; the second visitor had been introduced to the first. While Dave drew Townsend towards the rear of the hall, Jeff shook hands with the more recent arrival.

"How are you, Uncle Gil? When did you get back from Baton Rouge?"

Grown somewhat craggy of feature in his late forties, though gray scarcely yet tinged the dark hair, Gilbert Bethune as ever was cordial without being effusive, all intelligence and restrained energy.

"Late last night," he replied. "Or, rather, early this morning. I phoned Melchior to see whether he might have any news for me, and he had. So I drove back; here I am. There can't be any complaint about my health, young fellow; nor, I see, can there be any of yours. How's Paris?"

"Very much as usual. They've done a lot of talking about some

Americans who'll try to fly the Atlantic and make for there when the weather improves. But the Atlantic's been flown, hasn't it?"

"Yes, of course it has. Two Englishmen, Alcock and Brown, made the crossing by dirigible as long ago as 1919. What people mean when they say it hasn't been flown is that it's never been flown by one man alone, and never in a heavier-than-air machine. Now, with so many candidates lining up for a shot at that twenty-five-thousand-dollar prize, somebody ought to do the trick before long."

"It would seem so. Anyway, Uncle Gil, I've brought you a small present of your favorite reading."

He held out the book, which the other took and inspected.

"*The Secret of Father Brown*, by G. K. Chesterton. When was this published, Jeff?"

"It hasn't been officially published. Those are advance page-proofs of the English edition. And the mysteries are first-class; I thought you might like 'em."

"Thanks; it's much appreciated."

Uncle Gil thrust the book into his pocket. Then a shadow crossed his face.

Dave and Malcolm Townsend had gone on up the stairs, the latter examining every tread. Towards the front of the lower hall, on your left as you entered but on your right in the direction Jeff now faced, another arched door led to the companion of the drawing-room opposite, a kind of minor drawing-room less austere because less desperately confined to period furniture. Beyond this, at the southwestern angle of the house, you could see the shelves of the great dusky library.

Putting his hand on Jeff's arm, Uncle Gil drew him to the doorway of the minor drawing-room. But he did not go into the room; he lingered in the doorway, lowering his voice.

"I'm not surprised to find you here," he said, "but I wish you had come to my apartment. We may have a first-class mystery of our own, if it doesn't blow up like a booby trap; things are bound to be awkward whatever happens.

"At City Hall this morning I ran into Harry Minnoch, who told me he'd met you on the boat and said he'd hinted at our problem.

You're old enough to hear the truth; you'd better hear it. Now hearken, young fellow! Dave's friend Townsend isn't entirely a stranger; I heard him lecture in Richmond last fall; they'll be occupied for some time. As for me, I'm tied up this afternoon and most of this evening. But why not come along back to town and have lunch with me? Then I can tell you."

"Lunch?" exclaimed Jeff, glancing at his watch. "It's well past eleven already, and I've hardly finished breakfast! I may get a sandwich later in the day, but I couldn't face lunch. Besides . . ."

"What is it? What's wrong?"

"Ira Rutledge! Every single person has been plaguing me with mysterious allusions or references not one of 'em will explain. And Ira, since he wrote me a cryptic letter in March, has been the most evasive of all. But now I can have my mind set at rest. I've promised to meet him in his office at two sharp this afternoon. At least I'm going to learn how the death of Harald Hobart can affect me and one other person outside the Hobart family. Ira Rutledge is maddening at times, but he does what he says he'll do. Ira—"

At the rear of the hall, shrilly, the telephone rang. Cato, hovering near, picked it up and answered. Then, bowing smilingly, he held out the phone towards Jeff, who took over.

"Yes?" he said to the mouthpiece.

"Jeff?" returned an unmistakable voice. "Ira Rutledge speaking." The phone whirred in its throat. "Much though it distresses me, circumstances have arisen which make it impossible for us to meet this afternoon."

Jeff refrained from swearing aloud. "We don't meet at all, then?"

"On the contrary, my boy, it's imperative that we do meet; and as soon as possible."

"Well, when? I'm at your service."

"Let me see, now." The telephone deliberated. "For one of my age and sedentary habits, I fear, I have fallen to keeping shockingly unpredictable hours. I shall not be free until this evening. Would ten tonight, and at the same place, be too late for you?"

"No, not at all! But you won't put me off *again*, will you?"

"If the President of the United States requested my presence at that hour, Jeff, I should have to plead a previous engagement. You have my solemn promise for it."

"One other matter. I've only got to say something can't or won't happen, and immediately it does happen to prove I'm a liar. This business which so much affects me and one other person, now. Will you explain what you wouldn't explain in your letter or yesterday evening? In short, will you explain everything?"

"I will explain everything. You have my solemn word for that too. The door of the anteroom shall be left unlocked; just walk in. Until ten tonight, then, my apologies and goodbye!"

Jeff replaced the receiver. Whereupon, as though diabolically inspired, the phone rang again. An unfamiliar voice asked if it might speak to Mr. Gilbert Bethune, who had said he would be there.

"For you, Uncle Gil. It sounds like your office."

Taking over in his turn, Uncle Gil listened to some diatribe with the receiver close against his ear, replying only in monosyllables until he said, "Yes, immediately," and put down the phone.

"It *was* my office!" he fumed. "They've nailed a character we've been after for some time, provided we've actually got him nailed. The boys have been at him all morning, but without much success; they think I should have a try. And it'll have to be a devilish good try, mind, if we're to send Luigi up the river for as long a term as he deserves. Where's my hat, Jeff? I must run along now."

"This lunch proposition, Uncle Gil, and the first-class mystery of our own. Lunch doesn't matter; and I can't interfere with business, of course. But I could ride into town with you, couldn't I, while you gave some outline of the mystery?"

"No, young fellow; I'm afraid that won't do."

"If it's to be the brush-off or the runaround even from you . . . !"

Gilbert Bethune himself could assume lordly airs when he chose.

"And they call *me* impatient!" he declared, as though preening himself on monumental patience. "No, Jeff, no! These things must be approached in good order, one perplexity at a time, or a harassed public official will never come to the end. I want you to see the original of a certain letter: the original, not a copy. For another thing . . . well, that can wait. Keep in touch; you know where to find me."

Cato gave him his hat and ushered him out. The big front door was closing as Dave Hobart and Townsend, deep in conference, descended the stairs and joined Jeff. Townsend, less subdued than he had been, hesitated before addressing Dave again.

"May I ask one question?"

"Yes, ask a hundred; ask anything you like!"

"At this juncture," said the amateur architect, running a finger along his narrow moustache, "more than one won't be necessary. As I understand it, you're looking for what must be a considerable weight of gold bullion, concealed but not buried. Very well. But you've just finished telling me there is nothing hidden inside or between the walls. How can you be sure of that?"

"Last Monday night," Jeff interposed, "Dave told me the same thing. I wondered, but didn't pursue the point. How *can* you be sure, Dave?"

Dave held his hands a few inches apart.

"Air spaces," he said, "between the inside of the outer wall and the wall of the room next to it, that's how!"

"Oh, furring strips?" murmured Townsend.

"If that's the term for it, yes. They didn't build air spaces in the sixteenth century, I believe. They just slapped plaster on the inside of the outer wall and reared their panelling against that; it's one reason why houses got so damp. When my grandfather had this place transplanted and air spaces built in '82, it required some readjustment but not a great deal of readjustment: nothing at all that showed after they'd finished."

Here, facing Jeff, Dave levelled his forefinger for emphasis.

"Moreover!" he added. "I told you, didn't I, my parents had electricity and a telephone installed in '07? As architect in charge they used old Pete Stanley, who wasn't a young man then but is still very much alive and alert to testify."

"You said, I think," Jeff consulted memory, "the workmen 'opened' the walls?"

"They had to. For the proper wiring, of course, they opened the partitions between the individual rooms inside, where there aren't any air spaces, as well as those in the walls around the place. Pete Stanley was interested enough to make a careful examination of everything. He can tell you, and will tell you if you ask him, there's not one damn thing hidden inside or between the walls."

"Yes, but—!"

"I was forgetting," interrupted Dave, almost in a dance of excitement. "There's confirmation close at hand. We don't need to guess at the weight of the gold, if there is any gold. We don't need to guess the size of the air spaces. It's all down in the commodore's log, the ledger he kept for years to jot down notes from time to time. I've talked about that log practically *ad nauseam*, and yet neither of you has seen it! Care to come along and see it now?"

"With pleasure," Townsend agreed, "though after so many years it probably won't . . ."

"You're right; it probably won't. But it may. This way; follow me!"

"That staircase out there," said Townsend, "is a sixteenth-century staircase. That's all it is, though that's enough for stimulus. So far, at least, I have seen nothing to provoke wonder or suspicion. Where are we going?"

Striding ahead, throwing remarks over his shoulder, Dave led them through the minor drawing-room into the great library, with its mullioned windows facing south and west, and its oak mausoleum of bookshelves.

"This library, Jeff, used to interest you of yore. You might see what you can unearth in more mature years. We turn to the right here. That door at the back . . ."

The door at the back opened into a lofty billiard-room, where two tables stood shrouded under rubber covers. There were racks for cues and balls on either side of western windows.

"One table for billiards," Dave explained, "and one for pool. Both come from the original Hall. The nearer one, on which we play pool," he tapped it in passing, "was meant for an English game called snooker. It's harder, trickier than our domestic pool, though any pool shark (Billy Vauban is one, and Ira Rutledge isn't half bad either) can be a whiz at snooker too."

"There are two rooms in a line beyond here, aren't there?" asked Jeff, beginning to place memories. "The first is the gunroom?"

"It used to be called a gunroom," replied Dave, leading them through it, "in Victorian days when country houses contained a small armory. The Delys heir of 1882 kept his own array of sporting

109

weapons when he sold the house. Those glass-fronted cabinets now contain a collection assembled but almost never touched both by my grandfather and my father. This room is smaller than the library or the billiard room, as you see, even if the ceiling's just as high. The study just beyond corresponds to it. I open the door of the study—so. And it's a dark day; we'd better have some light."

Dave touched a switch just inside the door on the left. Then he went on in, while the others watched from the doorway.

The soft light which bathed the study came neither from its western windows nor from the central chandelier. On a table in the middle stood a student's green-shaded lamp. Victorian sporting prints adorned the walls; there were armchairs of black padded leather bunched into leather knots, and what older generations called a smoker's stand, with ashtray above and cigar-boxes in the cabinet underneath. Catercornered on the room's northeastern angle, a rolltop desk loomed beneath its hanging lamp. Catercornered in the northwestern angle stood a smallish safe of very antiquated pattern, with a tarnished combination dial and above the door Fitzhugh Hobart's name, as well as the Roman numeral V, in gilt so faded as to have become almost invisible. The glow of a floor lamp shone on the safe's door.

Dave's two companions followed him as he approached the safe.

"Here we are, you see," he went on briskly. "It's never locked, as I told Jeff; there's nothing of value inside. The famous log, as you also see, is on the lower . . . it's on the lower—"

Seizing the tarnished handle, he had dragged open the door to reveal a compartment divided into upper and lower compartments by a metal shelf.

Jeff could see nothing inside except some papers in both compartments. But he had more than an intimation. After one glance inside, Dave dropped on his knees and began to scrabble among the papers. Then Dave sprang to his feet. Darting at the desk, he rolled up its top, finding nothing except a bare desk surface and almost bare pigeonholes.

Instantly Dave made for the center table. He picked up and threw aside the few magazines that lay there. Finally, after inspecting the table drawer, he faced them with consternation.

"Somebody, no doubt," Dave declared, "might think this was a good joke. I don't think it's a joke, rot my soul if I do! It's gone, you hear? The log is gone! It was here last night, because I almost went blind poring over it. But it's gone now. Whoever took it . . ."

Malcolm Townsend had drawn back. His open countenance, which might even have been called handsome in an irregular, non-classical way, wore an almost comical look of dawning alarm.

"*I* didn't take it!" he said. "Accept my assurance: *I* didn't take it! Why not look inside my brief-case?"

Unfastening the catch of the brief-case, he held it open so that they could see it contained only some measuring tapes, two very small, light hammers, and a screwdriver.

"Sensational fiction, Mr. Hobart—"

"Look, why don't you call me Dave? I won't call you Malcolm; you're almost old enough to be my father. But why not call me Dave?"

"Sensational fiction, Dave, suggests that any man carrying a brief-case is probably using it for some nefarious purpose. And I am a stranger, the only stranger. All I can tell you is that I'm not guilty. I didn't take it!"

"Oh, I know you didn't. Not that I think you would. But as a practical fact, sir, you've been with me every second of the time since you arrived. If you didn't take it, though, who else would? I wouldn't take it; Jeff wouldn't; Serena wouldn't. There's been nobody else here except . . ."

"If you want me to prove an alibi for the District Attorney," answered Jeff, as Dave's eye strayed towards him, "I can tell you my esteemed uncle was with me whenever he wasn't with you."

"Who'd have taken it, then? Who *could* have taken it, for Pete's sake?"

The glowing lamps here in the study seemed to accentuarte the dark weight of the sky outside.

"Since we seem to have eliminated everybody," Jeff said, "it follows as a logical proposition that the ledger can't be missing at all."

10

So, that night, Jeff borrowed the Stutz and drove to town. What happened during the interval, between the discovery of a loss before noon and his own departure at half-past seven, seemed singularly meaningless.

After their frantic search of the study, to make sure the missing ledger had not been mislaid, there had been a general inquisition of all available servants. Dave, carrying on like a tough private detective in a pulp-magazine story, thoroughly cowed everybody he failed to scare. All professed ignorance; they said they knew nothing.

"And I believe 'em," Dave summed up. "Actually, as far as progress is concerned, losing that log doesn't amount to much. I can tell you everything the commodore wrote: weights, dimensions, remarks, everything. I've read it so often I know the contents practically by heart. What gets me is the utter *senselessness* of stealing a relic like that!"

"How much gold," asked Jeff, "is believed to be hidden?"

"About five hundredweight."

"Five hundred pounds of gold? A quarter of a ton?"

"That's a rough estimate. Possibly a little more, possibly a little less."

Jeff tried without avail to reach Penny by telephone, being informed that Miss Penny had gone out for the day and wouldn't be back until evening. Though nobody showed much appetite for lunch, they had a sketchy buffet of sandwiches and coffee.

At four o'clock tea was served in the open on the flagged terrace behind the house, overlooking a garden combining formal English box-hedges with Louisiana's near-tropical luxuriance. Serena presided like a divinity at the polished urn.

"Cream and sugar, Jeff? Or would you rather have lemon?"

"Not lemon, thanks; that's a Russian habit I want no traffic with. A little milk or cream; no sugar."

"Then you don't approve," Serena asked, "of Russia's beautiful new communistic experiment or its various five-year plans?"

"I loathe their communistic experiment and everything it stands for. There's more than that: I don't like Russians. I can't like Russians since I tried to read their novels, which highbrows rave about but which to me seem mere humorless hogwash, as pretentious as clumsily inept."

Serena handed him the cup. Without a word she filled other cups and handed them round. Avoiding any mention of mystery, she steered the talk to current films, which Dave suggested might become talking films in a year or more.

Much earlier Townsend, on the plea that they could always run him back to his hotel in one of the cars, had been persuaded to send away a taxi-driver too long waiting, whom he dismissed with a generous tip.

Permitted to explore on his own, he spent some time measuring lower and upper hall. Jeff examined the library, finding little except a first edition of Gibbon's first two volumes, while Dave sat in the study and jotted down what he could remember from the missing log. Afternoon became evening and then night. Townsend accepted an invitation to dinner. But Jeff, growing more and more restless, could not sit still.

"If you don't mind," he said at length, "I think I'll have dinner in town. I don't meet Ira Rutledge until ten o'clock, as you already know. But I can eat at one of the choicer places and take my time. Will anybody be using the roadster tonight?"

It seemed nobody would. So he took the Stutz and set out.

He took his time about driving, too. There was one address he must at least look at before he need choose a restaurant. Approaching the city from the south, he drove up Canal Street and turned to the right into the thoroughfare along which he and Penny had walked the night before.

If he drove some way up Bourbon Street, and then turned to the right to go back along parallel Royal Street in the opposite direction, Royal Street's odd numbers would be on his right-hand side.

At your convenience, try 701b Royal Street. Fear nothing, but remember the address.

Murkily lighted, all but empty at well past eight on a Saturday night, the Bond Street of New Orleans seemed lifeless, even a little sinister.

But that was nonsense; it couldn't be! Then he saw the address he sought.

Number 701b was a shop-front, next door to another shop-front at the intersection of St. Peter Street, closed and dark. Briefly the car's headlights, no less than the stray gleam of a street-lamp, picked up the display of pipes, tobacco, and cigars behind window-glass across which ran gilded lettering, *Bohemian Cigar Divan, by* —by somebody whose name Jeff could not quite read as he cruised past. More distinct loomed the figure of the wooden Highlander, bigger than life in kilt with colorful tartan, towering up beside the door.

One or two old-fashioned tobacconists in England still chose a wooden Highlander for their sign, as some cigar stores in this country still used a wooden Indian. But even in England, today, they wouldn't call it a cigar *divan.* If some Briton had set up shop here in the French quarter, it must have been a long time ago.

Again headed for Canal Street, Jeff found himself troubled by a memory that just eluded him. That tobacconist's sign had been in some way familiar; it struck a chord; he ought to remember and didn't.

Other troubles attended this. Tonight he need only identify the place; he could visit there later. But why an invitation, even a challenge, to visit what must be the most harmless premises in harmless Royal Street? Harmless, eh? Every feature of this affair had a trick of seeming harmless or without meaning until suddenly it turned on you from ambush.

Realizing he was jumpy, telling himself it must stop, Jeff drove across Canal Street and parked the Stutz in University Place, where Penny had left her car the night before. Though he had meant to eat at a French restaurant in the Vieux Carré, he compromised for Kolb's because it was so very close here on the American side.

To make the time pass more quickly, he dawdled over broiled lobster with butter sauce, over coffee and the evening paper. He must restrain impatience. On the other hand, if Ira Rutledge really had some communication of importance . . .

But you can't make time pass more quickly. At half-past nine Jeff paid his bill, left the restaurant, and went for a walk. Crossing to the French side, he strolled up Bourbon Street with a vague half idea of looking in at Cinderella's Slipper. This latter notion he discarded. He walked as far as the Esplanade, encountering nobody except two panhandlers and a *nymphe du pavé*, and returned by way of Dauphine Street just north. A few minutes before ten found him entering the small lobby of the Garth Building on the west side of Canal Street.

Old Andy Stockton, who used to operate the Garth Building's one elevator, still presided there.

"No, Mr. Rutledge ain't here yet. Toldya to go up and set; door'd be unlocked? It's a good thing I knowya, Mr. Caldwell; knowed your dad and your granddad too. That's it; that's got it; go right on up and set!"

On the third floor, where Andy let him out, was the familiar door with its ground-glass panel lettered *Rutledge & Rutledge, Attorneys at Law*, the other Rutledge being Ira's son. The neat if somewhat dusty waiting-room, dark except for a pale radiance from Canal Street until Jeff found the light-button, contained four severe wooden armchairs, a stenographer's modern desk in greenish-colored steel, with telephone but no sign of the typewriter folded up inside, and a dictaphone stand nearby.

Ten o'clock rang from several steeples, but Ira Rutledge did not appear. In the adjoining law library Jeff found a glass ashtray, returned with it to the anteroom, and chain-smoked. Ten fifteen; still no Ira. At half-past ten the telephone rang. If overbusy Mr. Rutledge, damn him, had phoned to make more excuses . . . !

But it wasn't Ira; it was Penny Lynn.

"Jeff? I hoped you'd be there! They seemed to think—"

"Where are you, Penny?"

"At home; I've just got back."

"Yes, the maid said you wouldn't be home until evening. She didn't say it would be as late as this."

"I don't mean I'm home for the first time. I got back before dinner. When Hetty told me you'd called, I thought I'd better get along to the Hall. They were sitting down to dinner, and insisted I must have dinner too. After dinner . . ."

"How'd you get on with Townsend, the secret-passage fellow?"

"Pretty well, I think. He's not there now."

"Not there now?"

"After dinner, Jeff, who should turn up but Kate Keith? Kate seemed terribly taken with Mr. Townsend; she was all over him. She had her car there, and said she *must* show him some night life. If she did take him out, Dave said, she'd have to drop him at his hotel. It seems Isaac, their chauffeur, had asked for the evening off; Dave lets Isaac use the touring-car when Isaac's got a heavy date. Off went Kate with the old-houses expert; you might almost think she'd met him before. Then . . ."

Jeff could visualize Penny bending close to the phone.

"Serena and Dave!" she breathed. "There's something awfully peculiar—yes, and upsetting too. They weren't themselves, either of 'em, though it's hard to say how or why. Things were so odd I didn't stay as long as I might have stayed. Since they said you'd gone for an important conference with Mr. Rutledge . . ."

"I haven't had an important conference with Mr. Rutledge; I haven't even seen him. If the slippery old so-and-so keeps me waiting just five minutes longer . . . !" He broke off as a humming noise indoors rose above the rattle of traffic from the street. "There's the elevator now, Penny! See you tomorrow, I hope? This must be the wandering prodigal at last!"

And so it was. Stoop-shouldered, cadaverous, a derby hat on his head and a raincoat over his arm, Ira Rutledge opened the door of the waiting-room.

"Yes, my boy, you needn't remind me; it's unforgivable. These domestic matters, after all, can be worse than business. I can only apologize for the second time, and suggest we get down to it at once. We shall be more comfortable in the law library, I think. If you will precede me there . . . ?"

Every room in this suite overlooked Canal Street. To the right a windowless little corridor led first past the small office of Ira junior and then past the larger office of Ira senior. While Ira senior doddered into the corridor, Jeff carried his sustaining ashtray into the longish, narrow law library on the left.

In the library, its left-hand wall of sectional bookcases containing impressive calf-bound volumes behind glass, he pulled the chain of a green-shaded lamp on the boardroom table. Framed on the walls hung humorous legal drawings of unhumorous aspect. Jeff sat down and studied these until Ira, carrying a buff-colored cardboard folder, joined him and sat down at the head of the table.

The lawyer still seemed in no hurry. For some moments he tapped the folder, musing over it, after which he pushed aside the extension telephone on the table.

"Our meeting," he said at length, "concerns certain unusual aspects of the will left by the late Harald Hobart."

"Yes?"

"The provisions of this will are extremely simple. Everything of which my poor friend died possessed is divided equally between his issue, Dave and Serena. There are no other surviving relatives and no other bequests, the children being merely enjoined to 'take care of' certain specified servants. May I suggest," and Mr. Rutledge looked hard at him through the spectacles, "that you hear me out before offering objection or even comment?"

"Why should I object?"

"I anticipate no real objection. But I do seriously suggest it."

"If you'll tell me what this is all about . . . ?"

"To be sure; forgive me. What might be called the will's corollary provisions, though also simple as regards disposition of property, are so unusual as to require a word of explanation.

"Before the heart attack that carried him off, my friend Harald, who knew it might happen at any time, had reflected much on the past. You may perhaps have heard that many years ago Commodore Fitzhugh Hobart had two close friends: your grandfather, for whom you were named, and the (also late) Bernard Dinsmore, formerly of New Orleans. Commodore Hobart quarreled with Bernard Dinsmore, who went to New England and made a considerable fortune. You had heard of this?"

"Yes; Dave sketched it out some nights ago. Dave said his father always thought Bernard Dinsmore had been very badly treated. Correct?"

"That, my boy," said Mr. Rutledge, whirring in his throat, "so sums up the case that I need scarcely elaborate. Now hear the rest of the testator's provisions."

Cars hummed and hooted in the thoroughfare below, threaded through by a distant clangor of streetcar bells. After a brief glance inside the folder without opening it fully, Ira Rutledge rose and went to one of the windows, where he stood looking down. He did not turn when he spoke.

"If death should overtake either Dave or Serena, the survivor inherits everything. On the other hand, should neither Serena nor Dave be alive by Hallowe'en of this year . . ."

"Hallowe'en!" exploded Jeff. "Why *shouldn't* either of 'em be alive then? And what's Hallowe'en got to do with it?"

"Did I say Hallowe'en?" the lawyer murmured. "Dear me, dear me! That's bad; I must not grow fanciful. And yet the word, if legally ill-chosen, is not inexact."

Here he did turn from the window.

"Fitzhugh Hobart, as you may or may not be aware, was born on October 31, 1827. He would have lived for a century had he achieved October 31st of this year."

"I'd heard the commodore's dates. But I still ask . . . !"

"Here is your answer. Harald's son and his daughter, though to much less an extent, have both inherited the cardiac weakness that killed their father. So much must be news, I take it?"

"Not exactly news, no. Dave did tell me a very slight heart condition had kept him out of the Navy during the war. Serena . . ."

"Serena, you were saying?"

"She's always shown athletic tendencies. Yesterday evening Dave remarked that she used to be an expert gymnast until the doctor made her give it up. Then again . . ."

"Some other memory, Jeff?"

"I don't actually know. The first time I saw Serena this morning, she walked into the refectory dressed for tennis. Dave got up as though for some sort of protest, and burst out, 'Look, Serena, you're not—?' before he stopped. He might have meant anything. But it did cross my mind that it might have been, 'You're not going to play tennis, are you?' or something of the sort. Which she didn't."

"Come, this is capital!" said Mr. Rutledge, rubbing his hands. "I don't refer to a cardiac weakness, naturally. The reference was to your own mental processes. For one of your wildly imaginative profession, Jeff, you are not altogether unobservant."

"Thanks for that saving 'altogether.' Have you anything else to tell me?"

"Yes: the reason you are here."

Returning to the head of the table, Ira Rutledge sat down, opened the buff-colored folder, and considered some papers inside before closing it again.

"Harald Hobart," he presently continued, "did not expect some fatality to overtake his children; he merely sought to guard against contingencies. Now bear witness that poor Harald, erratic and unpredictable though we might call him, was most anxious to do what he believed to be the right thing! Should neither Dave nor Serena be alive on October 31st, 1927 . . ."

"Yes?"

"In that unlucky and unlikely event, Jeff, the entire estate is to be divided equally between yourself and Bernard Dinsmore's sole surviving descendant: his grandson, the Rev. Horace Dinsmore of Boston."

The cigarette Jeff had just lighted slipped through his fingers and fell on the table. He snatched it up before it could inflict too much of a burn, and crushed it out among other stubs in the ashtray.

"No, not on your life! You can't mean that!"

"But I do mean it. Why should I not mean it?"

"Because it's impossible! I don't need money; I don't want money; certainly not that money! This won't do!"

"I was right, was I not, to anticipate some slight objection? But yours, my boy, is not a real objection. Will you excuse me for just one moment?"

Revisiting his office on the plea that he had left something there, carrying the buff folder with him, Jeff's host was gone for so long a time that the visitor considered taking down one of the law-books from the shelves. But their formidable appearance defeated him. Ira returned to find him still in mental chaos.

"Mr. Rutledge," he said, "what do you know about Horace Dinsmore? Beyond the fact that he's a clergyman whom Dave describes as very pious and sour-faced . . ."

"Let's be accurate, shall we? His piety I have no reason to question. To call the gentleman sour-faced would be unjustified and might even be actionable; I have never seen him. Neither has Dave. No doubt it occurred to Dave, after the fashion of youth, that any Boston clergyman must answer some such description."

"But—"

"Again let's be accurate, if you don't mind. Though an ordained minister of the Congregational Church, Dr. Dinsmore has held no pastorate subsequent to his original one in upstate Massachusetts. He is now professor of religious instruction at Mansfield College, Boston. He went up the usual academic ladder, but they think so well of him that he went up swiftly; in 1919 he became a full professor. What's troubling you, Jeff?"

"Well! As regards Dave and Serena, is there some suggestion that I, *I* of all people, might want to hasten their departure?"

"Hasten their departure? My dear boy," cried the lawyer, clearly taken aback, "so grotesque a fantasy never entered my head! Why should it enter yours?"

"Because there's been so much loose talk about fatalities that weren't accidents."

"At least, Jeff, you have the good judgment to recognize it as loose talk. Suspect *you* of evil designs? Nonsense! Nor, since we are on the subject, must we look askance at a middle-aged parson of quiet tastes, especially one already so wealthy in his own right (I have investigated Dr. Dinsmore with care) that he would scarcely be tempted by a depleted estate like—"

It was Ira's turn to stop dead.

"Is it a depleted estate, Mr. Rutledge? Forgive me, but *is* it a depleted estate? Serena and Dave swear to the contrary; it seems to me they protest too much and too often. And Penny Lynn quotes her father about Harald Hobart's losses. If I'm not entitled to know . . ."

"No, you are not entitled to know. Not yet, at least. Under the circumstances, however, I feel justified in intimating that—"

Again the lawyer checked himself, but not this time because he had almost made a slip. He held up his hand for silence.

Traffic noises from the street had dwindled to a murmur. Somewhere inside the building footsteps could be heard ascending stairs and drawing nearer.

"Andy Stockton," Ira said, "will have gone off duty. Whoever that may be, at this hour of the night he's not likely to come here. And I sincerely hope not. The anteroom door is still unlocked!"

He said this as those same footsteps, approaching in haste, bore down on the offices of Rutledge & Rutledge. The door stood open between law-library and brightly lighted waitingroom. Into the latter room, with an air of storming it, burst a plump, round-bodied man of somewhere past fifty, whose businesslike shell-rimmed glasses made some contrast to his festive green-felt hat with Tyrolean feather.

Ira Rutledge went out to join him, closing the library door. But Jeff could hear clearly.

"Remember me, Counsellor?" demanded a voice of carrying tenor. This newcomer in his fifties sounded like a frustrated small boy. "My name is Merriman, Earl G. Merriman of St. Louis. You're a hard man to catch, seems to me. I phoned your home; they said you were at the office. And I could see lights up here, but the elevator's not running!"

Ira spoke with dignity.

"Since it's after eleven at night, my good sir, could you expect anything else? To what do I owe the honor of this unexpected visit?"

"These clients of yours: have they got an answer for me? I'm only here for a coupla days; got to get back home, y'know, and it'd be just jim-dandy if I could have an answer to take back to my wife. Well, what about it?"

"My clients have promised you their decision, Mr. Merriman, by a date to which you agreed. That date has not yet arrived. Meanwhile, since at the moment I am fully occupied with another client . . ."

"I want that place; my wife wants it; I've already offered more'n it's worth to me. There's a lot of dough tied up in this deal, Counsellor: you can't sweep it under the rug like dust. But I don't think you get me; I don't think we're talkin' about the same thing!"

"What we are discussing should be fairly evident. Your offer to buy Delys Hall . . ."

"Didn't I say we weren't talkin' about the same thing? My offer's there; my offer stands. But it's come to my ears, one way or another, that maybe somebody else wants to beat me to the deal. I hear it's some guy with a French name; however they pronounce it, they spell it V-a-u-b-a-n. But his first name's Bill, which I *can* pronounce. Well, Counsellor? *Has* this Bill Vobbin propositioned 'em, and *are* they givin' him the inside track?"

"Already, sir, I have provided you with such information as I have been instructed to give. I am not instructed to volunteer more. And now, if you will excuse me . . . ?"

But Earl G. Merriman wouldn't excuse him. For what seemed half an hour he raved, repeating in various ways that after all his trouble and fair dealing it would be the dirtiest, scummiest trick ever played on an honest businessman if some French son-of-a-bitch were allowed the advantage.

The senior Rutledge listened with exemplary patience, though sounds indicated he was gradually edging his visitor towards the outer door.

After a final, "*Good* night, sir," from Ira, hearing that door whish as it closed on its air-cushion, Jeff opened the library door in time to hear Mr. Merriman stamp towards the stairs at the back of the hall outside, still raving to such an extent that, as he descended, Jeff expected him to bid goodbye by kicking at the banisters in a tantrum.

Ira turned round.

"If in fact Mr. Vauban has made any such offer," he said, "I have not been informed of it. Probably it is only rumor and canard, because—well, never mind."

Still with great deliberation, he wandered round the anteroom, as though tidying up what did not need to be tidied, before switching off the lights and joining Jeff in the library, where only its green-shaded lamp burned on the table.

"Now what were we discussing? Ah, yes: the financial affairs of the Hobarts!"

The minutes ticked on; Ira sat down.

"As an interested party, my boy, at least you may be informed that neither Dave nor Serena will be reduced to poverty. Delys Hall is theirs to dispose of as they see fit. My recent colloquy with Mr. Merriman should provide sufficient evidence of that."

"Then I was entirely mistaken?"

"If not entirely mistaken, you jumped to too many conclusions. —It's a curious thing," the lawyer added musingly, "that your own uncle should recently have concerned himself with one aspect of Hobart finances. Being himself a lawyer, he asked no question either unethical or injudicious. He did not care, he said, what the family holdings might be at present. But in the past, even the long past, had they ever had a financial interest in state or local industry?"

"And had they? Could you answer?"

"Yes, without embarrassment. They held shares in your own family's Dixieland Tobacco: which, though operating from North Carolina, is controlled here. They owned almost a controlling interest in the Vulcan Ironworks at Shreveport, once the largest in the South after Tredegar at Richmond. Poor Harald himself tried for a controlling interest in Danforth & Co. of Baton Rouge, and at one time I believe he had it."

"This Danforth & Co.: what do *they* manufacture?"

Ira drew designs in the air.

"Fine woodwork of all kinds: panelling, elaborate bookcases, highly skilled reproductions of antique furniture. There are no imitation antiques at Delys Hall, I might say! Even Danforth & Co. could not have made that notable sixteenth-century harpsichord in the drawing-room. If I am not musical, I have a discriminating eye for antiques."

"What did Uncle Gil want? What was he really up to?"

"I can't say." Mr. Rutledge, who for some reason had hesitated as he mentioned the harpsichord in the drawing-room, now seemed to wake up. "But all this is hardly to our purpose, is it? These suspicions of yours, Jeff! Dave and Serena, I gather, let you believe they were as financially comfortable as they have always been heretofore. They did not tell you, perhaps, that you yourself would be co-heir should misfortune befall them?"

"No."

"By their air of strain and disquiet, when I met the three of you yesterday evening, I more than suspected they had not told you. I guessed, and somewhat injudiciously hinted as much."

"*They* knew, didn't they?"

"Yes, of course they knew! We can both understand their reluctance to speak out. But they likewise knew it would be my duty to inform you fully. They left the job to me; I have done so; and the hour grows late. When I think of those two: alone in that big house, lacking judgment, with even Harald gone and nobody to advise them but an old hulk like myself, I sometimes wonder . . ."

Against night stillness, shatteringly, the telephone in the outer room began to ring.

Ira Rutledge pointed to the telephone extension here on the table at his elbow, and took it up.

Jeff rose to his feet and moved closer. It would not be true to say that a premonition of dread struck him as soon as he heard the phone ring. But he felt something like it when Ira answered and the voice of Dave Hobart rose as clearly as though the phone had been at Jeff's own ear.

"*Ira?* I—I—"

"Yes, this is Ira Rutledge. What is it, Dave? Why are you calling at this time of night?"

"I called you," Dave cried, "after I'd called the family doctor. Not for the same reason, but I want to know what to *do!* The place is upside down; the police are here; there's hell to pay in *every* direction!"

"Dave, control yourself. I beg you for heaven's sake to control yourself! You must not upset your sister by wild behavior and talk still more wild. Serena! Think of Serena! Where *is* Serena?"

"Well, that's the main reason I called," replied Dave. Then, just before his voice soared and cracked, he added, "Serena's dead."

11

Under an overcast night sky, with wind a-rustle in foliage, Jeff left the Stutz in the garage behind Delys Hall and walked slowly round to the front. Several cars stood in the drive. Though most ground-floor rooms seemed to be illuminated, upstairs he could see lights only in the bedroom above the front door. And the front door was opened by Uncle Gil himself.

Alert, keen-eyed, carefully dressed even at this hour, Gilbert Bethune studied his nephew with some concern.

"How is it, Jeff? How do you feel?"

"A little numb and light-headed. Nothing seems to be quite real. Sorry; I can't help it."

"There's nothing to apologize for. You've had a shock; it's only natural. But if you've had a shock, you can imagine what it did to Dave. It's knocked him endways, poor devil; I can't say I blame him."

"What happened, Uncle Gil?"

"You don't know?"

"I know it's Serena, that's all. I was at Ira Rutledge's office when Dave phoned, as you must have heard. And I knew the time must be getting on, but I hadn't realized it was past midnight. Dave blurted out a few things, including the fact that the police were here. After saying Serena was dead, he seemed to collapse."

"He did collapse."

"Then who should come on the phone but Lieutenant Minnoch? The lieutenant asked Ira if I wasn't there, and then said *you* said to get on out here as soon as possible. What happened to Serena?"

Uncle Gil jerked his head ceilingward.

"She fell, jumped, or was thrown from a window of her bedroom up there. She fell on the flagstones out in front."

"Well, that's quite a drop. But—" Jeff recoiled from the picture in his mind. "Was she—badly smashed up?"

"She wasn't smashed up at all. Her heart gave out, Dr. Quayle says. When you've known a person almost all your life, as you've known Serena, it'll be hard to think of her as 'the body.' But the body's been removed; there are no grisly sights. Now tell me. Do you want to turn in and try to forget all this for the time being? Or would you rather hear what we've managed to learn so far?"

"Turn in? I couldn't sleep now if my life depended on it! I'd rather hear anything there is to hear."

"Then follow me."

Striding ahead at his long-legged pace, Uncle Gil led the way through lighted minor drawing-room, lighted library, dark billiard-room and dark gunroom to the lighted door of the study at the rear. In the study he stood with his back to the rolltop desk, now closed.

" 'Fell, jumped, or was thrown,' " Jeff quoted bitterly. "Are the superstition merchants at it again? If some power can throw one victim downstairs and break his neck, is it all over the house? Is somebody suggesting the same power can pick up another victim and pitch her out of an upstairs window?"

"No," retorted Uncle Gil, "and nobody's going to suggest it while *I'm* in charge. This was a human agent, but how did the agent work?

"Here are the facts. It seems there was quite a gathering here earlier in the evening. We can clear that up when we question everybody tomorrow; I mean today. The last visitor to leave was Penny Lynn, who said good night not long before ten-thirty."

"I know; she phoned me from home."

"Very well!" Uncle Gil squared his shoulders. "It also seems Serena had been out very late the night before. It wasn't eleven o'clock when she said they'd better call it a day. Dave agreed; evidently *he* hadn't got much sleep Friday night. They went their separate ways, Serena to her room at the front and Dave to his own room at the back, the same room he's occupied since he was a boy.

127

"The whole business might not have been discovered until much later, possibly not until this morning, if it hadn't been for one of the servants. The chauffeur is a young fellow called Isaac, new since your time. They're a good deal more lenient with the help than a lot of people would be. This chauffeur . . ."

"Penny mentioned that too," Jeff interrupted. "The chauffeur had asked to go out; Dave gave him permission to take the touring-car. Yes?"

"Isaac was supposed to be back by eleven o'clock or catch it from Cato, who's quite a disciplinarian. He wasn't back by eleven; he did make it at eleven-twenty. There was a light in Serena's room, which wouldn't have roused curiosity. But the headlamps of the car picked up someone lying on the terrace.

"He found Serena there, so recently dead she was still warm, a little to the right of the extreme right-hand window in the window-panel above; it would have been the extreme left-hand window to anybody looking out of the room. Serena wore pajamas with something over them; there's argument about what she wore over the pajamas.

"Isaac put the car away; Cato met him at the back door; together they carried Serena into the house and upstairs. They shouldn't have moved her, of course; but we've got to make allowances for their state of mind.

"The door of Serena's room was bolted on the inside. For that moment they put her in another bedroom, while Cato woke up Dave. Then the uproar started. Following me so far?"

"Closely."

Gilbert Bethune took a cigar out of his upper left-hand vest pocket, but did not light it.

"Dave phoned Dr. Quayle," he went on. "Kenneth Quayle and I are both old friends of the family. Before the doctor paid his visit he phoned me, saying he wouldn't be able to issue a death certificate under the circumstances. I got in touch with City Hall and managed to catch Harry Minnoch. With others following, we chased out here as fast as a police car could bring us.

"By that time the whole place was in an uproar. They'd pried open the door of Serena's room so they could take her there. We questioned the servants and sent 'em to bed. When I'd got some sort of coherent statement from Dave—it was in the library out there—he ran to the telephone and rang Ira Rutledge. Then he almost literally keeled over; he'd have dropped the phone if Minnoch hadn't caught it. Dr. Quayle put him to bed and injected a sedative; Dave needed one. I like that young fellow; I've always liked him, though he doesn't seem to trust me much in return.

"And now, if you can face the contradictory evidence in Serena's room," said Uncle Gil, making for the door of the study, "come with me again. Keep your eye on Harry Minnoch. Harry's a pretty good cop, an honest cop. But I once told him he lacked subtlety, and he can't forget it; he's determined to be subtle if it chokes him. How *do* you feel, Jeff?"

"Like a completely useless intruder. I can't do any good here; whatever happened, it's as though I hastened the whole trouble by accepting Dave's invitation."

"You *can* do some good here, you know. Before that sedative took over, the last thing Dave said was, 'Jeff 'll rally round, won't he? He won't desert the ship even before it begins to sink?' "

"I'll stand by, of course, if that's what anybody wants. But—"

Once more Jeff followed Uncle Gil. In the lower hall, under a soft glow of electric candles, they met a silver-haired, worried-looking gentleman descending the staircase with his black bag in his hand.

"I have just told your lieutenant," Dr. Quayle informed the District Attorney, "that I can't testify as to what poor Serena may have been wearing over her pajamas, or what kind of slippers may have been on her feet. I was concerned with the victim, not her costume. When I saw her on the bed up there, to the best of my recollection she wore only pajamas; no footgear of any kind. Since they've taken her away now, and I can be of no more service . . ."

"Cause of death, Kenneth?"

"In non-technical language, Gil, her heart gave out. That's why there were no external injuries. Good night."

Lights had been switched on in the upper hall; more lights shone through the open door of Serena's bedroom at the front. Jeff hesitated before entering in his uncle's wake.

The door had been burst open, by all evidence with a chisel, splintering out the closed bolt in its socket so that both hung drunkenly down. There was a dusting of gray powder over the bolt and on both knobs of the door.

As with those downstairs in front, each room up here had a panel of diamond-paned casement windows divided into four lights by stone mullions: every light immovable above, but hinged below and opening out like a door. Three window-lights remained closed; that on the extreme left stood wide open, making a not inconsiderable gap. Gray powder had been dusted over window-fastenings and glass.

Despite sombre oak panelling, despite canopied bed and seventeenth-century dressing-table, Serena had tried to lighten it with a couple of overstuffed chairs, a floor lamp or two, a table bearing magazines as well as a generous-sized ashtray, and some smallish copies of paintings by Renoir and Monet.

Jeff glanced towards the bed, its silk coverlet undisturbed except for the indentation where a body had rested. In one corner of the room, as though brooding, stood elderly Sergeant Bull. Towards the newcomers, nodding recognition to Jeff, strode heavily moustached Lieutenant Minnoch.

"Mr. Bethune, sir!" he began with some formality. "This business o' subtlety, now . . ."

"No misunderstandings, if you don't mind!" said Uncle Gil. "It's your case, Harry; handle it as you see fit. I'm *amicus curiae,* and at the moment that's all I am. How do you read the situation?"

Lieutenant Minnoch, who did not wear his hat in the house, passed a hand over his bald head.

"Well, sir, we've both heard the testimony. First off, just for a starter, I'll tell you what didn't happen. However the young lady fell out that window, it wasn't suicide and it wasn't accident either."

"That seems fairly evident. Still, what are your reasons for saying so?"

"She came in here 'bout ten to eleven. She bolted the door. Her fingerprints are all over the bolt and on both knobs; Officer Richards dusted every surface that would take prints. She got undressed;

130

she put on pajamas and whatever else she did put on. But she wasn't interested in the window. Of her own free will, leastways, I doubt if she went near the window."

"How do you make that out?"

"Because she didn't touch the window! Not the one that's open, not the other three or any part of 'em!"

Lieutenant Minnoch went to the windows and peered closely before turning back.

"It's so high up here," he added, "that with these fancy windows they need curtains even less'n they need curtains downstairs. No curtains anywhere in front. And not a fingerprint o' Miss Hobart's anywhere here, though her prints are all over the rest of the room. And don't ask me who opened the window, sir; you heard it same as I did."

"Oh, of course!" said Uncle Gil. "That maid?"

"Got it, Mr. Bethune. The maid (I think her name's Josie) that was routed out with the rest and seems to be sweet on the chauffeur. Josie looked after the young lady. Every night she opens the window, always that same window, and did it last night. It's too early for many skeeters just yet, so she don't need to bother about screens or about a mosquito-net for the bed.

"I didn't want to scare the maid worse'n she was already scared, but Richards got her prints to play it safe. Her prints are on the window, on the catch and the frame too, a little bit blurred. 'Pears to me, sir, like there's only one thing that could 'a' happened."

"Yes?"

"The young lady, as I said, came in here 'bout ten minutes to eleven. She bolted the door—"

"Why did she bolt the door? They never lock or bolt doors at Delys Hall; they have no reason to."

"They had good reason this time, sir, if only they'd known it. Maybe Serena Hobart did know, and thought somebody was after her."

Uncle Gil drew himself up.

"As you so carefully pointed out, Harry, I heard the testimony too. At no time did Serena seem apprehensive: only determined, if a little absent-minded or remote. Her own brother said so, and the others agreed."

"If I were you, sir," the lieutenant said indulgently, "I wouldn't be too much impressed by anything young Mr. Hobart told us. He's a flighty sort o' gentleman, seems to me. And the nigras were all mixed up: not only that maid, but the chauffeur and the old butler too."

Uncle Gil, who had replaced the cigar in his vest pocket, stood pulling at his underlip with hideous indecision.

"I take it, Harry, you don't doubt this was murder?"

"Not a doubt at all, Mr. Bethune. Have *you* any doubt it was murder?"

"No, not really. But what happened here, exactly?"

"I was comin' to that, sir. The murderer got here tonight to do exactly what he did do. *He* wouldn't leave fingerprints; they all wear gloves nowadays. He just grabbed her and slung her out the window. Probably he knew about her bad heart, and knew she'd be dead before she hit the ground. Or maybe—"

"If Serena had bolted the door so that she couldn't be taken by surprise, how did the murderer get in?"

"Well, sir, that window's wide open."

"Quite right; the window is wide open. But that makes it all the worse."

Gilbert Bethune strode to the window and put his head out, peering first left and then right along the façade.

"I've already looked out here," he announced. "If you care to glance out for yourself, you can confirm what I say."

Jeff, following him, also looked and could confirm it.

"A very narrow stone ledge," Uncle Gil continued, "runs along the front about three feet below floor level of this room. A professional steeplejack *might* navigate that ledge by pressing flat against the wall and edging along. But there seems no way even a steeplejack could reach the ledge from below. Look out there!"

"I'm looking, sir," Lieutenant Minnoch assured him.

They had all concentrated on it.

"The walls are smooth brick smooth-joined," said the District Attorney, "with no crevice in the mortar for a fingerhold. There are no drainpipes to climb by. They've kept the walls free of ivy or other vines, as they've kept the oaks free of Spanish moss. Barring a professional job with ropes and hooks and tackle (and assistance), done by some expert team in broad daylight, it's a physical impossibility."

Uncle Gil drew in his head and faced the other two.

"No, Harry, that won't do. And what else do you postulate?"

"Well, sir . . ."

"Fearing attack, Serena Hobart has bolted the door. But she does not hesitate to undress and don pajamas. The behavior of your hypothetical attacker seems still more curious. In some fashion ascending the wall like Dracula, he carries out his purpose: in your own words, he grabs her and slings her out the window. All this, mark it, with no outcry or even protest from the victim! If those in the house tonight disagree on other matters, all agree there was no outcry. We observe for ourselves there is absolutely no sign of any struggle."

"But—"

"When they burst in here afterwards, witnesses also agree they found nobody hiding. What has our murderer done? Either he has descended Dracula-fashion, or else he has made himself invisible. How?"

Lieutenant Minnoch's face shone with a kind of radiance.

"God bless you, sir," he cried, "you can get as many notions as young Mr. Hobart himself! I'm the first to admit your ideas sometimes pay off, as in that Irishtown poisoning business where we caught the fake nurse who did it. But can *I* make a suggestion?"

"We are waiting for one."

"It's not dead certain she was afraid of the fellow who killed her. Maybe that's the answer to the whole business. I wouldn't want to say one word against the young lady's character, now. All the same, any cop knows these quiet ones can carry on and do things they oughtn't to do.

"Say she let the murderer in by the door, then bolted it so nobody else could intrude. She hadn't any suspicion he'd come to kill her. That's how he could get close enough to do what he wanted to do. Before she realized what was up, he just grabbed her and did it."

"How did *he* get down from the window, then?" demanded Uncle Gil. "Adopting your own conversational style, my friend, I might remark that, while tortures would not tear from me a whisper about your intellect, you can sometimes talk like a jackass."

"Easy, Mr. Bethune! E-easy, now! Don't *you* go flyin' off the handle, you of all people, or you'll wind up by proving this didn't happen and the victim's not dead!"

"Whatever I wind up by proving, we might at least make some small effort towards proving it. Fair enough?"

"If you say so, sir."

"I do say so. And I have already stated certain points on which the witnesses agree. It is further agreed . . ."

Musing, Gilbert Bethune sauntered to a dressing-table whose seventeenth-century Venetian mirror remained untarnished by time. Over the back of the straight chair facing it hung a light-blue dress with a white collar. More feminine apparel lay on the seat of the chair, together with folded flesh-colored stockings, and beside it on the floor stood beige alligator-skin shoes.

"That's the dress she wore at dinner," said the District Attorney, "as well as the stockings and shoes. I knew Serena Hobart as a girl of extreme neatness. But she does not seem to have put anything away, which is suggestive in itself."

"Suggestive of what?" asked Jeff.

"Well, let's see. When Cato and Isaac carried her upstairs, she had been lying on her back on the terrace. She was wearing something over her pajamas, and some kind of slippers. First they put her in another bedroom, because the door of this one had been bolted. When the door had been forced and the same two carried her in, as they put her down on the bed there Dave Hobart in a kind of daze removed the wrap and hung it up in the cupboard. He also removed the slippers."

"But that's where it gets mixed up!" Harry Minnoch said stubbornly. "Don't make much difference, I suppose, but . . . !"

"Dave says she was wearing a dressing-gown; the chauffeur agrees. Cato, on the other hand, thinks it was what women call a house-coat. Let's see whether we can determine which."

A very deep cupboard had been built out against the side of the bathroom in the southwestern wall. When Gilbert Bethune opened the cupboard door, several lights illumined its interior with fair clearness.

Both to left and right a long row of hangers held the great array of dresses, gowns, coats, and other outfits. A bank of closed drawers rose on the right. On the floor at the left shoes and slippers of every kind or description stretched in a line towards shelves at the rear.

From the first coat-hanger visible on the left depended a dressing-gown of dark-blue quilted silk. The first on the right held a black silk house-coat with faint gold embroidery down the front.

Lifting out the left-hand hanger, Uncle Gil held it up so that they could get a better view of the dressing-gown. Down the right sleeve from the shoulder ran a long smudge of dust or dirt. He reversed the garment and showed its back very broadly smudged in the same way.

"We are safe in deciding," said Uncle Gil, "that the girl did not fall head-first. She landed feet downwards, toppled on her right side, and rolled on her back."

"That 'un's the one, eh?" asked Lieutenant Minnoch.

"Not necessarily." Uncle Gil lifted down the house-coat, displaying a right sleeve and back also smudged; then he replaced both. "It might have been either the dressing-gown or the house-coat. Or else—well, never mind. As for the slippers, we have another if slighter difference of opinion."

Running the sole of his own shoe over the cupboard's rather dusty floor, he pointed to the parade of footgear.

"Dave and the chauffeur say the slippers were mules; Cato thinks they were a pair of moccasins, Indian or imitation Indian. Behold both in evidence here."

"Then there's no tellin', is there? And not much more we can do tonight, sir, if you ask me."

"The cupboard, if not entirely revealing, provides one or two suggestive points. You think we should adjourn? Very well, Harry; you adjourn. Before you go, however . . ."

Followed by Sergeant Bull, who had not said one word, Lieutenant Minnoch moved out past the partly shattered door into the upper hall. Overtaking him, Gilbert Bethune gave some instructions in a low voice.

"You'll do that, will you?"

"It can be done O.K., sir, if you think it's necessary."

"Oh, it's necessary; it may be vitally important. Coming, Jeff?"

Only too glad to get out of that room, Jeff went out and joined them. Together they marched along the hall and descended the main staircase.

"Before I myself leave," Uncle Gil observed on the way down, "I have one other small inquiry to make. You'll excuse me, Harry, if some of my remarks may have seemed rather cryptic?"

"Excuse *me*, Mr. Bethune," said the now-simmering lieutenant, "but they're just a little bit *too* cryptic! You keep talking about suggestive points, one after the other, and yet you won't come out with any of 'em!"

Uncle Gil had halted on the stairs, surveying the hall below.

"For one brief moment, please, forget what happened to Serena. Before I came here tonight, before I knew anything had happened, I thought I could see the clue to one minor mystery. Two generations of Hobarts, beginning with Harald, have been in search of the old commodore's hidden gold. Where must we look for it?"

"Well, where *must* we look for it?"

"I will give you a very broad hint. In what local or state industries have the Hobarts been financially interested for so long a time?"

He paused, studying each of his companions in turn.

"Now forget the gold. We return, as inevitably we must, to the wicked business upstairs. There was something in that cupboard I overlooked, but I can always refresh my memory. I would not have you think I myself am making mysteries or venturing on any flippancy at such a time. Nevertheless, at risk of being assaulted by the police themselves, I will conclude with still another question. In what way does Serena Hobart's death so much resemble the death of Thaddeus Peters seventeen years ago?"

12

Many hours later, on that dismal Sunday of rain gusts spattering and dying away, Jeff found himself again enmeshed in a net that seemed never to open for escape.

When neither Lieutenant Minnoch nor anybody else had been able to answer the question Uncle Gil flung out on the stairs, the lieutenant had gone into a whispered conference with Sergeant Bull and with a plain-clothes officer summoned from one of the police cars outside.

Beckoning to Jeff, Gilbert Bethune had led his nephew first into the library, then on through into the study. He waved Jeff to one of the padded chairs and sat down in another, where he clipped and lighted the cigar he had hitherto failed to smoke.

"And now, with your permission . . ."

"Uncle Gil," Jeff had insisted, "it's no use asking me in what way Serena's death resembles the death of the late Thad Peters. Except that both died of a fall, there's not one point of similarity between them. It happened in different places and under different circumstances. Finally—"

"After reflection, however, more than one similarity may present itself. But I am not now concerned with theories; my concern is only with information."

"What sort of information?"

"I rely," said the District Attorney, "on your phenomenal memory. For past events you have been blessed with what some might describe as total recall."

"Yes?"

137

"You journeyed downriver, I understand, with Serena, with Dave, with Penny Lynn, with Mrs. Kate Keith, and with a harmless if inquisitive journalistic character named Saylor. Be good enough to tell me everything you saw or heard between Monday morning and Saturday night."

"Everything?"

"Everything, at least, relating to any of those five persons. Perhaps relating to others as well; that will emerge in due course. If you are not too tired . . ."

Jeff did his best, even at that drugged hour of the morning. He touched only lightly on any private interview between Penny and himself, without mentioning the embarrassments of either. Otherwise he described and quoted at such length that he feared he might be talking too much. But Gilbert Bethune, far from seeming bored, more than once uttered an exclamation of satisfaction.

"You see, Uncle Gil, so very little actually occurred . . . !"

"And yet more may have occurred than on the surface seems evident. The preoccupation of Captain Joshua Galway merits close scrutiny. So does—but no matter. Go on!"

Jeff complied. It was a very long story; Uncle Gil had smoked a fair number of cigars, Jeff more than half a pack of cigarettes, and the hands of the clock crawled towards four A.M. before the narrator sat back.

"The shock of Serena's death," he summed up, "followed almost immediately after another shock that, in its different way, was almost as bad. I mean Ira Rutledge's news: if both remaining Hobarts should die before October 31st, their estate's supposed to be shared between myself and a New England parson who's already got more money than he needs. Damn it all . . . !"

"May I remind you," Uncle Gil spoke from a cloud of cigar-smoke, "that there is only one remaining Hobart? We must take good care no harm comes to Dave, and I have given orders to that effect. A plain-clothes policeman has been stationed outside Dave's door, with instructions not to be obtrusive or draw attention to himself. You should then be saved the awkwardness of an inheritance you don't want."

Crushing out the cigar in an ashtray, he rose to his feet.

"I have no idea," he added, "who wanted to harm Serena and may want to harm Dave. I agree with Ira that it's unlikely to be either you or the esteemed cleric from Boston. But I now have some of the facts and can draw certain inferences."

"Well, what next?"

Gilbert Bethune's eye strayed towards the safe in the room's northwestern corner.

"After your discovery that Commodore Hobart's log had been removed from there, I think you said, Dave himself made some notes of what he could remember from the log. Where are the notes now?"

"In that desk in the opposite corner, if they're still there."

Uncle Gil went to the desk and rolled up its top.

"The notes are here," he reported, lifting two small sheets of notepaper in Dave's impatient handwriting. "Though I hardly think I shall need these, I had better take them. The police will have gone long ago, except Officer O'Bannion; but if they followed instructions they left a car for me. Now try to get some sleep, Jeff. Tomorrow, not too early, I mean to rout you out and hale you away to town like Jack Ketch. Meanwhile, thanks; you've been very helpful. *A bientôt.*"

Thus it happened that, after troubled slumber—sometimes deep, sometimes with shocks or starts of wakefulness—Jeff rose and dressed to intermittent rain-noises at just past noon on Sunday.

Cato found him wandering aimlessly downstairs and insisted on serving him scrambled eggs in the refectory. Despite lack of appetite, he ate what he could. Cato, vanishing, reappeared after Jeff's second cup of coffee.

"Mist' Dave been wantin' to see you, Mist' Jeff. Say he *mus'* see you, no mattuh whut! You go on up and see him, Mist' Jeff?"

"Yes, of course I will! How is he this morning, Cato?"

"Still mighty po'ly, you ast me. Tuck up *bis* breakfus'; he ate less'n you did. Doctuh been and gone. P'leece offisuh gone too. Mist' Dave won' *say* how he feel; think Cato don' know?"

Momentarily the rain had passed over. Glancing out through one of the open windows, Jeff could see his uncle's Buick approach and draw up. Gilbert Bethune himself, in raincoat and soft hat, carrying a brief-case, unfolded his length out of the car. Jeff went to the window, tipping a hand to his forehead as Uncle Gil raised the brief-case in greeting.

"Cato, please tell my uncle I've gone up to look in on the patient. I shall be down again in a moment."

While Cato went to answer the front door, Jeff hastened upstairs. At the rear of the upper hall a transverse passage, like the transverse passage in front, stretched the house's full breadth. At the end of this passage, westwards and on the right, was the closed door of Dave's bedroom. At the left a back stairway led down to a similar passage and a side door on the floor below.

Replying to Jeff's knock, a somewhat fuzzy voice bade him enter.

The windows back here, smaller and less elaborate than those in front, all had curtains. Though these curtains were open, they admitted only the light of a murky day on comfortable furniture, pictures of sailing ships, a well-stocked, untidy bookcase, and the silver cup won by Dave for debating at preparatory school.

Pajama-clad Dave, propped up in another canopied bed with a breakfast tray hardly touched but a well-filled ashtray on the bedside table at his elbow, waved away all inquiries.

"Still full of that damn dope," he said. "I'm absolutely all right, old son, except when I get to thinking about what happened. Look, Jeff. Sorry about last night; sorry I acted like an old woman!"

"Easy, Dave. You didn't act like an old woman."

"And I can't see why they're so concerned about me. It's *Serena* they ought to be thinking about, not me!"

"Easy, I said!"

"You won't run out on me, will you? You *will* stay on for a few days?"

"Here I am, Dave."

"Speaking of staying in town," Dave continued, evidently not conscious of the illogic, "do you know they even had a cop on duty outside all night?"

"Yes."

"He looked in here before he went off duty. I asked him to do something for me, and I hope he has. Another thing, Jeff." Groping for his cigarettes, Dave found one and lighted it. "I can guess most of what Ira Rutledge must have told you. After Serena and me, anything left of the estate goes to you and old What's-his-name. We didn't tell you; we couldn't bring ourselves to tell you!"

"That's understandable, Dave."

"It's not all Serena didn't tell you, either. She kept making out she was so all-fired anxious to get rid of this house and get out; I backed her up. But that's not true; it never was true. She's as fond of the old place as I am, or more so. You sort of suspected that, didn't you?"

"Whether or not I suspected, Penny Lynn was sure of it."

"*Penny?* You didn't tell her . . . ?"

"At that time, early in the week, I didn't know anything to tell her. When I remarked that you were probably selling Delys Hall to one Earl George Merriman, Penny said, 'Serena won't like that; she won't like it at all.'"

"Last night, before all the hobgoblins descended, Penny was here. So was Kate Keith, who charged in and grabbed Malcolm Townsend. Which reminds me, Jeff. This fellow Townsend is all right; I like him. But should you say he's a man the women would go for in a big way?"

"No, not particularly. Why?"

"Because you'd be wrong. It's the same damn thing with any women you talk to! A woman will say some man is attractive, prefacing it," Dave mimicked, "with 'awfully' or 'terribly,' and challenge you to name somebody you think they'd go for. Then, when you do name somebody, she looks at you as though she'd been asked to find great sex appeal in the hunchback of Notre Dame. Kate Keith . . ."

Whereupon Dave again went off at a tangent.

"I myself, *moi qui vous parle,* wasn't entirely frank when I spoke to the cops or your uncle. Maybe I ought to correct that, but—"

"You might try to be frank with Uncle Gil, at least. He wants to help; he's on your side all the way. And he's just arrived to take me on some sort of errand in town, so I've got to go. Why weren't you frank with him?"

"All of a sudden, out of nowhere, I got a suspicion of something I've lived with as long as I can remember. It scared me; it scared the pants off me. So I didn't mention it, though *you* ought to guess what it is. And I'll take your advice. If you say it's safe to trust Uncle Gil, I'll trust him. Feel free to tell him anything I've said. I'm getting up soon; I'll tell him the rest later. Meanwhile, there's a copy of Palgrave on that chair by the floor lamp; throw it over here and go your ways."

Jeff closed the door behind him. In the lower hall Cato bowed and nodded towards the library.

On the long table in the middle of the library, under stained-glass windows and tiers of ancient books, burned a lamp with a yellow silk shade. Gilbert Bethune, Mephistophelian eyebrows raised, stood on the far side of the table's length, opening his brief-case. He pulled up a carved Jacobean chair and motioned Jeff to a similar chair opposite.

"I myself," Uncle Gil began, "have been up since eight this morning. It may be reported with some smugness that I have made and received several phone calls. Harry Minnoch has been gathering information with equal industry. He has also been fending off reporters, as Cato has been doing when they phone here. Our good lieutenant, furthermore, now broods over some weight on his mind (subtlety, perhaps?) about which he can't yet be persuaded to speak. Before we set out for town . . ."

"Yes, Uncle Gil?"

"You may recall that yesterday I mentioned a mystery of our own, at present unquestionably allied to the mystery of what happened in that bedroom last night. I said I wanted to show you the original of a certain letter. Before we set out for town, you might care to look at it. It was sent from New Orleans late in March, addressed to me at City Hall, and marked 'personal.' Though unsigned except for the two words at the end, and informative in only one respect . . ."

"You mean the business Lieutenant Minnoch was talking about on the steamboat? You let yourselves get stirred up by an anonymous letter?"

"The letter itself provides partial answers. Here it is."

From the brief-case Uncle Gil took a folded sheet of paper and handed it across. Unfolding the paper, seeing typewritten lines already much studied, Jeff spread it out under the lamp and sat down.

Dear sir:

This communication draws your attention to the murder of Thaddeus G. Peters at Delys Hall on the night of November 6th, 1910. Before you fling my letter into the wastepaper basket, impatiently exclaiming that you will pay no heed to anonymous correspondents and that anyway the victim's death was an accident, have the simple justice to read further.

Momentarily Jeff's eye stopped. Reaching into his inside breast pocket, he found and unfolded the much smaller typewritten sheet pushed under the door of his stateroom during the journey downriver.

"It's not the same typing!" he announced. "The one addressed to me has smaller letters, and was probably done on a portable."

"Ah, the mysterious note directing your attention to number 701b Royal Street? From your description it seemed unlikely they would be the work of the same hand, or at least of the same typewriter. The letter to me was typed on a standard Remington by one who left no fingerprints. But you neglect your duty; continue reading!"

Jeff did so.

The number of those who meet serious injury through falling downstairs, even an ancient staircase, is very small. That the victim should *break bis neck* in this way is an occurrence so rare as to be almost unheard of. Confirmation of my claim will be found in statistics provided by any insurance company.

Again Jeff's eye paused; he read the last sentence aloud. Despite that warm day, the atmosphere of the library seemed suddenly chilly.

"But he did get his neck broken, didn't he? Is there any doubt of that?"

"No, there is no doubt of that," said Uncle Gil. "On the other hand, it leaves us with a fairly miraculous accident.

143

Anonymous or not, crank or not, my correspondent is right. Those *are* the insurance figures."

"But a freak accident—!"

"After that sentence about the insurance company, Jeff, there is only one more paragraph. What does it say?"

Should any guest in your own house arise at dead of night to explore downstairs, it must surely provoke your own curiosity? This guest, apparently, then found it necessary to march upstairs with a silver pitcher on its tray. Why was Mr. Peters there? What could he have been doing? When you have examined all the circumstances, sir, I suggest you will adopt the view taken by

Yours sincerely,
Amor Justitiae

Jeff folded the letter and handed it back.

"You take *Love of Justice* seriously, do you?"

"Seriously enough, at least, to examine what he says. Your 'freak accident,' supposing it to have been that, befell a famous athlete in first-class physical condition, who for no apparent reason seemed to behave like a lunatic."

"According to Dave, those details about Peters carrying silverware, which he dropped, didn't come out at the inquest or get into the press. Who could have learned all that?"

"Anybody, at any age, with ears to hear. In 1910 I myself was only a young lawyer struggling to build up my practice. But I have not forgotten: the whole town buzzed with rumors, true as well as false."

"Anything worth remembering?"

Turning away towards the bookshelves, Gilbert Bethune clipped and lighted a cigar. Again more Mephistophelian than avuncular, eyes sardonic, he turned back to the table.

"Whenever I meet you, Jeff, I seem to smoke far more than is good for me. But then so do you, and neither of us has the least intention of giving it up."

His tone grew businesslike.

"In 1910, technically," he explained, "Thad Peters was managing director of Danforth & Co., Fine Woodwork. In actual fact he had far more power than that. His elder sister had married Raoul Vauban. With the backing of a rich and powerful clan, Thad was trying to get full control of Danforth's. So was Harald Hobart, who eventually got it. For a time there was rivalry between them.

"It seemed the friendliest kind of rivalry. Harald professed great liking for Thad, and always maintained there was somebody in the background, somebody whose identity he couldn't guess, trying to make trouble for them both. Were you well acquainted with Harald Hobart?"

"I'd met him, of course. That's about all."

Uncle Gil pondered.

"Strange, anomalous character: combining the close-mouthed with the overtalkative, good-natured but unpredictable! It's not well known that on occasion Harald drank heavily. He never went on a spree or misbehaved in public. But he might confide to some total stranger in a bar what he'd never have told a close friend, and next morning forget he'd said anything at all.

"One close friend was Dr. Ramsay, a brilliant surgeon who lived and still lives at Bethesda, Maryland. I don't think he did much drinking at Ramsay's, the doctor being one of those strong-minded Scots who object to booze. Serena, Harald's favorite of his children, struck up quite a friendship with Laurel Ramsay, the doctor's daughter, and has visited there too."

"These later remarks, of course, must refer to some time after the year 1910?"

"They do, Jeff, they do; I was anticipating. However, as regards the charge made by *Amor Justitiae* in this letter," and Uncle Gil returned it to the brief-case, "I can tell you what we've done."

"According to Lieutenant Minnoch," said Jeff, reflecting hard, "he interviewed a retired detective named Trowbridge, who had been the lieutenant in charge of the Peters affair. Minnoch didn't elaborate."

Gilbert Bethune blew a smoke ring and watched it dissolve.

"There's very little for me to elaborate," he answered. "Zack Trowbridge, getting on in years but still alert, couldn't give much help. He could add only one additional and random bit of testimony, which may or may not be significant."

"Oh?"

"Seventeen years ago it seemed generally agreed that Thad Peters hadn't cried out when he fell; there had been only the mighty crash of silver. All agreed to it, that is, except one maidservant, since dead and unavailable, who had been sleeping at the top of the house. The maid thought she *had* heard a faint cry of some kind. But she *thought*, she wasn't certain, she'd heard it a little time before the crash of silver, and thought it came from outside the house."

"That doesn't seem to—"

"Perhaps not; interpret it as you like," said Uncle Gil. "And yet it brings us round in a circle, don't you see, to poor Serena, dead last night under circumstances equally grim and senseless? Whether we like it or not, present facts must be faced too. We had better be on our way to question some witnesses."

"Speaking of witnesses, Uncle Gil, who else among those concerned in this business has heard of Serena's death?"

"Everybody must have heard it; it was in the Sunday papers this morning. When the reporters were chased away from here, they had to be content with a police handout in town."

"Thanks for the warning. I had meant to phone Penny Lynn, but I won't do it just yet. Penny will be so shocked and upset that . . . that . . ."

"Yes, better wait." Then the District Attorney meditated on his own concerns. "Last night, as already remarked, I neglected to look for something in Serena's room which clearly must be there. The oversight has been corrected today, with satisfactory results, and an interesting discovery as well. There is still one more obvious line of inquiry; but, this being Sunday, it must attend the working week. I will just bet—"

He did not finish, pausing at the clear peal of the doorbell. Through the open doors of library and minor drawing-room they could see Cato moving past to answer it.

"For what I was about to say," resumed Uncle Gil, pointing with the cigar, "substitute the statement that I will just bet I know who that is. It's Ira Rutledge, or I am a veritable Dutchman rather than whatever hybrid I do happen to be! He phoned this morning, and said he thought his duty lay here."

It was in fact Ira Rutledge. After handing hat and umbrella to Cato, who murmured some words, the lawyer crossed the minor drawing-room and entered.

"I did not even go to church," he said, "after the impact of last night's appalling news. Funeral arrangements, no doubt, will devolve upon me. Well, that's as it should be!"

"Before any funeral, Ira," Uncle Gil reminded him, "there are certain unpleasant but necessary formalities to be carried out. Regrettable, of course, and yet . . ."

"To be sure, to be sure; don't apologize! In the meantime, though, a wreath for the front door would be neither premature nor unseemly? And—Dave! Poor Dave! Where is he, Jeff, and how is he?"

"Poorly, Cato thinks. But he seems steady enough most of the time. He's in his room, and says he's getting up."

"If you'll excuse me, then, I will just offer my condolences. In his room, eh? I think I remember—"

"Before you go, Ira," interposed Gilbert Bethune, "one question about rooms. Often though I have visited this house, I never spent a night here; you have. Harald Hobart's wife, if memory serves, died about 1911 or 1912. When she was alive, which of those bedrooms upstairs did they occupy?"

"Poor Amy? If it matters, they occupied separate bedrooms not long after they were married. Amy was in the so-called Queen Bess's Room at the southeastern corner, and Harald in the Tapestry Room at the southwestern end."

"Though he never practised it, I believe Harald by profession was an engineer?"

"He studied electrical engineering, but never graduated. He was too preoccupied with—with other matters. Excuse me, excuse me!"

Out bustled Mr. Rutledge. Uncle Gil, eyes narrowing, still studied the doorway.

"Even apart from his concern as family lawyer, Jeff, our friend has some personal worry on his mind. It sounded very clearly over the phone. Ira has little to worry him, I should imagine. But the fact that he lacks cause has never prevented any man from worrying, particularly Ira. Whether he chooses to tell me may be another thing."

"In that respect, Uncle Gil, Dave himself has something to tell you. Dave's decided to speak out; he may clear up much. Will you see him now?"

"I will see Dave, I think, when I have seen some others first. For our journey to town, Jeff, you needn't trouble to borrow the car you have been using. I will drive you and return you. As regards clearing things up . . ."

About to close the brief-case, Gilbert Bethune hesitated. Cigar in right hand, he thrust his left hand into the inside breast pocket of his coat and drew out an envelope on whose back he had copied a few lines in pencil.

"Already," he said, "I have been forced to revise one pronouncement I made last night. Dave wrote down what he could remember of Commodore Hobart's log. When I removed those notes and took them away, I remarked that probably they would not help me. On the contrary, they have been of immense help. The old commodore did leave one more clue, a thundering clue, a clue that should open and reveal."

"Clue?" Jeff blurted. "Thundering clue? What clue?"

"Listen! After estimating the weight in missing gold, Commodore Hobart wrote as follows. 'Distrust the surface; surfaces can be very misleading, especially from that workshop. See Matthew VII, 7.' "

"Matthew? Workshop?" Jeff stared at him. "You mean you had an idea, but you've had to revise it because the idea was wrong?"

"No, by all the Magi!" said Uncle Gil, returning the envelope to his pocket and shutting up the brief-case. "I mean the idea was dead right. Commodore Hobart's reference to the gospel of St. Matthew, far from being curious, is so confirmatory as to be almost inevitable. The real clue will be found in his preceding sentence. 'Distrust the surface; surfaces can be very misleading, especially from that workshop.' " Uncle Gil drew himself up. "There you have it. Correctly interpret those words, Jeff, and you will have solved half the riddle of this case."

13

As they swept along the River Road in Uncle Gil's Buick, Jeff presently gave it up.

"All right!" he said. "Since every question gets turned aside with some further enigmatic comment—you're worse than Father Brown!—then it's apparent that questions are useless."

"Don't force me to paraphrase Dr. Johnson," begged his uncle, "and say I must provide information but not the understanding to grasp it. You're an intelligent man, Jeff; the evidence was before your eyes. Surely . . . !"

"Very well: information. Where are we going?"

"To Mrs. Keith's. Though I am not well acquainted with the lady, knowing her mainly by repute, at least I have met her."

"Why to Kate's?"

"You will see. A rain-splashed Sunday afternoon should find her at home and will find her at home; Harry Minnoch has made sure of that.

"Further information, nephew! Among the phone calls I myself made this morning was one to Westchester County, New York. I wanted information about Malcolm Townsend and, if possible, about Charles Saylor too."

"Townsend? Are you thinking—?"

"No, Jeff. It's not to be anticipated that an outsider like Townsend would have much interest in the Hobart family beyond his natural interest in their house. But I sought information and found it."

"To what effect?"

149

"Townsend's book, as well as a previous work of the same sort, was published by the small but reliable firm of Furness & Hart, Fourth Avenue. And Jerry Furness, whom I caught at home nursing his Sunday hangover, is an old friend of mine."

"Well?"

"Townsend, of whom Jerry speaks highly, delivers lectures under the auspices of Major Pond, Inc., one of the biggest Madison Avenue outfits. He began lecturing only last fall, and with some reluctance; it prevents him from spending so much time abroad investigating picturesque houses. Townsend has an independent income, which may be accounted as fortunate. His books are widely and favorably reviewed, but they don't sell."

"What about Saylor?"

"My informant," replied Uncle Gil, "had never even heard Saylor's name. But he promised to look into the matter; and, if he picked up anything, to phone me collect."

Whereupon Gilbert Bethune fell silent for so long a time, his attention apparently fixed on the road ahead, that it was sandpaper to Jeff's curiosity.

"Are you mulling over anything else, Sir Oracle?"

"Well, yes. If we look for suspects in a murder case, we find ourselves stymied at every turn. Regarding facts gleaned by Lieutenant Minnoch, consider our really remarkable collection of alibis."

"Alibis?"

"You and Ira Rutledge, to begin with. You yourself are not likely to be suspected; neither is Ira. In any case you were together from ten-thirty until past midnight. Townsend and Mrs. Keith have an alibi still more incontestable."

"When Penny phoned me at Ira's office," Jeff recalled, "she said Kate had lured Townsend away from the Hall soon after dinner."

"Correct. She lured him to a night club."

"Cinderella's Slipper, was it?"

"No, not Cinderella's Slipper. This place, poetically called *Le Moulin de Montmartre*, provides food and liquor as well as a dance floor. Many witnesses testify he was there with Mrs. Keith from about ten o'clock until after one in the morning. As for Penny, with whom I also talked today . . ."

"You phoned Penny?"

"Penny phoned me. She had seen the morning paper, and was much distressed."

"Uncle Gil, you never mentioned—!"

"I warned you, did I not, to let the girl alone for the time being? She lacked the courage, she said, to phone Delys Hall or approach anyone there. So she chose me. Was the news about Serena really true? It couldn't be true, could it? I soothed her as much as possible, to no great effect. After speaking to you at Ira's office last night, she played three-handed bridge with her parents until close on twelve."

"You don't think *Penny* needs an alibi?"

"Not at all; I merely commented on so impressive a collection of alibis. If we can manage to include Saylor too, the roster will be almost complete."

Again Uncle Gil fell silent. Except to repeat the substance of what Dave had told him, Jeff himself spoke few words until his uncle presently drew up at a house on the north side of St. Charles Avenue, just before the intersection of Jackson Avenue in the Garden District.

Of brick faced with white stucco, sleekly kept behind its hedge, the place had four slender white pillars on the ground floor and four more for the iron-railed gallery above. There had been another break in the wet weather; Jeff, lacking a raincoat, did not even need to hurry.

A maid admitted them to the wide central hall and thence, after taking Gilbert Bethune's hat and coat, to a drawing-room on the right.

Amid the Louis Quinze opulence of the drawing-room, amid a profusion of flowers in bowls, Kate Keith rose to greet them. If subdued and somewhat uncertain, she had an unmistakable air of sleek, satisfied well-being. Malcolm Townsend, equally subdued but perhaps less satisfied, also rose in greeting.

"Yes, Mr. Bethune?" Kate began. She presented Townsend to Uncle Gil, and was about to present him to Jeff when both murmured that they had met.

"You're here, I imagine," Kate rushed on, "to question us—they call it grilling, don't they?—about that dreadful business last night. Well . . ."

"Accept my assurance, Mrs. Keith," Uncle Gil informed her, "that nobody is to be grilled or even brought near the fire. But you had heard of Serena's death, had you?"

"Oh, indeed I'd heard! It was in the papers.·And Lieutenant Somebody, that awful man from the boat, has been here already!"

"You, sir," and Uncle Gil turned to Townsend, "had heard of it too?"

Courteous, uneasy, Townsend shifted from one foot to the other.

"*I* had heard, in fact," he answered, "even before I saw the newspaper or met Lieutenant Minnoch. Shall I explain?"

"If you will."

Kate almost interrupted this by becoming a good hostess. After installing Townsend on the brocaded sofa beside her, she insisted that the others should take chairs and offered refreshment, which they refused.

"You see," continued Townsend, pinching at his under-lip, "together with this lady, whom I now take the liberty of calling Kate . . ."

"Honestly, Malcolm," Kate murmured, "it's about *time* you got around to that, isn't it?"

"Kate and I, then, set out for the purpose of seeing some of the town's sights. We saw, to be exact, only one of the town's sights. I'm not quite sure whether I'm safe in telling this to any representative of the law . . ."

"You are safe enough, sir," said Uncle Gil, "in telling it to this particular representative of the law. You went to a night club, *Le Moulin de Montmartre,* where you found the drinks of better quality than you had expected. The police are satisfied regarding your movements and whereabouts at any important time after you both arrived there. But what can you tell me about events earlier in the evening: events, say, immediately before and after dinner at Delys Hall?"

Kate clenched her hands.

"Now, Mr. Inquisitor!" she burst out. "I don't want to seem uncooperative or be uncooperative. But I never heard such rubbish in all my life! Did *you* ever hear such rubbish?" she demanded of Jeff, and then whirled back on the inquisitor. "What earthly *differ-*

ence can it make what Malcolm or I or anybody else was doing *earlier in the evening?*"

"Nevertheless, madam, the question has interest."

"When *I* got there," Kate retorted, "Penny Lynn was with them. They'd just finished dinner, and were talking about taking indoor photographs."

"Penny Lynn," said Uncle Gil, "has already mentioned it to me. Perhaps there was something else. Mr. Townsend?"

Townsend drew a breath of relief.

"The process of taking indoor photographs," he replied, "had begun before dinner. Miss Hobart produced a large folding Kodak, and her brother a reflector with a special new kind of flash bulb which will burn with great brilliance for many seconds at a time if plugged in at any ordinary light socket.

"Miss Hobart proved an intense perfectionist at choosing backgrounds and posing subjects. Dave took the pictures, which almost invariably she said he did wrong. Dave further insisted on taking so many photographs of Miss Lynn—Miss Lynn in the doorway, Miss Lynn at the harpsichord—that both Miss Lynn and Miss Hobart strongly protested."

"Anything else?"

"I can't recall anything else. Towards the end of dinner there was some talk of resuming the picture-taking. But it was never done. Kate arrived, as you must have heard; she and I presently left for Montmartre's Mill. When I think that, as we sipped brandy at our table or I very clumsily squired Kate over the dance floor, Serena Hobart . . . !"

He let the words rise and die away. Uncle Gil nodded.

"Yes, to be sure! You left the night club—when?"

"I took no particular note; it was past one o'clock. Some time later Kate with her car dropped me off at my hotel. And now," said Townsend, "we come to the part of my story which may have some slight interest."

"Yes?"

"When Kate left me at the hotel, she had very kindly invited me to have lunch here today. I slept unpardonably late until almost nine o'clock, and decided to miss breakfast after I had gone down-

153

stairs. I had asked for mail at the desk; I was on my way out to find a taxi when . . ."

"Malcolm," interrupted Kate, "you must *not* take taxis all over the place! There are two cars in the garage here; use either of those when you need it. After all—!"

"Thanks, Kate, but—! As a matter of fact, sir," Townsend continued to Uncle Gil, "I had started in search of a taxi when I met a well-spoken, well-mannered young man who said he had just arrived and heard me inquire for mail. After introducing himself as Detective Terence O'Bannion of the police, he told me of Miss Hobart's tragic death. He did not elaborate. If for a moment the news seemed so incredible as to suggest some grotesque hoax or joke, young O'Bannion soon resolved doubts by delivering a message from Dave Hobart. Dave, collapsing last night, now asked that I would not desert him at a time like this; that I would stay on in New Orleans until he found his feet.

"My first impulse was to phone Dave or go out to the Hall and see him. But Mr. O'Bannion advised against either, saying Dave would be much better left alone for the rest of the day."

"So Malcolm did find a taxi," Kate amplified in a rush, "and did come out here. There was a fair amount in the paper, with one or two times of night referred to, but nothing much; mostly what they wouldn't or couldn't say. Then that other detective, the dreadful one with the big moustache and the bald head, walked in *before* lunch. *He* was the one who started talking about murder; murder, for pity's sake? It's crazy, that's what it is; don't tell me anything else!"

Townsend spread out his hands.

"I appreciate your offer of a car, Kate, even though I can't avail myself of it. And it's gratifying to think Dave believes I may be of some use to him. But I can't stay on here much longer; it's out of the question."

"Why is it out of the question, Malcolm?"

"Next week, for one thing, I am booked to sail from New York by the *Ile de France* . . ."

"We are told, Mr. Townsend," struck in Uncle Gil, "you spend a good deal of time abroad."

"In summer, yes; always in summer. Even the English climate is usually tolerable then. And those with historic houses, either in the British Isles or elsewhere, are in the proper mood to be approached. But my journeyings abroad, sir, are only small potatoes, the very smallest potatoes on the table! The real reason I cannot and must not remain in New Orleans much longer . . ."

"Well, sir?"

"Already," returned the other, with embarrassment mounting to his almost-handsome face, "I have proved the worst and most officious of intruding meddlers. Having tried to assist Dave, have I actually assisted him? You know I have not; nor can I."

Townsend rose up from the sofa. Wandering towards the two windows that overlooked St. Charles Avenue, he stood between the windows, his back to the wall, a picture of groping indecision.

"What looked important yesterday, gentlemen, has no importance today. Yesterday Dave Hobart's whole life seemed concentrated on only one thing: the search for his grandfather's hidden gold. He begged for a suggestion, any suggestion in any direction."

"And you could make no suggestion?"

"I did make a suggestion, Mr. Bethune. Since Dave was positive nothing had been or could be hidden between the walls, I wondered about the space between the floors."

"What did Dave say to that?"

"He ruled it out at once. The floors, he assured me, had once been taken up for the installation of some wiring. The floors held no secret either."

"You were present, I believe," Uncle Gil cleared his throat, "at the discovery that Commodore Hobart's famous log had been removed from the study. Afterwards, as you are probably aware, Dave made notes of his memories from that log."

"We all knew he had made notes. He did not show them to anyone, at least not in my presence."

"Here," pursued Uncle Gil, taking the envelope from his pocket, "is a direct quotation, another part of the commodore's challenge. 'Distrust the surface; surfaces can be very misleading, especially from that workshop. See Matthew VII, 7.' How are we to interpret that?"

Townsend stared into the distance.

"'Ask, and it shall be given you; seek, and ye shall find; knock, and it shall be opened unto you.' What odd scraps of memory stick at the back of any man's brain! The reference, I agree, is clearly to that ancient challenge. But what is the surface we must distrust? We have no clue there. Is the surface of brick, of stone, or of wood?"

"Suppose it were none of them?"

"*None* of them?"

"I state a conjecture, no more; it cannot yet be proved. Should the surface prove to be wood after all . . ."

"Wood, brick, stone, even cardboard or Brussels lace, it does not alter a situation now grown intolerable; Miss Hobart is dead, Dave momentarily shattered. Any search for hidden treasure becomes as meaningless as it is morbid. What about Jean Laffite's treasure? Or Captain Flint's? If I were to stay on here much longer, it would show a state of mind approaching the ghoulish."

"Honestly, Malcolm—!" protested Kate.

"I don't sail for Europe until next Saturday. If you insist, if Dave insists, I will stay until Tuesday night or Wednesday morning. I prided myself on only one thing in life, and I have failed in it. Let that serve as my warning for the future."

"Perhaps you have not failed," suggested Uncle Gil, returning the envelope to his pocket and getting up, "though you may as yet have neglected to realize in what you should take most pride. Sir and madam, my thanks to you both. Since I have no further questions with which to trouble you at this time . . ."

A few minutes later, as he and Jeff climbed into the car, Jeff gave voice to a certain despair.

"You didn't learn much, did you?"

"On the contrary, I learned much of value. That man has *no* idea where to find the commodore's gold; he has no idea at all!"

"Did you think he might have?"

"It was a possibility for consideration. I had a test to apply, and I applied it. As soon as I heard truth ring in his voice, I knew the direction we ought to look."

"For the lost hoard?"

"For the answer to a question which has been much neglected."

"Well, where do we go from here?"

"To my club, I think. We have both missed lunch; it's much too late in the day to bother. But the club can supply us with a sandwich even on Sunday."

Uncle Gil's club, the Blackstone for men of law, had been so long nicknamed the Wranglers' that most non-members believed it thus christened. Located well downtown, it reared three floors of double bay windows at the corner of Gravier Street and St. Charles Avenue.

Another rain squall had come and gone before Gilbert Bethune left his car in the parking lot just north. Following him into the club, down a dusky hall towards the staircase at the rear, Jeff thought he saw a vaguely familiar figure enter the front door behind them.

In the lounge upstairs, a large comfortable room of deep leather armchairs and sofas, its double bay windows overlooking Gravier Street, Uncle Gil waved his guest towards a chair. They had not yet seated themselves when in shouldered that familiar figure: the burly man grown somewhat overweight, ruddy of face and expansive of nature, whom Penny had pointed out on Friday night as Billy Vauban.

"Ah, Mr. District Attorney!" he said.

Uncle Gil introduced Jeff, who at once became conscious of the newcomer's likable qualities.

"Pleasure!" declared Billy Vauban, shaking hands cordially. "If you're wondering what a common-or-garden businessman is doing at a lawyers' club, I *am* a lawyer. Passed my bar examination years ago, even if the family did push me into a job once held by an uncle of mine. —What's the good or bad word, Mr. District Attorney?"

"I was about to order sandwiches and something to drink, if it's possible to get them served in here. Join us, Billy?"

"Thanks, but I can't. Got to pick up my wife at the Wentworths', out on the River Road beyond . . . Here! Shockin' business about Serena Hobart, wasn't it? Is it true she fell from her bedroom window?"

"That, at least, is what the evidence seems to indicate." Uncle

157

Gil sat down lazily, reaching for a cigar. "You've never held a grudge against the Hobarts, have you?"

"No; why should I? It's no fault of the family if Uncle Thad slipped and killed himself out there. Can't say I've ever been intimate with any of 'em, it's true. But many's the game of pool I've shot with Harald, and had a few drinks with him too. One other funny thing, Gil. Somebody's been industriously spreading the rumor *I* want to buy Delys Hall."

"It's only a rumor, then?"

"It's worse than a rumor; it's a damn lie," the burly man said with great heartiness. "We've got a country place of our own, and that house on the Esplanade in town. What we'd do with an imported English museum, all decked out as though they expected Queen Elizabeth or Sir Francis Drake to drop in at any minute, it would take some inspired crystal-gazing to tell you."

"A prospective buyer named Merriman . . ."

"I don't know who's spreading the report; I don't care. But I must run along now to get Pauline, and that reminds me. Two nights in succession, first Friday and then Saturday, I've walked into domestic hot water that almost boiled over. The first time was at a public night club; I admit I did some carrying on. Last night we attended a formal dinner at the Wentworths'. The trouble started much more quietly; it didn't really work up until we were on our way home, and I was cold sober. But . . ."

"When you were on your way home at what time? Do you by any chance remember?"

"Oh, round about midnight. Yes, easily that!" Then Vauban exhaled a deep breath as though to blow the matter away. "You never married, did you? You can thank your lucky stars you didn't! Anyway, goodbye now. Glad to have met you, Jeff; you keep out of matrimony too!"

When the non-practising lawyer had gone, as self-assured as ever, Gilbert Bethune rang the bell for a waiter.

"That little interview," he commented, "at least provided us with additional information and one more suggestion. What do you make of Forthright Billy?"

"I can tell you what I make of both the information and the suggestion."

"Yes?"

"Outwardly," Jeff replied, "there is no reason to connect either Vauban or his wife with whatever happened to Serena. But, if they didn't leave their friends' home until midnight, which should be easily established, it gives us another complete and unanswerable double alibi."

"Perhaps we're not thinking of the same suggestion," said Uncle Gil.

At his request they were served with chicken sandwiches, potato salad, and iced lager which tasted like real Pilsener. Afterwards they both sat back, smoking, as evening shadows began to darken in the lounge. Gilbert Bethune, like a sort of legal Sherlock Holmes, studied the tip of his cigar.

"Shall we argue this business a little?" he suggested. "Most of the facts, let it be repeated, are in full view. One such fact, in itself apparently of no importance, has been repeated more often than almost any other. And yet nobody seems to have noticed what it may mean."

"Some clue to the missing gold?"

"This fact, Jeff, bears no reference to the missing gold."

"*No reference to . . . ?*"

"Consider!" Uncle Gil urged in a low voice. "The commodore's gold is a fact of importance; it has been acknowledged as such. But it is only of partial importance to the solution of the mystery. If I betrayed the whereabouts of the gold at this minute, as I am inclined to think I could, we should be no nearer learning who killed Serena or how the murderer approached her."

"Are you telling me there's something so obvious I can't see it?"

"Forget paradoxes; they will lead us only into a blind alley. No, Jeff! There is something so commonplace, so everyday, so much to be expected, that of itself it would rouse nobody's suspicion or even curiosity. And yet, harmless though the fact may be, its attendant circumstances buzz with rattlesnake warning at any unwary tread. We must be warned and take care. We must—"

He was interrupted by the entrance of the waiter, who, in clearing away the dishes, told him he was wanted on the telephone.

"I can take it up here, can't I?" demanded Uncle Gil.

He indicated a telephone on the wall of the lounge at right angles to the wall with the big marble fireplace. When the waiter assented, Uncle Gil rose, strode there with some haste, and addressed himself to responsive carbon.

"Yes, Harry?" Jeff heard him say. "What's that? *When?* But he's . . . ?"

Despite gathering dusk that made faces hard to read, Jeff could not have missed the alarm in his uncle's voice. Foreboding entered the lounge as palpably as a sentient visitor. After monosyllabic questions and comments, a perturbed District Attorney hung up the receiver.

"There's been another attempt," he said, striding back again. "No, it did not succeed; Dave is still alive. But it might have succeeded; the murderer has almost shown his face. We must go out to the Hall, and in a hurry. Come on!"

14

It was Lieutenant Minnoch who opened the front door. Again the lower floor of Delys Hall gleamed with lights, from the main hall to the rooms on either side. At the lieutenant's elbow Cato waited patiently to take Uncle Gil's hat and coat.

Harry Minnoch himself, with a red stain of wrath across his forehead but the air of one lurking in ambush behind some weapon he will use at the right time, beckoned the two newcomers.

"This way," he said. "I wasn't here when it happened. All day," he passionately addressed the District Attorney, "all day, sir, I've been chasing over town to establish a few things, and I reckon I've established 'em. No, I wasn't here when it happened. But O'Bannion was; he'll tell you."

Thus Minnoch led them through minor drawing-room, library, and two more rooms to the lighted study at the rear.

At the table with the lamp stood a broad-shouldered, neatly dressed young man whose dark hair contrasted with his fresh complexion and Celtic blue eyes. Lieutenant Minnoch made an encouraging gesture.

"All right, O'Bannion; fire away!"

"Well, Lieutenant—"

"Don't speak to *me*, young fellow; I know what you're gonna say. Speak to Mr. Bethune and this other gentleman, who's Mr. Bethune's nephew. That is, sir, if it's all right for your nephew to hear it?"

"Yes, he may hear it," Uncle Gil assented. "What is it we have to hear?"

Terence O'Bannion obeyed orders.

"Well, gentlemen, it was this way. Last night the lieutenant posted me to guard young Mr. Hobart's door. When I came off duty, after I'd gone home to get some sleep, I was to return here and keep an eye on things. No specific orders; just 'keep an eye on things.' When I did come off duty this morning, Mr. Hobart asked me to take a message to a friend of his at the St. Charles Hotel—"

"You shouldn't 'a' done that, Terry!" Minnoch admonished him. "A cop's no errand-boy to take messages; leastways, not without he gets permission from his superior officer. Still! No great harm done, I reckon, so we'll forget about it this time. Go ahead; take it from there."

"When I did get back," continued O'Bannion, with one eye on his superior officer, "it was fairly late in the afternoon. The lieutenant had said I needn't hurry, so I took my time. But I expected to find *him* here when I returned. He wasn't here; there was no other officer on the premises."

"I can't be every place at once, can I?" demanded Lieutenant Minnoch. "I've done enough running around to wear out two younger men; but I don't complain; I've got the job done!"

"One question at this juncture," said Uncle Gil, putting his brief-case on the table. "When you returned, Officer O'Bannion, who was here? Apart from the servants and Dave Hobart himself, that is, who *was* here?"

"Only their family lawyer, sir: Mr. Rutledge. Mr. Rutledge told me what the butler had already told me. Mr. Hobart had got dressed and had even come downstairs for a little while. But he was still feeling rocky after last night. So he said he'd go on back up to his room and rest, maybe take a nap."

"Yes? And then?"

"Not knowing just what I was supposed to do, sir, I wondered. The lieutenant hadn't said anything about keeping guard during the day, but I thought it mightn't be a bad idea."

"Your suspicions," Uncle Gil told him, "would seem to have been justified. What did you do?"

"I went upstairs, sir, and tapped very lightly at Mr. Hobart's door. When he didn't answer, I opened the door. He was stretched out on the bed: fully dressed, sound asleep, and breathing peacefully.

"I went out and closed the door. I got a big chair from the main part of the upper hall; I pulled it up near the door of the young gentleman's room; I sat down to wait. It couldn't have been more than ten or fifteen minutes later . . ."

Clearly approaching the climax of the narrative, Officer O'Bannion tried to speak without allowing nerves to show in his Hibernian face, but without loutish stolidity in evidence either.

"It couldn't have been more than ten or fifteen minutes later," he said, "that the doorbell rang. I thought it would be Lieutenant Minnoch, probably, and I'd better be on hand. The butler had opened the door when I got downstairs. But it wasn't the lieutenant. It was a young lady, very pretty and also very nervous, named Miss Lynn.

"She asked after Mr. Hobart but wouldn't come inside. When I told her Mr. Hobart was asleep, she said she wouldn't stay and couldn't stay. She said it as though she meant she couldn't bear to stay. Oh, yes!" O'Bannion turned towards Jeff. "If you're Mr. Caldwell, sir, the young lady also asked after you. I told her there was nobody of that name here now, and she ran back to her car and drove away.

"There's not much more, gentlemen.

"I thought I'd glance through the downstairs rooms before I went back up; I don't know why I did. The main drawing-room's to the right of the front door as you enter this house. Mr. Rutledge was there. For some reason that room seems to fascinate him; he's almost always there when he's on the premises. But he said *he* had to be going.

"After I'd looked through the rooms on this side of the main floor, it was time to return to my post upstairs. It's a funny thing, Mr. Bethune. I don't want to lay any claim to . . . to . . ."

"What is it you don't want to claim, Officer O'Bannion?" prompted Uncle Gil. "Prophecy? Divination? Second sight?"

The young Irishman uttered what was not quite a laugh.

"If you'll excuse me, sir, I don't hold much with this second-sight business, or being born with a caul, or other things I've heard about in my family. All I can tell you is this. As I went back up the stairs, I started to walk a little faster. I didn't run, you understand. I just walked a little faster. And I did it, so help me God I did it or thought I did it, just *before* I heard a choky kind of cry from the direction of Mr. Hobart's bedroom, followed by a crash as something tipped over.

"Then I did run. You make a lot of noise on those stairs, and there's no carpet in the upstairs hall. But I didn't hear any other noise, or see anybody on the move.

"The door of Mr. Hobart's room stood wide open. Beside the bed I'd already noticed a table and a tray with some half-eaten food. The table and everything on it had been upset: broken dishes, cold coffee stains, quite a mess. Mr. Hobart himself was crumpled up on the floor beside the bed, with one hell of a lump—sorry, sir—!"

"We note it was one hell of a lump," said Uncle Gil. "Don't apologize; explain!"

"—with one hell of a lump, sir, on the left side of his forehead just below the hairline. On the carpet to one side of him was a pillow off the bed; to the other side was a blackjack, a crook's blackjack of weighted leather, such as you'll find when you frisk 'em.

"There was nobody in that room but the victim. He's got a weak heart, as his sister had. You'd have thought being knocked cold with a blackjack would have finished him, to say nothing of what else might have happened. He was alive, all right, though I didn't like the sound of his breathing. By that time the old butler, Cato or Seneca or something Roman, had run in and joined me. Together we hoisted him up on the bed. Cato gave me the phone number of the family doctor. On my way down to phone it occurred to me . . . but you don't want to know what I was thinking, do you?"

"On the contrary," Uncle Gil corrected, "it would interest me to hear your thoughts. What were they?"

"Well, sir," answered O'Bannion, clearing his throat, "somebody hit Mr. Hobart and ducked out of the room. The murderer or would-be murderer couldn't have run along that side passage towards the main part of the upper hall, or I'd have seen him.

There's only one thing he could have done."

"Yes?"

"In the passage, not far from the bedroom door, there's a back stairway. The murderer ducked down those stairs, and out of the house by a side door that's never locked until late at night."

"Or else—" Lieutenant Minnoch began with great portentousness, but checked himself. "To teach you a little about police work, me lad, I'll just stay quiet for a minute. Now that Mr. Bethune's heard your deep thinkin', you might stick to what it was you did."

"I went downstairs to phone Dr. Quayle. Old Mr. Rutledge had already gone, as he said he was going to. I was on the phone to Dr. Quayle when the lieutenant and the sergeant arrived. The lieutenant took over. And that, Mr. Bethune, is all I can tell you of my own knowledge."

"Thanks; it was very clear." Uncle Gil squared his shoulders. "Whereat, Lieutenant," he added formally, "a still small voice whispers that *you* have much to impart."

"I have, sir; it's gospel truth I have! In a short time, if you don't mind, I'll ask you to step upstairs . . ."

"What for? To question Dave Hobart?"

"We can't do that just yet; not tonight, anyway. The doctor's still with him. I wondered if they'd call an ambulance and take that young fellow off to the hospital. But Dr. Quayle said he wouldn't need to; he said he could handle it. There's something upstairs I'd like you to see, that's all. Meanwhile," said Lieutenant Minnoch, taking out a notebook, "we might clear up a few odd bits and pieces that ought to be helpful."

"Such as?"

"Alibis for last night, which is the key to the whole business. We mustn't neglect a murder last night just because of what looks like a near-murder late this afternoon."

"I have no intention of neglecting it."

"Good for you, sir! Much earlier today, you remember, I told you both Mrs. Keith and Mr. Townsend are absolutely ruled out. Too many witnesses will swear they never left that night club between ten o'clock and after one in the morning. She didn't drop him at his hotel until nearly three. While I wouldn't say one word against

the lady's character, it's dollars to doughnuts she took him home
with her between the time they left the night club and the time she
brought him back to the St. Charles. But all the dirty work was over
long before then. Besides, I've talked to both of 'em today . . ."

"So have we."

"And I'm satisfied, Mr. Bethune, if you are. Anyway, I could 'a'
told you no woman had anything to do with this murder in the first
place."

"No woman had anything to do with it in *any* way?"

"No woman had anything to do with it in a guilty way. Next,
there's Mr. Rutledge and Mr. Caldwell here."

"Are you satisfied of their innocence as well?"

"I'd like to see the cop who *wasn't* satisfied! That's so plain it
don't even need to be argued or talked about. Finally, if you remember, you asked me to get a line on this fellow Saylor."

"And did you?"

"Yes, sir. He's out of it too."

Lieutenant Minnoch opened his notebook and flicked over a few
pages.

"It was through you, sir, I got my first line on Townsend and
Mrs. Keith. Early this morning, you said, Miss Penny Lynn had
telephoned you and told you those two left this house together after
dinner last night, Mrs. Keith remarking they'd probably go to the
Montmartre Mill. So I could rout out the night-club people, much
as they hated seein' a cop on Sunday morning, even before I tackled
Townsend and Mrs. Keith."

"Yes; you've explained that. What about Saylor?"

"Saylor was harder to get a line on; nobody knew anything about
him. But I found he was registered at the Jung Hotel. It seems he's
a complete stranger here. After dinner at the hotel last night, he
asked the desk clerk for the shortest way to the Grand Bayou Line
Pier."

Uncle Gil snapped his fingers.

"Saylor, as Jeff described him, is both inquisitive and intelligent.
He wanted to find Captain Joshua Galway, did he?"

"By the Almighty's britches, sir, that's just what he wanted!

166

How do you know he was looking for Captain Josh?"

"One part of the evidence indicated it. Did he see the captain?"

"Not right away he didn't." After consulting the notebook again, Lieutenant Minnoch returned it to his pocket. "Saylor took a taxi to the levee. Captain Josh had gone out on the town somewhere, so Saylor talked to the purser. Didn't seem to have much on his mind, the purser says, but I don't believe it.

"And why don't I believe it? I'll tell you. These steamboat people are a friendly bunch; they'll talk your ears off if they get half a chance. The purser brought out a bottle; they had a few and chewed the fat until ha' past eleven, when Captain Josh got back to the boat."

"Serena Hobart," said Uncle Gil, "was found dead at eleven-twenty. Saylor's whereabouts can be accounted for until eleven-*thirty?*"

"Until much later than that, sir! The captain no sooner gets back, you see, than Saylor takes him aside for a mysterious confab in private until after midnight. I talked to Captain Josh today, and then I went to the Jung Hotel and saw Saylor. Both of 'em claim they talked about nothin' important, but this magazine writer from Philadelphia looked almighty wise when he said it."

Gilbert Bethune began to pace back and forth between the table and the door.

"Lieutenant," he declared, "this is sheer lunacy! Two others you will probably eliminate are a nephew of the late Thad Peters and that nephew's wife. Let's suppose, for argument's sake, *their* alibis hold up. Eliminating Saylor too, and throwing in Captain Galway for good measure, would seem to eliminate every single person even remotely concerned in this affair. No, I am not forgetting Mr. Earl Merriman. According to Jeff's story, our good businessman from St. Louis must have called at Ira Rutledge's office at a time very close to eleven-thirty. And that would seem—"

"Ah, but does it eliminate everybody? Just think for a minute, sir. *Does* it eliminate everybody?"

Lieutenant Minnoch, who had spoken of Saylor as looking wise, himself now looked so wise that he seemed almost bursting.

167

"I said, Lieutenant, it would 'seem' to eliminate everybody: that's the saving qualification. However, take things at your own summing up! It's conceivable, of course, that some total stranger killed Serena last night and attacked Dave this afternoon. At the same time—!"

"I still ask, sir, whether you've even *seemed* to eliminate everybody? Will you and Mr. Caldwell come along with me, please? You might tag along too, O'Bannion."

Carrying his moustache like a war banner, full of internal snorts that indicated satisfaction, the lieutenant led them out into the main hall and upstairs.

Many electric wall candles burned here, throwing soft light into the hall and into the transverse corridor across the house's breadth. Marching towards the closed door of Dave's bedroom, beside which stood a large chair of carved oak, the somewhat smug Minnoch altered his direction and turned to face them at the head of the back stairs.

"Maybe I'm not very subtle, Mr. Bethune. Then, again—"

"Are you still going on about subtlety, man? I've said this is your case to handle, and it is. I've already told you that, haven't I?"

A sense of grievance rang in the lieutenant's voice.

"You *say* it's my case, I know. You've said that more'n once since last night. But when you get started, sir, nobody's got a Chinaman's chance to handle things except you yourself. And when I've finished, Mr. Bethune, maybe this time you'll say I'm bein' too all-fired subtle for my own good. I claim it's only common sense, which is all a cop needs.

"So I won't get too much off my chest right now; I'll wait till I can be dead sure. I'll just call your attention to one or two things that may be worth thinkin' about. When I came out here today, I didn't expect trouble and didn't bring our fingerprint man. But, as soon as I saw that blackjack they found in on the bedroom floor, I grabbed it."

"You—?"

"Oh, I don't mean I grabbed it in the way that sounds! I packed it up in a box, as careful as I could, so nobody else would grab it or touch it, and I told Fred Bull to take it in and have it tested for prints."

"What do you expect to find, or expect the blackjack to tell us?"

"The blackjack, sir, may tell us a whole lot by not tellin' anything at all."

"The subtlety you have in mind, Lieutenant," Uncle Gil said courteously, "need not rise or descend to Chestertonian paradox. That's my department; I claim first rights."

"You can always claim first rights, can't you, sir? Hell's bells, *am* I allowed to say what I want to say, even if it's only common sense?"

"Yes, of course; sorry."

"You're the D.A., sir; no need for *you* to apologize. Now O'Bannion here," Lieutenant Minnoch went on, "has been claiming all along that the would-be murderer sneaked in by an unlocked side door near the foot o' these stairs here, sneaked up to this floor, walloped young Mr. Hobart, and ducked out again the same way."

"You doubt that?"

"I just want to show you something, that's all. Now it's rained all day, off and on; the grounds outside are soaked. Will you follow me, sir?"

Taking out his pocket lighter and kindling its broad flame, the lieutenant went slowly down the stairs. Gilbert Bethune descended after him, and then Jeff, while O'Bannion remained at the top.

The staircase, though long and steep, in daylight would have been well illumined by a small panel of windows above the side door at the end of the transverse corridor below.

Minnoch opened this door and held up the flame of the lighter. Outside, under a stone arch like a kind of hood to protect the entrance from wet weather, stone steps led down to the western arm of the driveway past Delys Hall.

Again rain had passed over, leaving only darkness, wet foliage, and a prowling wind. Lieutenant Minnoch held the lighter outside.

"Still quite a pool o' water," he commented, "at the foot o' those steps out there. Now back up the stairs again, gentlemen! And you might keep lookin' at 'em as we go.

"If I've still got the go-ahead sign, Mr. Bethune," he added, after they had reached the top of the staircase, "I'll sort of sum up. I've been all over the stairs, I've been up and down 'em. I've been all over the floor of the side entrance down there, and the floor of this passage up here. *And* the floor of the bedroom too. And there's not a trace o' mud, water, or even dirt anywhere on the steps or on the floor!"

"Oh?"

"On a day like today, sir," the lieutenant proclaimed with energy, "not a man alive could 'a' gone in and out without leavin' some kind of trace or track to show he'd been there. See what I mean?"

"You are saying, then," Uncle Gil returned in a strange voice, "that whoever attacked Dave Hobart must have come from inside the house?"

"Kind of looks that way, don't it? And that's not all it proves! With your permission, sir, I have a little plan in mind. Just to show I always take precautions, we'll keep the young gentleman well guarded from now on."

Seeing the lieutenant's eye stray towards O'Bannion, Gilbert Bethune cleared his throat for attention.

"I also," the District Attorney said, "am beginning to have a plan in mind. To carry out all aspects of this plan, I shall need professional help of several kinds and in several directions. For instance! You're about to post Officer O'Bannion as a constant guard, aren't you? If so, is there somebody you can use for that duty in his place?"

"Yes, sir, course there is! Why do you ask?"

"Because, if I can clear it through Captain Kelly without having to go over Captain Kelly's head to the Police Commissioner, I want to borrow O'Bannion for a little errand that must be carried out. Tell me, young man: have you ever done any flying?"

"*Flying, sir?*" O'Bannion stared at him.

Uncle Gil, it seemed to Jeff, just restrained himself from doing a little dance.

"There has been so much talk of transatlantic flying," he replied, "that the thought naturally jumped into my head. But I meant

170

nothing so ambitious or far-reaching. The proper question is: have you ever been up in a plane?"

"I've been up once or twice, sir, with those barnstormers who used to take you on very short spins at five dollars a time."

"Already," said Uncle Gil, "they have begun to fly the mail. Within twenty years or even less, it's been predicted, there will be regular passenger flights from city to city. Meanwhile, in a much more modest and restricted way, a similar kind of service is provided by our own Ted Patterson here in New Orleans. *You* won't mind too much, Lieutenant, if I borrow your subordinate?"

"If you say so, Mr. Bethune, borrow him and welcome! *But*——"

After a thunderous kind of pause, as though holding himself in check before he hurled a thunderbolt, Lieutenant Minnoch settled down to continue.

"I asked you, sir, what else the evidence proves. And I'm a little bit surprised, maybe, that anybody as keen as you didn't tumble to it right away. I mean the noise."

"The noise?"

"Well, the lack o' noise. Like this! Whatever happened in that bedroom over there, it'd seem, somebody had to get in and then out again. O'Bannion, as he's told you, heard a kind of cry. He heard the table and dishes go over with a smash. But that's all he did hear, and he didn't see anything. He himself made a lot of noise running up the main staircase, and there's no carpet in this passage. How was it the attacker, whether from outside the house or inside it or wherever the attacker came from, didn't make any sound at all?"

Gilbert Bethune regarded him in something like consternation.

"Lieutenant, I greatly fear—"

Uncle Gil did not finish. Quite literally he put his hand over his mouth as the heavy door of Dave's room opened and closed behind silver-haired Dr. Quayle, who joined them near the back stairs and spoke in a low voice.

"That will do for the present," he said. "I hope I'm not needed here again tonight. If the whole situation weren't so serious, I might have just cause for complaint. Any questions?"

"One or two," Uncle Gil told him in the same tone, "but mainly: how is Dave's heart?"

"The one predictable thing about such an ailment is that you can't make predictions. He'll do, I think. Organically Dave is in better shape than his father; and his father, cardiac condition or no, lived until the fairly ripe age of sixty-seven."

"Did Dave say anything?"

"Oh, yes. He kept trying to talk until the sedative took effect. I hate to give him so much sedation, but I had no choice."

"Could he—talk coherently?"

"Yes, to a degree." Dr. Quayle swung the black bag against his leg. "The boy's had a bad shock, of course; but apart from physical causes his principal emotion seems to be one of anger. Before hitting him with that weapon, the murderer you're after first tried to smother him with a pillow."

"To smother him? Then that explains—!"

"The pillow on the floor? Yes, to be sure. The bed had two pillows. Dave's head was on one of them. He lay stretched out, eyes closed and resting, but not asleep, when all of a sudden the other pillow came down on his face with the full weight of somebody's hands and arms and shoulders.

"He didn't take it, if I may say so, lying down. Dave's a very powerful young fellow. He jumped to his feet, tearing the pillow away and down, and stood up to face the assailant."

"He saw who it was?"

"He couldn't see the fellow's face, though he must have been as close as I am to you now. His assailant let go the pillow, and swung up a left arm—in some kind of loose raincoat, Dave says—to hide the face. Anyway! On a dark day, startled and confused like that, what happened isn't surprising. He saw the man's right arm go up. Something hit the boy; he knew he was falling against the table, but that's all he knew before the light went out."

"He can't say anything else?"

"No, I'm afraid not." Dr. Quayle drew a deep breath. "I begged him not to excite himself, but you know Dave. And I asked only one question. Late on a drowsy Sunday afternoon, with not a noise in the house, the unknown attacker creeps in and takes his victim unawares. 'You mean,' I said, 'you didn't hear a sound to warn you?' "

"Did Dave answer?"

"Yes, if you can make anything of it. The boy said, 'I couldn't have heard anything, Doctor. He wasn't even wearing shoes; he was in his stocking feet.' "

15

Jeff pulled the Stutz Bearcat in at the curb and switched off the ignition.

"This is the third time in four days, Penny," he said to the girl at his side, "that a car in which I was riding will have been left here in University Place. The first time, Friday night, we were together in your Hudson. Saturday night I was alone, driving this car, and on my way to Ira Rutledge's office. Yesterday, Sunday, Uncle Gil and I paid several visits without touching here. This afternoon . . ."

"On the way in," Penny conceded, "you've told me about yesterday afternoon. But what about last night? I know I oughtn't to be so horribly curious, but I can't help it. Some unknown man attacked poor Dave and got away. What happened then?"

"Very little, as I've also tried to tell you. Lieutenant Minnoch, afire with some great idea he won't explain, said he *would* explain today when he could be dead sure. And Old Nemesis isn't the only one. Uncle Gil, with two separate sets of great ideas—they go in different directions, he says—won't explain until *he's* dead sure. Seeing you today, Penny . . ."

"I—I do wish you wouldn't say *dead* sure!"

"Sorry; there was no intent to . . ."

"Of course there wasn't!" Penny assured him. "I—I did drive up to the Hall yesterday afternoon, which must have been just before the attack on Dave. But I couldn't go in. It may have seemed cowardy-custard, when I was so fond of Serena and like Dave a lot too; but I couldn't!"

"There's no reason why you should have. And you did manage it today."

"Yes, because I was resolved not to be such a 'fraidy cat! Then, when I'd no sooner got out of the car, you insisted I must leave it there and drive to town with you. There's no need to be so masterful, you know; I'll do *whatever* you ask whenever you ask it. But, now that we are here, what are we doing here?"

"That can be explained, Penny, by rounding out last night. Dr. Quayle left. Lieutenant Minnoch left, still muttering to himself. Cato persuaded Uncle Gil and me to have something to eat. When we finished eating . . ."

Under the clear blue sky of Monday afternoon, April 25th, Jeff had a sharp memory of Gilbert Bethune in the refectory the night before.

"Dr. Quayle, Jeff," Uncle Gil had remarked, "pays high tribute to Dave Hobart's courage and presence of mind, saying Dave was very much like his father. It's a fair verdict. My late friend Harald had presence of mind and undoubted courage. All his life, so far as I know, Harald feared only one thing."

"Oh?"

"He feared heights," Uncle Gil had said. "Harald might have gone up in a plane, because you can be strapped into your seat. But he wouldn't have walked near the edge of a precipice, even a very low precipice."

"Is that important?"

"If you use your eyes and your memory, Jeff, I think you'll find it very important. Tomorrow, shoving aside all other business except the Hobart affair, I mean to pursue my two lines of investigation. What's your own program?"

"It's to visit number 701b Royal Street, according to the invitation of the anonymous note. Am I likely to find anything interesting there?"

"It's possible, it's at least possible. For I think I have remembered those premises," Uncle Gil had answered, "and the rather curious character who inhabits them."

"Curious or not, is he a sinister character? Need I look out for squalls if I buy tobacco there?"

175

"Sinister, Jeff? No, quite the opposite! Whatever else may be said of him, old—the gentleman in question won't carry a blackjack in his sleeve. It's safe enough, physically speaking, to do business with him."

And so, behind the wheel of the Stutz in University Place that warm Monday afternoon, Jeff looked at Penny Lynn.

"As you say, here we are. There's now no reason why I shouldn't tell you about the anonymous note on the steamboat, so I've told you. On Saturday night I drove past 701b; not unnaturally, it was closed. Knowing your dislike of taking a car into the Vieux Carré, I'll leave this one here. If you'd care to accompany me to the address in question . . ."

More alluring than ever in a white summer dress, Penny climbed out of the car and joined him on the pavement.

"Of course I'd like to go, Jeff! It's a cigar store, I think you said?"

"The proprietor calls it a cigar *divan,* which is a term I associate only with—!" Jeff hesitated. "If I could just understand some little part of what's going on, and prove I'm not as dense as I must sound—!"

"You couldn't sound dense whatever you said or say." Then Penny made a despairing face. "But then nothing at all seems to make much sense, does it?"

Jeff did not reply until they had crossed Canal Street and turned south along the border of the Old Square.

"It makes still less sense," he announced, "every time my worthy uncle delivers some judgment which he claims is meant to enlighten me. Last night, as Uncle Gil was leaving the Hall, he made almost his final pronouncement."

"What was it?"

" 'Several dates, Jeff, are of great importance in this business. One of the most important may be the year 1919, when considered in relation to the present.'

"I said, 'What's 1919 got to do with it? In 1919 I went abroad to write, but you don't mean of importance to me, do you?' Whereat Uncle Gil at his most oracular said, 'It was an important decision to you, and may have been still more important to somebody with plans not quite so innocent; I mean its end result today.' "

"That's all he said?"

"Not quite all. He switched on a flashlight and sent its beam up over the front of the house. 'Eyes and memory, Jeff! Remember to use your eyes and memory!' Then away he stalked to his car as though it all ought to be clear."

Throngs of shoppers strolled or dawdled along Royal Street, where a carriage full of sightseers clopped at its leisurely pace. Nobody seemed in a hurry except Jeff, and Penny did her best to keep up with his long stride.

They passed jewelers, furriers, rather dusty shop-windows displaying antiques. On the south side of the thoroughfare rose a green-painted board fence, once the site of the demolished St. Louis Hotel, which now surrounded an automobile parking lot.

Moving thus along the northern banquette, Jeff counted house numbers growing higher, from the five hundreds to the six hundreds. Then the yellow stucco and elaborate ironwork of La Branche Building loomed up southwards . . .

When they crossed the intersection of St. Peter Street, the shop-front at the corner of Royal and St. Peter was that of a leather-goods merchant. Neither Jeff nor Penny had eyes for it. Just beyond, in garish hues of kilt and plaid, the tall wooden Highlander stood beside a window whose gilt lettering could now be read in full: *Bohemian Cigar Divan, by T. Godall.*

Ignoring pipes, cigars, and tobacco, Jeff stared at this sign.

"On Saturday night," he said, "I missed the proprietor's name. But that's no excuse, Penny! 'Bohemian Cigar Divan' should have told me."

Penny, hitherto all eager interest, now seemed merely bewildered.

"Speaking of being dense, Jeff, I'm afraid *I'm* it. What should the sign have told you?"

"Bohemia, once an independent kingdom and then part of the Austro-Hungarian Empire, since 1919 has been a province in the Republic of Czechoslovakia, which—"

"I still don't understand," Penny faltered, "but there's the year 1919 cropping up again! If that's what your uncle meant . . ."

"Whatever Uncle Gil meant, Penny, he couldn't have meant

177

that. The Bohemia of the sign bears no references to any real Bohemia that ever existed or ever will exist. Think, Penny! You read romances too!"

"I do have a hazy idea it ought to mean something, and yet it doesn't! Or are you just trying to be as oracular as your uncle?"

"No, my dear; you'll soon see. Let's go in."

A bell pinged over the door as he opened it.

" 'Small, but commodious and ornate,' " Jeff quoted, surveying the premises when he had followed her in. "Yes, Penny; it's a divan in the further Oxford Dictionary sense of smoking-room or cigar-shop. There's the sofa, which ought to be—and is!—of 'mouse-colored plush.' Originally this room must have been decorated not many years after old Commodore Hobart transplanted Delys Hall from England, and it's been kept in period ever since. The nerve of some people!"

Though he had been speaking only in a very low voice, he said no more. At the back of the shop a heavy baize curtain over a doorway was drawn aside. Into the room stepped a smallish, well-shaped, brown-haired girl of eighteen or nineteen, who halted behind the counter. Plainly but trimly dressed, she belonged to the present day as much as this cigar divan belonged to Victorian commercial elegance. Despite bright sun outside, the shop remained dusky.

"Yes, miss? Yes, sir? Can I help you?"

She smiled at Jeff, who returned the smile.

"*You're* not British, are you?" he asked.

"No; I was born here. I . . . Oh! You must want to see my grandfather, don't you? Just a moment, please."

Smiling again, she lifted the curtain and let it fall behind her. Faintly, afterwards, they could hear her speaking somewhere else. Then heavier footsteps approached.

Into the shop sauntered a stout, comfortable-seeming old gentleman with close-cut beard, moustache, and hair of iron gray. He had an easy manner and a knowing eye. His speech, in every intonation or turn of phrase, was that of the cultivated Briton. Taking up a position behind the counter, he addressed Jeff with great courtliness.

"Had you merely wished to make some purchase, sir, my grand-daughter could have served you. But, since Anne seemed to think my presence might be required . . . ?"

"I do in fact need cigarettes, if you stock cigarettes?"

Jeff named the brand and was supplied with it.

"However," Jeff continued, with a courtliness like that of the singular tobacconist, "your shop-sign so provoked my curiosity that I shall be glad of a word with its proprietor. I take it, sir, your name is not really Theophilus Godall, as these premises are not really in Rupert Street, Soho, for the reception of such customers as Messrs. Challoner and Somerset?"

"Your assumption is a just one," said the old gentleman, looking pleased. "I am called Everard, John Everard, as was my father before me. Those designations on the window," his gesture indicated them, "my late father adopted as a kind of trade name when he opened the business in '85. Perhaps you distrust whimsicalities, sir: a distrust your whole generation seems to share. But to me it seemed a harmless kind of deception, not undignified, which I have been pleased to continue and cherish. May I congratulate you on spotting the reference?"

"A literary reference, isn't it?" Penny cried out. "It's silly to feel I'm so very close to understanding that one little hint would probably tell me! The reference, surely, is to some book?"

"I will give you the broadest possible hint," Jeff answered, "by telling you the reference is to two books of stories by the same author, both published in the early eighteen-eighties, and both dealing with the same protagonist. This protagonist . . ."

"Shall we call him," suggested Mr. Everard, "less a protagonist than a kind of *deus ex machina* who sets all things right?"

"Thanks; that's a better definition," Jeff agreed. "This *deus ex machina*, Prince Florizel of Bohemia, was meant as a tongue-in-cheek, near-libellous skit on the then Prince of Wales, afterwards King Edward VII. At the beginning Prince Florizel, disguised, is roaming London with his aide, Colonel Geraldine. We meet him in an oyster bar off Leicester Square. He makes the acquaintance of the young man with cream tarts, and hears of an institution called the Suicide Club. The author of these stories . . ."

Penny's eyes were shining.

"Robert Louis Stevenson!" she exclaimed. "And the first book was *New Arabian Nights!* At the end of it Prince Florizel, for reasons never explained, has to abdicate and leave Bohemia. He returns to London, doesn't he?"

"He returns to London," supplied Jeff, "and sets up in business as Theophilus Godall of the Bohemian Cigar Divan, 'Godall' being short for Godalmighty. There the ex-prince serves as master of destinies behind another story collection, *The Dynamiter,* which Stevenson wrote in collaboration with his wife." Jeff broke off the summing up. "Mr. Everard, Miss Lynn," he added. "There's not much doubt about *you* being British, sir?"

"I am now an American citizen," returned that dignitary. "But I was born and brought up in England, where I had the pleasure of taking my degree at Cambridge before joining my father here in 1891. Come to think of it, sir," and he looked very hard at Jeff, "we need feel small surprise that you so instantly identified the work of an author no longer approved by those who prefer the savor of the dustbin. Several times, though not recently, I have seen your photograph in the press. You yourself, Mr. Caldwell, have made some reputation as a romancer in the grand tradition. You *are* Mr. Caldwell?"

"I am."

"And each of your historical novels contains some small element of mystery which is cleared up at the end?"

"Yes, that's so."

"Speaking of mystery," pursued the tobacconist, "we have near this city a house, Delys Hall, to which attaches more than a slight element of the mysterious. From somewhat confused accounts in the press yesterday, I gather, there has been another suspicious death."

"In the forty-five years between 1882 and 1927, Mr. Everard, there have been more than two deaths at Delys Hall. That would be true of any house you care to name."

"Ah," the other objected, "but how many *suspicious* deaths? In that regrettable affair twenty years ago, for instance, why should a cry have been heard *outside* the house some little time before the death occurred *inside?* Are you acquainted with the house, sir?"

"Well acquainted with it; I am staying there. But I fear I can't discuss—"

"Of course you can't; nor should I wish it. At the same time . . ."

Distantly, somewhere towards the rear of the premises, a telephone began to ring. The ringing was cut off; light footsteps hurried along what seemed to be a passage behind the curtained doorway. The girl called Anne pushed aside the curtain.

"If your name is Caldwell, Mr. Jeffrey Caldwell," she said to the right person, "you're wanted on the phone. Is it all right, Grandfather?"

"Indeed it is, my dear, nor must I complain if it interrupts a promising discussion. Follow the girl, sir; she will show you."

Jeff followed her along the passage into a cluttered sitting-room with one wall of books and two windows overlooking a weedy yard. He picked up the telephone from a book-strewn table under a letter rack stuffed with correspondence above the covered typewriter waiting to deal with it.

"You said you'd be there," the unmistakable voice of Gilbert Bethune reminded him. "I could only hope old Everard—or Florizel, or the Prince de Galles, whatever he cares to call himself—would keep you talking. Has he bewailed the decline in cigar-smoking, so that customers no longer sit on the couch to puff a choice regalia?"

"To puff a what?"

" 'Regalia,' Jeff, is the fancy term for a large cigar of good quality."

"He hasn't mentioned cigars. He wants to talk about the deaths at Delys Hall."

"Yes, he'd do that too. I'm at Delys Hall; I need a witness for support and sustenance. Better come back at once."

"Uncle Gil, has some other damned thing . . . ?"

"No, there have been no more fatalities or near-fatalities. It's Harry Minnoch. When he thinks he's right, there's no holding him; he's as stubborn as all his Scots forebears put together."

"Can't you control Minnoch?"

"I can control him officially. But we've had to chase more reporters away from here. My plans are dished if he drops an unguarded word before I'm ready. If Penny Lynn's still with you—Cato says she left in your company—bring her back here but don't let her into the house. What you'll find won't be pretty."

Having hung up the receiver and returned to the shop, Jeff had some difficulty in getting away. For all his blandness or courtesy, old Mr. Everard threw out conversational gambits as tenacious as the coils of an octopus.

"I had almost forgotten," he concluded, "that District Attorney Bethune is your uncle. Ah, well! If I can't detain you for discussion, then I can't. I will send Anne to the chemist's for a headache powder, and go on pondering according to my wont. A hearty good day to you both! As they say in the South, come back soon!"

In the street outside, with Penny on his arm, Jeff was surprised to see an empty taxi, which carried them back to University Place.

"You dragged me into Mr. Everard's," Penny commented on the way, "and now you've dragged me out again. That's all right; I don't mind being dragged. But you've got such an awfully odd, set look, as though you'd discovered a whole lot in there!"

"Maybe I have. On the steamboat, Penny, there was a debate with Saylor about the difference between British and American pronunciations of the same word. Didn't you ever note the difference between British and American words for the same thing? Our Stevensonian host said dustbin where you and I would have said garbage can. He said chemist's where you and I would have said drugstore."

"You mean old Mr. Everard said something peculiar or suspicious?"

"No, Penny. He didn't utter one peculiar or suspicious word; that's the point. I think I know what he would have said if he'd had occasion to say it."

"Are you going to explain *that?*"

"Not now, anyway. Since you haven't seen one blatant clue that was shown to me yesterday, it wouldn't mean much if I did explain."

"Where are we going after you've picked up the Stutz?"

"I'm driving you back to the Hall. But, on strict instructions from

Uncle Gil, you're not to go inside. He didn't tell me what's going on there, but he did say it's not pretty."

Penny made no further remark, and talked little on the return journey to Delys Hall. Though she seemed withdrawn into some remote world of her own, more than once the gray-blue eyes would turn towards him and disturb his judgment.

Late afternoon had almost become early evening when he stopped the car in the driveway so that she could get out. Penny climbed down, slammed the door of the car, and appealed to him.

"One request, please! If things in there aren't *quite* as bad as people seem to be afraid of, you *will* phone me?"

"You shall be the first to hear."

"Thanks, Jeff. I was just thinking . . ."

What she might have been thinking, to him the most welcome of all ideas, shone briefly, receptively in her eyes. Then she sought her own car and drove away.

After leaving the Stutz in the garage, Jeff tramped round to the front again.

'It's not quite dusk,' he said to himself, 'but dusk is so close you can feel it. At almost every dusky hour, it would seem, we get a new shock of some kind. So Lieutenant Minnoch's in a dither, is he? Has he put everybody else in a dither too?'

Evidently he hadn't. Cato, who opened the front door, seemed heavily puzzled rather than upset or in any way apprehensive, except on his own behalf.

"Been a heap o' comin' and goin', Mist' Jeff! Cain' say too much; mus'n' say too much; no, *sub!* "

Mr. Bethune, Cato more or less explained, would skin him if he said too much. After making some dread, uneasy reference to a furniture van—at least, it sounded like furniture van—he added that Mr. Bethune was in the library.

Once more the lamp with the yellow silk shade burned on the long table in that library. Again Uncle Gil's brief-case lay beside it. Uncle Gil himself, cigar in hand and eyebrows as Mephistophelian as ever, rose up from the carved chair at the far side.

"Mind telling me what this is all about?" Jeff greeted him. "And why must Cato go on about a furniture van?"

"Did he say what was in the furniture van?"

"No; he's too frightened of you to say anything."

Momentarily Uncle Gil had looked less like amiable, beardless Mephistopheles than like a Grand Inquisitor preparing to order torture. But some degree of amiability returned, and he sat down.

"That's just as well," he said. "At the same time, it's not Cato who gives me great concern now."

"It's Lieutenant Minnoch?"

"Yes. Our good lieutenant will be joining us at any moment. I have challenged him to state exactly what is on his mind . . ."

"It would be helpful if you did the same."

"Much of what is on my own mind," returned the District Attorney, "will be demonstrated as soon as I receive a phone call I have been expecting. Harry's demonstration is to be in full. 'And this, if I mistake not, is our client now.'"

Heavy footsteps could be heard descending the main staircase in the hall. Lieutenant Minnoch, trying hard not to look pleased with himself, strode through the minor drawing-room into the library. Gilbert Bethune took the cigar out of his mouth and balanced it on the edge of an ashtray.

"Well, Harry?"

"Before I say anything at all, sir, are you sure you want your nephew to hear it?"

"Yes; Jeff may remain."

"But you don't know what I'm gonna say!"

"Perhaps I can hazard a guess. You've got the murderer, haven't you? Got him all sewed up and ready for the law?"

"Oh, I've got the murderer! Whether there's enough evidence for an arrest right now—I don't know; maybe not; you're the judge o' that. But I do know who's guilty. I've been pretty sure since yesterday evening, and I'm certain sure today."

As though with ear alert for Cato or anyone else who might be moving in the house, Uncle Gil got up, closed the heavy door to the minor drawing-room, and returned to his chair.

Lieutenant Minnoch now sounded aggrieved.

"Whether we do or can make an arrest, sir, is up to you. If there's any justice in the world, though, we ought to. Honest, sir, do you think it's right for you to cross-examine me like a hostile witness?"

"I am *questioning* you, Lieutenant. Try to understand the meaning of cross-examination before you so badly misuse the word."

"Well, you know what I mean!"

"I am trying to be clear about your meaning. What worries you so much, Lieutenant Minnoch?"

The other spread out his hands.

"It's this young fellow Dave Hobart, sir. You like him, I know; but right from the start I haven't trusted him an inch. He killed his sister; he's lied every step of the way; he staged that fake attack on himself; and now I'm afraid he may get away with everything. He's as guilty as hell, Mr. Bethune! If you'd like me to show you what's real proof if not jury proof, I'm ready."

16

Breaking off, Lieutenant Minnoch looked very hard at the District Attorney.

"Any comment, sir?"

"Not before I've heard what you call real proof," said Uncle Gil, leaning back in his chair. "The floor is yours, my friend. Why not sit down and be comfortable?"

"If you don't mind, Mr. Bethune, I'll stay on my feet. And I'll do what you always do; I'll take it up point by point." The lieutenant nodded at Jeff. "Last Thursday night, on that journey down-river, your nephew kept asking me why I took such an interest in their group, specially in Dave Hobart and his sister. Did I suspect anybody, asks your nephew, of being concerned in a crime?"

"And you answered?"

"I answered, sir, that I hadn't said I suspected anybody of anything; leastways, I sort of qualified it, of anything that would ever get into court. And at the time, Mr. Bethune, that was God's truth."

"But you did suspect something?"

"Yes, sir, I did. We'd already had our attention directed to this house, and to the Hobart family, by that anonymous letter about Thaddeus Peters breaking his neck in 1910. By accident, see, Fred Bull and I landed on the same boat with the two Hobarts. So I had my eye on *anybody* of that name, and their friends too."

"You're not suggesting . . . ?"

"No, sir. I may lack subtlety, but I'm not a damn fool. I've never suggested or even thought Dave Hobart or his sister could have had anything to do with a death that happened seventeen years ago, when both of 'em were kids.

"But there was something very funny, and fishy too, about that situation on the steamboat. We'll take Dave Hobart, we'll take what he said, and I'll call your nephew as my witness to it. Fair enough, Mr. Caldwell?"

"Fair enough, I suppose," Jeff admitted.

Lieutenant Minnoch again addressed himself to Uncle Gil.

"Dave sneaked aboard that boat at Cincinnati, and persuaded Captain Josh Galway to keep quiet about it. But he soon changed his mind about hiding, or pretended to change his mind, after he'd had a little talk with your nephew on Monday night. He *pretended* he didn't know his sister was aboard, just as she pretended she didn't know he was there. But let's remember what he told Mr. Caldwell—what he confessed, you might say—that very first night on the river.

"He invited your nephew down to his stateroom on the texas, where he broke out a bottle of Scotch. Mr. Caldwell asked him what was the matter, why he was as jumpy as a cat and acting like a wanted criminal. Dave admitted there was a woman in his life; he did confess that much. He also said that, whenever he did what he oughtn't to do, his guilty conscience wouldn't give him any rest. And you could see . . ."

"Yes, Lieutenant," Jeff burst out, "now we can all see. *You* were the sinister figure lurking outside and listening!"

Minnoch came very near sputtering.

"I'm a lot of things, maybe," he declared, fist lifted for emphasis, "but my worst enemy couldn't call me sinister. I'll just remind you, young fellow, what happened in the middle of all this. In walked Miss Serena Hobart. Remember?"

"I remember."

"Immediately Dave, on the defensive, shouted out that he hadn't said one word of what mustn't be said. And she told him, with an odd kind o' glance between 'em, there was one matter that must never be touched on or even hinted at. Well, what did it mean? Who was the woman in his life? The law's got an ugly name for that kind o' business, and it's an ugly thing too."

"If you mean incest . . ." Uncle Gil began.

"Yes, I do mean incest," roared Lieutenant Minnoch. "Let's put the right name to what every experienced cop has seen for himself.

Just because we usually find it among poor nobodies from the slums is no reason why it can't happen among rich somebodies from the society news." He turned on Jeff. "When you went back up to your stateroom that Monday night which was Tuesday morning, you left those two together. Who's to say what they did through the rest o' the dark hours? Hell's fire, sir," and the lieutenant appealed to Uncle Gil, "won't you even admit the *possibility?*"

"Oh, I admit the possibility. Indeed, it was the first thing that occurred to me."

"It did, Mr. Bethune? Why?"

"Because I am a great reader of detective fiction; no other reason. Having admitted the possibility, which would naturally suggest itself to any follower of Sherlock Holmes, Father Brown, and Hercule Poirot, I am bound to say I don't believe a word of it."

"Neither do I," Jeff agreed instantly. "Lieutenant Minnoch could buttress his case by pointing out that Dave once referred to Serena as Iris March, the notoriously loose heroine of *The Green Hat*, though the lieutenant wasn't there and couldn't have heard Dave say it. All the same, there are sound reasons, not detective-story reasons at all, why the theory is most unlikely."

"May we hear those reasons?" asked Uncle Gil.

"If Dave had been carrying on any incestuous affair with Serena, I don't believe he'd have been so anxious to have me stay here at the Hall. Then there was her hasty flight from here on Friday night after the mysterious phone call, undoubtedly to meet this unknown lover in town. Dave stayed at the Hall, didn't he?"

"Did he really stay here, Mr. Caldwell?" Lieutenant Minnoch demanded. "He told you a lot of things, and hypnotized you into believing him; he's a very persuasive young gentleman. He'd already thrown dust in your eyes by suggesting an unknown lover so you wouldn't think of him as the man. There were still several cars in the garage Friday night. After he got some innocent confederate to make a prearranged phone call, he could have followed Miss Serena wherever she went. Did you see hide or hair of either of those two until you saw 'em again Saturday morning? Can you swear Dave didn't leave the house on Friday night?"

"He did leave the house on Friday night. But it was only to buy cigarettes at Rupert's Corners up the road."

"That's what he told you, was it?"

Uncle Gil's cigar had been gathering long ash on the edge of the tray. Gilbert Bethune trimmed off the ash, took two deep inhalations of smoke, and then crushed out the cigar.

"You have promised, Lieutenant," he said formally, "that you would produce evidence in your support. So far, whether you are right or wrong, we have heard theory and no more. Is there evidence?"

"You bet there's evidence, sir, and I'll line it up in just one minute! Before I do, though," and the stocky man bristled, "I'd like to ask your nephew a question. You, young fellow, just won't go along with the idea—the certainty, I'd call it—that Dave Hobart had been carryin' on with his own sister?"

"No, I won't go along with it."

"But he said there was a woman in his life, didn't he? You don't deny he said that, do you? All right! If the woman wasn't Serena Hobart, who in the name of sense could it 'a' been?"

"That's not easy to answer, I'm afraid. There's been Kate Keith, of course; it's no secret. But Dave has never taken her very seriously; she can't qualify as one who troubles the waters. What Dave meant, I think, is that there's a girl he'd like to be the woman in his life, but he's upset because she refuses to accept him as the man in hers."

"Oh? And who would that girl be?"

"Penny Lynn."

"Miss Lynn, eh? The beautiful little lady who *is* a lady?"

"Yes, Lieutenant. Dave's made more than one remark indicating that he's got Penny on the brain, and would go overboard for her if she'd give him any encouragement at all. But she won't. Apparently Penny's interested in—in somebody else. And Dave knows it. Late Friday afternoon he said nobody else had a chance with her as long as this other fellow is around."

"Would you mean yourself, by any chance?"

"I'm answering your questions, Mr. Minnoch; interpret the answers as you like. If you ask for my interpretation of Dave, I've told you. The woman in his life wouldn't *be* the woman in his life, which is what upset him."

"Ho!" roared Lieutenant Minnoch, so carried away that he teetered up on his toes as well as raising his fist. "Dave Hobart was upset, all right, though it was for a different reason. These Hobarts have always been a funny lot; that's no secret either. Don't ask a plain man like Harry Minnoch to sympathize with what's mortal sin in anybody's religion. But at least a plain man like Harry Minnoch can see through 'em."

"And so?" prompted Uncle Gil, studying the police officer through half-closed eyes.

"It's as plain as print, ain't it? Dave Hobart was upset because of what he'd been up to for some time with his own sister. But that flighty, smooth-tongued young gentleman just couldn't bear the hell he went through from his own guilty conscience. So he killed his guilty partner in hopes he'd get rid o' the burden, like other men have done before him in cases I can quote from the record.

"He killed her so sneakily, you can call it cleverly too, that if he'd left it at that we might never 'a' proved anything against him. We might 'a' suspected and did suspect; we couldn't 'a' proved. But would he leave well enough alone? Oh, no! These clever guys never *can* let well enough alone. He had to put in extra touches; he had to make it look too good; he overreached himself, and we've got him."

Well launched, impassioned, Lieutenant Minnoch had allowed his words to become torrential as he addressed Uncle Gil.

"Harry," asked the District Attorney, "do I detect a note of triumph?"

"Maybe you do, sir. I hate to say I told you so; I hate to remind you he took you in. I knew *he* was in no danger; I knew he was the murderer. But, when you asked me to put a guard on him Saturday night, I obeyed the boss and left O'Bannion outside his door."

"You have already theorized, haven't you, that the attack late Sunday afternoon was a fake attack?"

"It's more than a theory, sir. He faked the whole attack; he told a pack of lies that oughtn't to 'a' deceived any babe in arms, let alone deceive you. I started to prove it before you and Mr. Caldwell yesterday afternoon, so I'll finish proving it now."

"This entails, no doubt, your attempted demonstration that no outsider could have entered the house by the side door, attacked Dave, and left by the same way?"

"That's part of it, yes; but it's just one part."

"Well?"

Now sure of himself, Harry Minnoch could afford to be indulgent.

"*Nobody* came in or went out, Mr. Bethune. Outside, as I showed you, only mud or water everywhere. No livin' soul, so help me, could 'a' gone up those stairs, crossed an uncarpeted passage, walloped his victim in the bedroom and got out again, all without one trace of mud and water on the floor, and without one sound heard by O'Bannion only a short distance away.

"Now what does Master Dave say to this? All he can say is that the alleged man with the blackjack wore no shoes. In Japan, maybe, they take off their shoes in the house, even when the weather outside's not first cousin to Noah's flood. But we don't do it in this country, sir, and I say Master Dave's story is a barefaced lie. If you still won't go all the way with me, I'll back it up with the evidence of the blackjack."

"Evidence of the blackjack?"

"I have here," said a triumphant officer, taking out his notebook, "the findings of our fingerprint man, who tested the blackjack found on the floor beside Dave Hobart."

"Yes?"

"There were *no* fingerprints on that blackjack, sir, no prints at all. Just some smudges that might 'a' meant it was handled with gloves, or wiped clean afterwards, or not properly handled at all." Lieutenant Minnoch flourished his notebook. "You were mighty sarcastic when I said the blackjack might tell us a lot by not telling us anything; you called it something-or-other paradox. But it was gospel truth just the same!"

Gilbert Bethune sat up straight.

"One moment, Harry. Is it your contention that Dave, wearing gloves, hit himself over the head for realism's sake? If so, what happened to the gloves afterwards? He was knocked out, you know. If he used the blackjack . . ."

"He didn't use the blackjack, sir; nobody used the blackjack! It

191

was only part of the fakery to mislead us. He had it ready in the pocket of his pajamas or dressing-gown, bein' careful not to touch it except through a fold of cloth."

"And then?"

"At the right time," Minnoch announced powerfully, "he let out a kind of cry, upset that table with the dishes, dropped the blackjack on the floor, and dived straight down on the floor to conk his own head for the injury. We can't get away from evidence, sir. I say that's how he did it, and I say we've got him!"

Through the silent house, despite a closed door between library and minor drawing-room, they could hear the distant ringing of the telephone. Not long afterwards a knock at the library door heralded the appearance of Cato, who said Mr. Bethune was wanted on the phone.

Uncle Gil, clearly awaiting this, strode away in haste. He did not remain long absent. After an interval of perhaps two or three minutes, during which Jeff and Lieutenant Minnoch stared at each other without speaking, the District Attorney returned at a springier step. Instructing Cato to turn on the lights in the study and leave, he again took up his position behind the library table.

"You look pleased, Mr. Bethune," Lieutenant Minnoch said in an accusing voice.

"I *am* pleased," acknowledged Uncle Gil. "A little of the mist begins to clear away."

"If you ask me, sir, it's all cleared away! I've built up a case against Dave Hobart, haven't I? Got any comments on that?"

"Indeed I have comments," Uncle Gil assured him with enthusiasm. "You are more than a zealous police officer, Harry. You are also a not inconsiderable poet."

"Poet?" exclaimed the other, as though he had been called a jabberwock or a hippogriff.

"I mean what I say. This romantic tale you have spun for us ..."

"*Romantic*, for the luvva Pete?"

"Distinctly romantic. Romance, by one definition, is a narrative in prose or sometimes verse with scenes, incidents, and love affair remote from everyday life. You have done it, my friend; your reconstruction fulfills every need. Furthermore, if you had not so often assured me to the contrary, I should suspect you of being a secret reader of detective fiction."

"Sir—"

"In murder stories, almost invariably, any character attacked without being killed will be the guilty wretch who has contrived this injury as part of his own plot. You score there too, with a sweep of imagination which—"

Lieutenant Minnoch squared himself.

"Look, sir, I'm begging you! Say what you want to say; say what you've got to say; just don't *orate* at me. Since you think I went wrong, where did I go wrong? Is there any question I can't answer?"

"Yes, there is. If Dave Hobart killed his sister, how did he kill her?"

"Well . . ."

"You yourself have doubts, I think. This romantic fantasy, with strange love affair as well as Jacobean guilt motive, lacks a central pivot. Since the door was bolted on the inside and the windows are virtually inaccessible, how did the murderer get in and out of the bedroom? Until you can answer that question, Lieutenant, you can't take Dave Hobart to court; you can't charge him; you have no case at all."

"Well, sir, can *you* explain how the murderer did it?"

"I think I can. I believe I can name the murderer, who acted alone and had no accomplices guilty or innocent. My original notion as to the murderer's identity, which at first I distrusted as being wilder than yours, would appear to be backed by sound reason. Tomorrow, with luck, I should have incontestable proof." Uncle Gil lifted his shoulders. "Meanwhile . . ."

"Meanwhile?" prompted Jeff.

Gilbert Bethune took another cigar from his vest pocket, bit off the end, and lighted it.

"It is now time," he said, "to read half the riddle: what might be called the harmless half, though something of a shock if you don't know what's coming. The recent phone call, which pleased me so much, did not come from my office. It came from a certain firm or company at Algiers over the river; I needed expert help of a certain

193

kind, as tomorrow I shall need expert help of a different kind; and they provided it.

"In leading up to the explanation of the harmless half, Lieutenant, I will call my nephew to witness as you called him. During the journey downriver, Jeff, you observed that both Dave *and* Serena Hobart suffered badly from nerves. They had a weight on their minds; they were both upset. What caused this?"

"Don't ask me, Uncle Gil! I've tried so hard to answer that one that I'm almost convinced there's no answer."

"And yet there is an answer. We need not star-gaze for an incestuous affair between brother and sister. What did *both* of them fear?"

"Well, what did both of them fear?"

"They feared they would lose Delys Hall," replied Uncle Gil, "though they had no wish to lose it. Serena told you too often and too vehemently she wanted to get rid of the place. Penny Lynn doubted this, and Dave later acknowledged that Serena was as fond of this home as he still is.

"But it seemed almost certain they would lose the Hall. Information grudgingly laid before you by Ira Rutledge in his office makes it clear that Harald Hobart had in fact dissipated most of the family fortune. If they had some few assets left, the only real, thumping asset that remained was the Hall itself. And to keep their heads above water they must sell to Mr. Merriman of St. Louis. Unless . . ."

"You know, sir," Lieutenant Minnoch struck in, "I've got to admit that does make sense. But I don't get it; I don't see where this leads. They'd have to face the losses and sell out, unless . . . unless what?"

"Unless," Jeff suddenly exclaimed, as he saw, "they could find Commodore Hobart's hidden gold? A weight of bullion worth three hundred thousand dollars would relieve any future anxieties and allow them to keep the Hall too."

"But they didn't find the gold?" demanded Lieutenant Minnoch. "Is that it?"

"They did not find the gold," Uncle Gil conceded. "Under such tragic circumstances, good friends, it's hardly a pleasure to tell you I have found it."

Two voices cried, *"Where?"* Gilbert Bethune, holding himself in, blew a leisurely smoke ring and watched it dissolve.

"Let us see," he continued, "what we can make of some cryptic hints left by an ingenious-minded old gentleman who himself would have been devoted to detective fiction if it had then grown as sophisticated as it has become today.

"He found that gold in the summer of 1860, fully twenty-two years before he imported this house. Where could he have kept it, during that interval as well as afterwards, so as to have aroused no suspicion at all?

"With regard to the gold, remember his own comments. 'It's here,' he told his son. 'It's not buried; in one way it's not even concealed. It's in plain sight, when you know how to look for it.' Then again, carefully written, 'Distrust the surface; surfaces can be very misleading, especially from that workshop. See Matthew VII, 7.' Well, what particular workshop? The biblical quotation is from the Sermon on the Mount. Who but a— Well, never mind. Yesterday, wondering what surface ought to be distrusted, somebody asked whether the surface would be brick, stone, or wood. When I replied that it might be none of them, my own nephew seemed to doubt my sanity. But I was quite sane as well as quite serious. What surface, and from what workshop?"

Minnoch stared at him.

"Has all this got a point, sir?"

"It has. Come with me, both of you, and I will show you."

"Come where, Mr. Bethune?"

"Into the study, please."

Jeff swung round. The door to the billiard-room, to the gunroom, and to the study stood wide open. Though the first two rooms remained dark, a broad yellow path lay along that vista from the lights Cato had switched on in the study several minutes ago.

Uncle Gil led the way, with the other two following at his heels. Gilbert Bethune walked very slowly, talking over his shoulder as he traversed billiard-room and gunroom.

"Some time ago, as Jeff can testify, I asked Ira Rutledge some questions which (for once) that legal luminary readily answered. I was not concerned, I said, with the present financial holdings of the Hobart family."

"Are you telling us, sir," Minnoch threw at him, "their present finances don't matter?"

"For my particular purpose, they don't matter at all. But what had been their holdings in the past: the long past, when Commodore Hobart was still a young man? Had they any financial interest in state or local industry?"

"And that helped?"

"Indeed it helped. Among other sources of income, Ira responded, they had held an almost controlling interest in the Vulcan Ironworks at Shreveport, once the largest in the South after Tredegar at Richmond."

Crossing the threshold of the study, with Jeff and Minnoch immediately behind him, Uncle Gil stepped to one side and made a flourishing gesture with his cigar.

"Now tell me!" he said. "Does this room look the same as it did yesterday, or is there something different about it today?"

Three lamps, the central table lamp and both floor lamps, shed soft illumination over that nineteenth-century study of leather chairs and sporting prints. Jeff did not have to look far. When his eyes sought the room's far left-hand corner, he could only stare.

"Look, sir," Minnoch burst out, "aren't you going to show us where the treasure is?"

"I am going to show you where the treasure *was*," returned Uncle Gil. "But neither of you has yet answered my question. Is there anything different about this room?"

Jeff had to restrain himself from jumping or dancing.

"The safe!" he cried. "That iron safe in the far left-hand corner. It's not there at all; it's gone!"

"It is gone, Jeff, because it was removed this afternoon by the Fitzroy Scrap Metal Company of Algiers. One of their own trucks being unavailable, they shifted it with some effort and transported it in a borrowed furniture van. In the absence of the safe, will you kindly describe it for us? Particularly the front, and any letters or lettering you remember seeing there?"

"Old, very old, blackish and dingy-looking! Across the front, above the door with the combination-dial, it had Fitzhugh Hobart's name in faded gilt. Underneath that, for no reason I could see, it

DEADLY HALL

had the Roman numeral of V for 5, also in gilt."

"What looked like the Roman numeral for 5," said Uncle Gil, "was in fact the letter V for Vulcan, always the trade-mark of the firm which cast that safe late in the year 1860.

"The misleading surface, gentlemen, was not brick or stone or wood; it was iron. Not long ago I had the telephoned report of the Fitzroy foreman who made certain tests. Under a thin sheathing of iron, apart from an honest combination-dial and single shelf of base metal, the entire safe is made of gold; it was cast in gold and then covered."

Gilbert Bethune pointed with the cigar.

"You see, good friends, you have looked everywhere except in the right direction. You sought a missing ledger inside the safe, and never once stopped to think of the safe itself. It was almost too obvious to be seen. That safe does not hold the secret of the commodore's hidden gold; it *is* the commodore's missing gold, and has been for almost seventy years."

197

17

During the long pause that followed, Jeff could distantly hear faint rumblings across the sky. No doubt a brief spring thunderstorm, so characteristic of this uncertain climate, lurked there on its approach to town. Jeff studied the corner where Commodore Hobart's safe had stood.

"Let's acknowledge," he ventured, "that the commodore was an even craftier old schemer than anybody anticipated. Wherever he lived, he could take his treasure along unquestioned. The reason for a safe in any man's study seems evident; we don't have to explain it, and neither does the owner. When did you tumble to this trick, Uncle Gil?"

"Not long ago," Uncle Gil looked rueful, "and perhaps I should apologize. If I had bent my slow wits to the problem of the gold as soon as I learned that our Hobart family controlled the Vulcan Ironworks, instead of shelving it for future consideration as fallible humanity will do—"

" 'Slow' wits, eh?" exclaimed Lieutenant Minnoch, staring at him. " 'Slow' wits, for Pete's sake? Anybody who calls *that* slow-witted, sir, has got some kind of a leak in his own judgment to start with!"

"And yet had I acted sooner, it must be plain, Serena Hobart might still be alive. You see that, don't you?"

"Frankly, Uncle Gil," Jeff returned, "I don't think either of us sees anything at all. Finding the gold, you've said, is only half our problem, the harmless half. To get all the answers, to explain the half that's anything but harmless, we must learn who killed Serena and how the murderer got at her. You say you can explain that too?"

"I think so; I hope so."

"Was it done, for instance, by another ingenious trick like the trick of the gold safe?"

"By a trick of much the same sort, at least."

"Deriving its inspiration from the same source?"

Gilbert Bethune studied the cigar.

"If you ask whether long-defunct Commodore Hobart had anything to do with his granddaughter's murder, even in the sense of inspiring the person who killed her, my answer is a most thunderous 'No.' On the other hand—"

"As a practical man, sir," said Lieutenant Minnoch, "I've got a question for you. Whoever the murderer is, and however he did it (if you won't tell me, all right; you won't!), just what the hell do we do now?"

"Also as a practical man, Lieutenant, I reply that we lay plans to trap the murderer. Somebody, before all our eyes, has been leading a double life. Already, with still another phone call, I have received some desired information. A certain pursuit, as I suspected, is practised in fall, winter, and the edge of spring, but never in summer. Finally, if we can call in the expert advice I hope for, we may end our quarry's evil doing by this time tomorrow. Meanwhile, Lieutenant, can you by any chance be persuaded of my belief that Dave Hobart is completely innocent?"

"It don't come easy, Mr. Bethune; I admit it don't come easy. I was dead set on that young fellow bein' as guilty as Old Nick; I went all out to nail him, and thought I had. Still! You proved your point about the old commodore's safe; you've been right before this, and I'll go along. If you say Dave wasn't even mixed up in the funny business, that's good enough for me."

"Good!" beamed Uncle Gil. "Dave is in the house now, remember; up in his room, I think. When Jeff saw him yesterday morning, if memory serves, he said he hadn't been entirely frank with us. But Dave promised to be frank. If I have a word with him now, perhaps I can clear up one or two still doubtful points. When you see him, Lieutenant, will you be tactful? You won't let him know you had such strong suspicions of incest, murder, or anything else?"

Minnoch, drawing a deep breath, slapped at the sleeves of his coat as though dismissing all care.

"I'm no fool, sir, but I can *play* dumb with the best of 'em. Sometimes I think I could 'a' gone on the stage and got away with it; you trust me! As for Dave Hobart, if he's not guilty then he's all right. Once they haul that load o' gold back here, and I reckon you've made certain they'll haul it back . . ."

"Oh, yes; I have made certain of that."

"Then he's sho' nuff in good shape and ought to thank you. He *bas* come into a fortune after all!"

Once more Uncle Gil had turned, and was striding away towards the library with the other two after him. Again he spoke over his shoulder as he traversed intervening rooms.

"The question, of course, is whether Dave will admit—or can admit—he has come into possession of his grandfather's treasure. That gold was illegally removed from British territory without being declared to the proper authorities. At so late a date the British authorities, or any authorities, would have a hard job in proving that sunken gold from the Ambrogian Reefs became a gold safe in Commodore Hobart's study. It would present legal headaches fortunately of no concern either to the police or to my own office.

"A very vicious murderer, being aware of Dave's own weak heart, thought a blow from a blackjack would kill him. We need not worry about the lack of fingerprints on the weapon; somebody took the simple precaution of wearing gloves. Our own job, since we agree on Dave's innocence, is to make sure the same murderer does not try again. The motive for these crimes . . ."

Reaching the library, Uncle Gil paused only long enough to extinguish his cigar in the ashtray on the table. Then he made for the door to the minor drawing-room, still closed as Cato had left it on departing. Gilbert Bethune had just opened it when Jeff spoke.

"Yes, the motive!" he said. "Somebody killed Serena and tried to kill Dave. But with what possible motive? The only ones who stand to profit by killing Dave and Serena are either myself, definitely not guilty, or a quiet Boston cleric already very wealthy in his own right. The motive can't be gain, can it?"

"That would seem most unlikely, let's agree. And yet, if we examine the evidence with care, we may see traces of some motive other than financial gain."

"Uncle Gil, there's one fair question you've completely dodged! In your opinion, was Serena murdered by the secret lover both Dave and Penny think she had?"

"In my opinion, she was."

"Then are you suggesting some personal or emotional motive? That Serena tired of the lover, or that the lover tired of Serena, and in either event decided to get rid of her? If so, why try to kill Dave?"

"Tut!" Uncle Gil clucked his tongue. "I am suggesting no personal or emotional motive of the sort you mean. A certain person we have all met obviously covets something which would be attainable only after two deaths. You see, Jeff—"

A short peal from the front doorbell was followed by a longer peal which seemed to cry alarm through the house. Gilbert Bethune, his hand on the knob of the open door to the minor drawing-room, roused from whatever thoughts occupied him.

"That doorbell, as heretofore noted," he said, "has a very penetrating ring. How does it work, I wonder?"

Dave Hobart's voice answered him from the hall beyond. Footsteps could be heard descending the main staircase. Dave, fully dressed, still rather pale but with much of his old bounce, turned to face them as Uncle Gil, Jeff, and Lieutenant Minnoch trooped through into the hall, where every light now burned.

"The doorbell, as it always has," Dave replied, "works off three ordinary dry-cell batteries which Cato replaces whenever necessary." He gestured at that faithful servitor, who was moving towards the front door. "Just a moment, noble Roman! I'll see to the visitor."

Cato drew back. Dave went to the door and rather dramatically threw it open.

Lightning flickered against the dark landscape; distant thunder rolled low along the sky. In the drive shone the headlamps of a taxi. But just outside stood nobody more alarming than Mr. Charles Saylor, large and untidy and sandy-haired, in another plus-four suit.

"Chuck Saylor, eh?" Dave greeted him. "So it's you at last, is it?"

"Look, Dave!" began the other, uncertain but determined. "I've kept away, you know; I haven't intruded until now, have I? This God-awful business about Serena: it's upset me almost as much as it must have upset you. Mind if I come in and say how sorry I am?"

Dave hesitated. Easy and urbane again, Uncle Gil strolled up beside him.

"If you don't mind, Dave," he said, "the law itself claims first call on your attention at this moment. Your guest here . . ."

"Chuck," blurted Dave, "this is Mr. Bethune, Jeff Caldwell's uncle. He's also District Attorney Bethune, so watch your step. Mr. Saylor, Mr. Bethune."

"There's Jeff himself," Saylor cried, "and also, unless these eyes deceive me, the police lieutenant who's already been on my trail. You didn't want to see *me*, did you?"

"As a matter of fact, Mr. Saylor, we do," Uncle Gil assured him. "We think you can help us a good deal. At this juncture, however, our business is solely with Dave. Could you manage to call at my office tomorrow morning? Ten o'clock, say? You'll find me at City Hall, which is . . ."

"Oh, I know where it is. Yes, I'll be there. All right, then!" Saylor's manner suddenly became sulky and pettish, as though he might fly into a tantrum. And he swung round towards the waiting taxi. "Hang on, Johnsy!" he bawled at its driver. "Nobody here seems to want me around, so you can just drive me back to town."

When he had gone, and the door closed, Dave turned to Uncle Gil.

"On the level, sir, do you really have business with me? You made it sound like an important conference."

"It *is* an important conference, Dave, in more senses than one. I have good news for you. And you, I hope, will have enlightening news for me. This way."

Taking Dave's arm, he led that apprehensive young man into the minor drawing-room, with Jeff and Minnoch still following. When they reached the library, Uncle Gil spoke pointedly to the last-named two.

"Try to occupy yourselves here for the next fifteen or twenty

202

minutes," he advised. "It's best, I think, that I should see Dave alone in the study."

"Like the headmaster," suggested Dave, "with a hell-raising sixth former?"

"You are a *little* old for the sixth form, Dave, and I wish you had behaved as such. But your sins are pardonable; I will try not to be too severe. Follow me, please."

They trailed through billiard-room and gunroom to the study, where Gilbert Bethune closed the door.

Harry Minnoch and Jeff Caldwell, who had nothing whatever to say to each other, did not even try to communicate. The lieutenant, pondering, perched on the edge of the library table and muttered to himself. Jeff wandered past the bookshelves, taking down an odd volume or two at random. But *The Art of Heraldry* failed to hold his interest; so did *Sermons from a Sussex Parish;* he replaced both.

Few distinguishable words could be heard in the mutter of voices from beyond the study door. Once, when Dave uttered an exclamation, Jeff did make out audible syllables. But since these syllables consisted only of a hearty blasphemy, he learned very little. The conference seemed to take a long time. It was much more than fifteen or twenty minutes, Jeff decided, before Uncle Gil returned alone, looking satisfied.

"Well?" Jeff asked him. "Your deductions were right, were they?"

"They were almost more accurate than I could have hoped for."

"What about Dave?"

"Dave wants to be left to himself for a little while, so that he can think. After all, he has much to think about."

"Did you tell him you found the gold?"

"Yes, of course. That's the point he most wants to consider. If he can't yet make up his mind about it, he's hardly to be blamed. As for ourselves," Uncle Gil consulted his watch, "it's past seven o'clock and time we adjourned for dinner. Before we break up our present proceedings, however, I should like to show you something I failed to show you on a Saturday night that had become Sunday morning. Ready?"

Shepherding the other two before him, he directed them out into the main hall, up the stairs, and along the upper hall to Serena's bedroom at the front.

Here he switched on several lamps. The room had been completely tidied up: furniture rearranged, clothes put away. No trace of fingerprint powder remained on any surface. Apart from the damaged door, it looked much as it must have looked at any time before violence erupted.

Uncle Gil surveyed the result.

"In this room, on the night we first examined it, I propounded many queries. I asked, among other things, what Serena was doing here and why she bolted the door. Eventually, as we were leaving, I asked in what way Serena's death resembled the death of Thad Peters nearly seventeen years ago. Interpret correctly the exhibit I am about to put in evidence, and you will have a corporate answer to all those queries at once."

As though on a wire of nerves, the District Attorney went to the very deep cupboard which had been built out along the side of the bathroom against the southwestern wall. He opened the cupboard door.

Once more, as light penetrated the cupboard, Jeff could see the array of dresses, gowns, and coats depending from hangers at either side. Nearest at hand, on the left, he could see the dressing-gown of dark-blue quilted silk, which, when Uncle Gil had held it out to them, was smudged with dust along the right sleeve and the back. Nearest at hand, on the right, he could see the black silk house-coat with gold embroidery, smudged in much the same way. From the floor on the right rose a bank of closed drawers. On the floor to the left stretched a row of shoes and slippers.

"But—!" Jeff began, but checked himself.

"There was disagreement among witnesses, remember," Uncle Gil pointed out, "about what Serena had been wearing over her pajamas. Dave Hobart and Isaac, the chauffeur, said it was that dressing-gown, so dark a blue as to seem almost black. Cato, on the other hand, said it was the house-coat. I remarked to you that it might have been either. 'Or else—' I added, stifling the suggestion that had come to me. What I meant was that, for obvious reasons, it was probably neither one."

"Obvious reasons?" Lieutenant Minnoch echoed blankly.

"Yes, very obvious. Now see what she actually wore."

Gilbert Bethune, hunching his shoulders, moved into the cupboard, bent down, and pulled open the lowest drawer of the bank on the right. From this drawer he drew out, and held up for his companions' inspection, a woman's sweater of knitted wool, black in color, rumpled and heavily dust-stained. From the sweater's left-hand pocket, where they had been hastily stuffed away, he produced a pair of dark-brown cotton gloves, also dust-stained.

"Well?" prompted Uncle Gil.

The approaching storm had taken several strides nearer. Though all window-lights were now closed, they could hear the wind become a roar and hear the peal of thunder that followed a vivid lightning-flash.

Lieutenant Minnoch, as though half out of his wits, could only point at the sweater Uncle Gil was still holding up.

"That's what she did wear, is it?"

"Yes, Harry. Dave Hobart now admits she did. For he began to get a glimmering of what Serena had been up to on Saturday night. And, though he couldn't guess the details, it frightened him so badly that to conceal everything he hid the sweater in that drawer and told a lie about what she had worn."

Replacing the gloves in the sweater's pocket, Uncle Gil put it back in the drawer, closed the drawer, and stepped out of the cupboard to join them.

"Look, sir!" Minnoch said in desperation. "You mean she was wearing the gloves as well as the sweater? And, when Dave took the sweater off her, he took off her gloves and shoved 'em in the pocket?"

"No, not at all," Uncle Gil replied with great clarity. "Serena herself had removed the gloves at an earlier time. Kindly don't ask me how I know that; the reason should be apparent."

His Mephistophelian face now looking as pleased as it seemed wicked, Gilbert Bethune drew himself up.

"Well!" he added. "You have both seen the sweater and the gloves; you have marked their condition. Does either of you, like Dave, begin to have some notion of what Serena must have been up to? If you haven't any answers for me, have you some queries of your own? Harry?"

"Reckon I pass, sir."

"Jeff?"

"I have two questions, Uncle Gil," Jeff told him. "One of them is so very pertinent that you'll probably fob me off with more cryptic hints. The other question, which deals with the only aspect of this business I think I do understand, at first glance seems so irrelevant and inconsequential that I hesitate to ask at all."

"By all the saints and sinners," thundered Uncle Gil, "don't be daunted or put off by any seeming irrelevancy! Let's have both questions, if you will. And *begin* with the apparently inconsequential, which is an approach after my own heart."

"Yes; nobody could deny that. But, since I've been out of local circulation for eight years, I'm compelled to ask. Is old John Everard, the philosophical tobacconist of 701b Royal Street, a well-known character in New Orleans?"

Uncle Gil made a flourishing gesture.

"Yes, Jeff. To those who pride themselves on their literacy, at least, he has become a very well-known character indeed. John Everard is an asker of questions, a dabbler at curious problems, forever active with tongue or pen. If I had remembered that from the start, instead of being distracted by extraneous matters, I should have been spared much unnecessary wonder. Now, then! What's your very pertinent question?"

"You keep suggesting," Jeff flung at him, "that there's evidence for everything on every side. You do definitely say Serena's secret lover is also her murderer. It's the identity of this secret lover which has been driving me round the bend!" Now it was Jeff who shook his fist. "If there's evidence of the secret lover's identity, who provided that evidence?"

"Serena herself."

"Serena?"

"Oh, indubitably. Jeff, how do you take your tea?"

"What?"

"When someone offers you tea, how do you drink it? With milk and sugar, or with lemon?"

206

"With a little milk but no sugar, and never lemon. Didn't I tell you, Uncle Gil? We're back at cryptic hints again!"

Gilbert Bethune looked stern.

"It is no hint, cryptic or otherwise; it is the clue that should tell you. If you will just stop vilifying your saintly uncle and think back for a moment, you are sure to see the connection."

"Well, I don't see it. Who *is* this unknown lover?" Jeff yelled. "Who in Satan's name *is* it? The self-assured Serena lost her heart and her head, did she? She lost 'em to some bastard who's been lurking behind the scenes all the time?"

"A bastard in the vulgar sense of the term, no doubt. But not unknown, Jeff, and certainly not lurking behind the scenes. The person in question . . ."

Jeff experienced a kind of psychic fit.

"I've got a feeling, rightly or wrongly," he said, "that we haven't yet finished with unpleasantness. There's an ambush ahead; some damned thing or other lurks in it. Maybe you're waiting to spring on your quarry, Uncle Gil, but so is the enemy. When he does show his hand . . ."

Every window went white with lightning; thunder smote hard and close; still the storm would not break. Since the broken door still hung drunkenly open, they heard the clear ringing of the doorbell.

Footsteps, too light and quick to be Cato's, hurried over stone towards the front door. There was a rush of wind as the door opened.

"Penny!" exclaimed the voice of Dave Hobart, instinctively raised.

A low-pitched female voice said something indistinguishable. Dave's reply was equally indistinguishable until Dave raised his voice again.

"Yes, he's here. —Cato!"

"Suh?"

"They're all up in Serena's room, probably. Will you ask Mr. Jeff if he'll come down here and see a friend of his?"

Jeff waited no longer.

Hastening out into the upper hall, he made for the head of the stairs. Cato, on the way up, saw him descending and turned back. Dave's voice continued.

"What do you mean, you can't stay? Come on in, Penny! Come on in and take off that slicker!"

Penny, in a hooded yellow waterproof, was edging round the left-hand side of the doorway, whose door stood wide open. Dave, his left hand extended, had turned in that direction and stood almost in profile against the tumultuous night outside.

A small flame-spit from that tumultuous night was followed by what could only have been the report of a firearm. Two more flame-spits, two more blurred reports, whacked out of nowhere as Jeff neared the foot of the stairs.

Dave had not retreated; he did not even try to close the door. Lightning-dazzle briefly illuminated terrace and drive. An enormous crash of thunder, exploding above Delys Hall, split in tumbling echoes down the sky. As the skies opened and the rain tore down, Lieutenant Harry Minnoch plunged past Jeff and raced out into the deluge, shouting orders at somebody.

Penny Lynn cringed away. Dave Hobart closed the front door. Jeff Caldwell stood staring at the gouge made by three bullets which, missing Dave by inches, had lodged in the newel post on Jeff's right.

"Well, well!" he said to nobody in particular. "I seem to have made an accurate prophecy for once."

18

"You made an accurate prophecy, all right!" Saylor declared on the following afternoon. "How did it turn out, though? This joker who fired the shots, I gather, was in a car of some kind. The whole place was lousy with cops, and they chased him. But they lost him in traffic out on the main road, and didn't even pipe the car's number. Is that a fair summary?"

"It's an accurate summary," conceded Jeff, "without being strictly fair. The attack took 'em off balance; it took everybody off balance. Though they anticipated some move against Dave, they didn't expect him to be treated like a duck in a shooting gallery. Now that we've told you our side of it . . ."

Four persons—Saylor himself, Jeff, Dave, and Penny—sat over the remains of lunch at Henri's Restaurant, Toulouse Street just off Bourbon Street, towards three P.M., on Tuesday, April 26th. In the sedate central room at Henri's, with its dark-red wallpaper and its unhurrying waiters, Jeff found his mind toiling back over the events of last night.

Three bullets had been dug out of the newel post. Only Gilbert Bethune seemed untouched by the attendant confusion or chaos. At the height of the confusion Saylor, having evidently arrived back in town, had phoned with urgency.

Would Dave and Jeff, he had begged, have lunch with him tomorrow at Henri's? He knew Dave was in mourning; but, since Saylor might have something very important to communicate, would both of them accept? When Dave conveyed this message to Jeff, the latter at first had replied that he couldn't make it because he had invited Penny to lunch on the same day.

Though he had issued no such invitation, Penny's look showed her willingness. Whereupon Saylor had urged that they *all* join him, stressing the importance of what he might have to communicate.

And so it had been arranged. The question of Dave's mourning was settled that same evening, when Uncle Gil haled away the same three guests for dinner at *La Louisiane*, prolonging the meal until a fairly late hour.

"Do what you like tomorrow," he had said on parting, "but be sure you are all at Delys Hall by four o'clock in the afternoon. I am inviting a little party of interested persons. And we are preparing a surprise."

"What kind of surprise, Uncle Gil?"

"On the wall of some famous scientific rooms in London, honoring the achievements of Sir William Crookes, there used to be and perhaps still is a motto that reads, *'Ubi Crookes, ibi lux.'* When Sir William so earnestly espoused spiritualism, one would-be humorist suggested changing the motto to *'Ubi Crookes, ibi spooks.'* I also have hopes of shedding a *little* light."

"What's more, when we meet Saylor tomorrow," Dave had warned, "not a word about that gold being recovered! I've told Penny, but it mustn't go any further until I've made up my mind what to do. Agreed, Jeff?"

"Agreed. Do we also hide the fact that somebody shot at you from the drive?"

"We may not be able to hide it. So far they've pretty well kept the newspapers at bay; nothing's been published about this joker walloping me on the bean Sunday afternoon. Shots fired in public may belong to a different category."

They did belong to a different category. Mention of the shots, without factual elaboration but with every possible sensational hint, appeared in the press Tuesday morning. Saylor, meeting his guests at Henri's Restaurant, wore an air of great mystery and portentousness, like some Balkan diplomat at secret negotiations.

Their host ordered lavishly, but did not refer to the present until they sat over coffee. Then he called for some explanation of the shots, and Jeff told as much as seemed discreet.

"What about the gun?" Saylor instantly demanded.

"No gun turned up," answered Jeff, "but the three slugs they dug out of the newel post were .38 pistol bullets. —Now that we've told you our side of it," he repeated, "why not tell us yours?"

"*My* side?"

"Look!" said Dave, fiddling with silverware. "Mr. Bethune wanted to see you this morning, and there can't be much doubt you went. Well, what did he want to see you about?"

"Ah! That's part of the problem, isn't it?"

"One of these days, sooner or later," Jeff observed broadly, "some straight question is going to get a straight answer. Even my esteemed uncle has begun to loosen up. Why can't our esteemed magazine writer loosen up too?"

"Oh?"

Jeff caught and held Saylor's eye.

"As you yourself remarked at the front door yesterday evening," he continued, "Detective Lieutenant Minnoch has been on your trail since Sunday. At the Jung Hotel he found that on Saturday night you'd asked your way to the pier of the Grand Bayou Line. Uncle Gil said you were probably in search of Captain Josh Galway, and that something in the evidence indicated you must have been in search of him.

"Well, that's just what you'd done. Saturday night, at first not finding Captain Josh aboard the *Bayou Queen,* you sat down and talked with the purser. Then Captain Josh turned up, so you went into very hush-hush conference with him. Later both you and the captain said you hadn't talked about anything important. But Harry Minnoch wouldn't buy that explanation, and neither will my uncle. What *did* you and the captain talk about?"

Impressively Saylor rose to his feet.

"Since District Attorney Bethune has been playing detective," he commented, "it might have occurred to him that I was playing detective too."

"It has occurred to him, as I've just explained. Now don't confine your answers to sibylline comments like, 'Oh!' and 'Ah!' On what subject *were* you questioning Captain Josh Galway?"

Still on his feet, Saylor regarded them with an air of persuasive frankness.

"All right!" he said. "All right! I never intended to fool you or confuse you or sound like the Delphic oracle; I meant to speak my piece when the time came. I've been leading up to it gradually, that's all.

"First, though, forget that hot air I talked aboard the steamboat: killer staircases, bodies in a secret hiding place, guff like that. It was only a little play of the imagination, and didn't mean a thing. I never really expected there'd *be* a crime, still less any danger to Serena Hobart.

"But I wasn't very bright, it must be confessed. There were several little things I ought to have noticed last week. And yet we'd reached New Orleans before I suddenly realized what they meant, what they had to mean. Didn't it ever strike you that somebody in our party on the *Bayou Queen* was behaving rather strangely?"

Penny Lynn spoke for the first time in many minutes.

"Oh, now—!" she began in a voice of protest.

Facing Jeff across the table, Penny wore the same costume—orange-colored sweater, skirt of light-brown tweed—she had worn after their strange reunion on Tuesday just a week ago. There was another similarity too. In the turn of her eyes, in every shade of expression, Jeff could sense a return of that eagerly receptive mood which on him acted like strong drink. Through the skylight in the roof a stray beam of sunlight caught glints in yellow-brown hair.

"Do you object to something, Penny?" he asked. "If so, you've got every right to object. From one person after another we've heard little but vague talk about somebody behaving guiltily . . ."

Up went Saylor's forefinger, admonishing him.

"I didn't say 'guiltily,' remember!" Saylor corrected. "I didn't say 'guiltily' at all; I said 'strangely,' and I stick to it. The things I saw, and you saw too but didn't seem to notice, have nothing to do with anybody's guilt. They're not vague either; they fit together. I don't claim to be Old Sleuth himself, but they do fit together and they do start the explanation. They even explain why Captain Josh, as that boat docked, stamped past Serena groaning, 'How many of 'em? Dear God in heaven, how many of 'em?' "

212

"Mr. Saylor," Jeff queried, "how do you know Captain Josh said that? You weren't there when Serena heard him say it."

"Somebody told me afterwards, I guess. Anyway . . ."

"Anyway," interposed Dave, hammering on the table with the handle of a fork, "what difference does it make and why are we arguing? Somebody's behind this; somebody's guilty; that's the one we're after. You got us here because you said you had something very important to tell us, but we haven't heard it yet. What's the good of fancy talk if it proves innocence rather than guilt?"

Saylor teetered back and forth on his heels.

"Ah," he said wisely, "but relatively innocent behavior on the part of one person may lead straight to someone else who's actually guilty. Now I must correct *you*, Dave. I said I *might* have something very important to communicate. At that time I couldn't be more definite; I hadn't yet tested my ideas on District Attorney Bethune. But I've tested 'em and I'm sure. As a matter of fact, friends and guests, it was an innocent suggestion, innocently made, that showed me the direction in which we've got to look. Shall I tell you about it?"

"Well, at least," Dave almost yelled, "you might tell us *something*."

Few still lingered over lunch at Henri's; they had the big room almost to themselves. In leisurely fashion Saylor lighted a cigarette, blew out smoke, and stared into the middle distance.

"If I remember correctly," he addressed them all, "it was a week ago today, in the Old South Lounge of the *Bayou Queen*, that Dave told us he'd made a special trip north to see Malcolm Townsend, the investigator of old houses, and that Townsend had promised to be in New Orleans for the week-end."

"He's here," Dave assented. "We've seen him."

"I know; so have I." Saylor nursed the cigarette. "Towards the end of January, as it happens, I heard Townsend lecture in Philadelphia. When the lecture was over, I introduced myself and shook hands. So I know him by sight."

"Well?"

Their host looked still more portentous.

"On Sunday evening, all on my own and not knowing quite

what to do with myself, I decided to have dinner at the St. Charles Hotel. In the dining-room was Townsend, all on *his* own, having a meal with a book propped up in front of him.

"I'd promised not to pester you or your family, Dave; you can testify I've lived up to it. But in spite of all the tragic circumstances —sorry!—there was no reason why I shouldn't use my talent for questioning to pump somebody who might have information. So I went over; I said hello; I reminded him we'd met before. And he very hospitably invited me to sit down."

"What information did you get?" Dave asked quickly.

"About Delys Hall or the Hobart family, very little. He *hasn't* found any secret whatdyecallit, I gather . . ."

Resisting the temptation to interject, "No, *he* hasn't found it," Jeff cursed himself and kept quiet.

"As regards anything you or I would call significant," Saylor went on, "Townsend was as close-mouthed as Silent Cal. He's protecting Hobart interests, Dave; he likes you; he's only stayed on here because you asked him to. But, about any place other than Delys Hall, he'll talk a blue streak. Old houses aren't his only hobby. He's enthusiastic about a secondary hobby, and wants to write a book on that too, only his publisher discourages him."

"And what's this other hobby?" queried Dave.

"Disguise."

"Disguise?"

"Some people, Townsend swears, can make 'emselves completely unrecognizable without any mummery of wig or dyed complexion or false beard. As a younger man, you see, he became interested in the late Sir Herbert Tree, the actor, famous even offstage for being able to change his whole appearance and personality.

" 'I myself couldn't do it,' Townsend said. 'Probably you couldn't do it either. But I've met more than one person who with the simplest effects, plus acting ability, could deceive anybody except a close friend. Sometimes merely changing the hair style, together with putting on or taking off glasses, can work a surprising alteration.' And that's where *I* got *my* great idea!"

"Is it your suggestion, as it's Uncle Gil's," Jeff demanded, "that somebody in this affair has been leading a double life?"

Saylor stared back at him.

"What if I suggested, Jeff, that the guilty party is somebody we haven't even met so far? What would you call that?"

"Frankly, I should call it a damned poor detective story."

"Who's talking about detective stories?"

"Everybody, and my uncle in particular."

Dave, fuming, could not sit still.

"Whether real life does or does not follow detective stories, Chuck, this endless monologue of yours hasn't told us one damned thing! Haven't you led up to the revelation long enough? If you've got something important to communicate, why can't you just communicate it?"

"I intend to, Dave, as soon as we've had the entertainment."

"Entertainment, for God's sake?"

Saylor stubbed out his cigarette and signalled their waiter to bring the bill.

"Every good host, you know, will prepare a little entertainment at the end of a meal. I thought it would put you in the right mood —soften you up, sort of—for the inevitable end and climax."

Dave leaped to his feet.

"Jesus H. Christ, man, do you think we've *got* to be 'softened up' before we're in any shape to hear you?"

"Easy, Dave! E-easy now! I never did know a guy so quick to fly off the handle and hit the ceiling!" Saylor counted out money on the table. "I'm taking you to a place so close to here you could almost throw a stone and hit it from the door of Henri's; then you'll see what I mean. Ready?"

"We're all ready."

"Right. You go first, Dave, with Old Sleuth to guide you; Jeff, you follow with Penny. This way, then, and let everybody be merry!"

From the restaurant's rather dark foyer they emerged into narrow Toulouse Street between Bourbon and Royal streets, but much closer to the former. Golden sunshine, as well as a temperature in the middle seventies, lay drowsily on the pastel-colored houses of the Old Square, itself at its most somnolent now.

215

Dave and Saylor strolled ahead. Jeff, a short distance behind with
Penny's left arm touching his right, observed that the other two did
not stroll far. A few paces brought them to Bourbon Street, where
they turned to the right on its south banquette. Following the same
way, Jeff instinctively glanced back over his shoulder.

When he and Penny and Dave came in from Delys Hall, they
had taken two cars. Penny drove him in her family's Hudson; Dave
drove the Stutz. Despite Penny's dislike of driving in the Vieux
Carré, it had been convenient to leave both cars in the parking lot
now occupying the site of the demolished St. Louis Hotel close by.

But Jeff, as he guided Penny to the right on Bourbon Street, did
not concern himself with those cars. He glanced down at Penny;
their eyes met; they both instantly looked away. But their arms still
touched. So strong between them had grown the sense of communication, even of intimacy, that it brought outward embarrassment.

He would have liked to be leading her into some romantic garden where, in warmth and secrecy, he could have spoken his mind.
Penny, he knew, felt the same. Instead he was leading her . . .
where?

Saylor and Dave had gone only a short distance when Saylor
stopped, drawing himself up like a showman.

"Behold!" he exclaimed.

"Behold what?" asked Dave, also stopping.

"We are here!" the other said. "On your right, ladies and gentlemen, the south side of not-so-stately Bourbon Street, behold stateliness indeed!"

"What stateliness? And is this the entertainment?"

"It is, as you'll all soon agree."

"Well, what is it?" demanded Dave. "If there's supposed to be
anything stately about a shop that sells pralines . . . !"

"Not the shop that sells pralines, dammit! Beyond it; just beyond.
That noble façade, uprearing higher than most houses hereabouts,
with the electric sign unlighted in the daytime. Look at it, can't
you? Don't just stand there griping; look at it!"

They all looked.

The square façade, no doubt of brick faced with white stucco, rose to something more than a two-storey height. It showed no windows looking out. Instead, above broad green double doors inscribed 'ENTER in gilt letters, the front had been realistically painted to represent the skyline of a city on several hills, handsome buildings dominated by one impressive structure with a gold dome.

Saylor pointed to the unlit electric sign, which read SAN FRANCISCO.

"It has been remarked," he was proclaiming, "that in these United States there are only three 'story' cities to capture the imagination: New York, New Orleans, and San Francisco. By a natural transition we pass from the second to the third. If the lady will precede us, pushing open the right-hand double door . . ."

Penny glanced at Jeff. "Shall I?"

"Yes; why not? For once, during our forays into the Old Square," he reminded her, "we're entering a building on the south side of the street. Cinderella's Slipper, the Bohemian Cigar Divan: each was on the north side, respectively, of Bourbon and Royal. We can't be far from Mr. Everard at this moment."

Penny went on through.

Jeff, Dave, and Saylor followed single file into a foyer, broad if not very deep, of subdued interior lighting. In the glass-enclosed paybox against the left-hand wall sat a decorative young lady wearing clothes of some unidentifiably old-fashioned sort.

The rear wall of the foyer had been painted and decorated to represent the ground floor, together with partially the floor above, of a massive brownstone house, abode of the very prosperous. Though the house's front door was a practical door, a second glance showed the windows at either side to be dummies of painting and carpentry. Such subdued lighting might have been the glow of street-lamps. Beside the house door stood a ticket-taker in comic-opera uniform. Distantly, Jeff thought he could hear a cart rattling over cobbles.

Saylor gestured towards the paybox.

"Don't go near that ticket-window, anybody!" he ordered. "It's all been arranged and paid for. Usually, when a party goes through this exhibit, they're accompanied by a spieler to give the description. On the present occasion, good friends, *I'm* doing the spiel."

"This show had better be good, whatever it is," growled Dave, eyeing their host without favor. "You couldn't sound more complacent if you were Kubla Khan showing off Xanadu to the visiting Elks, so this show had better be good."

"There'll be no cause for complaint," Saylor assured him. "I promised you entertainment, didn't I?

"My name," he pursued in a ringing voice, "is Meldrum, Barnabas T. Meldrum. I'm a successful stockbroker with a home on Van Ness Avenue. Before you is my home, and you three are my guests. We've made a night of it in wide-open San Francisco; dawn is just coming up; I bring you here for a final drink before we separate."

Nodding towards the uniformed ticket-taker, who nodded in reply, Saylor leaned past him and turned the knob of the front door.

"Into the lower hall, please, where a light has been left against our return."

Then Saylor closed the door behind them.

They stood in a very fair simulacrum of the hall so described, with a floor which appeared to be squares of black and white marble, and a heavy staircase at the back. The whole place was so shadowy, from a mere faraway lamp-gleam, that Jeff could distinguish only the outlines of furniture which seemed old-fashioned without being ancient: it suggested the furniture in his childhood home.

"A hearty welcome, good friends," that stage voice continued, "to the house of Barnabas T. Meldrum! If you will go forward, and up those stairs . . ."

"Just a moment, Barnabas T. Meldrum!" interposed Jeff, with more than the glimmering of an idea. "You said 'wide-open' San Francisco, didn't you? If we've been making a night of it, what's the date?"

"That, sir, you will soon learn. Up the stairs, please, lest I seem to be lacking in hospitality!"

The stairs, if somewhat scuffed from usage, at least seemed solid. Dave went first, then Jeff with Penny at his left side, and Saylor bringing up the rear.

"If I tried hard enough," Jeff ventured, "I think I might guess the date. Probably it doesn't matter, but . . . you might stay close to me, Penny."

"Do you even need to *ask* that?" she whispered, taking his arm. "Here I am!"

"They build well in this town," declared the pseudo Barnabas T. Meldrum, "and especially here on Van Ness Avenue. They build for now and for the future too." Suddenly he dropped his stage manner. "This might really *be* a private house, mightn't it?" he asked in a normal tone. "The illusion is perfect."

The illusion could not have been called perfect, since they found no hall or landing at the top of the stairs. Instead they stepped straight through an open doorway into an oblong room where near-perfection of illusion had really been attained.

Through two large windows opposite, which had every appearance of being real windows, filtered a bluish pink light evidently representing dawn. That eerie glow lit up heavy furniture, wallpaper in a design of multicolored cabbages, and a long-necked chandelier.

"This room," Barnabas T. Meldrum proclaimed, "is used as an office away from the office. Note the stock-ticker in the corner, the massive table-desk, the absence of fal-lals or other fripperies. As for our view from the windows . . ."

He strode to the left-hand window, whose curtains had not been closed, and stood peering out.

"I've never been in San Francisco," said Saylor, again dropping his Meldrum role, "so I can't guarantee the accuracy of the topography. But the people who built this display have taken a lot of care with perspective effects, light and sound effects, models that work to deceive the eye. Look there!"

The others gathered round him.

"We're supposed to be fairly high up, seeing out over rooftops. Down there—east, roughly—is San Francisco Bay, with the foot of Market Street and the spire of the Ferry Building. Closer at hand, though still some distance away, that's the gold dome of City Hall. You can see smoke going up from some chimneys; you can hear wagons moving. And, in the area called South of the Slot . . ."

Here he turned, addressing Jeff.

"You wanted to know the date, didn't you? All right! Take a look at the wall opposite."

Jeff followed a pointing finger. The wall opposite, in addition to the doorway by which they had entered, had a second doorway with a closed door. At one side of this doorway hung a wall clock that at first sight appeared to be a real clock. At the other side hung a large tear-off calendar whose exposed leaf showed the date of Tuesday, April 17th, 1906.

"Get it?" Saylor leered.

"I think so," said Jeff. "It's too early in the morning for anybody to have changed that calendar. The real date is Wednesday, April 18th."

"And the time, as you see by the clock, is 5:12 A.M. Well? What did happen at twelve minutes past five in the morning on that date? Get that too?"

"Yes, undoubtedly," Jeff told him. "It seems we're just in time for the San Francisco earthquake."

And then it began.

19

At the outset it was sound alone: swelling sound like the rumble of a gigantic train that raced towards them from the direction of the bay. Next its first shock smote. The floor jerked and shuddered; the whole room seemed to jerk and shudder; the chandelier swung with it. That same shock flung Dave against the table-desk, which had not moved.

"Earthquake?" Dave blurted.

"Of course," affirmed Saylor, chortling to himself. "Why do you think I brought you here?"

"And this is *entertainment*, for God's sake?"

"Sure; what else? Look, Dave! You didn't turn a hair, Jeff says, when somebody fired three shots straight at you! Don't get upset by a make-believe sideshow that can't do anybody the least harm!"

"Maybe so, but the damn floor's having a fit! It'll be still more fun, won't it, when bricks from the ceiling come down and conk us?"

"Nothing like that," Saylor staggered a little as he turned back to the window, "nothing like that happened then or will happen now. The houses in this part of town were too solidly built. A few cracked windowpanes; some broken dishes in the china closet; that's all. They'd had earthquakes before, though never a bad one: good old Meldrum took precautions; the heavy furniture is fastened down. If you look out there—"

More shocks had thrown Penny into Jeff's arms, where she stayed. With his arm around her waist, as Saylor paused, he guided her over a rocking floor to the other window.

221

Rooftops near and far now seemed to writhe before some crumpled. The rumble from that phantom train had been succeeded by a crash and roar of falling timbers or masonry. Through dust-cloud effects Jeff caught what appeared to be the yellow flickering of fire.

"They've got the place so soundproof," exulted Saylor, "that nothing's audible outside. Hell of a lively show, eh? There goes most of a six-million-dollar City Hall, leaving the dome on top of the skeleton. But it's all right, Dave! Those flames are only lights; there's no real fire. And most people on Van Ness Avenue were asleep; they hardly knew it had happened."

"If they slept through *this*," raved the scion of the Hobarts, "they must have been dead drunk or just plain dead. Have it your own way, P. T. Barnum; I have only one question. How long does the bloody show *go on?*"

"Well . . ."

There was a distant, collapsing roar of breakage, with flames curling up. The floor ceased to tremble. Dave, who had perched on the table-desk and gripped its edges, rose to his feet.

"O.K.!" he said. "If a pin-headed master of ceremonies has now stopped entertaining us to the top of his bent, suppose we haul our freight out of here?"

"*I* don't want to be a spoilsport," ventured Penny, looking up at Jeff and speaking in a low voice, "but that does seem a very good idea. It *is* over, isn't it?"

"From what I remember reading, Penny, the first wave lasted about fifty-five seconds."

"The *first* wave?" yelped Dave.

"Then there was a pause of ten seconds, after which—"

"The rest of you may not be counting," Dave cut in, "but I'm counting as though I had a stopwatch at the ready. And it strikes me those ten seconds are just about—"

Again the floor rocked and the earthquake walloped, with a din as shattering as before. Saylor himself all but lost his balance.

"Though it may seem the wrong time to mention this, Dave, you haven't a notion what happened on that steamboat, now have you?"

"How's that?"

"Well," cried Saylor, "who *was* she sleeping with? Who was she *really* sleeping with?"

"What the hell are you talking about? And who's the 'she' in question?"

"You don't know that either, do you?"

In Saylor's manner there seemed something so sinister, even maniacal, that Jeff thought it best to intervene.

"How *do* we get out of this place?" he asked. "By the same stairs we came up?"

"No; it's forbidden to leave by those stairs; rule of the house. There are two other exits; I'll show you."

Separating Jeff and Penny, he grasped Jeff's left arm and Penny's right.

"If both of you want to leave," he went on, "maybe that's best. The second wave of the earthquake lasts only ten seconds, like the pause between 'em. There! It's over now, see?"

Across a steady floor he guided them to still a third door, a very broad door, in the same wall as the windows but some eight or ten feet to the right. Releasing Jeff's arm, he opened the door on near-darkness. Jeff hesitated.

"Where does it lead? And what becomes of your perfect illusion? This is supposed to be the back wall of the house, isn't it?"

"It's *all* illusion, all a box of tricks; but with nothing that could hurt a child, so help me! Just inside, one to the left and one to the right, you see two little padded seats facing forward. Step in; each of you take a pew; you'll be ushered out with some ceremony, and I'll guide Dave by a different way. Since the lady doesn't want to be a spoilsport . . ."

"All right; I think I understand," Penny agreed. "I'll take the one on the left; Jeff, you take the one on the right. If that's the end of the show, Mr. Meldrum or Mr. Barnum, we both thank you."

She entered and sat down. Jeff followed her example. The door closed behind them on total darkness. He had just reached out his left hand, which Penny clasped in her right, when without bump or jar both seats collapsed beneath them. Together, feet first, they went sailing down a broad slide of smooth, polished wood under dim red gleams too faint to be called lights, and landed on their feet at the end of the slide.

Though they landed on their feet, they did not separate; nature had its way. With Penny again in his arms, by design rather than simulated earthquake, he gripped her as tightly as though he meant to crush her, kissing her mouth with a concentration she fully shared. After a chaotic interval they both spoke in whispers.

"Penny, does this mark a beginning of some kind?"

"I hope so! Oh, I do hope so! May I—may I ask a question, Jeff, and then make a request?"

"Yes, my dear?"

"When do you go back to Paris?"

"As soon as we get some logical answers in this infernal murder case."

"When you do go back, will you take me with you?"

"If you mean what I think you mean . . . !"

"I mean everything you can possibly think I mean, and even more! Poor Serena said—"

"Does that matter now?"

"It'll always matter to me, because it's true. If ever you—you approached me like this, Serena said, it wouldn't be fair. Because, she said, I wouldn't even make a pretense of resisting. That's gospel truth, Jeff, and if I hadn't been such a coward I'd have told her so at the time. But you haven't answered the question. *Will* you take me?"

"Since I love you, damn your soul, the answer is so roaring an affirmative that I could shout the house down. Speaking of shouting the house down, in our own particular earthquake . . ."

He could now discern in the dark wall ahead a very narrow vertical line of light. He could also hear voices close at hand: Dave querulously complaining, Saylor serene and triumphant. Disengaging with reluctance, Penny and Jeff moved ahead. Jeff pushed open the right-hand section of double doors, each with an inner bar across it. Afternoon sunlight flooded down as they joined Dave and the showman in an alley that stretched south to Royal Street. Jeff faced them.

"How did you two get here?" he asked. "You didn't go down the slide."

"We went down a different slide, customarily not used," Saylor said with a touch of grandeur. "Did you notice another closed door up there, with the clock on one side and the calendar on the other?"

"To which you so dramatically called our attention? Yes."

"We went down that, Jeff, and landed at the blind front of the premises. Then back through a corridor under the display to another exit like this one. A certain character here," Saylor's thumb indicated Dave, "is still mocking and reviling a loftier intelligence. All right! But don't say I'm putting you off or dodging the issue. If we can sit down somewhere over a cup of coffee, I'll indicate to your bemused minds what must be several truths about the mystery at Delys Hall. Fair enough?"

Penny, it gratified Jeff to observe, had uttered no complaint. She had not said her hair was mussed or that she needed makeup repair, which she didn't. But she did seem to be suffering from a certain constraint.

"The cup of coffee is impossible, I'm afraid," she told Saylor. Then, suddenly, "Jeff, what time is it?"

"Twenty minutes to four, if that matters either."

"Oh, it matters! Jeff, Dave, have you forgotten what we promised Mr. Bethune?"

Then Jeff remembered.

"He's inviting a party of interested persons to Delys Hall," Penny went on. "He more than intimated, without actually saying so, that we'd hear the whole truth. And he made us promise to be back at the Hall by four o'clock. Considering traffic at this time of day, we can't possibly get there by four . . ."

"The *whole* truth, eh?" exclaimed Dave, casting off all querulousness. "We may not be able to get there bang on the hour, m'gel, but we can have a damn good try! Both cars are close at hand, thank God! You'd better make good time, Penny; I intend to drive like Barney Oldfield on the loose." He turned to Saylor. " 'Fraid you've got to excuse us, old son. The whole truth *is* a lot better than just part of it, let's agree."

Saylor, who clearly had received no invitation but just as clearly hoped for one from Dave, followed them to the Royal Street parking lot. When they collected the Stutz and the Hudson for their return journey, they left him fretting and muttering to himself, a sulkily indecipherable look on his face.

That drive to Delys Hall was not quite the breathless race of

Dave's prophecy. Dave drove fast, but with reasonable care; Penny matched his pace a little way behind. By tacitly mutual consent, both Penny and Jeff refrained from any discussion of their own emotional state. They remained grave, even sombre, perhaps with premonitions.

"It hardly seems possible," Penny said, "that the end of the wretched business is in sight, and the end of anxiety too. How *will* it end, Jeff?"

"I wish I knew."

"Not a glimmer?"

"Uncle Gil talks about evidence all over the place. But, except for one bit that doesn't help with telling us who's guilty, I don't see the clues at all. Also, if Uncle Gil can explain everything, it won't be an end of anxiety for somebody. Have you any ideas, Penny?"

Penny ruminated.

"As a matter of fact," she answered, "I did have a wild, irresponsible half-notion of who *might* be guilty. But it's so silly I won't even tell you. It's no reason at all; it's only what you might expect at the end of a detective story. And, since this isn't a detective story . . ."

"If it did happen to be a detective story, on the other hand," Jeff pointed out, "I think I can predict what the crafty author might well have in mind."

"Oh?"

"Uncle Gil, it would seem, didn't invite Saylor to his gathering this afternoon. Dave didn't invite him either."

"I don't think Dave likes him very much, Jeff. But Saylor can't be *guilty* of anything, can he?"

"No; he's got an incontestable alibi for the time of Serena's death. That's the point I'm making: everybody has got an alibi except Dave, to whose complete innocence Uncle Gil swears. According to the technique of the craft—this still refers to fiction—we immediately stop suspecting any person whom a know-it-all detective seems to have cleared. But some wily qualification has been slipped in without our notice; the detective didn't really say what we thought he said; and Dave Hobart turns out to be the murderer after all."

"You don't really believe that, do you?" cried Penny.

"No, of course I don't believe it; it's a writer's trick and no more. But, detective story or real life, what's the alternative? Say the murderer is any person you like. Say it's some apparently unconcerned character like Billy Vauban or Mrs. Vauban. Unless it's some person who hasn't even appeared on the scene so far, how do we get round the fact that everybody has an alibi?"

They said little more in the course of the journey.

Long shadows were gathering—another fateful dusk?—when Penny maneuvered the Hudson up a driveway so crowded with parked cars near the house that she had to find a place well removed. Arriving at the front door, she and Jeff encountered a nervous Cato just opening it for Dave.

The gathering planned by Gilbert Bethune, like many gatherings purposeful or purposeless, had not yet got down to business. Police, some uniformed but mainly in plain clothes, prowled through the lower hall, fidgeted in the minor drawing-room, and even spilled over into the library beyond. At Cato's indicative bow, all three newcomers went through to the last-named room.

Here, in an atmosphere at once oppressive and expectant, Uncle Gil stood behind the long side of the library's long table. At the right side of him stood Lieutenant Minnoch and Officer O'Bannion. At the left of him stood a smallish, alert, sharp-faced man whom Jeff had never seen before. Also in attendance were Ira Rutledge, Kate Keith, Malcolm Townsend, and, somewhat to Jeff's surprise, old John Everard, the philosophical tobacconist.

"Jeff," whispered Penny, "what *are* you thinking about?"

"I'm thinking," Jeff whispered back, "more about those who aren't here than about those who are."

"No talking in the ranks, please!" said Uncle Gil, rapping his knuckles on the table. "Now that we're all assembled," and he indicated the sharp-faced little man, "may I present Mr. Gregory Winwood, of the Arkwright Company, who has been kind enough to provide some much-needed technical advice? I next request that all those now in this room, but nobody else, will follow me upstairs to the bedroom occupied by the late Serena Hobart, once the principal guest bedroom at Delys Hall."

A very fair-sized parade did follow, with attendant police falling back to make way. If you heard some muttering among those being led, nobody spoke out until the procession entered Serena's room. Even then Dave, who did not raise his voice, threw away the words as though speaking to himself.

"What the hell," Dave said, "*is* this all about?"

"I will tell you," volunteered Uncle Gil.

Though he seemed to be answering Dave, he ran his eye over the whole group.

"There is plenty of daylight left," he said. "But, lest *any* shadow should be confusing, we might have one or two lamps turned on. Officer O'Bannion!"

O'Bannion, with an anticipatory expression Jeff could not interpret, kindled a table lamp and a floor lamp. Once more the extreme left-hand window-light stood wide open, projecting back into the room like a little door.

"We have had some difficulty in finding a theory which would fit all our facts," continued Uncle Gil, "because, unfortunately, the truth was almost too obvious to be seen."

"*That* makes sense?" Dave blurted.

"*I* think it does!" observed Mr. Everard, rubbing his hands together.

"Some confusion seems to have been caused," said Uncle Gil, "when your mentor asked in what way the death of Serena Hobart in April, 1927, resembled the death of Thaddeus Peters in November, 1910. Well, there were several resemblances."

"Indeed, sir?" prompted old Everard.

"Each victim had occupied the same bedroom. Thad Peters, a principal guest during his visit, was put into quarters which, as many of you have been informed, Serena took over at some later date. But does anyone remember what the male victim was *wearing* at the time he apparently fell downstairs and broke his neck?"

"I remember," Jeff said instantly, as his uncle turned towards him. "Dave told me on the steamboat. Thad Peters, that noted all-round athlete, was wearing a sweater and sports flannels and tennis shoes."

"Do you also recall one discrepancy in the evidence? A little while before the great crash of silver which seemed to mark his fall downstairs inside the house, some maidservant testified she had heard a cry from outside?"

"Yes!"

"Let's look for further parallels with Serena's case." Gilbert Bethune went to the wide-open window light, put his head out, and glanced to the left before turning back to the room. "I now draw your attention to some exterior decoration. Between every panel of windows on both floors stretches a row of ornamental iron brackets, each in *fleur-de-lys* shape.* And up here, a few feet below floor-level, a very narrow stone ledge runs along the whole front of the house."

Ira Rutledge spoke suddenly.

"We've all seen the decoration!" he exclaimed. "We could hardly have avoided seeing it if we'd tried! But what in heaven's name do you want to tell us?"

"On Sunday night, old friend, I stood out on the terrace with a flashlight and sent its beam up over those iron brackets, bidding Jeff use his eyes and memory. Since he was at the front door looking out, however, he may not have observed. And I fear I must trouble you all with another question. Serena Hobart, herself once an expert gymnast: what did *she* wear on the night she died?"

It was Dave who spoke then, as though shying back from something in his mind.

"I see the direction you're going," he said. "I can't quite see where it leads or can lead, but I see the *direction*. Some notion of it came to me late Saturday night; it scared me green. That's why I lied and misled you at first, as I've since acknowledged. Serena? She had Indian moccasins on her feet and wore a sweater over pajamas."

Gilbert Bethune strode to the cupboard. Throwing open its door, from a drawer on the right-hand side he took out the woman's sweater of black knitted wool, rumpled and heavily dust-stained, which he had displayed last night.

*The presence of these brackets has been stressed with a special footnote on page 80.

"This sweater, Dave?"

"That's it! I couldn't face what she might have been up to. So I took the sweater off her and stuck it away in there; I swore she'd been wearing the very dark-blue dressing-gown. Cato and Ike, the chauffeur, were almost as upset as I was. Ike backed me up; I'm boss of the house now, and he'd have backed me up whatever I said. But Cato wasn't having any. He knew the garment had been short, like that house-coat hanging on the other side; both the sweater and the house-coat are black. When Cato said it was a house-coat, that's what he believed. Both the dressing-gown and the house-coat might have got a little dusty from falling on the floor, but not as dusty as the real thing."

Uncle Gil held up the sweater.

"This pair of gloves in the pocket. When they carried the body up here, were the gloves on her hands or in the pocket?"

"They were already stuffed in the pocket, believe it or not!"

"Of course they were, Dave. They had to be."

At this point, adding to the ripple of tension through the whole group, Kate Keith almost had hysterics.

"Why did they have to be?" shrilled Kate. "What *was* she doing in a sweater, to get all that dust on her? I can't stand this any longer! Malcolm . . . Malcolm . . . !"

Townsend tried to shush her, not altogether with success. Uncle Gil swept aside incipient hysterics by ignoring them.

"We now propose to reconstruct," he said. "Is Sergeant Parker here?"

Harry Minnoch lumbered to the door and beckoned. Into the bedroom came a lithe, wiry, middle-sized young man, wearing a dark sweater and stepping lightly. He saluted Uncle Gil, who had grown Mephistophelian again.

"Sergeant Parker," Gilbert Bethune told the others, "is also something of a gymnast. You know what to do, Parker?"

"I know, sir."

From his trousers pocket Sergeant Parker drew a pair of loose-fitting brown cotton gloves, not unlike those in the pocket of Serena's sweater. Putting them on his own hands, he approached the extreme left-hand window space and with much agility hoisted himself through it.

"We thus observe," pursued Uncle Gil, "that one climbing out that window in gloves would leave only such smudges as were actually found on frame and glass."

Sergeant Parker had lowered himself to stand on the stone ledge below, having turned so that he now faced towards the left and partly into the room.

All others crowded towards the line of windows. Penny stood close to Jeff, with Dave just beyond. Uncle Gil raised his voice.

"When I say, 'Now,' but not until then, Sergeant Parker will begin to move along the ledge between this room and the next. To do so, of course, he will press close to the wall and support himself by gripping each iron bracket in turn. Once he is outside, however, such clumsy gloves will impede his movements rather than help. He will strip them off, as Parker is doing at this moment, and thrust them into his pocket.

"We are following what Serena Hobart did on Saturday night, as Thad Peters had done before her. Each sought something which each hoped to locate, because each had been persuaded it was there. We shall soon see what they found."

Uncle Gil put down on a chair the sweater he had been holding.

"Meanwhile," he said, "let's remember some facts. If one reference has been constantly thrown at our heads, it is a reference to some form of electricity."

"*But—!*" Dave began wildly.

"Electric lights and a telephone, we learn, were installed in the year 1907. The doorbell then worked, as it still works, off three ordinary dry-cell batteries, such as were advertised in the Sears, Roebuck catalogue as early as 1902. Mr. Gregory Winwood, whom I introduced downstairs and who has given so much technical help, is New Orleans manager of the Arkwright Electrical Supply Company." Uncle Gil bent forward. "It's time to demonstrate, Parker! Now!"

Bare-handed, gloves in pocket, Sergeant Parker began to edge along that perch. His right hand reached out and up for the iron *fleur de lys* nearest him in the row. As the sergeant's fingers closed round it, Uncle Gil straightened up.

"Oh, no!" he announced. "The mechanism has been destroyed. When Parker grasps the bracket, pulling slightly as anyone would do for support, its shaft will not move out that solitary eighth of an inch. Before it moves back again on its prepared spring, the trap inside the air space will *not* administer a startling and painful shock to topple him from his narrow ledge.

"Remember, finally, that the body of Serena Hobart was found on the terrace a little to the left of the open window. And now, Lieutenant Minnoch, the final move is yours."

Minnoch's eye fastened on one member of that group. In a loud voice he said:

"Horace Dinsmore, alias Malcolm Townsend, I arrest you for the murder of Serena Hobart. I must warn you that anything you say will be taken down in writing and can be used against you at your trial."

20

Penny, the only woman among seven persons assembled in the library at Delys Hall three nights later, addressed their master of ceremonies.

"Please, Mr. Bethune!" she begged.

In a carved chair at the head of the long table sat Gilbert Bethune. Ranged behind one side of the table, facing east, sat Ira Rutledge, Lieutenant Minnoch, and Gregory Winwood of the Arkwright Company. Ranged behind the other side, facing west, sat Dave Hobart, Jeff Caldwell, and Penny Lynn. Softly illumined by the glow of the yellow-shaded lamp, they looked like a board meeting at which Uncle Gil was presiding.

"Please, Mr. Bethune!" repeated Penny. "You'll tell us *all* about that dreadful gadget, won't you? The one with a wire stretching to the batteries of the doorbell? The one so cleverly hidden, in the air space between the walls, that any person replacing the batteries would never suspect it was there? The one you alone discovered?"

Uncle Gil, cigar in hand, contemplated the lamp and spoke from behind a smoke-cloud.

"The one *I* discovered, my dear?" he said gently. "You give me far too much credit."

"But—!"

"Without the least pretense to scientific ability or scientific knowledge, I felt only that an electrical device of some sort must in some way be attached to an iron bracket, in all probability the bracket nearest that open window. Lacking help from Mr. Winwood, a Georgia Tech graduate with much enthusiasm for such

233

matters, I should never have known how our device operated or could operate. Mr. Winwood found and explained the trap. He has so drilled me in explaining it, as though I were getting up my case for a jury, that I am almost parrot-perfect. Let's try to summarize."

Uncle Gil was silent for a moment, inhaling deeply.

"You've all seen that iron *fleur de lys,*" he went on, "which has a square shaft projecting from the wall. This shaft fits easily in a porcelain insulating 'bushing' (do I use the correct term, sir?) through the wall. The front face of the 'bushing' is hidden by the flange of the *fleur de lys;* this one can't be distinguished from any like *fleur de lys* in the row. When the bracket is grasped and slightly pulled, its shaft moves outwards only an eighth of an inch, but that's enough. The other end of the shaft extends through the wall into the air space we find between every outer wall and the rooms behind it on both floors.

"This inner end of the shaft carries a hard rubber piece which will cause a small electric switch to close when the shaft is pulled. The switch connects a wire leading from the house doorbell batteries to the primary winding of a Ruhmkorff coil also concealed in the air space. Do I speak accurately, Mr. Winwood?"

The sharp-faced little man answered at once. He had a voice as sharp as his face, but he was far from being without humor.

"If I were inclined to be pedantic," he replied, "I should insist that you refer to the *battery* rather than the batteries. The three dry cells of this mechanism are in fact only cells of a single battery. But it's become popular usage to call them batteries, so I allow it. Therefore we are safe in saying—"

"We are, are we?" Dave burst out.

Dave, seeming more hounded or haunted than ever, had been sitting with his elbows on the table and his head in his hands. Now he peered up.

"Not so fast, anybody!" he protested. "As far as science is concerned, I'm more than an ignoramus and want to be no better. But what in Satan's name is a 'Ruhmkorff coil'? "

Uncle Gil made a polite gesture towards the technical adviser, who cleared his throat.

"The Ruhmkorff coil, sometimes also called a spark coil," said

Gregory Winwood, "is used to produce a high voltage from some low-voltage source, such as a small battery of dry cells. Four of these provide the ignition for Mr. Ford's Model T, which he has now ceased to manufacture.

"To activate the mechanism in this house, as the chairman of our board was about to say a moment ago, the high-tension terminal of the coil is attached to the inner shaft of the *fleur de lys*. When the bracket is pulled, even lightly, whoever has gripped it will receive a very painful shock. The shock is not lethal and leaves no mark, having so brief a pulse; but the victim on that narrow ledge must inevitably pitch over. Finally, the inventor of the trap has supplied a spring which returns the shaft to its normal position once pressure has been released, opening the switch and cutting off the current. We have now come round in full circle from topics mechanical to topics personal, so I return you to the chairman of the board."

He inclined his head towards Uncle Gil, who frowned and took up the tale.

"Let's go back a little," Uncle Gil suggested. "Having suspected an electrical device *of some kind*, even before calling in Mr. Winwood we had to ask ourselves where such a device could have been installed, when it was installed, and who installed it.

"The most probable time, I thought, would have been just after the advent of electric power in 1907. Once the official workmen had finished their wiring, the unofficial workman had a clear field; air spaces were available since 1882. The person who installed it was someone of deviously ingenious mind, skilled at using his hands and with the requisite technical knowledge."

Dave pressed his hands over his eyes.

"Requisite technical knowledge, eh? 'I'll cross it, though it blast me!' You're talking about my old man, aren't you?"

"It seemed inescapable, Dave. I knew Harald Hobart had studied engineering. To learn it was electrical engineering confirmed the trend of this thought. I now hazard a conjecture for which there is no evidence at all. He prepared his trap but did not yet connect it, against some future day when it might be needed.

"On other points we do have evidence. In 1910 he became involved in rivalry for control of Danforth & Co. with Thad Peters, favorite in-law of the Vaubans. The trap *was* needed, or he thought it was. How would he approach his prey? 'If I could find Commodore Hobart's hidden gold,' he would say, 'I need never trouble myself or you or any other person on earth. They've been looking in the wrong direction for access to that hoard. They've been looking for access inside the house; real access is from outside.

" 'Provided I had the courage to walk along the ledge outside the principal guest bedroom, I could put my hand on a fortune. But I can't do it; I can't bear heights, as everybody knows.' Whereas, he suggested, if a noted athlete lent assistance . . ."

"I mustn't be too hard on murderers, must I?" Dave said. "Since my own father seems to have been a murderer—!"

"I like to think he had no such intent," said Gilbert Bethune. "It's a long drop from that ledge, but it should not have killed a young man in prime physical condition. I don't think your father believed it would kill. But it would hurt Peters a little and scare him badly. Peters, with the physical courage to walk that ledge, might well lack the moral courage to resist Harald Hobart any longer; he would yield; he would give Harald what Harald wanted. Not a pretty story, though a much more human story.

"By unforeseen chance, then, the victim broke his neck. What happened next?

"Though there had been a single cry from outside the house, Peters must seem to have died inside. The instigator of this plot worked entirely alone; he did not even share a bedroom with his wife. Last Friday night, Dave, I believe you yourself showed by a trick fall on the staircase that someone rolling downstairs makes almost no noise. Is that right?"

"Absolutely right! But—"

"Peters's body was dragged into the house. Heavy silverware, deliberately dropped, provided false evidence of what seemed to happen. Afterwards a conscience-stricken plotter covered his tracks. He forbade his son to mention even what had *apparently* occurred. In later years he would allow no examination of the premises."

Here Ira Rutledge intervened.

"One who asked to examine these premises," he queried, "being the smooth-faced skulker who did use Harald's trap with homicidal purpose?"

"Oh, yes. With homicidal purpose from the start. Townsend-Dinsmore had much charm, as so many murderers have had. He had considerable power over women, or at least over some women. All this hid the utter callousness of his tribe."

"And yet, Gil, it still seems incredible that the man you knew as Malcolm Townsend should really have been the Rev. Horace Dinsmore. Come, now! A Boston clergyman!"

Uncle Gil pointed with the cigar.

"Unthinkable but true," he replied. "The Rev. Clarence Richeson, who murdered his mistress and then emasculated himself in jail, was also a Boston clergyman."

"In addition to being an ordained minister," Ira remained stubborn, "Townsend-Dinsmore or Dinsmore-Townsend was a professor at highly respectable Mansfield College."

"And Dr. Parkman was a professor at Harvard. But they hanged him just the same."

"They won't execute this murderer," cried Penny, "after that awful business night before last. Townsend *was* Dinsmore, as we've got good reason to know now. I know *I* oughtn't to butt in; I know I ought to keep still and be good." She appealed to Uncle Gil. "But how did *you* know he was Dinsmore, or that he must have been the one who killed Serena?"

Gilbert Bethune meditated.

"Let's return to your journey downriver by the *Bayou Queen*, and to some rather curious behavior on the part of Kate Keith. Mrs. Keith is fond of male company; she will find it where she can. To all persons, male or female, she is forever friendly, forever obliging, as she was aboard the steamboat. But one thing she would not do: she would not invite anyone to her stateroom. On the first night, I am informed, Dave invited her into *his* room for a brief visit with Dave and Jeff. She excused herself in haste and almost ran; it was as though she had something on her mind.

"Several days later young Saylor asked her if she wouldn't invite all of you to her room for a drink. Though she provided the liquor (she had gone ashore and bought a bottle), she carried that bottle to a public lounge so that it could be poured there.

"When I remembered the attention she paid to Captain Josh Galway, as though persuading him of something and keeping him persuaded, I could not help wondering whether there might have been another paying stowaway who remained a stowaway throughout the whole journey. In that event, we had a better explanation than Jeff's for the despairing cry of Captain Josh, 'How many of 'em? Dear God in heaven, how many of 'em?' "

"Townsend in Kate's room?" demanded Jeff. "But how could you have suspected Townsend? And in what way did any of this affect *Serena?*"

"Perpend; you will see in a moment. Townsend, outwardly, did not appear on the scene until Saturday morning. He came here in a taxi, professing to have reached New Orleans by train. Serena and Townsend, each gave you to understand, had never met before. You discovered the loss of Commodore Hobart's log; Townsend instantly opened his brief-case to show he hadn't taken it."

"And that was suspicious, Uncle Gil?"

"Oh, no!"

"Well, what was suspicious?"

"The four who were there, you and Serena and Townsend and Dave, afterwards had lunch. It was a buffet lunch, at which each person served himself and only coffee appeared on the board. Then, presently, you had tea. Serena, presiding, asked you whether you took tea with lemon or with milk. After serving you, without a further word of any kind she prepared cups for the other two. She would have known, of course, how to serve her own brother. But the same question she had asked you she would also have asked a total stranger," Uncle Gil shot out the words, "if in fact he had been a total stranger."

"Good for you, sir!" crowed Lieutenant Minnoch. "You're under way now; keep rollin'!"

"Yet I need not roll with undue haste." Uncle Gil's eye sought Penny. "That same evening, Jeff, this young lady phoned you at the office of Rutledge & Rutledge. Mrs. Keith had turned up after dinner; and, as though *she* had known Townsend before, carried him off to a night club.

"Another link, you see. If Mrs. Keith had been hiding a stowaway in her room on the steamboat, Townsend might perhaps have been the man."

"Was that what Saylor suspected, Uncle Gil?" Jeff cut in. "And why Saylor went all out to question Captain Josh?"

"Saylor suspected the presence of a stowaway, yes. He never suspected Townsend of anything, and neither did Dave. But what did *I* suspect, your stumbling would-be sleuth?

"On Sunday morning, Dave," again Uncle Gil's gaze shifted, "you had a talk with Jeff. After dinner on Saturday night, it seemed, some woman had spoken to you of Townsend and called him very attractive. Penny Lynn had departed, after finding Townsend pleasant but not unduly impressive. The woman could only have been Serena, who by tea-table evidence knew Townsend at least pretty well.

"Supposing her to have known him more than pretty well, where could they have met? There was a possibility here: only a possibility, but it existed. Both Harald Hobart and his daughter had been in the habit of visiting the family of a surgeon, Dr. Ramsay, at Bethesda, Maryland. Bethesda is so close to Washington as to be a kind of suburb. And Townsend lived in Washington, where Dave went to see him."

"I hardly *did* see the so-and-so when I got there!" Dave fumed. "He was in and out; he was all over the place. We talked by phone, mostly; I wasn't dead sure I could recognize him when he turned up here on Saturday."

"In Washington, Dave, you hadn't a chance. This murderous Don Juan had been keeping two women on the string, Serena and Kate Keith, without either woman knowing the passion of the other. In Washington he devoted himself to Serena, who also had gone there. What a pity you didn't meet her!

"Well!" Uncle Gil pursued. "If at some time in the past Townsend could have met Serena, he could also have met Serena's father for a different kind of relationship. Harald Hobart, when on a quiet spree, would drop all defenses and confide in a stranger what he wouldn't have whispered to his closest kin. Townsend, the friendly fellow everybody trusted, could have learned of the electrical device in the wall.

"I must not too much anticipate the evidence. On the famous Saturday afternoon before the murder that night, however, bear in mind that Townsend prowled alone through this house while the others were differently occupied. He found the trap behind a wall panel in the southeast corner of Serena's bedroom, and reset its mechanism to work again.

"At this moment I would direct your attention to Sunday afternoon, when I questioned Townsend at Mrs. Keith's. I did not think this architectural amateur had located Commodore Hobart's hidden gold, and I was right; he never concerned himself with the gold. I did repeat Commodore Hobart's warning about distrusting surfaces, which ended with the reference to the Gospel According to St. Matthew, seventh chapter and seventh verse. Without hesitation Townsend quoted that verse in full, remarking that odd bits of memory will stick at the back of the mind.

"So they will. And yet an odd idea had just leaped into my own mind. Any devoted Bible reader might have remembered that passage as being part of the Sermon on the Mount. At the same time, who but a parson could instantly have spotted the verse and quoted it word for word?"

"A parson?"

Uncle Gil surveyed them all.

"There had been mention of only one parson, Dr. Dinsmore of Boston, co-heir to the Hobart estate if both Dave and Serena were dead. Absurd, no doubt? Still, before dismissing the notion as utterly fantastic, I must ask myself whether this remote clergyman-professor, himself wealthy in his own right, could by any wild chance be the architectural amateur called Malcolm Townsend.

"Townsend commenced lecturing only last fall. But he had taken that trail, under the banner of a large Madison Avenue bureau, at a time when academic duties would have prevented the Rev. Horace Dinsmore from gallivanting over the country as a speaker.

"So it would be quite impossible; it must be ruled out. Unless . . .

"Mr. Rutledge there, who investigated the Rev. Horace, had told me several facts about him. The Rev. Horace became a full professor at Mansfield College in 1919. Reckoning from 1919, an important date, the year 1926 to 1927 would have been his seventh and therefore . . . therefore, Jeff, would have been what?"

"His *sabbatical,*" Jeff almost yelled. "He would have been free to do as he liked between about mid-June of '26 to about mid-September of '27! Yes, Uncle Gil?"

"Though technically possible, it still seemed most unlikely. And yet Townsend, answering my questions at Mrs. Keith's, was less than candid.

"He had told his New York publisher that he took up lecturing reluctantly because it interfered with spending so much time abroad. Now an authority on any given subject may and often does speak free of charge to some learned society, at the occasional dinner here and there, at almost any time. But the same man's professional services are required, by a big outfit like Major Pond, Inc. (as I thought then, and later confirmed with a phone call to New York) only through fall and winter up to the end of March; never in any other season. Whereas Townsend, either slipping up or thinking it didn't matter, swore to me he travelled abroad *only* in summer: the very time he had no lecture platform.

"Yes, it was less than candid; he had been telling lies to somebody. Though it failed to show any connection with the Rev. Horace Dinsmore, and that prospect remained unlikely, it had to be investigated.

"Already we had a good line of investigation. Here at the Hall on Saturday night, before Mrs. Keith arrived to hale away Townsend, the four of them had occupied themselves with taking indoor photographs by flash bulb.

"I found the camera they had been using, an intriguing discovery. Those photographs should, as they did, contain some clear shots of Malcolm Townsend, who offered no objection to posing. I had the photographs developed. Then, with full permission of Lieutenant Minnoch—"

"Didn't throw any chairs in your way, did I?" that official demanded happily.

"With Lieutenant Minnoch's permission, and employing our own Ted Patterson of Patterson Aircraft, I sent Officer Terence

O'Bannion by charter flight from New Orleans to Boston. He arrived there late on Monday with some full-face pictures. Early on Monday, before dispatching O'Bannion, I had taken one necessary precaution." Again Gilbert Bethune addressed his nephew. "Do you see what the precaution was?"

Jeff nodded.

"I think so, Uncle Gil. Attempting to identify Horace Dinsmore as Malcolm Townsend would have been pointless if the Rev. Horace had never left Boston. So you telephoned Mansfield College and on some pretext asked for Dr. Dinsmore. They told you, probably, that Dr. Dinsmore was absent on sabbatical leave but could be reached by mail in care of a friend, Mr. Malcolm Townsend of Washington. Have I followed it?"

"Exactly; well done! It seemed safe to send O'Bannion with the photographs, which made their point. Horace Dinsmore was clean-shaven and wore glasses he didn't need. Townsend, though sporting a narrow moustache and lacking glasses, incontestably was the same man."

"But what about Townsend's faith in the efficacy of disguise? Was that why he didn't mind being photographed?"

"At that time," replied Uncle Gil, "I had not yet learned of his preoccupation with disguise; Saylor told me later. Our man had used very little disguise; he faced the camera confidently because he never dreamed anybody would associate Malcolm Townsend with a New England parson-professor. Those easy airs of his, I fear, hid swollen and arrogant conceit. He really and fatuously believed he could disguise himself beyond recognition when he chose. He would have tried something more elaborate in the future. But there was no chance to try anything; we had him cornered. On Tuesday, once O'Bannion returned with signed testimony and other preparations had been made, we were ready to pounce."

Uncle Gil's cigar had burnt down to a stump. He dropped it into the ashtray at his elbow.

"And now, ladies and gentlemen, we had better recapitulate.

"At the unexpected climax of the whole business on Wednesday night, some twenty-four hours after our quarry's arrest, the police had learned all details of his plot. Let's follow every step he took, marking clues along the way.

242

"For some time he had not been happy as Professor Dinsmore of Mansfield. Though his scholarly interests were real enough, he felt almost too constricted to breathe. Under the scrutiny of academic life, this womanizer could not womanize; this lover of high living must eat and drink as his colleagues did.

"About 1921 he created the *alter ego* of Malcolm Townsend, who lived in Washington and lived as he pleased. Of course Townsend had an independent income, derived from the same source as Dinsmore's. But he could be Townsend only during summer vacations or at odd intervals of the school year. And the sense of constriction grew worse as time passed; Townsend, an actor *manqué* who enjoyed lecturing, was receiving offers of lecture tours he could not accept.

"Why not end an intolerable situation? Why not get rid of Dinsmore and become Townsend for good? To accomplish this he need not 'die' or even disappear. As his sabbatical leave approached, he agreed to begin lecturing in the fall. But, on leaving Mansfield in June of '26, he would not and did not offer his resignation. Expected to return in September of this year, he would actually if briefly return. *Then*, with much regret, he would tender his resignation. After taking affectionate leave of his erstwhile colleagues, he would 'retire' to meditate on lofty matters, leaving no forwarding address.

"That was his plan and remained his plan until the end, though it underwent one slight change. This spring, by a letter forwarded from Mansfield to his apartment in Washington, he learned from the senior partner of Rutledge & Rutledge that, if both Harald Hobart's children were dead by October 31st, with my own nephew he would become co-heir to the Hobart estate."

Ira Rutledge drew a deep breath.

"Yes, I so informed him," the lawyer declared. "I told Jeff that would be my course and I adopted it, though I gave no details. And the noncommittal answer, signed Horace Dinsmore, was postmarked Boston and written on the stationery of Mansfield College. He had some *confidant*, then?"

"No, he had no *confidant* at any time. To answer your letter meant only a quick visit to the Hub City for that requisite postmark. If at any time he had to confess he was on sabbatical leave, he could always claim he kept in close touch.

"A moment ago, you remember, I spoke of the slight alteration in his plan. He was embarked on his affair with an all-too-willing Serena. Some time ago, from Serena's father, he had learned the secret of Delys Hall. So he resolved, quite coolly, that neither Dave nor Serena must survive."

Penny had been fidgeting for some time.

"But *why?*" she cried out. "What was his motive? If he already had more money than he needed, why hurt anybody? What did the man *want?*"

"He wanted this house. And he believed two deaths were necessary for him to acquire it.

"His fondness for picturesque old houses," Uncle Gil resumed after pausing, "amounted to a passion, among the few authentic passions of his life. He never concealed that or needed to conceal it. Otherwise this murderer presents a curious psychological study.

"The fellow's belief in the power to disguise himself I have called fatuous. He had other fatuous ideas as well. It can be established that Dinsmore-Townsend, despite so much surface cleverness, was essentially a stupid man.

"For no deaths were necessary. If he had investigated, he might well have discovered that Dave and Serena, far from inheriting a large estate, had comparatively few assets besides the Hall itself. But they were not likely to tell him, nor would a close-mouthed lawyer. If he had further learned they were about to sell, he himself had the wherewithal to buy. This consideration did not occur to him. To the born criminals of this world, I fear, such considerations never do occur.

"Hear the rest of his scheme, the essential *ignis fatuus.* Having disposed of Serena and Dave, 'Malcolm Townsend' would have left New Orleans. Nobody who had known him in Boston as Horace Dinsmore was likely to meet him here. After a decent interval, wearing some *other* elaborately impenetrable disguise, 'the Rev. Horace' would have turned up to claim his rights as co-heir."

"Just a minute, sir!" interposed Dave. "If he's gotten rid of Serena and me, does he also polish off Jeff to make the tally complete?"

"Oh, no. For all his arrogant delusions, credit the fellow with at least some restraint. Two suspicious deaths would have been bad enough. Three suspicious deaths, with Horace Dinsmore as sole beneficiary, would have constituted raving lunacy. He would have offered to buy Jeff's share of the Hall, as he could afford to do. Had he made such an offer, Jeff, would you have accepted?"

"Yes, at once!" Jeff answered. "If ever I crave an old English house, Uncle Gil, I'll buy one in England."

"Our murderer, then, would have resumed his happy life as Malcolm Townsend of Washington. When he visited New Orleans, of course, he must play Horace Dinsmore at all times. But what of that, to a man who enjoyed disguise anyway? He would *own* this house, his heart's desire; he could afford to come and gloat.

"Such was his plan, worked out in Washington this spring. Dave and Serena almost dished him at the outset, when they both appeared on his doorstep at the same time. Nevertheless, with his usual dexterity he kept them apart. Where or how he met Kate Keith we have not yet ascertained; and, in the lady's present state of mind, I am unlikely to ask her. But he travelled downriver in Mrs. Keith's arms. He could not have learned, of course, that the police had already been stirred up about Thad Peters's case by an anonymous letter signed *Amor Justitiae.*"

"Who did write that letter, Mr. Bethune?" asked Penny.

"I think I can tell you," Jeff said, "if Uncle Gil will allow me. It was written by old John Everard. I should have suspected what to look for as soon as I saw the thing, though I didn't suspect until you and I met the gentlemanly, harmless busybody at his cigar divan. Part of the text read, 'Before you fling my letter into the wastepaper basket,' and so on. Any American would have written just *wastebasket*, as we all do. Only a person brought up in England would have written *wastepaper basket*, the invariable form there. And I saw a large standard typewriter in the back room of his shop. But who wrote the other anonymous letter, Uncle Gil? The note on the portable typewriter, which sent me to Everard's in the first place? If Townsend himself wrote that, what was his game?"

Uncle Gil nodded.

"Already he was confusing his trail, as he often did, to confuse any who might follow it. In that respect, Jeff, recall our interview with Townsend at Mrs. Keith's last Sunday. Any search for hidden gold, he said virtuously, would be meaningless and ghoulish. 'What about Jean Laffite's treasure?' he added. 'Or Captain Flint's?' That was a slip.

"Our city has several legends of Jean Laffite, but knows no Captain Flint. Captain Flint, a figure of fancy, was the pirate cut-throat who buried his hoard only in Stevenson's novel, *Treasure Island.*

"Dinsmore-Townsend, who heard so much, had heard of the well-known local character, asker of questions and prober of problems, at the Stevenson-inspired cigar divan in the Vieux Carré. It would do no harm, it would serve admirably as confusion, if he roused the curiosity of somebody—of anybody; it scarcely mattered whom—about the inquisitive old man who presided there. But our murderer had Stevenson at the back of his mind, and he made that unconscious slip.

"Let's follow him. Arriving in town with the rest of you on Friday afternoon, he carried out the next step. Having finished using Mrs. Keith for the moment, he turned to Serena. That night he phoned her and summoned her to the city. When they did meet, we are informed, it was Serena herself who suggested Cinderella's Slipper. The owner-manager of that establishment, Marcel Nordier (his real name is Mario Petucci), has since confessed that he keeps several upstairs rooms for the convenience of the amorous.

"You see, Jeff, when you and Penny visited Cinderella's Slipper without finding Serena in either of the downstairs rooms, you looked no further because you never thought of any speakeasy as containing a house of assignation."

"I thought of so much," Penny said with a shiver, "that it frightened me silly! I—I nearly fainted when that flower-pot dropped and smashed. Do you mean What'shisname did it deliberately, aiming at Jeff?"

Gilbert Bethune shook his head.

"He dropped the flower-pot deliberately, from the window ledge of a room above, though without intention of killing or injuring. To kill unnecessarily would have been against his own interest, something he never did. But Dinsmore-Townsend had begun to taste power, a heady brew. He exulted in the thought that he *could* have killed if he had wished, and he could not resist the gesture.

"That same night, with Serena, he had given her instructions for what she must do the following night, Saturday. He told her that he, the authority on houses, had discovered the hiding place of Commodore Hobart's gold. If she would navigate the ledge between her room and the next, she herself would make the discovery. 'You don't need the gold, of course,' he said, 'but what a triumph if *you* found it!'

"We know, as Serena's murderer didn't, how much she wanted to find that gold and save her home. She would follow instructions to the letter, as she did.

"However, I must not anticipate. On Saturday morning he made his official entrance here. If you ask who removed Commodore Hobart's log from the safe in the study, it was Serena herself, on instructions from her mentor. Again he confused the trail, fouling it up for the benefit of any investigator. He was a little too quick to show us his brief-case, and there were other mistakes I have already indicated.

"Still, his plan seemed to go swimmingly. Having used Kate Keith before, he could now use her again. Mrs. Keith, on instructions from the same mentor, soon after dinner hurried in to claim him for his alibi. He had set his murder-trap, and that night the trap worked.

"Though he could kill Serena without going anywhere near her, the same would not apply to Dave. But it did not deter him. Serena's brother had a heart condition too; a blow with a blackjack should prove lethal. On Sunday afternoon, taking insane risks, he removed his shoes under the overhanging hood of the side door and went upstairs to finish his work. His luck had changed. He failed, as he failed Monday night with three bullets fired from the drive. Luck had run out."

"But, Uncle Gil," Jeff protested, "where did he get such mobility? He hadn't hired a car; and the police, I understand, can't trace any taxi he might have used. How could he be all over the place as he liked?"

"How could he be all over the place?" Uncle Gil echoed gently.

"You ask that, Jeff, although you were present when Mrs. Keith offered him either of the two cars in her garage? He declined, but he declined so cozily that it could not fail to rouse suspicion.

"Yes, his luck had run out; on Tuesday he was cornered. Photographs identified Malcolm Townsend as Horace Dinsmore. Captain Joshua Galway and several steamboat employees would identify him for us, which they wouldn't for Saylor, as the paying stowaway on the river. Mario Petucci, alias Marcel Nordier, could point out the amorous gentleman who had shared a private room with Serena Hobart. So we assembled our little gathering here."

"Forgive me for butting in again," volunteered Jeff, "but weren't several characters missing from that assembly? Just to round out the picture, shouldn't it have included Saylor himself? Kate Keith? Billy Vauban? Even Earl G. Merriman of St. Louis? Saylor had just finished so confusing me with an earthquake display that I almost asked about Earl G. Meldrum of San Francisco."

"My dear Jeff, where's your sense of fitness? Since we meant to show how Thad Peters had died, as well as how Serena had died, the gathering could scarcely have included Thad Peters's nephew. Already Mrs. Keith had suffered much; I would no more have summoned her here on Tuesday than I would have summoned her here tonight. We had small concern with the St. Louis businessman out of Sinclair Lewis. John Everard I did invite, because I rightly believed he could be persuaded to keep quiet. The irrepressible Saylor would never have kept quiet, so I omitted him too.

"And yet in one respect I judged badly. When Townsend was arrested, I expected him to fight; I expected a legal battle that might carry us all the way to the Supreme Court.

"I should have been most suspicious on Wednesday night when he offered to tell us everything and did tell us everything. To be present as he sat in jail, justifying each move he made—which he hadn't *wanted* to make, of course, but circumstances forced it—was not an experience I care to repeat. Having finished the recital, with a last gesture he swallowed the capsule which Kate Keith, faithful to the last, had secretly conveyed into his possession. He was unconscious in seconds and dead in two minutes."

"What was the poison, Uncle Gil? Potassium cyanide?"

"Even deadlier than cyanide, which is only one salt derived from what he used. The capsule contained hydrocyanic acid, the fastest-working poison on earth. It was provided, no doubt, by some obliging pharmacist with whom Mrs. Keith has been over-friendly. But we needn't hound Mrs. Keith; we needn't hound the pharmacist; we need hound nobody. Since there will be no trial, with its attendant publicity, I may be able to smother the story so that as little scandal as possible attaches to the Hobart name. As regards the evidence, at least, we have now explained everything."

Ira Rutledge spoke with dignity.

"Not *everything*, I suggest," he corrected. "What of my own suspicious behavior?"

"*Your* behavior? Suspicious? I observed that you had something on your mind . . ."

"You observed more than that, surely? Since Serena died by what might be called remote control, my famous alibi was worth nothing at all. And were there no suspicious circumstances? When Dave and Jeff arrived from the steamboat on Friday afternoon, together with Serena and the young lady who is now looking at me so strangely, I met them out in the hall. I said I had been looking at some papers in the study. But I emerged from the main drawing-room, which is in the opposite direction from the study.

"Others have remarked on my tendency to frequent that drawing-room. In point of fact, as I afterwards informed Jeff, it contains some very fine antique musical instruments, including a sixteenth-century harpsichord. But some of you may have thought I told an unnecessary lie." He looked straight at Penny. "*You* thought so, did you not?"

"Honestly, Mr. Rutledge!" Penny protested. "If some notion of suspecting you did cross my mind, I dismissed it as ridiculous. And the point of your being in the drawing-room never occurred to me."

"Well, it occurred to *me*," confessed the lawyer, "so I will speak out. Too long I have seemed a desiccated dodderer, acquainted with little except the law. But I know what's what. Though far from being as devoted to detective stories as Gil or Jeff, I have read my fair share. And no character is more often encountered than the solemn family lawyer, really an unmitigated old crook, who culminates embezzling activities with the murder of his client. It relieves my mind to be free of suspicion. At the same time—"

"Yes, Mr. Rutledge?"

"What of you, young lady? Have *you* something to say or something to reveal? If so, I move you say it forthwith."

"Let the motion hereby be seconded," agreed Gilbert Bethune.

Levelly Penny met Uncle Gil's gaze.

"Very well," she said. "If it's become a game of truth, I'll meet frankness with frankness and tell you. Too long *I* have seemed a dutiful daughter or even patient Griselda, which I'm not. Next week Jeff leaves for Europe. And, it's been decided, I leave with him. We sail by French Line ship from New York to Le Havre, then go overland to Paris." Her soft voice rose. "In conclusion, Mr. District Attorney: if you need to ask one single question about what we've got in mind, you're not the detective you've already proved yourself to be!"

NOTES FOR THE CURIOUS

1

APOLOGIA PRO SUA NARRATIONE

Since the events in *Deadly Hall* occur little more than forty years ago, a time many of us well remember, it seems unnecessary to buttress them with such elaborate notes as supported two predecessors, *Papa Là-Bas* and *The Ghosts' High Noon*. But some few explanatory words may be of interest. The book has been dedicated to my old friend Macon Fry, by profession an electrical engineer, who devised the trap at Delys Hall and gives assurance that it would work. Others deserve my gratitude as well.

2

ROLLING DOWN THE RIVER

The fictitious steamboat *Bayou Queen*, Grand Bayou Line, must not be taken for the actual steamboat *Delta Queen*, Greene Line, which now carries passengers on so many pleasant tours. Nor does Captain Joshua Galway, appearing briefly in these pages, represent the late Captain Thomas R. Greene, skilled commander and genial host, to whose vision we owe the luxurious service of the present day.

The *Delta Queen* was commissioned in the year 1948, over two decades after the date of the story. In October of 1948 I travelled from Cincinnati to New Orleans by this particular steamboat on what must have been one of her first journeys. It was inevitable that the real craft of '48 should suggest the imaginary one of '27. If any aspect of background or atmosphere has been accurately portrayed here, thanks are due to Miss Betty Blake, vice president of the Greene Line, who generously supplied information and river lore. Where I have erred through ignorance, as sometimes I must have erred, the sole culprit is your obedient servant.

251

3
COMMODORE HOBART'S GOLD

Those interested in lost cargoes under the sea will find many described in *Fell's Guide to Sunken Treasure Ships of the World,* by Lieut. Harry E. Rieseberg and A. A. Mikalow. 'Fell' means Frederick Fell, Inc., original publishers of a book now everywhere available in paperback from the New American Library. A certain Dr. Fell may be forgotten.

The Spanish ships lost off the Ambrogian Reefs were (and are) real treasure ships, most of whose cargo has never been salvaged. Commodore Hobart's diving operations would have been entirely practicable in 1860, and a banker friend has estimated the value of the gold bullion this treasure-seeker is assumed to have recovered more than a century ago.

4
NEW ORLEANS, 1927

Delys Hall, apart from its iron brackets, is not unlike North Mymms Park, Hertfordshire, a photograph of which can be seen in *English Country House Life,* by Ralph Nevill (London: Methuen & Co., 1925). Miss Margaret Ruckert, my valued New Orleans adviser, suggested transplanting the Hall to the River Road site of this story.

Other advisers provided local color from the nineteen-twenties. A speakeasy resembling Cinderella's Slipper did actually exist and served only absinthe, though the private room for purposes other than drinking is a low-minded embellishment of my own. A parking lot did in fact occupy the site of the old St. Louis Hotel, where now rises a modern hotel almost as stately as the St. Louis. If the Bohemian Cigar Divan had no more reality in New Orleans than it had outside the pages of Stevenson, some such tobacconist ought to have been there. Here is the city where anything can happen, and no adventurous soul will be surprised when it does.

›››If you've enjoyed this book and would like to discover more great vintage crime and thriller titles, as well as the most exciting crime and thriller authors writing today, visit: ›››

The Murder Room
Where Criminal Minds Meet

themurderroom.com

www.ingramcontent.com/pod-product-compliance
Ingram Content Group UK Ltd.
Pitfield, Milton Keynes, MK11 3LW, UK
UKHW040308180625
459803UK00005B/259